The Road Less Traveled By

Emily Tudor

A Hart Sisters Novel

For anyone who's trying to stay afloat every single day, despite feeling like you want to sink. I'm proud of you. I see you. Keep trying—it's all you can do, right?

And for all the folklore lovers, this one's for you.

Content Warnings

This book features on-page descriptions of sexual assault, sexual touching, and language during these situations which could be triggering for some. It also has undertones of depression, depressive thoughts, minor suicidal thoughts, and stalking. Bree is actively stalked throughout this book and taunted by her stalker. Some notes left could be triggering.

Specific Chapters:
Chapter 12
Chapter 39
Chapter 41

If you or anyone you know struggles with dark thoughts, call, text, or chat 988.

Dicktionary

For those who want to skip the spicy parts, or those who want to skip straight to them. Whatever you prefer!

Playlist

August — Taylor Swift

This Is Me Trying — Taylor Swift

Unsteady — Gracie Abrams

Walk Me Home — P!nk

I Don't Like Darkness — Chase Atlantic

Angels — Chase Atlantic

The Lucky One (Taylor's Version) — Taylor Swift

Not Strong Enough — Boygenius

Fake Smile — Ariana Grande

The Night We Met — Lord Huron

The 1 — Taylor Swift

Busyhead — Noah Kahan

Black Out Days — Phantogram

Hard To Sleep — Gracie Abrams

Mirrorball — Taylor Swift

Matilda — Harry Styles

Fear of Water — Noah Kahan

Delicate (Taylor's Version) — Taylor Swift

Die For You — The Weeknd

Only Angel — Harry Styles

The Archer — Taylor Swift

Something About Her — Stephen Sanchez

NDA — Billie Eilish

Smoke Signals — Phoebe Bridgers

If I Go, I'm Goin — Gregory Alan Isakov

Epiphany — Taylor Swift

Same Sea — Lights

My Tears Ricochet — Taylor Swift

Mad Woman — Taylor Swift

I, Carrion (Icarian) — Hozier

Nothing More — The Alternate Routes Ft. Lily Costner

Seven — Taylor Swift

Betty — Taylor Swift

The Lakes — Taylor Swift

Peace — Taylor Swift

Invisible String — Taylor Swift

Safety Net — Ariana Grande Ft. Ty Dolla $ign

As You Are — The Weeknd

Cardigan — Taylor Swift

So It Goes... (Taylor's Version) — Taylor Swift

Shake It Out — Florence + The Machine

Sometimes — Ariana Grande

Slow Down — Chase Atlantic

Would've, Could've, Should've — Taylor Swift

Ice Cream Man. — Raye

From Eden — Hozier

Gilded Lily — Cults

Daylight — David Kushner

Ptolemaea — Ethel Cain
Faithfully — Journey
Get Well Soon — Ariana Grande
Back Home — Andy Grammer
Forever — Noah Kahan

"I have been bent and broken—but I hope—into a better shape."

– EMILY DICKINSON

"No one pats them on the back every day, but every day they are actively fighting something, but there are so many days that nobody gives them credit for that. How often must someday who's in that sort of internal struggle must want to say to everyone in the room 'you have no idea how close I am going back to a dark place.'"

— TAYLOR SWIFT *on 'this is me trying' from Folklore.*

Prologue

October 2022

— AUGUST BY TAYLOR SWIFT

"So, I guess this is it," I say to my bodyguard as I watch him pack up his car. "You didn't leave anything at my house, did you?"

"No, I don't think so."

"Good." I grab one of his suitcases and load it into the black Tahoe as he goes back inside to finally check out.

Part of me longs to ask him to stay, even though the threat on my life is behind bars. Even though I know Ralph can't hurt me anymore, I still struggle to take full breaths when Vince is gone. It's going to take my body a few weeks to adjust to not having him as my shadow anymore, but I know, eventually, it'll get better. I have to remember that. Soon, it will be better. Soon, I'll be able to breathe normally again. *Not soon enough, though.*

I sit on the bench outside of the hotel as I wait, and I try to focus on anything other than the lingering feeling that something is going to go wrong.

Part of me is worried that this could happen again—having a stalker. Some celebrities have more than one, and even though I'm not at that status, the fact that I had one means there could be another. I could be stuck in this cycle of being stalked for the rest of my life. Who fucking knows what could happen?

"Bree? You okay, angel?" Vince asks as he sits down next to me.

Angel. I'm never going to think of that word the same ever again. "I'm alright."

"Are you sure?" he asks, those eyes seeing right through me. He's good at that—reading me. It's almost way too easy for him, and I guess that's why he made such a good bodyguard. He's got a natural way of reading situations, people, and the emotions they want to keep hidden.

"I'm as good as I can be right now."

"I made you a promise when we first met. Do you remember?"

Of course I remember. "Yes."

"I know Ralph only got five years, which sucks, but I'm glad they caught him before—"

I cut him off. "Yeah, I'm glad too. And you'll come back if he gets out? Or should I call the agency and ask for you?"

"I don't know where I'll be if that happens." *If*. Not *when*. *If* it happens, he'll be back. "Call or text me if you need me."

"And you'll answer?"

"Always, Bree," he says as he lays his hand over where mine clutches the bench we're sitting on.

Don't go, I want to say. *I don't feel as safe when you're not around, and even though Ralph was caught, I still think there are monsters out there. I still think I'm in danger. I don't think I'll ever feel safe or okay again, so please stay with me. Please protect me from anything bad that could come my way. Please stay.*

But I say nothing, because it would be selfish for me to say all that knowing the job he was assigned is over. It's strange how close we've become over a few months, and now that the job is done, it feels odd that he won't always be around. Vince is a good guy, and an even better bodyguard, but he was never *mine*. He was assigned to me, and I'm sure he sees me as some sort of case number he can finally close.

And let's not forget about his *rules*. Rule number three is no personal attachments, and my attachment means nothing to him. I'm his client—well, not anymore—but rule number four is to always see a case through, and with me, he has.

My case is closed—for now. Unless Ralph gets out, our story ends here.

"Bree, this is going to sound mean, but I truly hope I never have to see you again."

"Oh." I get what he means, though. If he sees me again, it's because I'm in danger again, and the idea makes my body shiver just thinking about it.

Vince stands and pulls his keys out as he walks to his car door.

"Where are you off to next?"

"Another case, I think. I have some calls to make, but that's what I assume."

I nod my head. "Gotcha. Well, thank you," I tell him, even though that seems too little to say after all he's done for me.

Thank you for making me feel safe. Thank you for protecting me. Thank you for treating me like a real human being and not some social media thing that people assume to know. Thanks for watching my videos before I uploaded them so I could make sure they were good. Thanks for being a friend when I desperately needed one. And thanks for being a shoulder to cry on when the world felt too big.

"Thank you for making my job easy," he tells me as he swings the door open. "If you need me, call me. I'll be back to you as soon as I'm able."

"I will. Take care of yourself, okay?"

"You too, Bree."

He shuts his door and drives out of sight, and I stand rooted to my spot for a few minutes.

It was good to know you, Vince Evans.

A few minutes later, I feel a hand snake through mine, and I jump.

"It's just me, sis."

Liv. "Sorry."

"It's okay. Are you ready to go?"

I take a long, deep breath before I answer her. "Yeah. I'm ready."

Chapter One

Bree

March 2026

— THIS IS ME TRYING BY TAYLOR SWIFT

I'VE ALWAYS BELIEVED THAT life is a series of choices.

Every day you're alive, you make a thousand decisions that lead you to where you are now. You might not even think about it, but any choice can have a thousand different ripple effects, like rain on a pond.

There are so many things to remember each day, and honestly, it gets exhausting. All these choices and different paths could come from them. What if I choose wrong and end up destroying a once bright future? What if I make one decision that, in my mind, feels small but ends up changing my life for the better? Or for the worse?

All the goddamn what-ifs could drive you crazy if you think about it too long and hard.

I never thought that choosing to post a YouTube video of a book haul one day when I was sixteen would lead me here—a conference room in Pennsylvania, being bored to death and on edge at the same time.

My leg has been shaking since I sat down, my heart beating so fast that I feel like it's going to explode, and not once in the past week have I felt calm. I keep zoning in and out of the conversation that doesn't really involve me. I might be the one to make the final call, but nobody ever really asks for my opinion anymore; they just tell me what to do, and I do it.

I used to have fight left in me, but I can't seem to find that anymore. I'm tired of fighting people and choices.

"So, that's about it. Bree, how do you feel about this arrangement?"

Shit. "Uh, good. I think it will benefit both parties."

"There's no way she was paying attention." A sharp voice I've heard before pierces the air, and suddenly, I notice a familiar face on the screen. Alexander Adams—an up-and-coming actor who made his name sleeping around with half his costars.

He's a decent actor, but most people know him for whichever girl he's dating that week.

"How nice of you to say, Alex. It appears you've only just joined the meeting as well." I glance down at the watch on my wrist. "A half hour late."

"It helps that I've already agreed to the plan, Brianna."

I roll my eyes before correcting him. "Just Bree."

"Can we get back to the matter at hand?" Connie directs what I assume is Alex's manager back to the topic they were discussing while I zoned out. "Bree, Grace and her team were telling you how this could help you."

"Fake dating a star of Alexander's caliber will help immensely," Grace tells me.

"And you want me to do this because…?" I trail off, the lack of sleep not helping my brain process anything. God, I'm a fucking wreck lately, and there's nothing I can do to help that.

"To get the press off your back about Ralph getting out."

My shoulders tense when I hear his name. My lungs suddenly forget how to work, and I want to shrink into the chair I'm sitting on and disappear. I start to twist the bracelet that lives on my wrist to try and calm down, but it doesn't work. I want to make myself so small that nobody can touch me, so nothing can hurt me.

But I don't, because I have to be professional. I take a short breath before I speak again. "And Alexander agreed to this for what? There's nothing he can possibly gain from dating someone a lot less popular than him." I don't mean to take a jab at myself, but there's a huge difference between being a *literal* movie star and an influencer with a large fanbase.

"My team has agreed that I need to...clean up my image. Plus, you have a different demographic than I do, which means more publicity for me in different areas." He smiles, one of those fake movie star smiles that he has probably perfected from years of acting classes.

I dislike him already, but before I can speak, Connie does it for me. "Bree's excited about the new reach and the media's distraction from her current situation. She'll do it." She looks over at me and smiles, and I shoot her one back, not wanting to upset her.

"It will be a great opportunity for sure," I grit through my teeth.

"Wonderful. I'll send over the paperwork for you and your people to look over," Grace says, scribbling something down on a notepad.

Alex is smirking like he has something up his sleeve, and I fake my best smile to pretend like I actually care.

I just want to be home. I want to curl up in my bed and hide away until something swallows me whole.

"I'll see you soon, Bree. Get that video camera ready, or whatever you use to film those videos of yours."

"I'll charge it right up," I say as Connie hangs up the call. "So, pawning me off on fake dates now, are we? This wasn't what I imagined when you said you had good news for me, Con."

Connie, my manager, is one of the only people I trust in this world. She's around thirty-five, with brown hair that's currently styled in a bob, and is about a head shorter than me. She handles all the confusing parts of being in the public eye, and we have a love-hate relationship because of certain things—like whatever today has been.

"Bree, you know how it is. I'm trying to get the media attention off—"

If I hear his name one more time, I might collapse. "I know, but is fake dating a movie star the right move? You know I would've said no if I knew ahead of time."

"That's why I didn't tell you. Wouldn't you rather have the attention on the boy you're dating than the man you've tried to forget for four years?"

No. As of right now, I'd rather have no attention on me when I'm relapsing into who I was after I met him for the first time. After what he did to me. After what he took from me. "Yeah, but is fake dating the way to do that?"

"I know you don't believe in love, Bree, but give him a chance. He might end up surprising you in the end."

I roll my eyes. "I doubt it."

I used to believe in love. I used to think that it could conquer everything—every bad day, every shitty feeling I had about myself, *everything.* Isn't that what every romance novel I read tells me? That, despite it all, despite being who I am and doing what I do, I can still find love?

But it doesn't work like that, and I would never drag someone into the life I have now, and I don't think anybody would willingly walk into it either.

Nobody wants a girlfriend with an active stalker, PTSD, anxiety, and a belief that love doesn't exist. *I* don't even like who I am most days. Ever since I got the call about Ralph's release a week ago, I've been ghosting through everything. I'm trying my fucking hardest to snap out of it, but I can't.

Every time I try to tell myself that I'm going to be okay, I panic. Any small sound I hear, I jump. I can't be alone in small spaces like elevators or my shower, not without feeling like the walls are closing in on me. Nobody wants someone who worries about leaving the house, who worries about her future. All of my time is spent worrying about things that haven't happened yet. I'm constantly on edge, panicked and on the verge of crying because my brain won't shut off.

Nobody would want that. Nobody would want me, so I guess fake dating is all I'll get.

"How are you holding up? Have you been sleeping lately? You look tired, B."

Tired is the understatement of the century. "I'm alright."

"Have you talked to Dr. Anna lately?"

Dr. Anna—my therapist. "Every single day this week, and I have a call with her later too."

She smiles at me. "Good. Make sure you start to get some sleep. You and Alex will have your first public outing in a few weeks. There's going to be lots of press tipped off about it."

Of course there is. "I'll try." It feels like all I'm doing lately is fucking trying, but nobody notices. Every fucking second of every fucking day, I'm trying not to break, not to look like I'm falling apart at the seams, but nobody notices. They only notice how seemingly put together I am for someone whose stalker was released from prison and is probably on their way back to finish what he started.

Nobody ever takes into account that the act of not falling into pieces on the floor because of how exhausted I am, is trying too.

That fucker ruined my life, but I have to pretend like he didn't. I have to pretend like I'm okay, that my order of protection will save me, but I know it won't.

I know he's coming for me, and I feel like a sitting duck.

"I'll see you later, Bree. I have another meeting to get to." She taps my hand as she gets up from the giant glass table we've been sitting at in her office. "Feel free to sit here and take it all in. I know it's a lot to digest, so take all the time you need. I'll keep the windows frosted so you can't see in or out."

"Thanks, Connie." She slips out of the room through one of the doors, and as I sit and stare at the glass walls surrounding me, I wait for something to come.

But the only thing that does is worry. Worry that I have to walk out of here alone, that I have to get back in the elevator and stand in the corner for eight floors as I hope and pray that nobody else gets on. I have to act natural, like I'm perfectly okay as I walk out of the building and get into my car, but I know there's probably paparazzi outside—there always is. I'm not the only semi-famous person who has meetings here. Connie's management firm is huge, after all.

To the media, I'm Bree Hart, the social media influencer who talks about books she loves, who always has a bow in her hair no matter what she's wearing.

To myself, I'm Bree, the 5'4", long blonde-haired girl, freckles on her face, green eyes, the book lover who doesn't believe in love. I'm just a girl from Pennsylvania who got big by talking about things I loved on the internet. I never imagined this would be what my life looked like as a twenty-five-year-old, but the decisions I made have led me here.

So, as I get up and place my hand on the door, I take a big deep breath and hope it will help calm me down, even knowing it won't.

Love doesn't exist. Worrying and looking over my shoulder is all I'll ever know now, and I might not be alive if he finds me in the next few weeks. I'm still living in the same area. It's only a matter of time before he gets me again.

I swing the door open and head down the hallway, the elevator looming at the end of it like a door in a haunted house. My steps drag along the tile floor, the luminescent lighting hurting my eyes, when I notice a familiar figure sitting on a bench by the elevator.

Is he real, or am I imagining him? His face meets mine—those hazel eyes I know so well look back at me like a lifeline in the middle of a storm. I didn't think I was going to see him so soon. I thought he was finishing another assignment. "Vince?"

He doesn't say a word; he only looks at me like he used to all those years ago—like he can see every thought running through my head.

"You're back." It's not a question.

"You needed me."

I did. I do. "I thought you weren't going to be here for another month?"

"Someone else took over for me. I'm needed here."

God, I want to cry. I want to break down because I know Vince would catch me. He's the only person other than my sister I trust to catch me when I feel like falling. I've been scared out of my mind for the past week, and seeing his familiar face is helping me center myself.

After everything, I never thought I'd be able to be alone with a man without freaking out, yet with Vince, I felt safe. I don't know what it is about him that makes me feel like that, but I still do, even four years later.

"Thank you for coming."

"I made you a promise, Bree. I'm not one for breaking promises." He stands from the bench and walks over to where I stand rooted in my spot. His over 6-foot frame, tattoo sleeve, and muscles bigger than I last saw him looms over me, yet I've never felt safer.

It's been years, yet my body isn't screaming at me to get away or hide. I'm starting to think he might be the only person I'll ever feel safe around since his job is to *literally* protect me.

His hand reaches out, touching the light pink bow that rests on the end of my braid. "It's nice to see some things haven't changed."

"I didn't mean to make you drop everything just for me."

His eyes move off my bow and lock onto mine. "Do you remember how we're going to do this, angel?"

Angel. My codename. Vince picked it out when I first met him. I asked why I needed one, and he said it's standard practice. I'm obviously not so important as to need one, but he insisted. He does it with all his clients, apparently. I nod at him. "You get in the elevator first, and you exit with me behind you, but only when you tell me it's all clear."

He cocks his head, a small smile gracing then disappearing from his lips. "And?"

"And listen to you at all times. You open all my doors for me, and no matter what, no arguing when it comes to my safety. I remember, Vince. It's not my first rodeo."

"I know, Bree. Are you ready to go?" I nod at him again, not having words for seeing him here after all this time. He puts his hand to his ear before he speaks again. "Angel is leaving the building. We'll be down in two. Get the car ready."

"Who the hell are you talking to?"

"My team."

"Your *what*?"

"I have a lot to catch you up on, Bree. But let's focus on getting you out of here safely first, okay?"

"Whatever you say, boss." I smirk, knowing he hates when I call him that. Before I know it, we're in the car headed back to my house, and I feel safer than I have in a week.

Chapter Two

Bree

One Week Ago

— UNSTEADY BY GRACIE ABRAMS

I FUCKING LOVE MY sister.

As I set my purse on the hook in my room and plop on my bed, I reminisce on the beautiful night I just spent with some of my favorite people. Liv released her second book a few hours ago, and Tristan—her everything—invited us all over to celebrate: his family and friends, me, Liv's college friends, and his sister, my best friend, Teags.

Teagen West is probably the only true friend I have in the world, and I'll never stop being grateful for her existence.

My older sister is officially a two-time author, and I couldn't be more proud of her. Since both of us have cut off contact with our parents, she's the only family I have left.

But she's the only family I need.

I'm glad Tristan and Liv decided to stay in Pennsylvania. I wasn't sure if Liv would follow him back to California, but after the rockiness of the last four years, they finally figured it all out. Even if I don't believe I'm destined for love in this lifetime, my sister has found it in Tristan. They met in their senior year of college and were going strong until my parents decided to break them up.

Liv was always the daughter who got pushed aside for all my shit, and I was the daughter who got smothered and overwhelmed by our parents.

I can say with my full chest that our parents were not meant to be parents. I don't even know why they had us if they were going to treat us like shit on the bottom of their shoes. But regardless, I have Liv, my beautiful, inspiring, and intelligent sister.

I decide to head straight for my shower, knowing that if I sit for much longer, I won't be getting back up. I turn it on to the hottest it can go before stepping out of my outfit from tonight. I stole Liv's jacket because I knew it would look great with some of the vintage pieces I have in my closet, and I set it in my walk-in closet before I hop in. Liv should know that I'm not giving it back—she didn't even ask for it, since she knows she never wore it.

After my shower, I turn my classical playlist to the lowest setting, turn my night light on, and hop into bed with my Kindle.

I may be twenty-five, but I still sleep with sound and a night light because of what happened four years ago. I hate being alone in this house, but being alone is better than being surrounded by a bunch of people I don't trust.

At least when I'm by myself, I know the only person who can hurt me is me and my own thoughts.

As I'm transported into the world of my book, my phone ringing interrupts my break from reality. Connie's ringtone—*I Will Survive* by Gloria Gaynor—hums from my phone, and I pick it up.

"Hi, Con. It's like one in the morning. Is everything okay?" She never calls me this late, not unless it's something important. *I wonder what it is this time.*

"Ralph is getting out of prison tomorrow."

I stop breathing. "N–No. What?"

"It's confirmed. He's getting out for good behavior. We knew this was possible, Bree—"

I hang up on her. I can't breathe. My chest is on fire. Tears are flooding my eyes and dripping down my face, but I have no control over them. I don't even feel like I'm inside my body. I'm somehow sweating and freezing at the same time. I have goosebumps, but my skin is on fire. I'm a walking contradiction.

He's getting out. My stalker is getting out of prison. I knew it was possible. He was only given five to ten years in the first place, which was bullshit considering what he did to me, but the judge went against everything my lawyer fought for. I assumed I would be in a better place and that he would've eventually forgotten about me.

But there's no way. I put him in prison, and there's no way he's going to just let this slide, especially after what he said to me that night.

He's going to come for me, and this time, he might actually achieve what he set out to do the last time I saw him.

I somehow make it out of my bed and onto the floor, my phone clutched in my hand like a lifeline.

"H-Hey, S-Siri, call Liv," I say, hoping that my phone dials her for me. She picks up on the third ring.

"What did you forget this time? I can try and drop it off before—"

"Liv, he's getting out. They're letting him out." I don't even know how I get the words out. I can barely breathe. I need to get out of my house, my body, my mind. I can't handle this. I can't handle being back in the same place I was four years ago. All it took was one call to catapult me back to who I used to be. I hate this. I thought I was stronger, but maybe all the progress I made was an illusion.

"That's not possible."

"Connie just called me. It's real and it's happening. What the fuck do I do, Liv?" I don't know who else to go to. Liv is the only person other than Teags who fully understands what I was like when all this started. My parents don't care—they made that clear when they kept the house I was assaulted in.

"We'll figure this out, Bree. I'm calling Vince tomorrow to see if he'll come back."

Vince. Just hearing his name makes me feel a bit safer, but I doubt he'll just drop everything and come back. He did promise me that if Ralph ever got out, he would be back, but he could be anywhere in the world right now. He's probably on a job, and there's no way he'll get here in time. Plus, I can't do that to him—especially because of those rules of his. "Thanks, Liv. I'll try texting him later, but I have to go. I hung up on Connie as soon as she told me, and she's calling me back."

"It's fine, sis. I love you."

I don't answer her before I answer Connie. "I understand this is tough, but please stop hanging up on me. He officially gets out tomorrow. It'll hit the news in the morning most likely."

"I-I'm sorry. I had to call Liv. I had to—"

"It's okay, Bree. I know this is a lot, but you still have an order of protection against him. He technically can't come near you or contact you without being arrested again. You're safe, Bree."

I hear the words, but I don't believe her. "No. I'm not."

Two Hours Later

Bree: He's getting out.

Bree: I don't know what to do. I don't even know why I'm texting you because I know you're probably working on another case.

Bree: I need you, if you're able.

Vince: When does he get out?

Bree: Tomorrow.

Vince: My current case has about a month left. Will you be okay until then?

Bree: Yeah. I'll figure something out.

Bree: See you in a month.

Vince: See you soon.

Chapter Three

— WALK ME HOME BY PINK

Fᴜᴄᴋ.

I didn't think that falling into our old patterns so quickly would hit me like this. She fell right into place as I escorted her from the building. Bree might be the best client I've ever had...but one I wish I never met.

A girl like her doesn't deserve to be going through this again. *Again.* God, I hate that word. I hate that this is happening, that I'm back here so soon.

If I could kill the fucker, I would. It would be much easier than watching Bree retreat into herself.

But I can't. All I can do is hope that my team and I can protect Bree to the best of our ability and pray it's enough. I've never lost a client, and I don't plan on my first loss being Bree.

I look at her in the rearview mirror, her eyes glassy and staring straight ahead, as if she's not really here. It reminds me of who she was when I met her—jumpy, scared, and very clearly traumatized. I still don't know exactly what happened, but I know enough. Bree never told me the nitty gritty details, and I never pressed. I knew enough to do my job, and that's all I needed.

He assaulted her in her own home, and it got to that point because nobody in her life—besides her sister and manager—thought the threats were bad enough.

I focus my eyes back on the road, trying not to think of the worst-case scenario, before I clear my throat. "So, has he tried to contact you since he was released?" Ralph was a big fan of leaving notes and what he called gifts for Bree. When I was first assigned to her, he left about one a week until the police eventually caught him. Bree saw every single one, even the ones that detailed what he was going to do when he got his hands on her.

My skin still crawls thinking about it, and I don't scare easily. There's just something about this case, about him, about Bree, that makes me extra protective. "Bree?"

She shakes out of whatever haze she was just in before she meets my eyes in the mirror. "Sorry, did you say something?"

Fuck. She's distancing herself again. When I met Bree four years ago, the first thing I pegged about her was that when reality got too tough to deal with, she'd enter a different one. Whether through a book, music, or her own head, she would go somewhere else that made her feel safe. I don't blame her, not after all she's been through.

She used to have this...glow about her, especially in the end after he was caught. Even though she felt broken, it was like all the pieces that made her who she was shined through. Even on her worst days, her light still lingered in the air around her. I don't see that anymore. I see someone struggling and trying to hide it from the rest of the world, but Bree should know that she could never hide from me. "It's nothing we can't talk about another time."

Her mouth opens as if she wants to say something, but she decides against it. "Did you want to ask me something, Bree?"

"You have a team now." It's not phrased as a question, but I nod. "How did that happen?"

"It's a long story, but a friend of mine, we created a company together—security and protection services. He handles the security aspect, and I run the protection side. We expanded so much that I needed more help." When Bree and I first met, I was employed under a different agency, and when I met Nico, we decided to team up. I wouldn't call us friends—Nico disagrees—but more or less friendly coworkers.

"I wasn't aware you let yourself have friends, Vince. What happened to no personal attachments? Or have your rules changed since I last saw you?"

I catch the smirk at the end of her sentence, and I feel my lips perk up as well. "I've added about six more since I saw you. Don't worry, Nico gives me as much shit as you do for my rules, but there's a reason why I have them." *And I've already broken one of them for you. Two, if you count how I touched your hair in front of the elevator.* I've got to get my head on straight and focus on the task at hand—protecting Bree.

"I know, I know. They're important to you, and it's why you're so good at your job. I'm just messing with you."

"When I move in, I'll put a framed photo of my rules in every room, so don't test me."

Her eyes widen. "Sorry, when you what?"

"I plan on moving into your house, Bree. I know you live somewhere different now, and it has more space, so I decided that's what's best for the time being. It's how I know you'll be safe, and I can protect you easiest from underneath your own roof. But only if it's okay with you, of course."

"It's okay with me, Vince." She takes a big deep breath. "Thank you for asking."

"I'm just doing my job, Bree."

"Right, but still, thank you for coming back. How's your sister, Aria?"

"She's okay. Currently living in Seattle with her husband."

"That's nice."

That's another thing about Bree—if you tell her something about yourself, she'll remember it. She's ridiculously good at remembering small details, and I have no doubt she'll ask for a full list of the names of my team members soon. She's never not thinking about other people.

Being here with Bree is much better than the last asshole I protected. I normally don't talk poorly about former clients, but now that I'm off his case, I can say he really deserved to get punched by his ex-wife. He was some high up official in Italy who needed a bodyguard because his wife found out he was cheating on her—with about twenty different women. I stuck Romero—another one of my guys—on his case when I dropped everything to get back here. I got her text a week ago, and my heart dropped. I tried to shake it off and focus, but I couldn't. All my thoughts were on her and if she was safe. Then her sister called me—apparently, Bree doesn't feel safe with anyone but me. I told her the same thing—that I was already on a case—but after that conversation, I could barely sleep. I wasn't focused, so I dropped my case early and handed it off—which is something I've never done.

I have an unwritten list of rules that most people acquainted with me make fun of. Rule number four is to always see a case through.

Which I didn't. I couldn't care less about what happens to the fucker. I'm right where I need to be right now, and I don't regret my decision.

Not one fucking bit.

"So, is Liv still here with you? Wasn't that the plan when you got this new house?" I'd feel better knowing Liv has been with her the entire time, that Bree hasn't been by herself in this house for years.

"She was, but she eventually got her own place, and now she lives with Tristan."

That's a name I haven't heard in a while. I've never met this Tristan guy, but I knew Bree talked to him, so I ran a full background check way back when. He was clean, and Bree seemed to trust him, but I was still cautious of anyone who wasn't Liv. Even Bree's parents were on my shit list. *I wonder if they're still around.* Bree always talked about cutting contact. "They're still together? Wow, good for them."

"Well, they haven't been together this entire time. A few days after you left, they broke up. It's a long story. They only recently got back together after four years apart."

Damn. I don't have the brain power to keep up with this. I'm thirty-three years old, but my mind might as well be a hundred. I work slowly and methodically, and the speed of this day and age is terrifying. That's why Nico handles the technological aspect of our company and I do the more physical component. It's much fucking easier for my brain. "Oh, wow."

"Yeah, it's been a crazy few years." She averts her gaze to the window, and I don't bother trying to keep our conversation going; I can tell she's somewhere else right now. It kills me that I can't help her, but I hope my presence is enough for her to know that she's safe.

A few minutes later, I pull onto her street and take the path to her driveway. Her new house is nice—and fucking huge. It's a bit secluded for my liking, but the gate in front of her house makes me feel better.

"The code is—"

I've already punched it in before she can finish her sentence. "Liv told me."

"You talked to my sister?"

"She called me the day after you texted me. Gave me all the information I needed for when I got here." I might hate most family members of my clients—they usually don't give a fuck about the safety of their loved ones—but Liv is one of the good ones. She genuinely cares about her sister and acts more like Bree's parent than their biological ones. If Bree trusts her, I trust her, plain and simple.

I park in her driveway, opting not to use the garage before I've had a chance to look around, and get out of the black Tahoe with tinted windows. My guys get out of theirs too, since they were following me here. I open Bree's door for her and escort her to her front porch as I look around. The property plans said she has around 4,000 square feet of living space, and a few acres surround her too. It's bigger than her old house, but my team can handle it.

I don't hear her key turning in the lock, and when I look at Bree, her face has gone pale. I follow her unblinking eyes to the front porch, where a manilla envelope sits, her name drawn in red marker on the front.

"Get behind me," I say as I pull her flush to my back. I don't know what this is, and if it's anything dangerous, I'd rather it hit me first. "You haven't ordered anything recently?"

I feel her shake her head against my back before I call Emerson over to inspect it. He has bomb squad training, and at least he can tell me if there's a device in or attached to it. It looks a little too small, and that was never Ralph's MO. He much preferred breaking Bree down psychologically with notes, letters, and *details*. The fucker liked messing with her head, and it doesn't surprise me that he's picking up where he left off.

"It's clear. It just looks like some pictures and a note." Emerson steps back, and I move toward the package, feeling Bree grip my jacket like a lifeline.

"Get Bree back in the car while I sweep the house. Take this and bag it so Nico can analyze it."

"I–I can't do this again." Bree's voice is shaking. I haven't heard her this scared in a long time.

I turn to face her. "Let's get you back to the car where it's safe, and I'll be back in fifteen minutes, okay? You remember this part, don't you?"

She can barely look at me. Her eyes are glassy, petrified, and her gaze is shooting all over the place. I place a hand on her lower back, and as we get back to the car, she lets me open her door so she can slide in, still breathing heavily. "Y-Yes. You search every part of my house, and when it's clear, I can come in. When it's clear, that means I'm safe."

I nod at her, happy she remembers. "I thought you had a security system."

"I did. I do. It should've notified me if the gate was opened or if there was motion at any of the doors, but I never got anything."

Fuck. "Then we'll get you a better one. I'll call Nico tonight and ask him to set one up. He's the only fucker I trust in terms of security, and soon, your entire house will be wired with state-of-the-art protection."

"Isn't that just you?"

Damn right it is. I turn to my team of four and look them all in the eyes. "Emerson, you're with me. Duncan and Chris, I want you to sweep the surrounding property. Kenner, you protect that girl with your life. Close the door to the car and make sure nobody else is around watching outside the gates. Let's go."

WHEN I OPEN THE package an hour later and a few photos of Bree fall out, my stomach drops. I feel Bree tense up beside me before she gives context to the pictures.

"This is from two days ago. I had to go to the grocery store."

Jesus. I pull the note out, and when I read it, my body goes cold.

Cat got your tongue? My shackles are gone, and now I'm back to setting my traps.

Sleep tight, Bree. I'll see you soon.

You don't know how long I've waited for this.

"I-I'm gonna go upstairs and shower," Bree tells me as she turns away from the table and heads to her room.

I look at Chris and Emerson as they watch her leave. "Make copies and send them to Nico. See if he can identify where they were taken and when." I turn around and catch up to Bree as she walks up her stairs.

"Are you okay?" I ask, but she ignores me, or she's too in her head to hear me saying anything. By the time we get to the top of the stairs, I grab her shoulder and turn her towards me. "Tell me how you're feeling, Bree. Tell me what's going through your mind."

"Nothing. I just need to go take a shower," she tells me, still not looking in my eyes. "I'm fine, Vince. Really. I'll be down later for dinner, okay?"

I can only nod at her as she speed-walks to her room and softly shuts the door behind her.

Chapter Four

— I DON'T LIKE DARKNESS BY CHASE ATLANTIC

Just when I thought I was falling asleep for the first time in a week, I'm startled awake by a loud noise. Soft white light filters in, and the silhouettes of my furniture and personal items surround me.

There's nobody in your house, Bree. You're safe.

I glance over at the clock, and it reads three in the morning. Wonderful. I fumble for my phone on my bedside table and immediately open my last text thread.

> **Bree: Are you awake? I think I heard something.**

> **Vince: On my way.**

It should only take a few seconds since Vince is just down the hall from me, and sure enough, I hear his heavy footsteps come towards my room before my door opens. *Dear lord.* He's wearing black sweatpants, no shirt, and his hair is all messy, as if I woke him up from a deep sleep. He does a quick sweep of my room, closet, and bathroom before he comes over to my bed, checking underneath it as well.

My room is big, but I keep it simple. My furniture is all white, including my bed frame, vanity, desk, and bookshelves. My walls are light gray, but you can barely see them since my shelves cover most of the space, and my carpet is light pink because that's my favorite color. Blankets cover my bed since I'm a cold sleeper—when I sleep, that is. On the other side of my bed is my closet, and through it is my bathroom. All the rooms connect, which brings more terror for me when I think someone could be hiding, watching me while I sleep.

I shake out of my haze when his hazel eyes meet mine as he sits down on the edge of my bed. "No sounds anymore, just the light?"

He was never one to beat around the bush. "Both, actually. My noise machine has a timer on it, and it turns off after two hours when I'm hopefully asleep."

"Ah." He glances around my room. "Your room is clear, Bree. Where did you hear the noise?"

"I'm not sure."

"I'm going to sweep the rest of your house. Will you be okay while I'm gone?"

I nod at him before he gets up and calmly walks out of my room, shutting the door behind him. I take a deep breath before I get comfy, yanking my light pink blanket up to my chest, trying not to panic.

But trying is not the same as succeeding.

Vince *just* got back here. It's not even been one full night, and I'm already freaking out about a noise I heard and sending him to check my whole house. God, I'm a fucking mess. When will I be able to hear loud noises without thinking of my front door being slammed open? When will I be able to stop looking over my shoulder? When will the fucking noise that clouds my brain stop?

I'm trying not to fall apart. I'm trying to pretend like I'm going to be fine and that this will be over soon, but deep down, I don't believe it. I'll never escape this fucking torment that my own mind conjures up.

A loud noise equals someone coming for me. Small spaces lead to me trapping myself in my closet before he opened the doors and grabbed my ankles. PR packages turn into notes detailing all the things he wants to do to me. Whistling leads to remembering how he whistled while he touched me that night.

A full shiver passes through my body before I feel myself slip into the overwhelming panic. *He's here. He's coming for me. I'm not safe. I'll never be safe ever again.*

He's going to kill me.

This is how it starts—the notes. Finding one on my front porch was just the beginning. He'll only get angrier, more agitated, more terrifying. At least this time, I know who he is and what he looks like, but I don't think that's enough.

I'm fucking terrified every second of every day. Since I heard he was getting out, I don't think I've taken a full breath. I don't know what to do because I'm not in control. He is. He's the one who calls all the fucking shots.

And then, there's the part where I try to grapple with what he did to me. I don't feel like I deserve to be upset about it. He didn't rape me, so why do I still feel the way I do? Why does hearing one little sound scare the fucking daylights out of me?

God, I can't breathe. I can't do fucking anything except trust the people around me to keep me safe. *But what if it's not enough? What if he still finds me? What if they get hurt trying to protect me?*

Fuck, I can't do this. I slither out of my bed and literally crawl to my bathroom, hoping I can get there without collapsing in on myself. My therapist taught me a trick to help get me through these attacks. She recommended a few things, but cold water—splashing it on my face, dipping my feet, hands, or neck in it, drinking it—has been the only thing that works. It gets me out of my head enough to ground me, helps my body recognize that I'm still here, still alive.

I get into my bathroom, chest still heaving, sweat dripping down my skin. I'm almost to the sink before I feel a pair of arms wrap around my middle and place me on my countertop. I try to swat them away, but a voice permeates my head.

"It's just me. It's Vince. You're safe, Bree. I'm just trying to help."

"P-Please help," I choke out.

"Tell me how, angel."

"C-Cold water," I say as I motion to the sink. I hear him turn the tap on, and a few seconds later, his cold hands wrap around the back of my neck and one of my wrists.

"Focus on the cold, my voice. Feel my pulse and breathe with me."

I muster enough strength to nod at him before I move my hand toward his pulse, feeling it beating beneath his skin. A few minutes later, my lungs unlock, and I let out a huge breath. "Am I safe?"

"You're safe." His stare meets mine, and it's now that I realize how much I missed him.

"Thank you for coming back for me." If anyone else was assigned to protect me right now, I think I'd be drowning, but somehow, Vince seems to know exactly what I need, and I'm grateful for his presence.

He doesn't respond to me; instead, he changes the subject. "My guys checked the whole property, including the guesthouse, and found nothing. It's a bit windy tonight, so that might be what you heard. I cleared the upstairs."

"You have people patrolling my house while I sleep?"

"Yes. I'm the only one who stays in here, and there's six of them out there on rotating schedules with the other six who are currently sleeping."

"You have twelve people watching my house? There were only four earlier, Vince."

"I called in my most trusted guys to help me out. Your property is huge, and I'm not taking any chances, Bree." His confident stare makes a shiver roll through my body all the way to my toes. "Are you cold? Do you want to get back to bed?"

I shake my head, knowing I won't be sleeping for the rest of the night. "Why is it just you who lives with me while the rest of them are in the guesthouse?"

"Because if someone manages to get past the twelve of them, they won't survive getting past me." His words sink in, the low tone making me shiver again. *Maybe I am cold.* "Trust me on this, okay? We've worked well together in the past. Do you trust me to keep you safe, angel?"

There's that fucking name again. I shiver at the insinuation he's making. *Vince will kill anyone who tries to hurt me.* I know he has some combat training and some advanced knowledge of weapons, but I never thought he'd kill *for* me.

The fact that it turns me on is ridiculously insane. I blame all the books I read where a man goes ballistic when someone threatens his wife or the slew of bodyguard romance books I read before getting one myself.

I meet his stare and try my best to be fearless when I speak. "Yes, I trust you."

I swear, I see his lips turn up for a second. "Then let me keep you safe how I see fit."

"Okay. You have my permission to do what you have to."

"Good. Now, I know you're not going to sleep, so go work out, and I'll call Nico to see if he can come over to install a new security system today. I don't like the one you have now, and the sooner I'm able to nip that in the bud, the better." And with that, he leaves.

Of course he knows I'm not going to sleep. I underestimated how much he remembered about me; I knew Vince was observant, but not *that* observant. I hop down from my counter, and my legs stagger before they start to feel normal again as I head to my closet.

I grab one of my favorite workout sets before I lace up my sneakers and head to my home gym, hoping to run out the anxiety that surrounds my body every second of the day.

Chapter Five

— ANGELS BY CHASE ATLANTIC

Vince: I'm sending you an address. Get your ass over here early so you can set the new system up. And don't be fucking late, or I'll break your ankles.

Nico: Someone's in a mood this morning.

Vince: See you at eight.

Nico: Why the fuck are you up so damn early? Do you ever sleep?

Nico: You're getting old, Vinny. It's important to get eight hours, or your dick might fall off. Or maybe it will anyway without proper use.

"You're late."

Nico and his team step out of their vans, and while his team gets to work, he comes to shake my hand. "I had to stop and buy more hair gel."

I hum in response as I bring him inside the house. "I don't want a single blind spot in here or on the property, including the guesthouse. I have my guys staying there."

Nico just whistles as he moves around the foyer, his hands shoved into the pockets of his perfectly tailored suit. He has always been a suit guy while I opt for more comfortable clothes that let me move easily. "Where are *you* staying while you're here, Vinny?"

Don't punch him. "Stop calling me that. I'm staying upstairs." I don't offer more because none of this actually concerns him. "How long is it going to take?"

"Probably all day with a place this size but pretend like we're not even here." Nico runs his tattooed hand through his jet-black hair as Bree comes upstairs. *Has she been working out since four this morning?* To be fair, if I had access to a home gym like hers, I'd use it as much as she seems to.

My gaze falls on her as she looks over at my business partner. "Are you the infamous Nico?"

Nico smiles at her, and for some reason, it pisses me off. "Guilty as charged. I hope Vinny told you some good things."

Bree reaches out, and they shake hands, Nico's smile still on his face. "Vinny, huh?"

"Or if you prefer to call him one-half of Wilder's Angels, he loves that too."

"Wilder's Angels?" Bree looks confused, and I remember I never told her the name of the company we founded.

"Our company," I say to her as her eyes widen.

She smiles, and I notice how red her cheeks are. "I like the name."

"Vince picked it out, and I have to say, I like how he used my last name instead of his. It has a nicer ring to it." Nico winks at her. *Prick.* Even he doesn't know why I picked that name, but I do know he likes being the face of the company over me. He prefers the spotlight, and I'm more of a silent partner. It's why we work so well together.

"How did you guys meet? You two seem very..."

"Different?" I finish her sentence, and she nods at me.

"Well, we do have different *tastes*, if you know what I mean..." Nico elbows me in the side. *Fucker.*

"I don't need to hear about your sexual escapades, Nico. I get enough of that in the emails you send me once a week. And stop fucking putting me back on your stupid newsletter when I've unsubscribed."

"But it's too fun. I always enjoy the emails you send back. I didn't realize that many bad words existed," Nico jokes.

Bree laughs as she runs a hand through her ponytail. "How much do I owe you for this? And do any of your guys need water or snacks? I can whip up something."

God, this girl—always worrying about other people before herself. Before Nico can speak, I cut in. "You don't owe us anything, Bree."

Nico meets my eyes and winks at me with a stupid fucking smirk on his face.

"No. Absolutely not, Vince. Let me give you guys something, please. I can't let you do this for free."

"Bree, this is for your safety, and it was my idea to call Nico." I don't tell her that I already paid Nico. I paid the usual amount I do when I bring him to a client. He gets them to use our security service while I guard them. It's a win-win.

"I take payment in the form of catching that Ralph motherfucker. How does that sound, princess?"

Bree's cheeks go red. Seriously? "Don't fucking call her that, asshole."

"Vince, it's fine. Does this system work the same as the last one?"

"It does. There's a passcode I suggest you change from the last one, and you have someone on your house twenty-four-seven. If anything is tripped or looks out of place, someone will notice and call authorities. There will also be panic buttons around the house, just in case. Those alert us as well."

I see Bree's shoulders relax when he finishes. "Oh. That's good."

"You'll be safe, Bree, especially with this one living down the hall from you. He's like a giant wall, and nobody I've seen try has succeeded in breaking it down." Nico pats my shoulder as I stare at him, hoping he catches the annoying glare I send his way.

"Do you guys think..." Bree trails off, her eyes looking hollower than before.

"Think what, angel?"

Nico snickers and covers it with a cough.

"Do you think it's still Ralph, or could it be someone new? He didn't sign the note he left like he used to."

"The timing of it all is too coincidental. It's him," I tell her.

"And if you remember our boy here, rule number nine is that coincidences don't exist." Nico pokes fun at my rules for the umpteenth time. "So, tell me about this guy. I'll put some feelers out for him, but I need to know more."

"Bree, you don't have to be here for this," I tell her as we move into my makeshift office, my files spread out all over the room.

"No secrets, remember?"

I nod at her, but I still feel this urge to protect her from seeing all this despite her having to *live* through it every single day.

"Ralph Nash is a thirty-five-year-old male, approximately five foot eight, with no living family members. Physically, he's fit enough to be able to lift a person, but he grew a bit of a stomach while he was in prison."

Bree shudders next to me, but I continue. "He's socially awkward since he doesn't contact face to face, and he manipulates his victims through the notes he sends. He likes to be in control and isn't a compulsive person." This fucker plays the waiting game a bit too well. The only reason he got to Bree before was because his patience was wearing thin and the police were almost onto him, which made him act more quickly than he would've liked.

"I believe he latched onto Bree because of her looks and personality."

"How so?" Bree asks, a note of false confidence in her voice.

"I dug up some files that were previously sealed," Nico says as he pulls out his tablet.

"How did you get access to them if they were sealed?" Bree asks.

"Princess, don't ask questions you already know the answer to. I hope Vinny here has told you *just* how good I am at my job. I get results, and sometimes the ways I do it aren't so..."

"Legal?" Bree questions, a slight smile on her face.

"I knew I liked you." Nico smirks before continuing. "As I was saying, his ex-girlfriend has the same hair type, color, and build as Bree. They could almost pass for twins. According to a police report I found, she went missing a year before the notes started. Police had Ralph as the main suspect, but no charges were ever filed. She's technically still a missing person."

"That plus his obsessive personality would make sense. He lost one obsession only to latch onto another," I say, all the pieces starting to fall into place. "He prefers knives over—"

Bree shakes her head. "No, he doesn't. He has a gun. It's a silver revolver. I think it holds six or seven rounds."

What? "And you're sure of this?"

"Well, when it's pointed at your face on the worst night of your life, you tend to remember little things like that. I'm sure, Vince."

Christ. I feel like an asshole for some reason. She never told me about that. Our eyes meet, and I can tell she's trying not to slip back to that night.

"That's all I've got." Nico pauses as Bree and I continue to look at one another. "I'm going to go check on the guys."

As he slips out of the room, I speak a few seconds after I'm sure we're alone. "I didn't want to make you go back there. I'm sorry."

"Vince, it's fine. If it helps you catch him faster, then I'll do whatever it takes."

"You say you're comfortable with that, but I'm not. I don't want to cause you any more pain or stress while I'm here." It pisses me off that I might've already. I'm supposed to be protecting her, not adding to her trauma.

"Vince, I can handle it."

"I know you can, but it doesn't mean you *have* to."

She only looks at me, her gaze flitting to my mouth and then back up to my eyes. For once, I can't tell what she's thinking. Her words say one thing, but her tense shoulders, tight jaw, and clenched fists say another.

She's been working out since this morning, yet she's still tense as fuck. "That's all we've got for now. If any other notes get delivered, you'll know about it."

"I'm gonna go shower. I have a brand meeting this afternoon that I have to get ready for."

"Sounds good." After she walks out the door, I take all the anger I'm feeling out on the desk as I swipe everything onto the floor.

Chapter Six

—THE LUCKY ONE BY TAYLOR SWIFT

"What do you wear on a fake date?" my sister asks through my phone.

"Normal clothes, Liv. It's just the relationship that's fake, not anything else." I swipe some blush onto my face before I braid my hair, throwing one of my favorite light brown bows on the end. This relationship is mostly for the media buzz it'll create and, according to Connie, I always have to look camera-ready when I leave the house.

So today, I opted for a simple sweater dress since it's still a bit chilly out. Spring is slowly moving into Pennsylvania, and pairing my cream-colored dress with my favorite brown boots is making me feel more confident already.

I've always thought that a good outfit and a few swipes of lip gloss make me more confident, and my theory is always proven correct. I feel less jittery already.

"Are you sure this is the best idea?"

"Liv, I know you're worried, but don't be. I'll be fine. Vince will be with me the whole time, and our managers called the paparazzi, so there will only be people there they want there."

"Bree, I'll always worry, but I just want to make sure you feel okay about this choice."

It wasn't really a choice. "I'll be fine. I have to go, or I'm going to be late. I love you. Tell Tristan I say hey."

"I will. I love you too." I hang up, and just as I zip my boots, Vince knocks on my door.

He's wearing his usual all-black attire, and when he sees me, his eyes do a once over of my outfit before stopping on the bow at the end of my hair. I grab my purse before throwing my lip gloss, wallet, sunglasses, and phone in it, and when I meet his eyes again, he's looking straight at me.

"Are you ready to go?" His voice doesn't match his expression. It's like he's straining his voice to speak, but his face is still as hard and tight as it normally is. *Is he okay?*

"Yeah, I'm ready." As I say that, my palms start to sweat, and I suddenly feel like my outfit is horrendous. "Do I look okay? I'm basically announcing a relationship to the world, and I feel like I don't look camera-ready."

"If I was him, I'd never take my eyes off you." His voice is *still* doing that weird thing. "Why do you have to do this again?"

"It was Connie's idea. She's trying to get the media off my...situation and onto something better. A lot of couples in Hollywood do this, so it's nothing new. She would rather have good press on me, and it was a mutually beneficial agreement. Alex proves to the public that he can settle down, and I get to stop seeing everyone only talk about Ralph rather than the good I've been doing."

"Ah."

We stand and stare at each other for a few more seconds before I remember we have somewhere to be. My heels click down the stairs, where I find another guy standing there waiting for us. "Emerson, right?"

"Yes, ma'am." He nods at me, and I hold my hand out to introduce myself.

"Bree Hart."

I feel Vince come up behind me before I see him. "Emerson is joining us today. Connie told me how much paparazzi she called, and he's one of my best. He'll drive, and I'll sit in the back with you and escort you into the coffee shop. Sound like a plan?"

"Sounds perfect, boss," I joke with him, and as we head for the car, I start to second guess whatever the hell I've gotten myself into.

⚶

As the car slows to a stop outside the quaint shop, I take a deep breath. *It's just a cup of coffee, Bree. You can do this.*

"Emerson is staying in the car the entire time, and I'll get you inside. Stay behind me and wait for my hand to let you know it's safe to get out of the car."

"Got it." And then he slides out, and I already see flashes of cameras going off. I throw my sunglasses on, wanting the bright lights to go away already.

I was never at this level before Alex, and now, I'm afraid that this whole fake relationship will change that forever. I used to be a girl who sat in her room and ranted about the books she loved, but now, it all feels different. I never could've imagined that this is what my life would turn into—camera flashes anytime I leave the house, my mail having to be sorted in case of any dangerous things, and guys threatening to do things to me without my consent.

I have the things I've always wanted—financial stability, people who care about my thoughts, a life of talking about the books I love—but it's not at all what I imagined it would be.

Vince's hand reaching back into the car breaks my spiral, and I put my hand in his as I get out of the car. That small amount of contact brings awareness to all my senses. Goosebumps travel over my skin, and

I don't know why. *Focus on what you're here for, Bree.* It's probably from my nerves. I'm hoping they'll settle, but I doubt it.

"Step back. You'll get your pictures, don't worry." Vince tells them as I follow him forward, my head down the entire time as they throw questions at me.

"Bree, did Alex fly all the way to Pennsylvania for you?"

"Bree, are you and Alex an item?"

"Is this a first date, Bree?"

"Care to comment on the rumors that Ralph was wrongfully accused?"

My steps falter as that last statement hits me in the face. *Wrongfully accused.* I pause before the door of the coffee shop, my head starting to leave my body before I feel a hand against my arm.

"Bree?" Vince asks me, eyes full of concern. "Let's get you inside."

I nod at him, regaining my composure as I put my fakest smile back on and act like that statement didn't rattle me as much as it did.

Good God, some days, I just wish it would all stop.

As I sit down across from Alex—in a window seat—I paste on my fakest smile and pretend like I'm happy to see him. "Hi."

He reaches for my hand and presses a kiss to my knuckles, the flashes still going crazy. I notice we're the only two people in the coffee shop, and I see a few of his bodyguards posted around as well. Vince has taken up his spot in the far corner, where he's able to see every entrance point. "Hi, baby."

"Did you rent out this whole place just for me?" God, I don't even recognize my own voice. This might be my version of a customer service voice. I sound like my sister at her old job.

"I did. I also got you your favorite drink." He slides the cup over to me, and I take a sip, letting the caffeine calm me down and erase my headache. "Boy, they really are going crazy out there, aren't they?"

"Well, you're you, and wasn't that the point of this? Cleaning up your playboy image, Mr. Adams?"

"Exactly right, Miss Hart, but I thought for sure you'd back out before this. I guess I underestimated you."

"That you did. I do what I'm told, and I do it well." God, I hate this already. Is this what real-life dating is like? If it is, I'm happy to know I'm not missing much. This is as close as I'll ever get to going on a date with someone, so I better make it count. "So, what does one talk about on a date?"

"Oh, honey, I have no clue. I'm not much of a dater per se. I much prefer my partners to be horizontal and silent during our time together."

Ew. "What a charmer you are." Part of me is confused as to his attitude. I did some digging on Alex after our initial meeting, and he had a long-term girlfriend. Granted, it was very on again and off again, but all the pictures I saw of them together, he looked at Lily like she was the only person in the world. I could tell he was in love with her—maybe he still is. They only broke up about a year ago, and I wonder what happened.

If I had that once-in-a-lifetime type of love, I'd do anything to keep it. Unless Alex fucked up pretty badly. I can only speculate since I don't believe all the rumors, but I wonder why he agreed to this if he could still love her.

Though he might not, since he's been fucking most of Hollywood's up-and-coming actors and actresses since the big split.

"So, you're really into books. I wasn't aware that so many people were hardcore readers."

I nod. "I do love escapism. I've read around thirty books so far this year, and—"

He cuts me off. "I don't think I've read a book since the second grade."

Not this. Anytime someone finds out what I do, that phrase is the most common one said back to me. It drives me insane because what am I supposed to say to that? Congratulations and here's a medal for being illiterate? "Everyone has their own hobbies, I guess."

He takes a sip of his drink before he continues the conversation, and I try my best to pay attention, but it's hard when all Alex does is talk about himself. He's not even that interesting of a guy, and I wonder how his fake charm works on so many people. That's the one thing I love about being an influencer: I think people can tell I'm genuinely just a girl and her books, nothing more, nothing less.

A sharp noise startles me, and all of a sudden, I can feel my skin start to crawl.

He's in the house. His steel-toed boots are thumping up the stairs. He's pausing in front of the closet door. He's dragging me out by my ankles, and I'm about to scream, but he puts a gun to my throat that I thought was a knife, and—

"Excuse me," I say as I get up from the table as elegantly as I can before beelining it for the bathroom.

I manage to get in, but my legs feel like jelly as I collapse to the cold tile floor, all the memories of that night rushing through my mind like a tsunami.

I'm not safe.

I'll never be safe.

I'm going to die.

He's going to shoot me, and I'm going to die.

Chapter Seven

— NOT STRONG ENOUGH BY BOYGENIUS

As I watch Bree and Alex on their first public outing, part of me is pissed off that she feels like she has to do this to distract the media. The other part of me is still walking into her room and seeing her smile at me.

Bree is a beautiful girl. Anyone who looks at her knows that, but she's my responsibility, and I need to shake whatever weird feelings I've been having about her off. I can't afford to be distracted because that's when mistakes happen. And when mistakes happen, people get hurt, and I'd rather die than have Bree get hurt because of me.

I shake myself out of my haze when I see her shoot out of her chair and head for the bathroom. *Dammit, Bree.* She should know that I'm supposed to clear it before she goes in, but she doesn't wait for me. All I see her do is head in before the door closes.

I get out of my seat and knock twice on the door, but when I get no response, I burst in, and what I see practically kills me.

Bree's back is against the wall, her head draped between her knees, both her hands covering her face. She doesn't even look up, and I can't tell if she knows I'm in here.

Doing my best not to scare her, I speak as softly as I can. "I'm here, Bree." She doesn't look up at me, so I move to her side. The bathroom is fairly small—two stalls—and I lock the door before I do anything. "Can I touch you?"

I always ask, but especially when she's like this because I don't want her to think I'm him. "Y-Yes."

I douse my hands in cold water from the sink before I grab one of her hands and bring it up to her neck, just like I did last time. "You're okay, Bree. You're safe. He's not here."

"I-I'm—"

"Shh, Bree. Just focus on my voice, focus on the cold, okay?" I feel her nod as her gaze meets mine—fear pouring out of her eyes along with tears. *God, she's shaking.*

A few minutes later, I hear her whisper to herself or me, I can't really tell. "I can't keep living like this."

"Like what?"

"Afraid of every loud sound. Afraid to leave my house. I shouldn't be terrified every second of the day. I should be stronger than this."

That one sentence kills me. Why doesn't she think she's allowed to feel how she does? She went through something traumatic. "You're trying your best, Bree. It's okay to feel on edge and scared. That doesn't make you weak."

"I'm young, my life is seemingly perfect to everyone on the internet, and here I am, falling apart in a bathroom because of a noise." She sniffles, and I grab some tissues from my pocket. She takes them from my hand and blots her eyes. "This was my first big outing after the news broke about his release, and I can't even keep it together for half an hour before something scared the shit out of me."

"You're trying, angel."

She shakes her head at me. "Not hard enough."

I've dodged bullets, punches, and all sorts of shit while on the job, but those three words kill me. I wish she knew that just because she's famous, it doesn't mean she doesn't get to hurt like the rest of us. Sure, Bree has never publicly talked about it, but that doesn't mean she has to force herself to be okay all the time.

She's a goddamn human being, and if she has to fall apart every once in a while, she should be able to without feeling guilty about it. "Do you want me to call Emerson and we can head out? The vultures should have enough pictures for a fucking lifetime."

"Yes, please." I grab my phone from my pocket, letting him know that we're headed out and to clear a path before I throw my hand out for Bree to grab. She takes it immediately, and when she's fully standing, her hand lingers in mine for a few seconds longer than normal before dropping it. "Thank you for helping me through one of those again. I'm sorry that you even—"

"Don't you dare apologize. I'm here for you, you know that." I look down at her and wipe a stray tear from her eye.

"I'm going to freshen up, and I'll be out in a few minutes. Will you—"

"I'll be in front of the door the entire time. Take your time." I exit the bathroom, standing in front of the door like I promised before one of Alex's bodyguards comes over to talk to me.

"All good?"

"Yes. We're ending early today. Bree will be leaving after she's out." He just nods and speaks into his wrist, walking away and whispering something in Alex's ear. I haven't been a big fan of this guy for a few reasons, but him not checking on Bree when he's supposed to care about her in the public eye already has me wishing this situation was over.

He also didn't ask permission to touch her, which I know was in the contract she signed because I read it over a few times to make sure he didn't try anything.

Bree knocks twice on the door, and I move away from the entrance as she steps out. "Is everything okay?"

"Everything's fine. Emerson pulled the car around, so all you have to do is say goodbye, and I'll escort you to the car."

"Perfect. I'm ready."

I head toward the exit as the cameras start to flash again. I don't know how anyone deals with this—the constant flashes and invasion of privacy. It's annoying the shit out of me, and I've only dealt with it today for around forty-five minutes. This is what it's constantly like for Bree wherever she goes now that she's more than just a YouTuber. She's expanded into other things and is one of the most recognizable influencers.

I'm proud of her and what she's done, but I know that she's still trying to make it seem like nobody needs to worry about her.

It's too bad I'll always worry about her, even when the job is up. Rule number six is that when the job is done, you walk away, but I don't see myself ever forgetting my time with Bree, and I don't know why. Part of me feels like there's been this line that pulls me to her, like I was always meant to meet her in some fucked up way.

I wish it wasn't under these circumstances, but no amount of wishing can change that. Plus, she's my responsibility—my client. I could never be with someone like her—good in every sense of the word, caring, thoughtful, *extraordinary*.

I doubt she would want to be with someone like me—cold, quiet, and someone who was literally hired to protect her.

Alex meets us at the door and takes one of Bree's hands in hers. Before he speaks, I beat him to it. "Ask permission next time. You know that."

"My apologies. Is everything alright?" he asks her, sounding like he doesn't really care.

"Everything's fine. Something came up. I'll call you to schedule another date," Bree replies in her sweet tone that really means she wants to get out of the conversation.

"Can I kiss you on the cheek? I think it'll seal the deal for the press outside."

I feel Bree tense even though she's not even touching me, but she agrees. The cameras go crazy as his lips touch her cheek before he pulls back and smiles. Just this kid's mere presence is starting to piss me off, so I head to the door, feeling Bree behind me as I search the area. Emerson has the car door open already, so Bree should be able to slide right in.

Thank fuck. The sooner I can get us out of here, the better. I know Bree is still a little shaken from her panic attack, and I want to get her out of her head as soon as possible. As we step outside, more questions are thrown at her.

"Bree, any comment on that kiss?" *Really?*

"How did you and Hollywood's hottest heartthrob meet?" *Hottest? Yeah, right. The kid's practically a twig.*

"Care to comment on how Lily might feel about this?" *Seriously?*

"How do you think your stalker will react?" *What kind of stupid fucking question is that?*

I slam the door of the Tahoe behind us and hear Bree let out a huge breath as she throws her sunglasses in her purse and stares out the window.

"Home?" Emerson asks me from the front seat, and all I can do is nod as I try not to reach out and comfort Bree, knowing that she needs it and not being able to give it to her.

Chapter Eight

— FAKE SMILE BY ARIANA GRANDE

As I KNOCK ON the door of my sister's house, I suddenly feel nervous.

I've been over here hundreds of times, but for some reason, this time feels different. Liv invited me over for dinner tonight because she missed me, and Teags is coming, too. Since the news about Ralph broke, I've been trying to keep my distance. I'm afraid they could become targets too, and that's the last thing I want.

Ralph wants me, but he would do anything to get to me—including hurt or scare those closest to me.

"Bree!" is all I hear before my sister engulfs me in a hug. I feel Vince step behind me as Liv pulls back and cups my face. "How are you holding up?"

What a loaded question, but I know if I'm honest, Liv will worry, so I lie a little. "I'm hanging in there. One day at a time, right?"

She smiles, understanding full well that sometimes, it's all one is capable of. "Exactly. Come in, you two."

Vince and I step into her house, and instantly, I feel calm. I never felt that way when I would walk into my childhood home—before and after what happened—but something about the atmosphere Liv and Tristan have created just feels like home.

Their three-bedroom home has a beautiful open floor plan that makes the entire place seem bigger than it is. The kitchen opens right into the living room, and the small dining room off the kitchen fits our small family perfectly. Liv's office is right off the living room, and all three bedrooms are upstairs. These two have created the perfect family house, and I'm so excited that they finally get to experience life beside one another.

"There's my favorite influencer," Tristan says as he sets down the knife he was using. He pulls me into a hug, too. "How are you?"

"I'm fine," I say into his ear.

"It's perfectly okay if you're not."

My throat locks up, and before my emotions bubble up, I shove them down as best I can. When I pull away and he sees my face, I know he knows, but he doesn't say anything.

If anyone knows how I feel right now, it's probably him.

Tristan's brother Tobias died last year. It was horrible, sudden, and it wrecked us all. I didn't know him very well, but I still felt the pain of it. Losing someone the way that they did is never easy, and Tristan blamed himself for not seeing the signs. He loves to run away from his feelings, according to Liv, but he's been working on being more open about them. I don't really know how to talk about my own feelings either. My therapist has helped a lot, but I've always avoided it because I don't want anyone to worry about me.

My sister and friends have enough to worry about without adding all my shit to the mix.

"How are you holding up?" I ask him, wanting to switch the subject off me. It's bad enough the media spotlights my trauma all the time; I don't need it to be the topic of conversation when I'm trying to have a nice dinner with my family.

"Some good days and some bad. I know it won't feel like this forever, but some days, it sure feels like it." His eyes sadden, but as he looks over at my sister opening the door for Teags, his eyes sparkle.

Liv is his anchor, and I'm glad they have each other while they adjust to their new life together.

Teags' eyes meet mine, and I know she can tell what's going through my mind, but before she joins us, her eyes move to Vince. He hasn't said a word since we got here, and I know he feels a bit out of place. When I told him he didn't have to come tonight, he just scoffed at me and got the car ready.

He's been attached to my hip, and I don't hate it, but I figured a family dinner wouldn't matter in terms of my safety. He disagreed, and now we're here.

Liv throws Teags' coat in the closet before she heads toward me. "Vince, how nice to see you again."

"Teagen," is all he says. He really is a man of few words.

"Actually, I take it back. It's *not* very nice to see you since you're back to protect Bree from that fucking psychopath."

I hear Vince laugh under his breath as Teags smiles at him. "I feel the same way."

"Vince. We've never formally met, but I'm Tristan." Tristan reaches out to shake his hand, and before I feel like this interaction is going to be awkward, Vince shakes his hand.

"Nice to meet you." This is their first time meeting in person, but I know Vince has an entire folder of everybody in my life with background checks and anything else he managed to dig up. So, Tristan might not know Vince that well, but Vince surely knows him.

"I need all the details about you and Alexander before dinner," Teagen says to me, dragging me by the arm to sit on the couch. I feel Vince behind me, and he sits next to us on the smaller couch.

"Teags, there's really nothing to tell. You and Gregory probably have more fun than I do. It's a *fake* relationship, remember?"

"First rule of tonight is no talking about my sister and her boyfriend. Got it?" Tristan says from the kitchen.

"Babe, what did I tell you earlier?" Liv asks him.

"I know, Liv, but if I hear about my sister and the things she does with her boyfriend, I might combust."

"Stop being such a dad, Tristan. I'm twenty-three years old, and this is what normal girls talk about when they hang out."

I stifle a laugh at how forward my best friend is. "You two are anything but normal, and you know that." Tristan points his knife in our direction, and I hear Liv laugh as she pulls out a few waters for us.

I wish I was normal. Somedays, I feel lucky to live the life I do, but other days, I wish I could've been a normal teenager. I wish I had the chance to go to the mall with my friends, to get coffee with a boy, and be nervous about him touching my leg under the table. I didn't have any of the normal experiences people go through as they age.

I get cameras shoved in my face every time I leave the house. I get so many notifications that I had to turn them off completely, and while I'm grateful for my platform and how I'm able to use it, some days, I just wish I got to be a normal kid.

"So, is Alex every bit of the dick everyone says he is?" Teags asks me.

"Well—"

"Yes," Vince says before I can answer and defend Alex.

"Oh, the plot thickens." Teags smiles, and when I look over at Vince to scold him, he's already looking at me. *Damn, that stare does something to me.* I've never seen a gaze that affects me like his does, and again, I'm blaming books. That's the only reason his heated stare seems to make my insides feel all tingly. No other reason.

"He's fine. We've only been on one fake date so far, with many more to come."

"I still don't understand this whole fake dating thing. Why did Connie do this in the first place?"

"Tristan, you don't really need to understand it. It is what it is," I snap, a bit harshly, and I immediately regret it. I'm just sick of talking about this.

"It just feels like bullshit. Why make you fake date someone to distract from the news about Ralph rather than focus on finding him? It rubs me the wrong way."

"You and me both," Vince speaks up, and for someone who's usually quiet, he sure has a lot to say tonight. His gaze meets mine again. "It's not fair to you, and that Alex kid sucks at following the fucking rules."

"The rules?" Teags questions, and I shake my head.

"It's nothing."

"No, it's not, Bree. He touched you without asking. The kid is a fucking prick."

"I'm sorry, he what?" Tristan shouts.

"I'll snap his wrist if he does that again, Bree. Just let me know which hand." Teags smiles, maybe a bit too joyfully at the thought of doing that.

"Can we please stop talking about this? It's bad enough that I'm in the situation in the first place. I want to know about your book, Liv. How's it going?"

"My girl's book is still in the top one hundred of the Kindle store." Tristan smiles, proud of everything my sister has accomplished.

"Thank you, baby. It's going well. Marketing has been kicking my ass, but I guess I'm doing okay." Liv's face flushes, and I instantly know she's uncomfortable. She always gets weird talking about her success, but I'll never stop shouting about my sister and how talented she is. Her books are like a breath of fresh air, and there's a reason why people love them so much.

"I'm proud of you, Liv. Did you see my video about the release?" I ask her.

"Yes. Your new vlog style is super cute. I love all the little doodles you add to the screen. It really makes things pop."

"My favorite part was watching all the guys cry when Liv read the dedication. I swear, Dom looked like he was going to start blubbering," Teags laughs, but I see right through her. That mention of Dom was no slip of the tongue. In fact, that was probably her favorite part of the video.

Teags has been crushing on Dom since she met him, but I doubt those two will ever happen. After all, she's in a relationship with someone else, whom she seems to like. *I think.* They've only been dating since January, so a few months, but this has officially been her longest relationship. Teags isn't one for staying attached to someone for long periods of time—at least romantically—so she must really like this guy.

Teags loves reading romance books, since her parents' relationship made her believe in love, and she believes it's possible for her.

I don't.

And I don't *want* anyone to be in love with me. It's too hard. I can barely deal with the invasions of privacy, and I doubt anyone else would.

It's not easy to love me, but Teags and my sister prove that theory wrong every single day. My sister is one of the only people in the world who makes me feel like I matter, and Teags is my one true friend. Most of the influencer friends I have are only in it to up their follow count by being seen with me. It's all superficial and fake—purely for social status.

But Teags has become someone I can't live without, and if I told her that, she would gag, but I know she feels the same about me. She doesn't do feelings well, but her actions show otherwise.

"Are you guys ready for dinner?" my sister asks us, and we all congregate around the table.

AFTER A DINNER FILLED with us making fun of Tristan, Liv pulls me into her office. I feel bad for leaving Vince, but Liv told him this was an important, sister's only conversation, and when he looked at me for confirmation, I nodded.

I take a glance around Liv's office, both of her books now lining the shelves behind her desk. I trace one of her shelves with my hand as I feel her gaze pierce my back. I know why she brought me in here. She wants to really talk to me, to make sure I'm okay.

I may be good at masking my emotions, but my sister is the one person I could never hide from.

Wanting to push that conversation off a bit longer, I head to a safe one. "I loved these two. I read them only recently even though they've been published for a while."

I trace the spines of two of my favorite reads from last year.

"That's my favorite shelf. I read those two because of you. I think you mentioned them in a video once, and they both piqued my interest." I turn to face her and see her leaning against her desk.

"Dinner was good. I didn't know Tristan could cook that well."

"Yes, you did, Bree." *Damn. I'm caught.* "How are you doing with everything? Have you been talking to Dr. Anna lately?"

"Yes, I have. I'm afraid she might block my phone number if I keep calling her." It's funny, but the truth. I've talked to her every single day, sometimes even twice. It barely helps, but if I don't talk about it with her, it'll fester. Sometimes, it's easier to talk to a complete stranger about how my life is falling apart rather than someone I know.

"It's good that you're getting it all out. Are you taking care of yourself? Are you eating enough? Tristan can wrap up some leftovers for you to take—"

I cut her off; Liv's a rambler when she's nervous, and in a minute she might start pacing. "Liv, I'm fine. I'm making do. Having Vince around has helped. He got me a new security system."

"So why do you sound like you're not sleeping? You better not be working out all night like you used to. I swear, you left tread marks on the floor at the old house from how much you used the treadmill. It's not healthy, Bree."

Speaking of our old house... "Have you talked to our parents lately?" I ask, wondering if they've tried to reach out to her. It's been radio silence on my end, and I'm fine with that.

"Nope, and I don't plan on it. They don't deserve to hear about my successes that they never believed in."

"Damn right." I smile, happy for my sister finally standing up for herself. My parents always knew how I felt—smothered and angry at them for their actions—but Liv was never one who stood up for herself. She deserved to let them have it after what they did to her and Tristan.

Liv's practically been my parent since I could remember. She always takes care of me, and I know if she decides to have kids of her own, she'll make a great mom.

"Bree, I want you to know I'll always be here for you. I know I don't really understand what you're going through, but if you just need someone to sit with you while you're having a hard time, I can do that. Just call me, and I'll be there."

Emotion clogs up my throat, and all I can do is nod. "I haven't been sleeping. My noise machine and the night light don't help anymore. Knowing he's out there is fucking with my head. I always feel like some-one's watching me while I sleep, and I can't shake the feeling that he's right around the corner."

"Vince stays in your house, right?"

"Yeah, he's down the hall."

"And how does that make you feel?" she asks, a hint of something in her voice.

"Safer, but I still can't shake the feeling. It eats away at me like a tapeworm."

Liv comes over to where I stand against her bookshelf and grabs my hands. "It's okay to feel how you're feeling. You don't need to be on all the time. You're allowed to crack and break apart as long as you trust that those who love you will be there to piece you back together."

Tears start to fall as what she says invades my bones. "Thanks, Liv." I take what she says into consideration, but I know there's no use. I've always been hard on myself, and this is no different. I still grapple with what Ralph did to me since it could've been worse, but that doesn't change that I'm still a victim of something horrible. Nothing I can do will erase that night from my memory.

"Promise you'll talk to me if it gets hard. I want to be there for you, Bree, but I can't do that if you're not being honest with me." She holds her pinky out, and I take it, solidifying the promise.

"I'll try my best."

"That's all I ask."

A few light knocks on the door make both of our heads turn. Tristan pops in, holding onto the door. "Livvy, the sun is setting. I'm forcing everyone onto the porch if you guys want to join."

"We'll be right out." She smiles at him as I try to discreetly wipe the tears from my eyes. Liv's hand stays in mine as she pulls me onto their front porch, five chairs already set up where there's normally two. My sister and Tristan have this tradition where they watch the sunset every night. It's a cute thing they started back in college, and whenever we all get together at night, they make us join.

Well, they don't force us, but sometimes it's nice to watch the day end when you know another is going to begin.

I sit down in my chair, Teags to my left, Vince to my right. I tap his shoulder. "Did you survive?"

"Yeah. I think I like Tristan."

Oh, wow. "Really?" I wasn't expecting that. Vince doesn't really *like* people. He tolerates them, which is why I was so surprised to hear he and Nico created a business together.

"Yeah. He's fine."

I drop it because that's all I'll get out of him tonight. When I watch the sun set in the sky, I hope to have more nights like this one in my future.

But that feeling in my gut won't go away. The fear will always creep back in just when I start to finally feel okay again.

Chapter Nine

Four Years Ago

— THE NIGHT WE MET BY LORD HURON

"Vince Evans? You can come on in." A slim man pokes his head out of the conference room, and I join him inside. I thought there would be more people here, but it appears to be just us.

I already regret taking this case. My handler at the agency said it was a rush job and that they asked for the best. Now that I'm here, I wish I wasn't. I wasn't given any details or anything about who I'd be protecting, and I'm hoping to get some clarity now.

"Connie will be right in. Can I get you some water?"

I shake my head at him, and he leaves, submitting me to the silence of this room. I notice that he frosted the glass, and I like the little bit of privacy. I did some digging about this place, and it's a public relations management firm, so I assume some rich socialite needs protection.

I hope that's *not* the case, but either way, I'll do my job.

A hard knock on the door comes, and I stand as Connie enters the room—I assume. I don't know who else it would be. At first glance, I notice the tension in her shoulders, the bags under her eyes, and I can almost feel the stress rolling off her. *Has she not slept?* That immediately causes my senses to perk up, and the weird feeling in my gut is telling me this is more serious than I thought.

And my own rule is that when you have a gut feeling, it's probably right.

She meets me where I stand and offers me her hand. "Connie. Thank you for getting here so quickly."

"No problem, ma'am," I say as she sits across from me.

"Please, just Connie. I'm not a ma'am, and I hate formalities." She takes a deep breath before she slides a folder over to me. "It's been a rough few days around here. That folder contains a bare-bones gist of information about Bree and what happened. It even has some of the notes he left inside, but I can explain it if you prefer that."

"I'll take anything you want to give me." The more information I have, the better, and I never take any chances. If I don't know everything, someone could wind up getting hurt, and I've never lost anybody I've protected.

Yet.

The little voice in the back of my head nags at me like always, but I disregard it for now, returning my attention to Connie.

"You'll be protecting Bree Hart. She's a social media influencer with around ten million followers across all social platforms."

I've never heard of this girl, but I'm nine years older than her, so it makes sense that I haven't. I doubt my older sister has either. It says in her file that Bree is twenty years old, and I wonder how long she's been doing this to have garnered that many followers.

The pit in my stomach is nervous to ask what happened for her to need a bodyguard, but I don't say anything as Connie continues.

"Over the past few months, Bree has received notes from an obsessed fan. We know it's the same guy because of the signature, and the police analyzed her mail so we could have every note he's sent on file.

"A few days ago, Bree was attacked inside her home by the man we believe has been sending her these notes. If you flip to the last one, you'll see why we think that."

I open the folder, and sure enough, photocopies of the notes rest right on the top. I flip through fifteen to twenty pages, and when I get to the last one, goosebumps race up my arms.

On the page, in detail, is what this guy wants to do to her when he finally gets his hands on her. He talks about how they're meant to be, that nobody else will be able to have her because he's going to make sure she's his forever.

My blood is running cold at the *detail* he gives.

"Oh," is all I can say.

"Yeah. The worst part is that it was completely preventable. Bree's parents didn't take it seriously, and well, you can see what happened in the report from the hospital. I wish we had you sooner, but there was nothing I could do."

Fuck her parents. They shouldn't be able to *be* parents after this. How do you fail to protect your own daughter? It's laughable—they get to be parents while mine died and will never exist again.

But this isn't about me. It's about her, and I need to do what they failed to—protect her from this fucker.

"The guy ran off before the police got inside, but not after he kept his promise."

Fuck. "What happened?"

"Bree was assaulted. She still has some visible bruising on her ankles and neck, and I ask that when she comes in, you remain seated."

What the fuck did this guy do to her? And why didn't they get her a female bodyguard? I assume this girl will run for the hills when she sees me. I'm not a soft guy. I'm a bit rough around the edges, and most people are scared of me when they see me. Even those I work with at the agency have told me I make them nervous, even after seven years.

I guess I'll just have to tone that part of myself down if I even know how to. Most of the people I guard are politicians, events that need an extra set of hands, and witnesses in criminal proceedings. I've never had to protect someone so young, famous, or one who has been recently traumatized.

"I can do that."

"Thank you. I'll go grab Bree." She gets up, and I set the folder onto another chair, opting to look at it later. A few seconds later, she comes back with two girls, both young looking, and I stay seated. They sit across the table from me, and I notice the blonde one is wearing a thick scarf around her neck despite it being warm and sunny outside. *That's gotta be her.*

The brown-haired one speaks first. "I'm Liv, and this is my sister, Bree."

"Vince Evans." I'd normally say it's nice to meet them, but it isn't. These girls are too young to be dealing with this.

"Connie told us you're the best," Liv says.

"Yes, ma'am."

"Good. We're not requiring you to live in our parents' house, but anytime Bree leaves or has some event to go to, you'll be with her. Does that sound okay?"

"It sounds perfect. There's a hotel across the street from your place, so I'll always be around."

"Great. I'm glad we're on the same page." She smiles, and I notice that Bree hasn't said anything yet. I hope I'm not scaring her. I usually prefer not to personally attach myself to my clients, but something about this case is different.

Something about *her* feels different, and I can't pinpoint why. It's probably because she's the youngest client I've ever had. Let's go with that. Rule number three is to never get attached to your clients, and most of the jobs I'm on, I don't speak. It's trickling into my daily life now, and most people are put off by my silence, so it wouldn't surprise me if they are, too.

"Could I have a moment alone with Bree?" I move to where her vacant eyes stare back at me, hoping she'll say yes. I like to get a basis of who each client is, but I understand if she doesn't want to.

Bree nods her head before Liv places her hand in hers. "If you don't want to, it's okay, Bree."

"It's okay, sis." Her voice comes out in a whisper, and I wonder if her vocal cords were damaged. I barely looked at the hospital records.

"We'll be right outside," Connie says as the two of them leave. The door clicks softly behind them, and neither of us speaks as silence blankets the room.

Before I explain myself, I try to make my voice a bit softer, with less edge. I can already tell if I spoke like I normally do, I'd scare her, and that's *not* what I'm trying to do.

"I have a few rules I like to go over with my clients before we start. Is that okay?"

"Yes," she whispers again.

"There's only five of them. Never be unreachable. I always need to be able to reach you, so you'll have my number saved. No physical contact unless it's an emergency. I won't touch you unless your safety is concerned, or I'm trying to help you. Is that okay with you?"

"Yes, actually. Thank you." The whisper comes out a bit hoarser, and I have to clench my fingers to stop myself from breaking this fucking table.

She's twenty years old. She shouldn't have to deal with shit like this, and it pisses me off more than my cases usually do.

"Number three is no personal attachments. We can make small talk, of course, but my main job is to protect you, and if I get attached, my judgment will be clouded."

"Understood."

"Number four: I'll be here until this is done. That means that until he's dead or behind bars, I'll be by your side."

"And if he gets caught and gets out? What happens then?" Her hoarse whisper is getting a bit more strained, and I notice her leg hasn't stopped shaking.

"Is that something you're worried about? Also, if writing your questions down helps your voice, feel free to do that."

I swear, I hear her say something to the effect of being worried about everything, but before I can speak, she writes something down and slides it over to me.

Felony stalking means up to five years in prison, but most get out before then on good behavior. It happened in most of the cases I looked at in Pennsylvania. So yes, I'm worried about that.

"I understand. Well, if it makes you feel better, if he gets out, I'll come back. How does that sound?" She writes something down before sliding the paper over again.

I'd rather him be dead, but yeah, that sounds good.
Thank you.

I clear my throat before I speak again. "No problem. Now, rule number five is to never go anywhere without a knife. I carry a pistol on my hip and will only use it if it's necessary. I always let people know that just in case."

"Does that mean I'll carry a knife as well?"

"Not if you don't want to, but I'll always have one."

"I don't need one." She shakes her head.

"Okay. That's all I have for now. Just let me know when you leave the house, and I'll be over."

"I probably won't be for a while, but if you want to just hang around, that's okay too." She gets up and heads for the door. "And next time, speak normally, Vince. You don't scare me like you think you do."

Damn. She's tougher than I gave her credit for. "Noted, ma'am."

"Bree."

"Noted, Bree. I'll walk you out."

She nods her head at me, and as I walk her and Liv out of the building, I find myself wondering more about what makes the youngest Hart sister tick, but I quickly shake that thought away.

Now

"Vince? Vince? Baby brother, did you go through a tunnel or something?"

I shake my thoughts out of that first meeting I had with Bree, and turn my attention back to my sister. "No, Aria, I'm still here."

"Good. I thought you were ignoring me."

"How could I with your incessant calls? I told you I'm working. I'm *busy*, not dead."

"Forgive me for worrying about you, Vince. You have no friends, you work too much, and you have no social life. I hate texting Nico to ask how you are because even he doesn't know. Isn't that sad? Your *only* friend, probably your best friend, doesn't even know how you're doing."

"I'm doing fine. How's that?" I smirk from across the line, and I hear my sister sigh heavily.

"Vince, I know you hate attaching yourself to people, but you're thirty-three, for God's sake. Your lifespan is going to seriously decrease if you don't form relationships with someone. You can't just have Nico."

Here we go again with this shit. My sister is one of my favorite people on the planet, but ever since she stepped up to raise me after our parents died, she feels more like my parent than my sister. Which, to be fair, she kind of was. I was only fourteen when our parents died, and she was nineteen, forced to become my guardian.

I can't imagine doing what she did. I can't imagine having to deal with her grief and raise my dumb ass. She had it harder than me, but sometimes, she forgets to turn the mothering part of herself off

"Sis, you know I don't need anybody else. I have all I need. I've got you, Nico, and my girl. How is she anyway?"

"*Your girl* is fine. I'm taking her on a walk later."

"Good. Did you buy her favorite treats? And did you—"

"Dude, calm down. Nellie is thriving, surviving, and having a wonderful time with me. She misses you, though. She told me herself."

"I bet she does. I miss her too." Nellie is my golden retriever who's currently living with my sister. I was going to grab her after my last assignment, but Bree's situation threw a wrench in my plans. I could bring her here, but I don't know how Bree feels about dogs. Still, moving my dog into her house feels a bit too...real. I wouldn't want Nellie to get used to the surroundings either, especially since it would only be temporary.

"Back to the subject at hand, though. Forming relationships with people has always been something you've sucked at. Not everybody is going to leave in the manner that our parents did. I'm just saying that you need to stop working yourself to death and actually have a life. That's all I'm asking."

"I'll think about it." I hate when she does this. In the back of my mind, I know that if I get close to people, they won't end up crushed under a semi-truck on the side of the road, but the little voice in my head always nags at me that it *could* happen.

Just like it did when I was young.

Plus, I can't get attached to clients, so where else am I supposed to meet people? It all sounds way too exhausting, and since what I do for work makes me happy, it's all I'll ever need.

"So, what case are you on? Or can you not tell me?"

I was afraid she would ask that. "Uh, it's kind of a boring one. Nothing too fancy."

"Vince, don't lie to me. Your voice just went up an entire octave. Why are you being so weird?"

"Why are you being nosy?"

"Because I'm your sister. Now, since you can't stare at me and get me to back down over the phone, tell me."

I run a hand down my face. "I'm back with Bree."

"Oh. The fucker got out then?"

"Yup."

I can practically hear her smirk from this side of the phone. "You've never gone back to a client before."

"Yeah, and?" I snap at her, already knowing what she's insinuating.

"Isn't that the reason you have eleven rules now and not just five? Rule number six is when the job is done, you walk away. You added that one after you left her the first time, remember?"

"Yeah, sis, I fucking remember. They are *my* rules."

"Slow your roll, Vince. I'm just pointing out that she's different. I'm not jumping to any conclusions."

"I bet you're not." She absolutely is. Sure, Bree is the only client I've ever returned to protect, but I promised her that if Ralph got out, I'd be back, and I'm not one to break a promise.

Especially to her.

I'm a naturally protective person, but with Bree, it's dialed up tenfold. Part of me wants to shield her from every bad thing that could happen, but I know I can't do that. I can only do my best to make sure Ralph doesn't ever fucking touch her again.

Given the chance, I'd kill him just so she could sleep soundly at night.

"Look, Aria, I have to go. Say hi to Max for me and give Nellie my love, okay?"

"I will. You should come visit soon. I miss you."

"After this case, I'll come up. I promise."

"Okay, good. And think about what I said, Vince. It's scientifically proven that people who have strong bonds with others live longer."

"I bet it is. I'll talk to you soon."

"Talk to you soon. Be careful."

"I always am." I smile as I hang up the phone. My sister and I never say goodbye; we prefer to use statements that don't feel so final. It's been that way since she got the call about our parents.

That's one thing my parents always told us—death may be final, but people live on in so many other ways. It's something I've always carried with me, and I know that anytime I'm struggling, my parents will be looking out for me, wherever they are.

Chapter Ten

— THE 1 BY TAYLOR SWIFT

"Ugh, this main male character is hot as fuck," Teags says from across my reading room. She's sitting on the beanbag chair I have in the corner of the room.

My reading room has bookshelves on either side of it, then a wall with windows because I love how the natural lighting looks, especially in the mornings. My shelves are about seventy percent full. Thank God I still have room, because having no shelf space is the worst thing in the entire world. If that happens, I usually stack my books in towers on the floor.

The walls are light pink, and fairy lights decorate my shelves. I like turning them on at night for a beautiful ambiance. It's like I have my own personal library, and this is by far my favorite room in the house.

I'm sitting on my futon as I adjust my body so I have a better view of Teags.

"What mafia man are you falling in love with this time?"

"Hey! Don't knock my newest book boyfriend. He just threatened to kill someone for touching his wife."

Oh shit. "Nothing gets you going like threatening murder."

"I know!"

"Does Gregory often do that?" I say, wanting to know more, but knowing Teags probably still won't budge.

"He's not like that, but that's fine with me."

"Are you sure?" I find it odd that Teags has been so secretive about this guy, and I know her girl crush on Dom still exists, so what the hell is going on inside her head?

"Yes, I'm sure. Gregory is nice and patient. I think that's what I need in a guy anyway. Someone who's not like me whatsoever. It brings a nice balance to things."

Yeah, right. She's lying through her teeth. For one, she's brushing through the ends of her hair while she speaks, which is her tell. If I know my best friend like I think I do, she wants someone who makes her feel as alive as the dark romance books she reads.

Teags needs to meet her match, and maybe one day she will, but I don't see Gregory being that for her.

"Understood. It's nice that you know you have a type. I don't think my type exists anymore."

"Oh, believe me, I know your type: emotionally unavailable, tall, has an arm sleeve, name rhymes with—"

I throw one of my pillows at her because I hate what she's insinuating. "He's my bodyguard, Teags. He's just doing his job."

"And? He's *beautiful* to look at. I swear, that stare is panty-dropping. He has aged quite nicely these past few years."

"Ew, Teags. Stop it."

She only giggles at me. Teagen West is *giggling* at me. "I'm just saying, girl. He came back for you. He kept his promise, and you can't ignore how he looks at you."

"How he looks at me is his *literal* job, Teags."

"Yeah, and you have always loved protective men, at least in books. Now that you have your own, who knows what could happen?"

"Nothing. That's what's going to happen. Now, this is a reading date, not gossip time, so hush."

"You're the one who started asking me about Greg," she mumbles, flipping the page of her book.

"You're a closed door about the guy, babe. Forgive me for wanting any crumbs you could give me. Plus, my relationship is fake. Let me live vicariously through yours."

"I'm happy you have your platform, but Gregory was my choice. You didn't have any say in the whole Alex situation. Doesn't that get annoying?"

"Yeah, it does." I wish I had choices over my life, especially about who I'm dating. Even though Alex and I are real in the media's eyes, we'll never have that connection.

This conversation is bringing me back to the only boy I ever loved—or thought I did—until he broke my heart.

Seven Years Ago

As I sit across from Tommy, gaze full of wonder, I notice that he looks a little nervous. We've only been dating for around seven months, but it's been going great. The two of us are only seventeen, but he's the first boy I've ever loved, and if life works out for us, he'll be the last.

We're sitting outside of one of my favorite places—a coffee shop around the corner from school. It's a fairly nice day out, and I'm wearing one of my pink sundresses. Tommy opted for his normal spring attire—black joggers and a simple blue t-shirt. His blond hair is messy, with some straight pieces peeking through on the sides.

"So, for my next video, I was thinking about doing a day in my life. Is it okay if you're in it? I know how you feel about your privacy, and it doesn't even have to be your face if you don't want it to be."

"Bree, listen—"

"Oh! I also had this idea where you pick the books I'll read for that month. It's a trend going around, and I *really* want to do it. I feel like you have pretty good taste, too." Tommy and I only started dating when my channel was first gaining traction, but now, I have over a million subscribers. It's *insane*, but I can't imagine not making it. I love being able to share my love for books, and most people have been so sweet.

Life feels like a dream lately, one I hope I never have to wake up from. I know I spend a lot of my time in different book realities, but one I never want to stray from is the one I live in. If this life is a dream, I hope I never wake up.

"That sounds fun, but—"

Before he can speak, I feel someone tap me on the shoulder. When I turn around, a girl my age is looking at me. "Hi, are you Books with Bree on YouTube?"

"Hi! Yes, that's me. It's so nice to meet you!"

"I knew it was you! I wasn't going to interrupt you, but I knew if I didn't at least say hi, I would regret it! I absolutely love your videos. You give some of the best recommendations."

"Thank you so much. That's so kind of you."

"Can I get a picture?" she asks me, and I nod. I take a selfie with her, and then she leaves.

That's one thing I'll never get used to—people recognizing me. It's always so weird, but I love meeting people who watch my videos. I wouldn't have my platform without them, and they're always so sweet.

"I'm sorry, Tommy. Where were—"

"I can't do this anymore, Bree."

My stomach drops. "Do what?"

"Us. It's too hard. I'm breaking up with you."

I feel tears start to fill my eyes, but I try my best to keep them at bay. I didn't see this coming. Everything has been perfect, and I thought we were happy, but maybe that was only me. Did I do something wrong? "Why? I thought everything was going well between us?"

"You're too recognizable. All you care about is your channel and books, and it doesn't feel like you care about me anymore. All you do is work, and you're never around. This is the first time in days where you're not preoccupied, and you still chose to talk to a fan over me."

"Tommy, it was barely a five minute conversation! Do you want me to ignore my fans? Because I won't do that. They're the reason I have my platform; I can't just ignore them when they want to talk to me for a second!"

He runs a hand through his hair before he scoffs at me. "It's just too much—the fame, your work. You don't seem to be in the relationship like I am. I think you need to do some serious evaluating if you get into a relationship after this. Don't fall in love with someone, because there's no way any ordinary person could deal with your job if it gets worse than this. Don't put someone through that, Bree. It's bad enough that I had to deal with it for a few months, but if you get bigger, I don't even want to think about that."

Don't put someone through that. Has he always been this much of an asshole, or am I only noticing that now? "What I do moving forward is none of your business, Tommy. I'm sorry I became too hard for you to deal with, but I thought being in a relationship meant that you stood by your partner no matter what, even if things got tough. So maybe *you* should think about that for your future."

"Maybe you should get a life instead of burying your head in those unrealistic books." He leaves me sitting at the table, tears brimming as I pick up my phone and dial my sister.

"Can you come pick me up?"

"I'm on my way. Are you okay? What happened?"

"I'll explain, just get here, please," I say as I wipe a stray tear from my eyes.

THAT DAY CHANGED A lot for me. Gone was the girl who believed in falling in love, in fairytales, in happy endings with someone you love despite it all. Gone was the girl who believed my favorite fictional boyfriends were setting the standard for real life, and in her place is a girl who just wants someone to choose her.

I want to be someone's choice. I want them to choose to be with me.

I've since grown like he knew I would, my heart has been kept under lock and key. Because deep down, I'm sure he's right—nobody would want to deal with all this. Somedays, I don't even want to. I'm exhausted in every way possible, and no person could ever love me how I am now. Nobody wants to love someone with a stalker on the loose threatening her every move. Nobody wants to love someone who can't even hear a loud noise without breaking down into tears, and someone who can't sleep without lights and sounds on.

I'm too broken to be loved. If Tommy thought I wasn't worth it, then what am I now?

Worthless. That's what I am. I'm destined for fake relationships and lackluster connections for the rest of my life. I'm stupid to even think that anyone could choose me after they get to know everything about me.

My road to love looks bleak. It's a path that nobody else but me is on, and I'm destined to find nothing at the end of it.

"I wish love like this existed in real life," Teags sighs as she flips the page.

"Is everything okay with Gregory? You know you can talk to me if it's not."

Her puzzled face meets mine. "Everything's fine. Why?"

"I don't know. You just seem really against love for someone in a relationship."

"I can be in a relationship and still think love is embarrassing. I mean, look at what my brother and Liv have. I adore their relationship, but it's almost hilarious how head over heels he is for her."

As he should be. It's what my sister deserves. The irony of Teags being in a relationship and saying all this is not lost on me, and maybe someday, I'll get the truth out of her. "Yeah, well, it's possible for them. It's never going to be possible for me."

"Bree, it *is* possible for you. You're the one too stubborn to even try. One day, you'll meet someone, fall in love, and create a beautiful life together. I just can't see myself ever loving someone, if that makes sense."

"You don't love Gregory?"

Teags just continues reading, swiftly avoiding my question. I decide not to press any further, but I can't help but smile. This conversation has been so normal, and I love it. I love sitting here talking about boys, books, and love like a regular girl would do with her friend.

I wonder if she knows I've never had anything normal, that I'm extremely thankful she's able to give me a piece of it every so often. I go to tell her that when her phone buzzes a few times.

"Shit, Tristan needs me. Theo just got home, and he's drunk again."

My heart lurches for the West family. Tristan and Teags have been holding their family up since Tobias left. It's only been six months, and all of them cope in their own way, but Theo has been struggling. He has good days, but lately, it feels like the bad ones are more frequent.

Tristan only recently started to heal, and Teagen is trying her best, but I know she still cries when nobody can see her. I know she hides her pain from the world because she hates talking about it. Emotions and Teagen don't mix well.

But I also know Teags is strong, and when she wants to talk to me about it, she will. I just have to let her grieve and deal with it how she knows best.

And like myself, I know how hard it is to be the youngest in a family, to feel like you have to be perfect. You feel like you have to be the person nobody worries about, so you shove your emotions down until they explode one day. You have to let your older siblings know that they did okay, and make sure they don't have to worry about you while they figure their own shit out.

"Have you thought about getting him help? He's been like this since the funeral."

"Yeah. Tristan and I have talked about it, but we don't think Theo would be too happy with us."

"Wow, a stubborn West sibling, I can't believe it," I joke, and she smiles at me. "I'm just saying that your family offered me help when I needed it, and even though I never took it, I'm always willing to help. I'm sure Dr. Anna could recommend a colleague for Theo. Just let me know."

"Thanks, Bree." She pauses, unsure if she wants to say something next. "Somedays, I wish we could just leave Pennsylvania and run away together. I think you're the only person on Earth who understands me and all my quirks."

"I have days like that, ones where I wish I wasn't who I am, that I could leave all of this behind and start a new life." I grab her hand even though I know she hates physical touch. "But then, I remember that if I went back in time and changed it all, I'd never have met you."

"I'm glad I know you too, Bree. You're my best friend. No matter what your ghosts are, you'll always be that for me."

"I love you to the moon, Teags."

"And back, Bree. I'll see you later."

"See you later," I say before I pick my book back up and get lost in a reality I know I'm safe in.

For now.

Chapter Eleven

— BUSYHEAD BY NOAH KAHAN

It's been two weeks of nothing but silence.

Besides the noise in my head, no notes have been left, no creepy packages, and that scares me more than actually getting stuff from Ralph.

I've gone on two more dates with Alex, and they've been fine. Nothing has made me have a panic attack like the first time. His company is still not the best thing ever, but I've barely seen anything in the media about Ralph, so I guess Connie was right.

Love and relationships *can* distract the general public. Still, I hate that I basically had no choice in this. My entire life doesn't really feel like mine anymore, and I don't know how to make it feel like I'm in control again.

Ralph has taken so much from me—my safety, sanity, control, but the worst thing he took was my ability to just exist. I was twenty when he did what he did, still a girl trying to figure out who she wanted to be, but he made that choice for me. I will always be a victim. I will always be the thing that happened to me. That's why I refuse to talk about it online. People can speculate all they want, but it's my story to tell, and I'll tell it when I want to. That day may never come, but it's my choice to share it, and nobody is taking that away from me.

He has already taken so much. He doesn't get to share *my* story with the world. He's just the man who hurt me, but I will always be the terrorized girl who watched him walk into my house with a gun at his side.

I've never been a big relationship girl before, but now, I can't see myself ever having any type of relationship with someone like everyone else can. I don't see myself ever experiencing that feeling of choosing to be with someone despite it all, of growing alongside someone else as you age and experience life together. That will never be in the cards for me because if Ralph gets caught, someone else could just as easily take his place.

I'm never going to be safe again, and nobody would ever choose this life over a quieter and more peaceful one.

As my brain starts to spiral, I dial my therapist. She picks up almost immediately. "Hi, Bree. It's wonderful to hear from you."

I scoff at that. "As if I didn't call you yesterday."

"You call me every single day, but it's always good to hear your voice. How are you feeling today?"

The question seems so simple, but it has a thousand different answers to it. "I'm here, I think."

Anna always makes me say that when I can feel myself wanting to slip into a safer reality—whether in my head, in books, music, or anything else. It's my coping mechanism, according to her. When I feel unsafe and scared, I bolt to another place that will make me feel safe.

"That's good to hear. Is there anything specific you wanted to talk about? Anything on your mind today?"

Anna's a very question-led therapist. She likes to get me talking, even if none of what I'm saying is making sense. She understands that my brain and my thoughts can often get overwhelming, and this helps me to just speak and not have time to lie or keep it hidden. I learned the hard way that if you try to bury everything, it doesn't end well.

"I'm feeling scared, a bit guilty. Same old shit, just a different day."

"That's part of the process, Bree. Remember what I told you on our first session?"

"That my mind is like a pot of boiling water. Sometimes, the temperature is high and everything overflows, and other times, it'll be on a low simmer, and those are the days I feel okay."

"Good. Today feels like an overflow day, so what's on your mind?"

"I've been thinking about this one conversation I had with Teagen two weeks ago." Anna is very familiar with Teags. She thinks it's good that I have someone like her, and I always agree. Even though Teags isn't a big emotional person, she's always there when I need her.

"And what did you two talk about?" I can hear her scratching something down on her notepad over the phone, and I let the words flow out.

"She told me how she thinks about running away sometimes, just the two of us. And I told her I think about that too, but I wasn't honest with her."

"Why?"

"I didn't tell her that what I think about is running away so the people I love aren't in danger, how I want to run away and have Ralph follow me and stay away from them." I'd do it in a heartbeat if I was brave enough, but the selfish part of me wants to stay surrounded by the people I love, even if it means Ralph could go after them to get to me.

"That's perfectly normal to feel, Bree, especially with everything you have going on, but remember what I told you. The people you're surrounded by, even though they might not understand what you're going through, are your lines. You're the kite flowing in the wind, whipping around and feeling like chaos, and they are the lines that anchor you back to reality. You have to have a support system while you heal."

Tears stream down my face. "But what do I do if one of them gets hurt because of me? How do I deal with knowing I was the reason?"

"Bree, these people have chosen you. They know all about your situation, and they stayed. They stayed by your side because they love you. If they didn't, they wouldn't be here—like your parents. They don't deserve to feel your love, but your sister and Teags do."

"But what happens if it gets to be too much? What happens if they leave, if nobody stays?"

"Don't let the what-ifs cloud your brain, Bree. Come back to right now with me, okay?"

I take a few steadying breaths before I feel my mind start to clear. Sometimes, I hate my mind. Scratch that—I always hate it. My anxiety and PTSD feel like this gigantic invisible thing in front of me, but I can't physically fight it because it's all coming from my own mind. All of these thoughts and feelings are just me. None of these feelings exist outside of my body, and nothing that I do will ever change that.

I am my own worst enemy. Every single day, I'm fighting a war within myself, and I can't get it to stop. I can only turn the burner off until something knocks into it again and my water starts to overflow.

"Did I lose you?"

I sniffle before I wipe some tears from my face. "No. I'm still here."

"Let's turn the stove off, okay? Do you have cold water near you?"

"I'm going to get some." *Take some deep breaths.* I get off of my desk chair before I head to my bathroom. I grab the cup I keep in here for emergencies and fill it up with cold water. When I sip it, I don't feel relaxed, so I try the next best thing—I start to fill the tub up with freezing water. I only fill it a few inches, just enough for my ankles to be under the water, before I grab my phone again. "I'm back. My feet are in the tub."

"That's good, Bree. Is it helping?"

I take a breath, focusing on the cold beneath my feet. "Yeah, it is."

"Good. Now, earlier, you mentioned feeling guilty. Is it about the same things we talked about yesterday or something different?"

"The same thing." I hate that my mind won't stop making me feel like this, but I can't stop it. "I keep coming back to this one thing."

"That you weren't raped? That it could've been worse?"

Her voice says the thing I can't say out loud, but it filters through my thoughts every single day. "Yes. I'm sorry, I feel like we have this conversation every time we talk."

"Don't apologize, Bree. It's a hard thing to grapple with."

"People have it so much worse than I do, yet I find myself constantly falling apart over what happened to me."

"You're a survivor, Bree. You went through something traumatic, and you *survived*. No matter what you went through, you're still here. Comparing trauma is not healthy. No matter how bad it was, no matter if other people have gone through worse, your trauma changed you. It changed you in a way that only you know, and you're allowed to feel however you want."

Tears are dripping into the tub like rain falling into a puddle. I know I shouldn't compare, that everything she's saying is making sense, but I can't stop the guilt from peeking through.

"I'll tell you that as many times as it takes, Bree. You survived something horrific, and yes, it could have been worse, but it wasn't, and thank God for that."

"You're right."

"I always am. How are you feeling?"

"Like I'm out of my head." I unplug the drain before I get out of the tub and dry my feet. "This helped. Thank you."

"It's what I'm here for. Call me anytime, okay?"

"I will. See you next time."

"Keep what I said in mind. Baby steps, Bree. Even the smallest ones can be huge leaps." And then she hangs up, leaving me standing in my bathroom while I stare at myself in the mirror.

My eye bags are worse than before since I've barely slept the past month. I look...tired, yet I can't sleep. Every time I sleep, I feel his hands around my throat, grasping at my ankles as he drags me out of my old closet. I feel his warm breath on my face, saying all the things he did to me while he touched my body as I tried to kick him off me.

It's been four years, and I can still remember every minute detail, every word he said to me, and nothing about that night will ever be forgotten, no matter how hard I try.

Chapter Twelve

Bree

That Night

— BLACK OUT DAYS BY PHANTOGRAM

As I DOODLE ON my next promotional post, I think back on today and how proud I am of my sister. She graduated *college* today. She probably doesn't feel like it's a big deal, but to me, it's huge. I'll never have the chance to do that. I graduated high school, but college was never in the cards for me, and that's okay.

Liv never really had an idea of what she wanted to do, but I know that if she wrote her damn book, she'd find out that being a full-time author is well within her reach.

I've never told her I used to secretly read her journal when we were younger, that every story she had started inside caught my attention immediately. My sister is a natural writer, but no amount of support from me could convince her to make the jump.

I've tried. I've brought it up practically every time I see her, and I know she's been writing again. After the stunt our parents pulled, I know her mind is going a thousand miles per hour.

I can only hope that Tristan can help her see how amazing she is, and maybe one day, she'll write the damn book. But Liv has always wanted our parents to notice her, to *really* see her, even though they never will.

I hate that they treated her like she barely existed when we were growing up, and I'll never forgive them for how they chose to parent us.

Our parents don't really deserve to have that title, especially since they couldn't go one fucking day without berating my sister about her future. Liv had been graduated for all of five minutes, and they still found a way to ruin it.

But she seemed to be having fun when I was over at Tristan's place earlier, and I'm glad she has him and all their friends to keep her afloat. She's embarking on a whole new journey with the love of her life, and I couldn't be happier for her.

Only, the tiny voice in the back of my mind wishes I had something like that too. Sure, I have my friend Ellie, but she's an *influencer* friend. There's no doubt in my mind that she's using me to gain more followers. Teags is all I have, really, and even that might change when she starts college.

The front door slamming open makes me pause. *Did my parents forget something?* Huh, maybe I'll have the option to yell at them about earlier before they leave for two weeks. I throw my covers off, determined to march downstairs and pick a fight, before I stop in my doorway.

Something doesn't feel right. I heard the door slam open, but I don't think it ever closed. The hairs on my arms are pricking my skin with awareness, and my stomach is turning. I'm sure it's nothing. *Maybe I left a window open somewhere.*

But in my mind, that doesn't feel right. Ever since my stalker surfaced, every window has been locked, every entry point sealed.

But the alarm isn't going off yet. You have a certain amount of time to punch the code in before police are alerted and the alarm sounds, so it could only be my parents since the only other people who have the code are Liv and Connie.

I shake off the tension covering my body, but when I peer downstairs, I know that my parents aren't home.

Because there's a person standing in my doorway, back to me, punching in the code to the alarm, something shiny in their right hand.

It looks like a knife.

It's him. He's here.

I quietly step back into my room, swiftly shutting the door behind me. I grab my pillows and turn my reading light off, hoping he'll think I'm asleep.

Maybe he's not here to hurt me. Maybe he's just here to scope my house out for next time. Maybe he's here to watch me sleep and nothing else.

No matter how many excuses come to my mind, I know they're all wrong.

I might die tonight. I might die all alone in my house, and since my parents won't be home for two weeks, Liv is probably going to find me.

Liv. I should call Liv. She'll know what to do.

I grab my phone and head for my favorite hiding spot, shutting the doors to my closet softly behind me as I try not to make noise.

I can hear his heavy footsteps downstairs from here. I wonder if he's looking for something or if it's just me he's trying to find.

Deep breaths, Bree.

But I can't breathe. There's not enough air in here, and I suddenly wish I'd die because of that rather than whatever he has planned for me.

When, not if.

His last note was angry. He's *angry* with me and how I've ignored him, so I know for a fact that when he finds me up here, it's not going to end well.

Please let me run out of oxygen and not die by his hands.

I dial my sister, turning down the volume in case he gets up here and can hear it. "Don't worry, sis, I have your bracelet. It must've—"

"Livvy, there's someone in the house," I whisper to her.

"Bree, what are you talking about?"

I try to sound as coherent as possible when I whisper again, "There's someone in the house with me, and I don't know who."

"What? Where are you?"

"I'm hiding in my closet. I heard the door slam open, and I thought it was Mom and Dad, but when I looked downstairs, I saw someone." My chest starts to seize as the words become hard to get out. I can practically feel my pulse thrum through my body. "I-I think they had a kn-knife, Liv."

"Stay where you are. Call the police, and they'll come in from outside. Hang up and call them, Bree. I'll be there soon."

Thump. Thump. Thump. His boots are on the stairs. I know for sure because the third step up on our staircase creaks. I think I even hear him whistling some sort of song—like this is a game to him. "Okay, I will. Liv, I'm scared."

I'm scared that I'm going to die. I'm scared that I'm going to leave this Earth without a trace, that nobody will remember me. I'm scared that I'll never see you again, that this might be the last time we speak. I'm scared that you're going to find my body and fall to pieces.

"Bree, you're going to be fine. It's just someone trying to scare you." *It's not. It's him.*

I hear my door creak open, footsteps slowly wading into my room as I try my best not to make a sound. "Wait, I hear footsteps."

"Bree, call the police right now."

I don't have time to answer her before my closet doors are ripped open, and I feel two bare hands grab my ankles, dragging me out of my hiding place. "No! Please!" I somehow flip myself over as he drags me out, and despite trying to kick out of his grasp, it's no use. I really hope the call hung up because the last thing I want Liv to hear is her sister being murdered over the phone.

I'm clawing at nothing. The carpet beneath my fingertips is useless. He's too strong for me.

I'm not getting out of this alive.

I feel his hand grasp around my throat as he flips me over, my back landing against the frame of my bed. *Fuck, that hurt.* I feel my bed move from the sheer force of my body. He's bigger than me, stronger, and has every advantage.

He's in control, not me.

It's now that I realize I can't see his face. He's wearing a ski mask over his entire face and neck, and the only thing not covered are his hands—the ones roaming all over my body.

No. No. No.

I see one of his arms shoot out against my bed, forcing it away so I can no longer lean against it. Tears fall from my face, from panic, terror, and I can't do anything but sit here. I'm frozen.

I've always heard that when you're in a dangerous situation, your body can react in two different ways—fight or flight. I guess I did fight a little at first, but now, I find myself frozen, laying against my carpet.

I don't feel him on me anymore, but when I lift my head, I hear the lock of my door click before he turns around.

Even in the dark, his gaze disgusts me. I can feel it running all over my body, every hair on the back of my neck standing up.

I'm the prey. He's the predator.

Shuffle away! Try to get out! Do something, Bree! The voice in my head is speaking, but I can't find myself trying to do any of that.

I know what happens next. I know where this is going.

I'm going to die. He's going to kill me.

I lift my head before I crawl back to where my bed sits. I need something to lean against, to tether me to this moment, so if I manage to get out of this alive, maybe I can help identify the guy.

But I doubt that'll be the case.

"My sweet Bree. You've been a bad girl." His words come out in a low voice, almost croaky, like a frog. I see his hand go into the pocket of his jacket, probably reaching for the knife.

"I-I don't even know you." I manage to get the words out, but I immediately regret them when he lunges for me, landing a punch on my cheek that's wet with tears.

"Don't crawl away from me. You know me, Bree! You love me!" This time, he kicks me on the side of my ribs, and I feel myself whimper at the pain. It feels like a firework exploded against my skin. My body hunches over, but his hand around my throat forces me back to sit.

Fuck, this hurts.

I can't breathe, and before I know it, he throws my upper body to the ground, removing my tether, and I feel him crawl on top of me.

His fingers are calloused and rough as they wander over my body. *Stop. Please stop. I don't want this.*

"Sit still, or this won't be that enjoyable. Haven't you dreamed of this day, Bree? Haven't you wished for me to do this to you? To sneak in late at night while you're alone and have my way with you?"

I can barely speak past the tears flowing down my face. "N-No. Get off!" I try to knee him, but his body is too much.

"I know you want this as much as I do, and you're going to take it, Bree."

"P-Please, get off me." I can't even tell if I'm making sense, but I need him *off*. I need to wake up from whatever horrible dream I'm having. I want to wake up and call Liv. I want to call Teags and have a reading date like we did last week and tell her how much it meant to me because none of my other friends ever just wanted to hang out. They always had to post about it for the entire internet to see. I want to tell Tristan that I'm glad he loves my sister, that I'm thankful he's offered so much support to us. He's the big brother I never had.

Maybe there's some way to tell them all this when I'm gone. Maybe I can make the breeze blow over their faces or send a ladybug to sit on their hand when they think about me.

"Shut the fuck up! You're ruining everything!" Another slap is delivered to my cheek, and it burns as bad as the last one. I open my mouth to speak again, and I feel something cold and metal against my face. *The knife.*

"Do it. Get it over with, p-please."

Click. Not a knife, then. A gun. *He's holding a gun to my head.* "I'm going to take my time with you. Your parents are away, after all. You're mine to play with, little lamb, and play we will. Don't make me use this on you. I'd hate to blow your pretty brains out before I've had time to enjoy you." I feel him press his hard-on into me, and I have to fight the urge to throw up.

"N-No."

"Bree! Stop ruining it!" His voice cracks as he yells before I feel his fingers trail down my body.

No, no, no, no. He rips my cotton shorts off, and I feel exposed. I don't want him to see me. I don't want him to touch me. I want his hands off me. His thick fingers tease my center as he touches me.

He's going to rape me, and then he's going to kill me. Tears are falling from my face, and I feel like a failure. I should thrash, scream. I should do *something*, but my body is frozen as I wait for him to change my life before he kills me when he's finished.

I feel my body start to tremble as the cold metal of the gun presses further into my face, his other hand exploring my rigid body.

It feels like forever until he stops. Something has forced him to stop.

"Did you call the cops, you fucking bitch? Did you ruin this for us?"

Cops? What cops? His sweaty hands wrap around my throat, and I can't breathe again, but this time, it's because of him, not me.

His hands are wrapped around my windpipe, and any minute now, I expect to hear it crack and break under the pressure. My eyes start to flutter, my lungs seizing for air that won't come.

This is it, I think to myself. This is all the time I'll ever have on this Earth.

I'm not ready to die. I have so many things left to say, so many years left to live. But it's not my choice. This man holds my life beneath his hands, and I'm sure he'll kill me before the police I don't hear seem to arrive.

He picks me up by my throat before he throws me onto my bed now in the corner of my room, and my throat starts seizing, needing air but not getting any. I stop coughing enough to hear him say something before he leaves.

"This isn't over, Bree. No matter where you end up, I'll find you. If you can't count on anything else, count on that. You're mine." He says those last words with a snarl before he rips my door open and runs out of my room.

I cough what feels like a thousand more times, wanting to crawl under my sheets and forget this entire night before I feel something touch my leg.

He's back to finish what he started. He's going to kill me.

"Please don't! Leave me alone!" I kick at whoever it is, finally finding the fight in me, before the sounds of my room get back to my ears.

"Honey, we're here to help. Do you mind if we take a look at you?"

"Is he gone?" I can barely get the words out, my throat feels like it's on fire.

"They're searching the house now, but it seems that way. Can you stand for me?"

The lady reaches her hand out to me, and I shakily take it, but as I get up, my legs give out from underneath me, and the last thing I remember is someone calling for assistance.

Now

I WAKE WITH A startle, my hands shooting up to my throat like they always do. "Get off! No, no, no, no." I run my hands all over myself, checking that I'm okay. My body is sweating, my lungs seizing like they normally do after a nightmare.

Even when I drift off to sleep, these invisible ghosts always seem to haunt me. I'm never going to have peace ever again.

When I'm awake, I'm looking over my shoulder, scared that Ralph is around every corner. When I'm asleep, memories of him and that night come back to haunt me, and no matter what time of day it is, it always ends in the same way.

The panic comes back and my throat closes up, both symptoms of what he did to me that night. Dr. Anna tells me it's residual—the feeling in my throat. He strangled me enough to leave bruises for a week and even damage my vocal cords for a bit. I could barely speak after what he did.

It happened four years ago, and I can still feel his hands around my throat.

"Bree, look at me, angel," I hear a voice say before I meet those eyes I know so well.

Vince. He's here. He's in my bedroom.

"Can I touch you?"

I somehow nod before I feel his cold hands run up and down my arms. Goosebumps prickle my body as I feel myself come back to reality. *How long has he been here?*

"You're safe. There's nobody else here. You. Are. Safe." He enunciates every word, trying to make my brain comprehend that it was just a nightmare. "It's just us here, Bree. Just you and me."

His voice is low and soft. If I didn't already have goosebumps across my skin, that would've done it too.

Vince is here. Vince says I'm safe. Vince always keeps me safe. I'm safe.

I take a few steadying breaths as his hands trail up and down my arms, still a bit cold. Unlike Ralph, Vince's hands are soft. They're not calloused or rough, but smooth, and that helps bring me back. I never thought I'd ever be able to handle another man touching me. I always assumed it would remind me of how *he* touched me that night, but with Vince, it feels safe. His touch feels warm despite his hands being freezing. And he always asks permission.

I feel safe with him, and I never thought I'd feel this way ever again.

I lock eyes with him, and it feels like he can see right through me and the tears that fall from my eyes. His hands stop where mine sit in my lap, and his touch lingers for a moment too long before he shuffles away from me on my bed.

He clears his throat before he speaks again. "Are you okay?"

There's no use lying to him. "No." My voice is low and defeated, and I hate how broken I sound. I hate that I'm constantly falling apart and he has to deal with it. Vince didn't sign up for this, and somehow, I feel more broken than I was four years ago.

"What can I do?"

I just shrug. There's not much anyone can do when it's my own mind conjuring up these things.

The two of us sit in silence for a few seconds before I feel Vince's hands grasp onto my comforter. His knuckles look white, and before I can ask him about it, he leaves my room, softly shutting the door behind him.

I note the time on my phone—four in the morning—before I swipe my contacts open and call Dr. Anna. Tears are still streaming down my face, but my body feels steadier than before. When she answers, I know I'm in for a long day considering this is how it started.

Chapter Thirteen

— HARD TO SLEEP BY GRACIE ABRAMS

I FEEL SOMETHING THROWN against my body before a voice permeates my ears.

"Good morning, sleeping beauty. It's time to wake up." When I open my eyes to see his bright, smiling face, I silently curse myself. *He's never going to shut up about this.*

"What the fuck are you doing here?" I rub my eyes, the light in the hallway too much for my eyes to handle. I note the magazines next to me, and a familiar face looks back at me as I grab one of them.

It's Bree. She and Alex are on the front page of a few different magazines, all of them from their last few outings as an official couple.

That word leaves a sour taste in my mouth.

"What the fuck is this?"

"I grabbed them at the grocery store this morning, but what I really want to know is why you're sleeping in front of her door?"

"It doesn't matter," I say as I get up, walking back to my room. I try to slam my door and avoid this conversation, but Nico stops it with his foot.

"Actually," he pauses to chuckle at me, "I think it does, Vince."

Vince. He used my name and not that stupid nickname, which means he's serious. One thing about Nico Wilder is that when he wants to have a conversation, the conversation will be had. He's an annoying fucker in that sense. He always seems to get all your secrets out, even when you don't want them revealed.

"The other night, I woke up to her screaming. I'm a few rooms down from her, but it felt like that scream was right next to me. It was guttural, terrifying. She was fucking petrified. So I ran to her room, my knife from under my pillow in hand, but there was nobody in her room. I don't even think she clocked me when I came in."

"Fuck," is all he can say.

I sit on the edge of my bed, my body unable to hold itself up as I recount the memory. "She was having a nightmare. She yelled for whoever was in her head to get off her." I'll never forget hearing Bree scream a few nights ago. It scared the fucking shit out of me thinking someone was in her room, that someone had gotten past me in the night.

And I'll never forget the split second of relief when I walked in and saw Bree by herself, shaking where she sat on her bed. The last time something like this happened, cold water seemed to help, so that's what I did.

"You thought someone got past you."

"Yeah."

"And now you..." He trails off.

"Yeah. I sleep in front of her door to ensure that if someone was to try and get in, they wouldn't get past me. And if she had another nightmare, I'd get to her quicker, too. I don't know why I can't seem to fucking sleep in my room, either. My bed feels like a rock, and the only way I fall asleep is when I'm sitting in front of her door."

When I meet Nico's eyes, he just smiles at me, a thought crossing his mind that he doesn't dare say out loud. If he did, he knows I'd punch him for saying it.

You're breaking all of your rules.

Well, not *all* of them. Most of the physical contact I've had with Bree is necessary in my eyes. I'm helping her through her panic attacks. I'm calming her down somehow, and that's not *technically* breaking that rule.

"So much for no personal attachments, huh?" Nico's unabashed grin breaks through my thoughts.

"I'm not personally attached. She's just a client."

He chuckles as he fully shuts my door, not wanting what he's about to say to leak into the hallway. "I'm gonna tell you something you don't want to hear."

"Are you going to leave after?"

"Yes."

"Then fucking say it."

"You've been personally attached to her since you came back here. Vince, in all the years I've known you, you've never handed a case off, but for her, you did. That tells me a lot, and if you can't see it, then maybe you are a fucking idiot."

"I'm not an idiot. She's my fucking client, Nico. *Our* client, technically. I'm doing my job, and I'm doing it well."

He nods at me. "I know, dude. You're great at your job, but you're the one who says feelings cloud your judgment. From my perspective, you care about her, and not just because she's our client."

"I can't listen to this right now."

"Because you know I'm right." His pearly white teeth shine in my direction, and I'm fighting the urge to punch them out of his mouth.

"Okay, fine. Is that what you want to hear? That it pisses me off that I can't do anything to help her? That I can't take her pain or nightmares away? That I feel this fierce urge to protect her from anything and everything that could harm her? It's my *job*, Nico. My job is to protect her, and that's what I'm doing."

Nico doesn't say a word as he steps toward the table, picks up the magazines, and throws them at me. "Just be careful. The media attention isn't going to make this any easier. I can try and get some of it taken down, but a shitstorm is coming, and you need to be ready. You need to be on your A game, Vince."

"And I will be, asshole."

"Good. I'm glad we're on the same fucking page. I'll get out of your hair. Just think about what I said."

"See you later, Nico." I sigh heavily as the door shuts, and I'm finally alone.

That fucker might be right, but nothing will ever come from digging further into whatever my feelings are concerning Bree.

Not that I *have* feelings for her.

She just gets under my skin in a different way than most. When I sat in front of her and saw the tears leak from her eyes, her body trembling, I had to force myself not to hold her until she came down from it.

She didn't pull away from my touch when I ran my hands up and down her arms. She didn't flinch, which means she wasn't scared of me. She feels *safe* with me, and that's all I could ever hope for.

I just wish I could fix her, even though she's not broken in the first place.

I groan as I stand up and head for my shower, but not before one of the magazines Nico brought catches my eye. It's a picture from that first outing; Alex is gazing at Bree from across the table, looking completely enamored with her as she laughs at something he said.

The words across the picture are what make me pause.

The headline reads, "New hot couple alert! But how does Lily feel about her long-time beau moving on so quickly?"

God, I don't have the energy for this. I knew the media attention would be bad, but I don't understand why people are so obsessed with celebrity relationships. I don't get the appeal of it, but I guess some people prefer to live vicariously through parasocial relationships rather than actually live their own life.

The next headline reads, "Bree Hart and how she can't find the love she reads about, but maybe Alex is the one!"

Jesus Christ. What the fuck even is this? I rip the magazine in half and throw it in my garbage can. This shit is so fucking ridiculous. I can't stand it.

I turn my shower onto the hottest setting it can go, and as I step into it, I hope it will burn away any remnants of the rage I feel.

But as I turn the shower off thirty minutes later, I know it didn't work.

I sigh again as I close the door to my bathroom, towel around my waist, but stop in my tracks when I see blonde hair turn around and meet my gaze.

Her eyes bug out of her head as she notices I'm practically naked. Her eyes roam down my body, stopping for a beat longer than they should on the area my towel covers before she meets my eyes again.

"I'm sorry, I—"

"Did you need something?"

She clears her throat before answering. "Sorry, uh," her gaze is shooting all over the place, "Nico texted me. He told me he left something for me in here, and I was trying to find it before you got out."

"Nico texted you?" *That sly motherfucker.*

"Yeah, he told me he left a book in here that he thought I would like." *Of course he did.* "I-I can leave. I'm sorry."

"It's okay, Bree. Just give me a minute."

"I'll just be in the hallway, then." I see her swipe her tongue across her bottom lip before she turns and leaves my room.

I grab my phone, ready to call Nico and give him an earful, before I see a message from him.

> **Nico: Check.**

> **Nico: Your move, Vinny.**

> **Nico: ;)**

I swipe my hand down my face, pissed off that this was clearly a calculated situation by him. I throw some clothes on, not before I remember Bree's eyes swiping over my body when I was half-naked in front of her moments ago. *Was she turned on?* There's no way. She would *never* look at me that way, so I must be imagining things. Plus, that's a line I'd never cross, especially with her. She deserves more than me.

I look around my room, and when I see the book Nico placed on my bedside table, I grab it before I open my door. Only Bree must've been leaning against it because she falls right into my arms before she can hit the floor.

The moment her skin touches my hands, my fingers feel like they're buzzing. "Are you okay?"

Her breath hitches as she looks up at me. "Yeah, I'm fine."

I lift her up, my hands lingering around her waist for a second too long before we break apart. "Here's the book."

She grabs it from me, holding onto it with both hands as if it's a shield. I sweep my gaze over her outfit because it looks like she's going out. I don't remember anything being on the schedule for today. Her black skirt is swallowed up by a long and flowy...blouse? I don't even know what to call it, but it's white and the sleeves are huge. Her black boots go up to her knees, and when she walked out of my room, she had a big black bow in her hair.

Bree looks magnificent, and the smile that graces her lips makes her look even more radiant.

"Uh, Vince?"

"Yes?"

"Did you hear what I said?"

Shit, she said something? "Yes, I did."

"Great. Then I'll have Alex's bodyguards send over the information you'll need about the fashion show next week. I know you want the layout plans and everything, so I'll be sure they send it all. Does that sound good?"

"That sounds great. Are you headed somewhere? I thought today was a content creation day?"

Her smile grows even larger when she realizes I have her schedule memorized. "It is, but Teags wanted to go for coffee. Is that okay?"

"It's perfect. I'll grab Emerson and we can head out in ten minutes."

"Great. I'm just going to put this in my room. Can you tell Nico thank you for me?"

"Yeah, I'll let him know."

And as her heeled boots click as she walks away, it hits me that Nico was fucking right.

I'm way more invested in this girl than I thought, but I know I can't fucking have her.

Fuck.

Chapter Fourteen

— MIRRORBALL BY TAYLOR SWIFT

I HATE FASHION SHOWS.

Why do you need strobe lights that have nothing to do with the clothes you're showing off? And when did clothes get so eccentric?

This isn't what I had in mind when Bree told me about the show. I figured it was going to be this huge thing, but I forgot how much I hated loud and crowded spaces. This was never my scene, and by the way Bree keeps fidgeting in her seat, it's not hers either. She keeps smoothing the fabric of her light blue mini dress, even though she steamed it four times before coming out tonight. She keeps crossing and uncrossing her legs, her white heels almost hitting Alex's leg every time she does.

She always preferred the safety and tranquility of her room over being in public. There's been a bunch of photographers in her face since Alex is with her, and I can tell how uncomfortable she is.

Despite that, she still looks radiant as always. I swear, Bree and her aura attracts every person in the room. It's hard to look away from her sometimes, and tonight is no different.

She reminds me of a disco ball in the middle of a dance floor because when she smiles, it reflects in everyone's faces—including mine. Even though I know most of her smiles are fake in public, I like being able to pull out her real ones when I can.

I force my gaze away from her when I see Alex move his hand onto her thigh, slowly trailing up while Bree tries to stop him. I could go over there, but since they're sitting in the front row, I decide not to ruin the entire show and go to his security instead. I head for where Jason is—his head bodyguard—and stand next to him. He's got a decent angle on Alex, and I don't bother lowering my voice.

"If he touches her without her permission again, I'll cut his hand off."

He doesn't turn his head to face me as he speaks. "Is that right, Vince?"

"Yeah, that's right. It's in the goddamn contract, and his blatant disregard for it is making Bree uncomfortable. Tell your boy he needs to take that clause seriously, or I'll make good on my promise." I don't wait for his reply before I head back to my spot.

Bree must've known where I was standing because I see her head moving back and forth, trying to find me, but when her eyes lock on mine, she takes a deep breath. She places her hand on her chest, all her fingers splayed out, and I know that means there's about five minutes left of the show.

Thank fuck. I don't understand the appeal of shows like this, and the sooner I can get her out of this building, the better.

After a huge applause, all the models walking back out and showcasing whatever the fuck they're wearing, I head over to Bree.

"Angel is on the move. We should be out in five," I say over comms and hope someone is getting the car ready. As we head out, and I don't feel Bree behind me like I normally do, Emerson speaks since he's the one who follows behind them.

"Boss, we've hit a snag."

I turn around to notice another girl talking to Alex. From what I can tell by this exchange, Bree looks insanely uncomfortable, and Alex almost looks...human. I've never seen his guard down before, but it looks to be now.

This has got to be the ex-girlfriend I've seen all the magazines talk about. If it's not, then this guy sucks more than I thought.

Wanting to get out of here safely, I head towards them.

"We've got to get going, Bree," I say as I lean down so she can hear me. I look to where Alex's team is, and they nod, understanding that this area is jammed and not safe at all. Before they have the chance to swoop in, camera flashes go off like lightning.

When I turn around, all the cameras are pointed in our direction, and I know this exchange with his ex, Bree standing by his side, is going to make the internet by tonight.

I decide that enough is enough before I lean down to Bree's ear. "We've really got to go."

She nods at me, and before she starts to walk forward, she turns to Alex. "One kiss on the cheek, and that's it."

"Well, then let's make it worth it." He grabs her chin and brings her face to his lips.

I know everybody else missed it, but I didn't miss the flinch before he did that.

After a thousand camera flashes, Bree says goodbye and locks eyes with me. "Shall we?"

I nod at her, clearing the path as we head for the exit.

"The car's in position," Kenner says from my ear.

"I'm driving me and Bree. The rest of you follow us."

"Got it, boss. I'll close Bree's door while you settle in the driver's seat," Emerson says.

"Sounds like a plan, boys," I say as I push the door open and head for the Tahoe.

A few seconds after I get into the car, Bree slides into the backseat and Emerson closes the door, tapping that we're good to go before I *finally* get us out of here.

I normally don't drive to these things, but tonight was different, and I needed a little bit of that control back. Plus, if we're followed, I trust my own driving skills over anyone else on my team. It's not that they're bad per se, but I can lose a tail far quicker.

I swipe my view to where Bree sits in the backseat, and by the way her leg is bouncing, her eyes all foggy, I can tell she's disappearing from everything tonight. *Not if I can help it.*

"Did you have a favorite look from tonight?" Bree loves clothes. Her closet is practically filled with a bunch of designers I can't pronounce.

She doesn't answer.

"I think my personal favorite was that light pink one. The dress, or whatever you call it."

"The jumpsuit?" Her eyes meet mine in the rearview mirror, a smirk creeping up her face.

"Yeah, if that's what it's called."

"That was my favorite one too."

I knew it would be based on the color. "I guess I just don't understand the appeal of something that looks like a dress but has pants attached to it."

That earns me a small laugh. *Bingo.* "It's not something you understand, Vince. It's fashion."

"Ah. Understood."

The drive is silent for a few minutes more until Bree softly speaks again. "I don't think I'll ever get used to all this attention on me."

"If tonight was too much, I can cancel whatever Connie has on your schedule tomorrow."

"No, it's fine, I just—" She takes a big deep breath. "It's nothing."

"If there's something on your mind, angel, I don't mind listening. Someone once told me I reminded them of a really shitty therapist."

Bree smiles at that, noting my reference to something she said to me after we first met. "You're not a shitty therapist, and can you blame me for saying that? I don't think you said a word for the first two weeks after we met."

"Incorrect."

"Oh, am I?" She smiles, her shine coming back as I goad her.

"We talked at our first meeting, and after that, I didn't want to—" I stop; I don't want to make her uncomfortable.

"You didn't want to what?"

"Your voice. I wanted it to heal, and I thought any unnecessary strain would make it heal slower."

"Oh."

Yeah. Oh is right. It's been my job to protect her ever since I met her, so I did, but admitting that to her right now is making me feel strange, and I have no idea why.

"It's just weird sometimes, all the flashes of the camera on me. Every time a picture gets taken of me, there's a light on me, and people are noticing me through that. But when they're gone, and I'm by myself in my room, I feel...lonely." She folds her hands in her lap before continuing. "I feel like my struggles were broadcasted across the internet four years ago, and now, it's happening again. It feels like this weird and strange cycle. Every time I'm broken, it's somehow used as another story, another headline, anything people can use to get clicks. My pain is broadcasted for the world to see, and I don't think I'll ever get used to that."

I don't even know what to say to her. I wonder if writing runs in the family, because the way Bree just described that was hauntingly beautiful.

"I'm sorry for dumping that on you. I shouldn't have—"

"Bree, don't apologize. You know I'm always here when you need someone to listen."

"Thank you."

The rest of the ride home is filled with silence, *Friday, I'm In Love* by The Cure playing in the background.

— MATILDA BY HARRY STYLES

AFTER TOSSING AND TURNING in my bed for what has felt like hours, I finally swing my legs to the side and get up.

Sometimes, I don't even know why I bother trying to sleep. I should know by now that my brain never shuts off, and sleep will probably never come again—at least with Ralph still running wild.

I slide my fuzzy pink slippers on and softly walk down to the kitchen, hoping I don't wake Vince up. I thought I heard him walking around as I crept down the stairs, and I remember he told me once that he's a pretty light sleeper, so I try my best not to make too much noise as I pull the strawberries from the fridge.

My favorite late-night snack has, and always will be, chocolate-covered strawberries. There's just something so perfect about chocolate at night, and the strawberries trick my brain into thinking it's a healthy snack. It's a win-win.

I grab the chocolate and place it in a bowl, throwing it in the microwave so they can melt while I wash the strawberries. As I'm placing the strawberries in the sink, the kitchen light flicks on, and I flinch a little.

I already know it's him before he says anything.

As I turn, I have to will my jaw to stay attached to my mouth, because leaning against the entrance to my kitchen is a shirtless, sweatpants-wearing Vince, his tattooed arm sleeve on full display, as well as his abs.

I might start drooling. Vince Evans is like a real-life bodyguard romance character come to life, and he's never been more off-limits.

He's my *bodyguard*, and I'm suddenly thinking about all the ways I want to climb him like a tree. I haven't had thoughts like this in a while—four years, to be exact. I'm in the world's longest dry spell because the thought of another person touching me in that way again makes me want to curl into a ball on my floor.

But right now, the thought of him touching me doesn't repulse me.

It *excites* me.

But I have to remind myself he has a job to do, and the last thing I want is to distract him from it.

If he notices me staring, he doesn't say anything. "Can't sleep?"

"Nope. I didn't wake you, did I?"

He just shakes his head. "Chocolate-covered strawberries?"

"I should've known you would guess that." I laugh as I turn back to the sink, placing the strawberries under the spray. A few seconds of silence later, and the microwave beeps. "Can you grab that for me?"

He doesn't answer, but I hear him stride along the kitchen floor before the microwave opens. I twist my head to catch a glimpse of him, only to find that he's swirling the chocolate in the bowl with a spoon before he places it back in the microwave.

"Thanks."

"It reminds me of before—catching you in the kitchen when you couldn't sleep."

I feign a smile. *Before.* Vince once barged into my parents' house because a light turned on, only to find me in my pajamas making my favorite late-night snack. He was worried Ralph had somehow gotten in the house, but any time after that when I wanted a snack, I would always text him before so he wouldn't get worried.

But he kept showing up, sitting with me while I made them. At first, we didn't talk much, but towards the end, we got closer and closer. One-word conversations slowly morphed into full sentences, and eventually, we talked like two old friends catching up.

My life wasn't any better back when we first met, but part of me felt a little lighter than I do now. It felt easier dealing with everything back then, and now, it feels insurmountable. "Yeah, same."

I grab the strawberries from the container and place them on the cutting board that appeared on my counter. I look over at Vince, and he's grabbing a knife.

"What are you doing?"

"What does it look like? I'm helping." He grabs a strawberry and cuts off the stem. "Unless you want to do it?"

"Well, no, I—" I sigh. "I don't want you to feel like you have to hang out with me."

He takes a deep breath, and I find myself staring at his arm veins for a beat too long. "Do you think I don't want to be around you?"

"Well, no. You're practically required to be around me at all times. But nowhere in our contract does it talk about us being friends."

"Bree, I'm *required* to protect you, but me being down here and wanting to spend time with you right now is because I'm choosing to. Is that okay?"

I'm choosing to. He'll never know how much those three words mean to me. "That's perfectly okay."

"Okay. So let me cut your strawberries for you while you grab the chocolate and the skewers."

I nod just as the microwave beeps, and as I take the bowl out, my mouth starts to water. "Do any of your men want some? I feel like I should do something to thank them for their hard work."

That earns me a small smile before he shakes his head. "After the assignment is over, you can make them whatever you want, but it's best not to distract them while they're on duty."

"Okay. I just feel bad that they have to watch my house all night. How do they stay awake?"

"They've trained for this exact job and, believe it or not, people like working for me and Nico." He continues cutting, and as I hop onto my kitchen island and let my legs dangle off the side, I realize how normal this feels.

Vince is cutting strawberries, and the two of us are talking about work. This might be one of the best nights of my life. "I'm glad you have Nico. It's good to know you weren't alone all these years."

"Bree, like I've told you before, I'm not lonely."

"Oh, come on, big guy. Believe me, I know what loneliness feels like, and I bet jumping from job to job and place to place feels the same. Have you ever thought about settling down?"

His eyebrows scrunch together as he scoops the strawberries up and places them into another bowl. As he does, I hop down from my counter and follow him to my kitchen table. I sit in my usual spot, and he sits next to me rather than across the table like he always used to. "That's not your usual spot."

"Do you want me to move?"

I shake my head. I like the closeness. It makes me feel protected. *Safe.*

Four years ago, after Vince and I got to know each other a bit better, Liv used to invite him over for dinner on the days my parents were gone—which was most of them. Sometimes, I would cook, sometimes Liv would, and Vince would help us out. He was a wonderful guest, and when we all sat down for dinner, he claimed the spot across from me. He sat there every time, and it sort of became a thing.

When we've had dinner together lately, he has sat in the same spot. But now, it's late at night, and he's sitting so close to me that I feel the urge to place my hand on his thigh.

Instead of doing that, I grab a skewer, stab a strawberry with it, and dunk it into the melted chocolate. When I pop it into my mouth, it's *perfect*. I swear, chocolate-covered strawberries can solve all my problems.

Well, most of them.

"I'm sorry about today," he whispers as he eats.

"What about today?"

"The fashion show and running into that girl or whatever."

Ah, yes. Lily. Running into your fake boyfriend's ex and one true love in front of a bunch of cameras is not the most comfortable moment. I know Alex and I are fake, but to the rest of the world, we're not, and I can only imagine how Lily felt when she saw us together.

I could tell she's still in love with him. I could see it in her eyes, written all over her face, and for a second, I swear I saw the same look on Alex.

"It's fine. I'm sure the entire internet will have something to say on those pictures, but there's nothing I can really do." I sigh before I eat another strawberry, trying to swallow the anxiety brewing in my gut.

"You talk about all this stuff as if it's not a big deal."

"I'm so desensitized to it at this point..." I trail off as all my thoughts swim. "Sometimes, my life doesn't really feel like mine. It doesn't really feel real, and I never know how to explain it to people, so I don't."

"I get that, but I've been told I'm a great listener."

I meet the hazel eyes I know so well, and my body shivers at his stare. It feels like he can really see me right now, and that scares me. I've been so used to pushing people away, but right now, I don't want to do that to Vince. He has seen every broken piece of me, and he's still here. So, for the first time in a while, I let someone in. "It all feels so normal to me—the invasions of privacy, the camera flashes, the fans. It has become part of my everyday life, and that's because I chose to upload videos for the entire internet to see. It feels odd to complain about where I've ended up when I made the decision in the first place."

"Just because you made that choice doesn't give everyone else the right to invade your privacy. You're still a human being, and I think the world forgets that sometimes."

"I guess it never really scared me—all the attention—until Ralph came into the picture. Connie shielded me from the mail I used to get, but then my parents didn't take the threats seriously, and it ended exactly how we were afraid it would." It took me a long time to realize that my parents never showed me and my sister love, and I used to think I needed a reason to stop talking to them. I never thought I could stop because it was what was best for me. I never thought that was even an option—cutting them off with no explanation.

That's the problem I've always had—I need explanations for things. I need a reason for why something happened the way it did.

My parents don't love me? Well, maybe their parents did something similar to them, so they don't know how to be parents.

I have a stalker threatening my life? Well, maybe I did something wrong to make him fall for me.

I don't believe I'm destined for love? Well, that's my own fault because I'd never drag anyone into the mess that is my life.

I only have one true friend who loves me for me? Well, Teagen West is all I'll ever need, so fuck anyone else who just uses me to get ahead.

"Even if it didn't scare you, don't discount your feelings and pretend like the life you live isn't a big deal. Going through this *is* huge, and you don't always have to handle it perfectly. You're allowed to break apart and allow your friends and family to put you back together."

"The only family I have is Liv."

"I know you don't believe that, Bree." His voice is low, like the first time I met him. He always does that—lowers his voice when he tries to appear less intimidating, but I've told him countless times that I'm not afraid of him. I think it's just a habit by now.

"I guess I've found my own version of a family after all these years of feeling used." I smile, thinking about how big our circle has grown. It used to be just the two of us, and now it has expanded to include the entire West family and Tristan's friends.

They show us the love we've been chasing our entire lives. In the race to grasp our parents who were always just out of reach, they carried us to a separate finish line.

"I'm sorry you've had to deal with how broken I've been these past few weeks. I know I should let Liv be here for these moments, but I can't stand the thought of her seeing me like this. And I don't want to give Ralph anyone else to target."

"You're not broken, Bree. I understand why you're pushing people away, but you should know you don't have to push people away to protect them. Sometimes, letting them in is safer." His eyes sadden, and I wonder what he's thinking. It felt like he was pulling from personal experiences, but I decide not to press, just in case.

"Vince, you've seen me break down a dozen times since you've been back. You know parts of my story that the rest of the world doesn't. You can't say I'm not broken when you've seen me fall to pieces."

His hand reaches for my chin, and he pulls my gaze back to his. "Is this okay? Because I'd prefer that you look at me when I tell you this."

I nod, his hand still holding my face. I note that I didn't flinch at the gesture like I did when Alex did it earlier. "You're one of the strongest people I've ever met. You're resilient. You are far from broken, Bree. So, yeah, while the entire internet thinks your life is perfect and knows your stalker's out, they don't know how you feel. I don't know how you feel most days either. Only you do, and you're allowed to feel however you want because you're the one going through it, not anybody else."

For some reason, right now, in the kitchen sitting across from Vince, my bones exhausted from the weight of the past few weeks, I tell him one of my biggest fears, one that only Dr. Anna and my video diary know about. "But one day, the world will know. Everyone will know what happened to me, and I don't think I'm ready for people to see me as a victim of something that could've ended up much worse. They'll think I'm overreacting, and I'll get ridiculed again, dragged through the mud even further."

"Bree, you're a fucking survivor, not a victim. You *survived* something horrible, and I think a lot of people can relate to your situation."

"You really think so?"

"I know so, Bree. Ninety-seven percent of women know too." He releases my chin before he skewers a strawberry, dips it in chocolate, and holds it up to my mouth. I close my lips around the skewer, and a weird look crosses his face before it quickly goes away.

My heart squeezes; I'm a part of that statistic now. "I just hate that everyone online thinks they know me, that they're allowed to have an opinion on my life without actually knowing what goes on behind closed doors."

"Well, I know I can't take down the entire internet, but maybe Nico can try."

"You'd do that just for me?" I smile.

He smiles back at me, something I don't see very often but cherish when I do. "I'd try my damn best, Bree."

For the rest of the morning, Vince and I sit at my kitchen table and talk about normal things as the sun filters through my kitchen and the world wakes up.

Chapter Fifteen

— FEAR OF WATER BY NOAH KAHAN

"Ellie, I just told you I've never worked with that brand because of how they treat their own employees. I think this is your agency's problem, babes."

I hear her scoff through my phone. "I don't ever remember signing anything! Ugh, this is a giant clusterfuck. Do you think I should address it? Lina said I should, just to be safe."

In the past few years I've known Ellie, she's the one who makes friends easier than I do. She's friends with mostly everyone I'm acquainted with, but it's easy to understand why—the girl practically throws up rainbows. "I think you should do what you think is best."

"Thanks, Bree. I'll keep you updated, but I have another meeting. We'll talk soon!"

I barely get to say goodbye before she hangs up on me. *Nice*. I throw my phone onto the kitchen table before it buzzes again.

Teags: Are you filming today, or can I come over and rant about this book?

Bree: I filmed earlier! Get over here. You know how much I love a Teags rant.

Teags: If the main character talks about how small she is one more time, I'm going to throw this book out of a window!

I laugh when she says that just as Vince comes up from the basement, looking all sweaty, disheveled, and beautiful, as always.

It's official: I'm lusting after my bodyguard.

I try to swallow, but the lump in my throat makes it difficult. His gray shirt is practically drenched from his workout, his hair messy at the top, but one strand hangs down in front of his face. *Good lord*. That one hair is one of the hottest things I've ever seen.

And to top it all off, I can see the outline of his abs through his wet shirt. My mind jumps back to when I saw him fresh out of the shower.

I almost saw him naked, and that's all I've been able to think about when I look at him. So, yeah, maybe me lusting after the man who's supposed to protect me isn't a great thing, but come on—how do I not? We have history together, he knows all about me and my favorite things, and on top of all that, he's protective of me.

That's his job.

But sometimes, it feels like *more*, like maybe he could feel the same thing about me.

Lust, of course. Not that he would want anything more. Maybe I need to grab my Kindle and put all this sexual energy into a smutty book. Actually, that sounds like a great idea. Before I can get up, he speaks.

"I'm gonna go shower. Call me if you need me, okay?"

Shower. "Mhm!" is all I can manage.

"Are you okay?"

I raise my eyebrows at him, hoping he can't see the thoughts swirling around my head. "Yup! Perfectly fine. Why?"

"Your face is all red. Have you been overworking yourself again? I told you, you need to calm down in the midst of all this chaos."

"And I am! Teags just texted me a bunch of funny things, and she's on her way over."

His gaze swipes down my body, and I think he knows I'm lying, but he doesn't call me out on it. "Okay. She's already cleared to come in, so she should have no problems this time."

Ah, yes. *This* time. Because the last time Teags came over, her name wasn't on the list of accessible people, and she ripped Vince's men to shreds for it. I, for one, had a wonderful time watching that security footage. It made me laugh so hard that my ribs hurt.

I've been laughing a bit more lately despite still feeling like there's another shoe ready to drop, and I couldn't be more thankful for the people around me.

"Are you sure you don't want to see her argue with Billy again?"

"Billy requested a transfer to the night shift, so Wilson would get it this time." I see a small smile form on his face. "Your friend is one of a kind."

"Teags is the best."

"I'm glad you have her." His eyes lock with mine for a beat too long before he shakes out of it and heads upstairs.

I grab my phone and swipe to Instagram, heading to my sister's profile to see what she's up to today. I know she started her next manuscript, but she refuses to share anything about it with me until the first draft is done. It's driving me crazy, but sometimes she shares snippets on her story about it, so I always check her profile during the day.

After finding nothing, I go through some of my messages and respond to some of them. I uploaded a new video yesterday where I had some of the authors I've worked with pick my reads for the next month. People are loving it so far, and I love it when they comment about how much they loved a book that I'm going to read soon. It gets me more excited to pick it up.

The doorbell ringing has me putting my phone down, knowing that it's probably Teags. I always tell my friends and family they don't need to knock or ring the doorbell, but Vince quickly changed that. He told me it's safer this way, and I agreed, knowing he's pretty much always right.

But when I swing the door open and Nico walks in, I'm surprised.

"Hey, Nico."

"Hi, princess. Where's the brood?"

"Showering. It looked like he had an intense workout this morning." I can feel my cheeks get hot when the image of him floods my brain. When I look at Nico, he has a weird look on his face, and that's when I register the package in his hand. "What's that?"

"It was on your porch. It says it's from a publishing house, so I figured I'd bring it in for you."

"That's nice of you. Tha—"

A low voice cuts me off. "Bree, what did I tell you about opening the door?"

"It was just Nico." I look to where he's stomping down my stairs, hair still wet from his shower, that one hair still dangling in his face.

"Yes, but you didn't know that. It's safer for me to open the door, and you know that. Next time, come and get me."

"I will. I'm sorry." I hold the package close to my chest, and when it doesn't feel like a normal book, I tense up.

"Princess? Is everything alright?"

"Bree? What is that?"

"I-I don't know." I examine the envelope, and it looks like a standard package I would get from a publishing house, but something feels off, and my gut is screaming at me that something's wrong.

Vince grabs the package from me, and Nico and I follow closely behind him as he places it on the kitchen table and carefully cuts open the package.

"Rule number five," I whisper, and Vince's eyes meet mine.

"I didn't think you remembered them all."

Nico just laughs. "Oh, please, Vinny. Anyone who knows you well probably has your rules memorized. I should think about getting some laminated cards made."

I stifle a laugh as Vince rolls his eyes and carefully dumps the contents of the package out. The sound of metal on the table has my eyes wandering, and when I see what it is, my heart stops beating.

There are two bullets on my kitchen table, rolling around as if they're taunting me.

"What the fuck?" Nico says as he goes to pick one up.

"Don't. They could have fingerprints on them." Vince goes to one of my cabinets and grabs a plastic glove, putting it on his hand as he reaches to inspect them. *It's from him.* It has to be. The packaging was just a ruse to let my guard down and get it past the gate.

Vince picks one up, and I swear, I see something on the side. "What's that?" He doesn't answer me. "Vince, is there something on the side of it?"

His eyes narrow at the bullet, and I watch his eyes go cold as he looks at Nico. They have some sort of telepathic conversation before I speak.

"No secrets, Vince. What does it say?"

He sighs heavily before he turns it so I can read it. Scratched on the side of the bullet is my name, and when I look at the other one, I see Liv's name.

"What about the note?" Nico asks, and I look around the table. Sure enough, I see a small piece of paper.

I feel my palms start to get sweaty, my heart starting to race, and I know that this might finally be my breaking point. Vince can't bear to read it out loud, so he just shoves it toward Nico and me, and as I read it, my body goes cold, my hands start to shake, and my throat feels drier than a desert.

One for you and one for your sister.
She's keeping you from me, her and that supposed boyfriend of yours, so why not make it a two for one special? He'll never look at you how I do, Bree. You know that.
You ruined our moment last time, and I'd hate to use one on you, but I'll still enjoy watching the life drain from your eyes while I finally have my way with you.
Your last moments will be with me, just like I've been dreaming of.
Sleep tight, Bree. I'll see you soon.
— R

I'm not in my body anymore. I can't *feel* anything but the cold fear that courses through my veins. *He's going to kill me.* Ralph has never escalated this quickly, and all I can think about is when he shoved his gun in my face and touched me without my consent. I have no energy. I'm drowning in the deepest end of my mind, the water starting to overflow, leaving me no room to breathe.

I feel disgusted. I want out—out of my body, my skin. I can't do anything but stand here and tremble because I'm too afraid to move.

"Bree? Bree!" I hear someone yell my name, but I can't seem to pinpoint who. I feel tears leaking out of my eyes, but I'm frozen where I am.

And that's when I feel a hand on my shoulder.

"Don't touch me!" All I can remember is him. Him touching me, him breathing in my face, his calloused hands grabbing my skin.

I need to get out of here. I need to get out of my old room. I'm not safe. I'll never be safe. The only voice in my head is his.

"Haven't you dreamed of this? Me sneaking into your room at night?"

"You've been a bad girl."

"You're going to take it, Bree."

"I'd hate to blow your pretty brains out before I've had time to enjoy you."

"S-Stop. Please, d-don't," is all I can manage to say before a pair of arms sweeps me off of my feet. *It's him. Ralph is here, and he's going to make good on his promise.* "Let me go! Please, I won't fight this time. I'll do whatever you want, just don't hurt me or my sister."

I hear a rumble from the chest I'm against, and I remember how he growled at me when I fought back.

"I'll be good this time," I say as more tears leak from my eyes. "Please, just get it over with."

"Nico! Turn the shower on cold for me."

Nico? He wasn't there that night. What's going on?

Before I can try to answer that question, cold water attacks me from above, and a strong pair of arms wraps around me while I try to regain my bearings. I look around at the familiar space and realize that I'm in my shower.

"W-what?" I say as I shiver, my body slowly coming back to reality.

"Leave, Nico. Go deal with how this got past the door."

I hear a door shut, and before I can say anything, another voice whispers in my ear, his arms anchoring me to my spot. "It's Vince. Come back. You're safe. Everything's alright."

"He was here." My body feels heavy, like weights are attached to my ankles. If Vince wasn't holding me up, I'd collapse.

"Just in your mind, Bree. It's you and me here now." The cold water and his reassurances are helping me come out of whatever tunnel vision I was in, but I'm still crying, still shaking, and it's not from being cold.

I'm terrified. I could've sworn I was back in my old house, that he was with me, but I realize it's just Vince and I here.

"You're getting all wet," I tell him. Both of us are fully clothed in my shower as the water cascades down my body.

"Don't worry about me, Bree. I'm not going to melt."

I burst out laughing before I can stop it, and instead of quivering with fear in his arms, I'm laughing as tears continue to leak down my face, mixing with the cold water from the shower.

"What's so funny, angel?"

"You made a reference to *The Wizard of Oz.*"

"And that's funny because?"

"I can't imagine you sitting down to watch a movie and picking that one."

I hear him chuckle in my ear, his arms still wrapped around me as if he can't bear to let go. "It's my sister's favorite movie. After our parents died, we must've watched it a thousand times."

I didn't know his parents were dead. I wonder how old he was when that happened. "I'm sorry."

I feel his head shake next to me. "We're not here to talk about me, Bree. Are you okay?"

No, and I never will be. I'm half in my body and half out of it. I'm so afraid of my own mind. It felt so real—being back in my house with Ralph. God, when will this end? When will it be over? "What happened?"

"You read the note, and your entire body went pale. Nico and I started talking about how best to go about this, and you started shaking. Nico tried to grab you to calm you down, and you yelled at him to stop."

"I wasn't yelling at him. Ugh, I feel terrible. I need to apologize." I try to get out of his hold on me, but he keeps me upright.

"Nico's fine. He understands, Bree. Just stay here with me for a few more minutes. I need to make sure you're okay."

"I thought it was him. I thought *he* was touching me." I feel more tears fall from my eyes, and he turns me around to face him, the water of the shower cascading between us.

"I figured," Vince says in a low voice. "I thought you were going to pass out right where you stood, so I carried you in here. I thought it would help."

"It did help, so thank you. You always seem to know how best to help me."

My mind is my biggest enemy. All it does is play tricks on me when I'm trying to retreat into myself, and I hate it. "I'm sorry if I hurt you."

"Not physically, Bree." His eyes glance down at the tile of my shower, and a few seconds later, he turns the shower off. "I'll grab us towels."

I nod, and before he leaves, his touch lingers on my waist, and he's looking at me as if I'm going to disappear into thin air. It sure felt like I did earlier, but once again, Vince helped me through one of the worst panic attacks I've ever had.

Because it's his job.

"Thank you," I say as he holds a towel out for me. He nods as I watch him dry himself off, ultimately giving up and heading back to his room to change.

I go to follow him to say more, but Teags barrels up the stairs and throws her arms around me.

"Teags?" I question the sudden physical touch.

"Nico let me in when Vince was carrying you bridal style up the stairs. Are you okay? I've never seen you so pale."

I pull back from her, only to meet Vince's gaze behind where she stands. "I'm okay, but I can't talk about it."

"That's okay, Bree. When you're ready, just know you can always talk to me. But buckle up because I have lots to say about this book." Teags pulls me into my room, wet clothes and all, and I hear Vince yell at someone that just walked in the house.

"Find out how that package got through the fucking gate! Now, or you're fired!"

I hope they find something, anything that can help catch this fucker before it's too late because if he's sending me bullets as a warning, I don't want to know what will happen if he actually gets his hands on me again.

Chapter Sixteen

— DELICATE BY TAYLOR SWIFT

My phone ringing interrupts the song I was listening to, and I turn the treadmill off as I answer. "Hello?"

"Bree? Are you in a wind tunnel right now? What is all that noise?"

I take a few seconds to calm my breathing. "You caught me in the middle of a workout. What's up, Con?"

"I wanted to talk to you about something."

"Okay..." I say, weary of how she worded that sentence. "About what?"

"I was wondering if you wanted to throw your own event this year?"

I take a deep breath. It's been a dream of mine to host an event that helped out a cause I care about, but is now really the right time? I already feel like I'm on the brink of exhaustion, and this could make it worse, but it's been something I've wanted forever. "Is now really the right time? Can't we wait until next year, when things have calmed down?"

"I don't know if I would ever describe your life as calm, Bree. I think now is as good of a time as ever, and it could bring some good publicity, too."

I take a sip of my water as I mull over what she said. If I say no, she'll keep hounding me until I say yes. Having no fight left in me, I agree.

"Yeah, you're right. Just let me know what you need from me, and I'll get it to you."

"Thanks, Bree. I'll send an email by the end of the day. Did you still want to do the Mental Health Foundation?"

"Yes," I say immediately.

"Great. I'll be in touch. Make sure to smile for the cameras with Alex later!"

"I will," I say as I end the call. I have another fake date with Alex in a few hours, and I've been up since three this morning, running my body to the point of exhaustion. Even though I'm exhausted, I know I won't be sleeping tonight, either.

My body is running ragged, and I don't know how much more of this I can handle.

I smile for the media when I'd rather be home in bed beneath my sheets. I pretend to be madly in love with Alex when I'd rather he admit that he still has feelings for Lily. I have to pretend like I'm fine with all the distractions from Ralph, but I'm petrified.

I'm handling this as best as I can on my own. Liv has her own shit to deal with, Teags is still trying to find her way back to herself after Tobias, and the last thing they need is to deal with my shit. They aren't famous, so why should they have to deal with the shitstorm that my life has become behind closed doors?

I take a big sip from my water bottle and trudge up the stairs, hoping that a long, hot shower will brighten my spirits.

⁕

Six hours later, I'm on my way to a bookstore to meet Alex. Connie thought it would be a good idea to show the media that Alex has taken an interest in the things I love, so we're going to wander around a bookstore and chat.

I've never wanted to not go to a bookstore before. I hate all this showmanship that comes from this deal. When I first agreed to it, I knew it would be like this, but I didn't take into account how exhausting it would feel. It turns out that pretending to be in love with someone is harder than I thought.

Normally, in the books I read with this trope, somewhere along the way, the lines get crossed, and things aren't as fake as the two of them thought.

With Alex, that will never happen. Eventually, maybe he and Lily will work things out. He *could* have his happy ending if he stopped being such an ass, but I'll probably never get one, and I have to live with that.

I'd rather spend my life without romance than be stuck in a sham relationship.

"Bree, we're here," Vince says as the car slows to a stop. I can see photographers outside the building already, and before I can calm myself, the car door opens, and Alex's face greets me.

"Hi, sweetheart. Care to join me inside? I already picked out some books I think you might like," he says as he offers me his hand.

"Thank you," I say as I step out of the car, the lights from the cameras practically blinding me. I see Vince clear the path for us, and I know he's already mad that Alex opened my door for me. It's protocol that Vince does it, and Alex broke it.

Just like he's broken a few other rules set into place when we signed the contracts. He always touches me without my permission, whether it's just a small touch or a peck on the cheek. It seems like he has a thing for breaking the rules, and even though I flinch every time his hand touches any part of my body, he doesn't seem to notice.

But Vince always does, and even though I'm looking at the back of his head, I can tell there's a scowl on his face. His back is tense, and when we finally get inside, he goes right to Alex's security team.

Alex and I begin to wander around the store, neither of us speaking as we hold hands and peruse the romance section. I trace the spines of some of the books with my free hand, and after minutes of silence later, I hear Alex clear his throat.

"Look, I wanted to apologize about all the coverage with Lily and me in the press. I know it can't be easy on you."

Wow, he actually sounds genuine. This is the first time I've heard him have any emotion besides that damn charisma. "It's fine, Alex. We're not real, remember?"

"Yeah, but we are to everyone else."

"It's okay. Really. Nothing about our lives is peaceful anyway. I knew what I was getting into when I signed that deal."

He smiles softly as he looks at me, and I think this is my first glimpse of the real Alex. "Yeah, you're right." He pauses as he searches my face. "You're a pretty cool girl, Bree. I wouldn't mind being friends after all this is over."

"If you stop hiding your true self from the world, I could see that happening." I laugh as I pull out a book.

"I wouldn't say that I hide, I just pick and choose who I show my real self to. It's easier putting on that stupid persona for the world."

"But you've shown me, and I assume Lily as well."

His face turns red when I mention her, and the fact that his pupils are dilated tells me he's still in love with her. "Yeah, she knows me better than most."

"Then why aren't you with her right now? It's obvious you two still love each other, at least to me."

"Yeah, well, you're the romance reader, Bree, not me."

I lightly tap his arm as I laugh. "What the hell does that mean?"

"It means that real life is much more complicated than it is in those fictional books of yours."

"Okay, pretty boy. I'm about to give you a lesson in literature."

He laughs at me as he runs a hand through his hair. "Bring it on, Bree."

"Romance as a genre is highly hated because most people think it creates impossible standards. Which it sort of does, but most things people love about romance books are the little things the characters do for one another. They listen, they talk about the hard topics that can be terrifying to open up about. Romance isn't always about big gestures."

"It's not?"

I smile as I trace the spine of my sister's book. "No. It's about all the little reasons you fall for someone, like how they remember little details about you or your favorite snack. Some of my favorite characters don't feel like characters; they feel like real people. Sometimes, I get so angry at them for making the decisions they do because I do the same things, and it feels too real, if that makes sense."

"It does."

"For example," I say as I hand him my sister's book. "My sister wrote this based on a relationship that went sideways. She thought he was the one, and they fell apart after a year or so, and this book follows a girl who goes through the same thing, except she doesn't end up with him. She ends the book single as she tries to find herself again. People loved it because there were so many others out there who relate to that feeling."

He smiles at me, a real, genuine smile. "That makes sense. People connected with her words and stories because they had felt them before, too."

"Exactly. And even though this is a fiction book, people still read it for the romance aspects."

He flips through the pages before he looks back up at me. "Alright, you've convinced me. Pick out some romance books you think I would like."

"Are you serious?" I ask, a smile bursting from my face.

"Dead serious, Bree. I think it could give me a new perspective, and I'm always willing to try new things."

"Well, buckle up, Alex. Movies might be your wheelhouse, but this is where I shine," I say as I grab a few books. As we're checking out, I look over to where Vince is standing.

He's moving his head back and forth, but he finds my eyes and pinches his eyebrows. I nod my head, letting him know that I'm okay. I love how we can read each other with only looks. It's like the two of us have our own secret language. That's probably why we work so well.

Alex grabs his bag from the sales associate and smiles at her before he grabs my hand, and we head for the door.

"Well, I can't believe it, but I actually had fun with you today," I tell Alex as I try to focus on him and this conversation, not all the shouting outside.

"Is being around me really that bad?"

"When you're pretending, yes. But today, you showed me a different side, and I'm thankful for that. Thank you for trusting me with your book choices. I can't wait to hear what you think about them."

"I'm sure I'll update you whenever I have time to start them."

"Good."

He leans in and presses a kiss to my cheek before he motions for our security teams to escort us out of the building.

Shouting ensues for a few seconds before Alex and I go our separate ways, and when Vince closes the door to the car, I find myself taking a breath before he gets in.

"Are you okay?"

"Yeah, I'm alright," I say, and I mean it. I genuinely had fun with Alex today, and I could see us being friends when all is said and done if he keeps being himself.

"You looked like you had a good time. He didn't do anything untoward, did he? I lost you guys between the shelves a few times."

"He was fine, Vince. I would've asked to leave earlier if he had done anything, but I think I got a glimpse of the real Alex today."

"Is he less shittier than the regular one?"

I stifle a laugh at his obvious hatred for him, but since he breaks all the rules Vince and Connie put into place, I don't blame him for it. "Yes, he is."

"Huh," is all I get out of Vince, and before I think we're going to spend the rest of the ride in silence, he speaks again. "Can I ask why you agreed to all this in the first place? It does seem like the media is distracted enough from the Ralph situation, but if it's extra stress on you, then why bother?"

Before I can stop it, the words flow out of my mouth. "I guess I don't really believe in love anymore—for myself."

"The romance reader doesn't believe in love? I'm surprised, Bree."

"I'm allowed to read it and not believe in it for myself. That doesn't mean it doesn't exist for anyone else. It's just myself I don't think it's possible for."

"Why not, angel? Why is it only you who doesn't deserve to feel loved?"

I can't bear to look at him when I say this, so I stare out the window and watch the sun disappear behind a cloud. "I could never give anyone the peace that comes with finding someone you love. You know that feeling? Where you love someone so much that your soul feels calm and serene?"

"I can't say that I do."

"Well, that's what I imagine it's like. It's how I feel when I look at Liv and Tristan. I can tell they bring each other that calm, and I don't think I'll ever be able to do that for someone. It's a choice to fall in love, and I wouldn't willingly put someone through all of this, the fame, the cameras, the life behind a lens. It's not easy."

I hear him sigh heavily as he turns the music down to a soft hum. "Love is a two-way street, Bree. If someone truly loves you, they would go through all of that because you're worth it. Someday, someone will do anything to prove to you that you're worthy of all the love you give others."

"But who's to say they would stay when things get tough? Who would stay if, month after month, the media starts to get too much? Or they can't handle all the people who point at me and take pictures with me?" I'm getting worked up for some reason. *What's wrong with me?*

"The right person will stay because they love *you*, not what you are to the world."

I lock eyes with him, his hazel ones meeting mine in the rearview mirror. "I want to believe you're right, Vince, but I'll believe it when I see it."

"One day, you'll see, angel."

The use of my nickname has me thinking he's talking about himself, but that would be crazy, right? I'm looking for things that aren't there, and I try to shake my mind off the topic, but it won't let go.

He's not talking about himself, Bree. He's literally your bodyguard. He would never think of himself that way.

"You deserve to feel that way too, Vince. You deserve to feel that peace when you find someone you love." I pause, feeling like I crossed a line, so I try to ease the tension I'm feeling. "Not with me, obviously, but with someone."

Vince only chuckles under his breath. "If I ever feel it, I'll let you know. Now, what song do you wanna scream-sing to on the way home? I can put on your usual playlist if you want."

"That works." I smile as he turns on the playlist, and I see him mouth some of the words on the way back as I quietly sing to myself.

That alone makes the pull toward him stronger. He knows me better than I know myself some days, and he even joins in on some of the ridiculous things I like to do when I'm stressed or in need of a pick-me-up.

But no matter what, we'll never cross that line. No matter how pulled I feel towards him, I'm going to have to sever that string at some point.

At some point. Not right now, though. I want to hold on to the end of my line a little longer because it feels good to pretend. It feels good to daydream that when I pull it toward me, Vince will be at the other end of it, waiting with a huge smile on his face.

Maybe in another life, I say to myself.

Chapter Seventeen

— DIE FOR YOU BY THE WEEKND

As I SIT DOWN across from Tristan at our usual restaurant, I notice that his face is paler than normal, and he's all sweaty. *Is he sick?*

"Hi, Bree!" He gets up to hug me, but I hold my arm out at him.

"Are you sick? We could've rescheduled, you know." Tristan and I hang out together, just the two of us, once a month. It's something we started doing when he and Liv got back together, and I've loved it. It helps to get me out of the house and see a familiar face.

It also helps that Tristan and I have some common ground—his grief, my life as a whole.

"I'm not sick, Bree. Just nervous."

Nervous? "Does lunch with me really make you that scared?" I don't even have to wait for him to answer because I know it does. Ralph running wild is making all my favorite people not want to be around me—especially in public, and I don't blame them.

"No, but what I have to talk to you about does."

"Okay, let's sit down and talk then." I motion for him to sit back in his spot, and before he does, he pulls my chair out for me. "Always such a gentleman, Tristan."

"You know how I like to maintain the image, Bree. Plus, it's fun seeing that bodyguard of yours squirm while he sits in the corner."

I move my eyes to where Vince is sitting, his eyes currently scanning the restaurant like he always does before they lock onto mine for a few seconds. Tristan's voice filters into my ears as I tear my gaze away from Vince.

"He doesn't squirm."

"Oh yes, he does. Have you seen those pictures online? In every single shot, it looks like he's ready to kill someone."

"He's just doing his job, Tristan."

His eyebrows raise at me. "And you feel safe with him?"

Safer than I do with anyone else. "Yes, I do."

"Then that's all that matters. Even if he scares the shit out of me, at least you feel safe with him."

I laugh at the fact that Tristan is afraid of Vince. He may look all broody and scary on the outside, but he's still the same guy who helped me melt chocolate and cut my strawberries. Vince is a secret softie, but I'd never tell anyone that. I'd hate to ruin his image.

The server comes over, and since we always sit at the same table—in the back, away from most people—she doesn't even have to ask for our order anymore. Tristan and I are officially regulars at this cute restaurant a few minutes from home.

"So, why are you so nervous? I'm on the edge of my seat here."

"Well, uh...I don't exactly know how to come out and say this, so I guess I'll just blurt it out."

Oh, he better not have done something stupid. "Okay..."

"I came to ask for your blessing because I want to marry your sister."

Tears flood my eyes instantly. Happiness blooms from my chest at the thought of Tristan becoming an official part of our family. "Are you serious?"

"Of course, I'm serious."

"And you're asking for my blessing? Why? You should know that you don't need it."

I notice his eyes are all glassy, too. *God, the way he loves my sister is once in a lifetime.* "You and Liv don't talk to your parents anymore, and normally, I'd ask your dad for his blessing. But I know the only true blessing Liv cares about comes from you, Bree. You're her sister, her favorite person on the planet—"

"Besides you."

"You know that's not true. The way Liv loves you is different from the way she loves me. You two have only had each other your whole lives, and that means something. Yours is the only blessing I want. It would be an honor to become an official part of your family, Bree. If you'll let me, I'll make Liv the happiest girl in the world."

I'm full on crying now. "Tristan, you already make her feel that way. Of course you can marry my sister."

He reaches across the table and grabs one of my hands, squeezing it. "Thank you, Bree. I promise I'll only be an annoying older brother some of the time."

Older brother. "I've never had a brother before, but I wouldn't want it to be anyone else, Tristan. Thank you for taking care of my sister. I know the road hasn't been easy, but I'm glad you guys found your way back."

"Me too. It's been rocky, especially this past year, but I'm excited to start this new chapter with her. I think it's going to be the best one yet."

I hope so. For their sake, I hope they know nothing but sunny skies and beautiful sunsets. If anyone deserves it, it's them. "Do you have the ring, and if so, can I see it?"

"I have a bunch of options, but I wanted to ask you about cut and size because I genuinely have no idea what I'm doing, and you seem like an expert."

I laugh at his insinuation, and for the next thirty minutes, we scour a few sites to try and find the best ring for my sister. I know Tristan likes silver, and so does Liv, but based on a few conversations from our childhood, I know she's not the flashy type. She prefers smaller diamonds over huge and heavy ones. We finally narrow it down to a few contenders before our food arrives.

"Thank you!" I say to our server before she gives me a weird look and leaves.

Tristan must notice because he immediately says something. "What was that about?"

"It's part of the job. It keeps happening when I'm out. I either get mobbed by cameras or stared at."

"I'm sorry, Bree. I can't imagine how that feels."

"It's fine. It's a part of what I do." I don't add that all the cameras make me jittery. I also don't add that I hate the situation I'm in—fake dating Alex. It feels like any time I leave the house now, there's a spotlight on me. I'm performing for the entire world when I'm in public, and it's all a big fucking lie.

"And how have you been doing lately? I know Liv asks you that every day, but you should know that you can talk to me, too."

"Thanks, Tris. I'm..." I trail off, unsure of if I want to tell the truth. Nobody close to me really realizes how dark my head can get sometimes, and I'm afraid if I tell them the truth, they'll see me differently, that they'll leave because being around me is too much. I decide to anyway, because I know Tristan understands the most out of everyone. "I'm not doing great."

"Is it all just too much? Maybe you should tell Connie you need a break," he tells me as he takes a bite of his pizza.

"I've been on an extended break from events out of state since the news broke about Ralph. Alex flies here for every fake date we have, and all I'm required to do is see him, upload as usual on my YouTube, and post my sponsored shit. I'll be fine, Tristan. It's just hard being in my head some days."

"I know the feeling, Bree." He takes a sip of his water. "It was a rough week for me."

"I'm sorry. I can't even imagine how it feels."

Before I think he's not going to elaborate, he says, "I lost one of the shirts Tobias gave me for my birthday. It was the smallest thing ever, but it sent my mind into a tailspin. I was worried that if it was gone forever, he'd be mad I lost it. The smallest, stupidest thing set me back so badly that I completely wrecked our bedroom and laundry room trying to find it."

My heart starts to ache for him, for his family. I can't imagine losing a son and a brother the way the West family has.

"Liv found it yesterday underneath some boxes in the basement. It fell while it was hanging up to dry. I apologized profusely for practically tearing the house apart, but she just wrapped me in a hug and held me until my tears stopped falling."

Liv has always been my favorite shoulder to cry on, and I'm glad he has her.

"It's a battle every single day, Bree. I miss my brother so bad, it feels like my body might explode, like my bones might crack under the weight of my own thoughts."

"Well, would you rather grieve or never love anyone enough to be able to?"

"I'd rather feel it all now, especially with Liv by my side. She carries me through the dark days until her light shines so bright, I can barely remember what the dark feels like."

God, you'd think he was the author with the way he keeps talking. "I'm glad you have her."

"You have her too, Bree. And me. You know you don't have to shoulder this alone. She knows you're struggling. Even my sister told me she's worried about you."

"Did Teags tell you about what she saw?" I already know she did. Last Monday scared me more than I care to admit, and with the way Teags hugged me that day, I know it probably scared her, too. Of course she would tell Tristan about it because nobody knows I've been falling apart at the seams since Ralph got out. Nobody but Vince and now Teags.

"Yeah, she did. Besides the day Tobias died, I've never heard my sister so scared, Bree. She said it was like you weren't even in your body. You were thrashing in Vince's arms as he tried to calm you down."

I lower my gaze from his, suddenly feeling guilty. "Please don't tell my sister."

"I won't, Bree. But you need to start talking to her because she's worried about you. Don't shut her out just to keep her safe. You need her as much as she needs you, especially now."

"I know, Tristan. I know all of that. I'm just worried about you guys. I don't want you to get hurt because of me and my stupid stalker. I never wanted to put you guys in danger, and—"

He halts my words with his hand on top of mine. "And those thoughts are valid, but we're practically family, Bree. Let us make those choices for ourselves because no matter what, we're on your side every single fucking time."

Before I can tell him how much I appreciate that, someone comes up to our table. "Bree Hart?"

I quickly wipe the tears from my eyes before I turn back around. "Yes, that's me. Hi!"

"Do you mind if we get a picture?"

"I don't mind," I say as I feel another presence come up to our table.

"Is everything okay?" Vince asks as he looks between the three of us.

"Yup. We're just getting a picture." I place my hand on Vince's arm as I look up at him. "It's all good."

But he makes no move to leave. As he continues to stare down at me, those hazel eyes burning into mine, my hand suddenly feels like an inferno where it touches his arm.

"I can take the picture if you give me your phone," Tristan says to the fan at our table.

"Thanks, bro."

"No problem." Tristan looks uncomfortable, his guard up like Vince's.

I don't have a lot of male fans, but since I started dating Alex, more and more have come up to me, wanting to take pictures. Which is fine, I don't mind, but there's something a bit more comforting about girls talking to me about books, rather than guys just wanting a picture. They can get a bit creepy sometimes.

I start to pose from where I sit, and the guy leans down, getting in the picture, and I hear Tristan clicking some pictures before the guy whispers something in my ear. "He's coming."

My body goes cold, but I try to shake it off. "What was that?"

"I didn't say anything." But the smirk on his face says differently.

"Is something wrong?" Vince asks me.

"Here's your phone, dude." Tristan hands it back to him before he pockets it.

"W-What did you say to me?" I question, knowing in my gut what I heard.

"Thanks for the picture, Bree." And as he walks away, I hear him start to whistle.

It's the same exact tune from that night, and before I have time to do anything, Vince is crouching down to meet me at eye level. "What's wrong, Bree?"

"He whistled. I–It was the same thing he whistled that night before he—"

"Fuck." Vince runs a hand through his hair. "We should go."

But before any of us has time to react, a loud pop permeates the air before I hear a whizzing sound by my ear. The sound of a glass breaking and screaming shocks me back to reality.

"Bree, let's go!"

"W-What?"

"Now!" Vince says as he grabs my head, ducking it down underneath the table.

"Wait, where's Tristan?" I shout, hoping he can hear me, but Vince is too busy talking through his earpiece, probably figuring out the safest way out of here. I don't see his legs across from me at our table, and my ears are ringing. *Is he hurt? Did I put Tristan in danger?* "Vince! Where's Tristan?"

"Over here!" I hear him shout from behind a potted plant.

Vince is still cradling my head away from danger before another whizz goes by our table. "Is someone shooting at the restaurant?"

"I think so. Emerson and Chris are trying to figure out what's going on and where the shots are coming from." Vince cranes his neck to Tristan. "You follow me, okay? On my count."

Tristan must comply because when Vince reaches three, he jumps up and shields my body as he heads for the bathrooms at the back of the restaurant.

Vince kicks open the bathroom door and checks it out. When he deems it safe a few seconds later, he turns to the two of us. "Stay here, and don't open this door for anyone but me. I'll be back."

My heart starts to race at the thought of him going out toward the danger. *Stay here. Stay here where you won't get hurt.* "Vince, where are you going?"

"I'm going to figure out what the hell's going on and who the fuck was shooting at you." *At me.* Not the restaurant, me. He unholsters his gun from his ankle before he clicks the safety off. I jump at the noise but shove it down because there's too much else to worry about.

"Be safe," is all I can say.

He nods at me before looking at Tristan. "If I'm not back in fifteen minutes, you get her out of here."

"I will."

"You fucking better because if I find out she got hurt because of you, I'll strangle you myself!" Vince *yells* at Tristan.

"Vince—"

"I'll protect Bree with my life. You have my word."

"Tristan, no—"

"I'll believe it when I see it," Vince shoots back at him, and I'm afraid this is going to turn into a fight if they don't stop challenging one another.

"Vince, go do your job. We'll be fine here." I turn to Tristan. "And you. Don't ever insinuate you'd die for me because you shouldn't even be in this situation in the first place. It's my fault you're in this mess, and it should always be me getting hurt over you."

Before Tristan can respond, Vince speaks. "If you ever blame yourself for this again, angel, don't do it in front of me."

What does that mean? But he's gone, and I'm suddenly worried that he might not come back. The thought of it makes my skin crawl, and it's then I realize my crush on Vince might be more than that.

Because as I stand in this bathroom and think about him getting hurt or killed, I realize I'd rather die before I see that happen.

If I was given the choice, I'd choose him—the man who makes me feel safe, protected, like my voice still matters. The man who helps me through the panic, the man whose face and eyes help me see through the fog.

I like Vince. I care about him, but I know that the two of us could never happen; he will never see me as more than just a client.

"Bree? Are you okay? God, what the hell is going on?" Tristan has started pacing around the bathroom, and I shake out of my terror enough to answer him.

"He sent me a bullet with my name scratched onto it." I leave out the part about Liv because Vince sent a few guys to watch their house. I think Nico is also planning on installing a system for them.

"He *what*?" Tristan throws his hands into the air. "Bree, what the fuck? Why didn't you tell us?"

"I-I was scared! I haven't been sleeping, and I can barely leave the house without panicking, and it's all too much! It's too much for me to handle, and I don't want to dump it on you guys because you have your own shit to deal with."

"You're not too much, Bree, don't you get that? Your sister and I love you, and we can only help if you tell us when you're having a hard time. After today, Liv is going to go crazy, and you're going to have to tell her everything. I mean *everything*, Bree."

"I will! I will, and I'm sorry you're in this mess."

His arms wrap around me as tears leak from my eyes. "Don't apologize again, Bree. None of this is your fault."

We stay like that for a few minutes until he breaks the eerie silence. "So, angel, huh?"

I laugh into his chest. "Don't even start with me right now."

"Oh, come on. I *had* to bring it up. Even *I* got all hot and bothered when it rolled off his tongue like that. Liv's been writing a bodyguard romance, and I swear, you two are ripped right from the pages of her Word document."

"She's writing *what*?" Tristan's eyes bug out of his head because he knows he wasn't supposed to tell me that.

Two long knocks on the door followed by two short ones make me breathe a little easier. *He's okay.* I open the door to the bathroom, and when I see blood dripping down his face, I panic.

"What the hell happened?"

"I knocked out the shooter until the cops could get here. He managed to get a punch in. It's not Ralph." He looks *pissed*, and I can't tell if it's because the guy managed to get a hit on him or just in general.

"What do you mean it wasn't Ralph? Who was it?"

"I don't know. Some gun for hire, I'd assume." Fuck, his entire body is so tense.

"Are you okay?"

"Let's get out of here. Chris has the car ready in the alley." Vince continues to look at me while he addresses Tristan. "You too, West. Let's go."

As the three of us walk out of the restaurant, my body is still shaking; any of us could've been shot while trying to enjoy something as simple as eating lunch together.

Will this ever end?

Chapter Eighteen

— ONLY ANGEL BY HARRY STYLES

"He's a fucking coward!" I say as I punch Nico's gloves. *God, this feels good.*

"I know, but damn, take it easy," he says as I get a few final hits in before we call this round.

Take it easy, he says. "Easy for you to say. You weren't the one being shot at a few days ago." I rip my gloves off and toss them aside, the workout not doing anything to calm the fire burning through my veins.

"You did your job, Vince. You did it well, and you even held the guy who was shooting at you. Stop beating yourself up over it."

I know he's right, but I'm not giving him the chance to rub it in. I swipe my water bottle from where it rests on the floor and take a few sips from it. My face scrunches a bit because of how hard that motherfucker punched me, but I shove the pain down; it could've ended much worse.

Bree could've been shot. She could've been killed. *Killed.* I keep replaying that day in my head, and I'm glad it ended how it did, but that doesn't stop me from thinking how else it could have ended.

I almost lost her. I almost lost Bree. I almost lost my first client.

"Have you talked to the cops? Have they updated you on anything?"

Shit. I forgot that's why I originally called him over here. "The shooter was found dead in his cell this morning. His tongue was cut out."

"Fuck."

"Yeah. Somebody wanted to make sure he couldn't talk. I'm assuming it was whoever hired him."

Nico drags his tattooed hand down his face. "This is a shitshow."

"Have you had any luck tracing the payment to his account?" Our shooter—Daniel Marsh—was a hired gun, like I expected, but I'm not sure who hired him in the first place. Ralph was never one to have other people do his dirty work for him, but I'm working under the theory that he made a few new friends in prison. He has become really good at the waiting game. So, while he is technically escalating from notes to shooting at Bree, I can't be sure that this is him.

The fact that it could be someone completely different scares me more than it should.

"I've got my best guys working on it, and when they find something, you'll be the first to know."

"Good," I say before I bring up something I haven't wanted to say out loud. "You know what has bugged me the most about all this? Daniel was a trained sniper. The fucker had a bunch of medals and shit before he was dishonorably discharged."

"You're nervous because he missed," Nico states, a look of concern flashing across his face.

"Yeah. If his target really was Bree, then how did he miss every shot he took? It almost feels like he was trying not to hit her."

Nico just grumbles something before he leaves to go upstairs, probably wanting to get back to figuring out where the money came from. I hear him talking to someone before he gets fully up the stairs, and when Bree comes into view, I feel a twinge in my chest.

She hasn't slept in days. I know that because she's been down here every day before I am, sprinting as fast as she can until her body practically collapses. She barely spares me a glance as she heads for the treadmill, but I can't take my eyes off her.

I think she's wearing my shirt. It looks like one of the band shirts my sister bought me that I lost when I moved. I assumed I accidentally left it somewhere, but now I think that she either stole it from me or it fell out of one of my bags.

"Where'd you get that shirt, angel?"

She breaks out of her haze before looking down at her attire. "It was in my laundry basket. Why?"

"It's mine."

Her eyes bulge, and I can practically see the thoughts racing through her head. "I'll wash it and give it back to you, I promise."

"It's okay, Bree. Keep it." *Why did I just say that?*

She shakes her head as soon as the words are out of my mouth. "No, Vince. I can't keep it. That's—"

"You wear it much better than I do." I ignore the way her cheeks flush before I walk over to her, grab her water bottle, and head to fill it up. Bree always forgets, and by the time she's done sprinting out the tension in her body, she won't feel like filling it.

By the time I bring it back to her, she hasn't moved from her spot.

I take the time to study her like this—headphones around her neck, blonde hair up in a ponytail, my shirt covering her entire body to her knees, her tattered sneakers on her feet.

She looks like a forbidden fruit standing here in front of me, and I have to physically stop myself from reaching out to her.

"Thanks," she says in a low whisper. I notice her pulse has started to beat faster, and I can't tell if she's nervous at our close proximity or scared. I take a step back before I speak again.

"I'll leave you to it."

She swallows hard before her gaze breaks mine and she looks anywhere else besides my eyes. "I'm still good to go to Liv's tonight, right?"

"Yes. Emerson is driving, and I'll be with you inside."

Her shoulders fall just a little bit. I've noticed that, out of all my men, she feels safest with Emerson—besides me, of course. "Her event in a few weeks is still under review. It's too out in the open, but I think I can figure something out."

"It's important to Liv, so I'd really love to go. If it's not possible, I'm sure she would understand, but I can't keep living like this."

"I know. I'll figure it out, Bree. He doesn't get to keep controlling your life like this."

"But he is, and he does."

I step toward her again, needing her to understand that this won't be forever. "*For now.*"

Bree surprises me by taking the loose strand of hair that hangs from my head and smoothing it back into place. "I trust you, Vince. It's him that I don't."

She's never voluntarily touched me before, and I don't dare move because I don't want to scare her off. *Her touch feels good.* I'm chalking all the weird feelings up to not having touched a woman in a few years. I can't even remember the last time I was intimate with someone. I tend to stay away from clients, and when I need any sort of release, random hookups have been fine.

But this feels different for some reason. I don't hate it, but nothing could ever happen between the two of us. Bree's drowning in her own mind most of the time, and she's my client. I would *never* put her in that position. She deserves better than me, and after all of this is over, I'll just be a distant memory.

We'll both move on, and I'll be okay with that.

But as I walk away from our interaction, the sinking feeling in my gut gets heavier and heavier with each step I take.

— THE ARCHER BY TAYLOR SWIFT

"Bree, you were shot at! Did you forget about that, or do I have to remind you?" My sister yells at me, rightfully so, as I sit on her couch. Liv is standing in front of me, pacing back and forth on the rug that sits underneath her coffee table.

"Livvy, baby, you're going to burn a line into the carpet if you keep pacing." Tristan gets up off the loveseat and grabs her shoulder, trying to maneuver her to sit, but she shrugs off his hands.

"Tristan, stop. You were shot at, too! Why am I the only one taking this seriously?" Liv's hands get thrown up into the air, and I shift uncomfortably. I *hate* that I worried her so much, but it's hard for me to talk about what's been going on in my head lately.

"Liv, it's been an insane few months. I think Bree just needed a little room to breathe," Teags tells her, and I'm glad she's here. Since she witnessed one of my episodes in person, she can help explain why I wanted to keep it a secret. I feel like shit for lying to her, but I also feel like shit for making her worry this much.

I shift again, not knowing if it's my clothes I'm feeling uncomfortable in or just my body in general.

"I understand that, I do. But Bree, I'm your sister! You should be able to come to me about these things. I'm not like our parents. I don't want to smother you. I just want to make sure you're doing okay."

"Liv, I know, but—"

Tristan cuts me off. "Livvy, just take a few breaths. Imagine you were in her situation—"

Liv cuts him off. "Tristan, you could've been killed! Both of you could've been seriously hurt! I could have lost both of you. So before you tell me I'm overreacting, put yourself in *my* shoes."

"Pretty girl, I—"

Teags cut him off. "Everyone is making valid points, but can you guys let Bree talk?"

I lock eyes with my best friend before I give her a small smile. Teagen is the youngest in her family, and she knows just as well as I do that barely being able to get two words in is a trait of being the youngest. Nobody ever really wants to listen to what you have to say sometimes, and it used to be a fight with my parents when they would never let me get a word in about *my* career.

"Thanks, Teags."

I hear my sister sigh before she grabs both of my hands in hers. "I'll never stop worrying about you, Bree. All I'm asking is that I'm kept in the loop." Her eyes flit to Vince, who sits at my right. "You promised me I was being kept in the loop."

What? "What are you talking about?"

"The only thing I promised you was that I'd keep her safe. My allegiance is to Bree, first and foremost. Her safety is the only thing I care about. That's all I think about twenty-four-seven," Vince tells her, his voice low and quiet.

I hate to admit that hearing him say that turned me on a little bit.

What is it about protective men?

"Look, Liv, I'm sorry I've distanced myself from you the past few weeks. Saying I've had a lot going on is the understatement of the century, but I didn't want Ralph to put a target on your back, too, especially after what he sent to my house—" I stop myself because the one thing I *didn't* want Liv knowing was that one of the bullets had her name on it too. I didn't want to cause her any more stress or panic, but it looks like I have no choice now.

"What did he send to your house?"

I sigh heavily before I run a hand through my hair. "Nothing. Just some notes and pictures. Can we eat dinner now?"

"You're deflecting. There's something you're not telling me. What did he send you, Bree?"

"Liv, just drop it. It's better if you don't know." I stand, ready to crawl back into my bed and never come out again.

"Bree, you should tell her," Teags says to me. "Especially after you *and* Tristan were shot at. It's not a coincidence."

"How the hell do you know about it?" I question. Nico told me he hid the bullets in his pocket when he let Teags into my house that day. *How did she find out?*

"Wait, what are you guys talking about?" Tristan asks.

"Can someone explain before I go insane?" Liv says, pacing once again. Before I can open my mouth to spill everything, Vince beats me to it.

"Ralph sent a package with two bullets in it. One with Bree's name on it." He pauses. "And one with Liv's name."

"Wait, back up. What did you just say?" Liv all but stops cold in her tracks. "He sent you a bullet with my name on it, and you didn't think you should mention that to me?"

"I was going to tell you that night! Tristan and I met for lunch, and he told me to open up to you, and I was going to! I swear, I was, but then we got shot at, and that took precedence, and it slipped through the cracks."

"How could you forget something like that? Bree, oh my God. This is nuts." Liv stops pacing and places a hand on the mantle to steady herself.

I'm a horrible sister. I let my own mental health take priority, and if something had happened to her that I could've prevented, I don't know what I would've done. "I'm sorry, Liv. I—"

"Liv, she's trying her best. You don't see the kind of pressure she's under, so give her some leeway." Vince stands up from his seat, heading to the fridge for water, and I hate that he's been dragged into my family squabbles. This is a fucking mess.

"Whose idea was it to keep this a secret from me? Because you clearly knew about it and could've told me, but you didn't." Liv points an accusing finger at Vince.

"It was—"

Vince cuts me off. "It was my idea. I had to keep Bree safe, Liv. It's what you guys hired me for, and that's what I did. To be fair, I had some of my guys watch your house, just to make sure that—"

Nobody sees it coming, not even Vince. His guard was down, and Tristan manages to land a punch right to his nose, a cracking sound echoing around the living room. Vince broke his nose when the shooter landed a punch, and by the sounds of it, Tristan just broke it again.

"You didn't think we needed to know about that? You son of a bitch!"

Vince centers himself, and when he lifts his head to look at Tristan, blood is running down his face. I swear, I see a hint of a smirk on his face, but it might just be my imagination. "I was doing my job, Tristan. If you can't understand that, then I'm sorry."

"Teags, go get some towels and an ice pack," I tell her, and she nods at me, rushing to the bathroom.

"I understand that, Vince." Tristan turns his gaze to me. "I just don't understand why all of a sudden you're keeping secrets from us, Bree. You omitted that detail."

God, I feel sick. I know I fucked up, but how can I explain it without breaking down? Words don't come easily to me. I'd rather just keep it all in than have to let everybody know I don't feel like myself, that some days, I wish I wasn't here anymore.

How do you tell the people you love that you wish you could disappear forever? How do I look Tristan and Teags in the eye and say that after they lost their brother how they did?

I can't. I couldn't do that to them, so burying all of my emotions has been the new normal for me, and it's worked out just fine until now.

"What happened to our pinky promise, Bree? Did that mean nothing to you?"

Crack. That's the sound of my heart breaking and slipping onto the floor in front of me.

"Liv, don't," Teags warns.

"Teags, stop defending her actions. She messed up, and—"

"And she knows that! Everyone needs to stop telling her what she should've done and just listen to her! I've seen firsthand how much she's struggling, and you could all give her a tiny bit of grace. None of us know what she's going through, and it sucks to be out of the loop, but she's the one *living* in this horror right now. Everyone take five and chill the fuck out!" Teags hands me an ice pack and some towels, and I take them over to where Vince is sitting on a kitchen stool.

"Fine. Liv, let's go outside for a second, okay?" Tristan says, and I hear the sliding door shut a few seconds later.

I all but drag Vince to the bathroom. "How does your nose feel?"

"Broken. Again."

"Yeah, no shit. My brother packs a hell of a punch," Teags says as she leans against the door frame. "I'm sorry for tonight. I didn't think it was going to be this heated."

"Thanks for sticking up for me. I don't deserve a friend like you, and if you want to distance yourself, I'll understand," I say as I clean the blood off of Vince's face.

"If you ever say that to me again, I'll be the one punching you," Teags says before she leaves the bathroom.

Vince is silent for a few moments as I fix his face up. It's comfortable—the quiet air between us. Sometimes, I wish my wounds were this easy to patch up. A band-aid here, some gauze there. But that's not how it works when the problems are in your head, when your memories are the things that haunt you. All my scars are invisible, unnoticed by the rest of the world. Nobody notices my marks. Nobody can see or feel the battle that goes on in my head every day. And no matter how hard I try, nobody is able to put me back together.

I'm the only one who can, but some days, I wonder if it's even worth it. Maybe I'm broken beyond repair. Maybe it's too late for me and there's no cure. There's no band-aid that I can put over my brain to make it all stop.

"Bree, I don't know where you got this idea that you don't deserve good people around you, but that stops now. The only reason Tristan and Liv are upset is because they care about you. A lot. I've never seen a client's family so passionate about knowing what's been going on."

"I know," I whisper, feeling again like a big fat failure. It seems like everything I do lately has been wrong, and I don't know how to fix any of it. I place a small bandage across Vince's nose before I clean up the mess I made. "You're all set."

"Thanks for taking such good care of me. You're a natural," Vince whispers as he gets up, and I follow him out to the living room.

The door opens a few seconds later, and Liv wraps me in a hug. My sleeve gets wet, and I feel even worse for making her cry.

"Go easy on me, okay?"

I feel her nod into my shoulder before she untangles herself from me and sits down, Tristan standing behind her. The four of them are sitting while I stand in front of them, and even though I feel really on the spot, I speak.

"I haven't slept through the night since I found out he was getting out. If I do sleep, I have nightmares so vivid that they haunt me when I'm awake. I don't know how to talk about what I'm going through because my brain can't even wrap around it. It's hard for me to put all my feelings into words. I'm not like you, Liv. I can't just take all my thoughts and make them coherent. It's fucking hard for me to talk about everything

I've been and am still going through. I also don't want you to worry about me because I'm doing the best I can."

Liv sniffles. "I'll always worry about you, Bree. I'm not wired any other way."

"I didn't want you guys to be forced into my shit. That's why I kept it from you. In my mind, if you didn't know, then you were safe from the shitshow that is my life." I take a small break, my throat burning from the tears I'm holding back. "I have panic attacks a few times a week. I jump when I hear a loud noise I wasn't expecting. I can't stand to hear people whistle because it all reminds me of that night. Of him. I'm afraid he's lurking around every corner, waiting to come back and finish what he started."

I notice my sister is full on crying, Tristan too. Vince has a somber look on his face, even though he knows all this, and Teags even has glassy eyes. *Look at what I'm doing to them. Look at the pain I'm causing them.*

"I keep waiting for something to get better. I keep waiting for my mind to stop playing all these tricks on me, but it hasn't happened yet. Everyone says that time heals all wounds, that it gets better, but it hasn't for me, at least not yet. I am drowning in my thoughts every waking moment of the day, and it won't stop. I didn't think anyone would want to stay by my side if threats kept being made, if the media kept publicizing the worst night of my life."

"Bree, I didn't know it was this bad. If I had known—"

"You didn't know because I didn't want you to. This is on me, not you, Liv."

"For future reference, we want to know it all. We're your fucking family. We care about you, and all we want is to help you through the tough moments. Got it?" Tristan asks me.

I shake my head. "You all have your own shit to deal with. I don't want to add to that."

Liv gets up and grabs my hands where they hang at my side. "Imagine we're all sitting at the same table. All four of us."

"Okay." I don't know where she's going with this, but I let her continue.

"Four years ago, I put my strength down on the table, and you picked me up. You carried me, and when I collapsed into your arms the day our parents tricked me with that note, you held me up."

I remember catching her as she sobbed. I had never seen Liv so broken before. She was always stronger than I was, though, and I'd carry her through that again and again if I had to.

"And eventually, I picked my strength back up. Then, Tristan and Teags put theirs down when Tobias died. The two of us are still helping them carry it, but each day, it gets a little lighter, and they can help shoulder some of it on their own. Right?"

Teags nods as Tristan says, "Yes."

"And then, Vince sat down at our table with us. Yet another person who wants to help carry you when the weight gets too heavy."

"Damn right, angel."

I'm sobbing where I stand at the picture my sister is painting.

"You can put some of your strength down, Bree. You never need to ask us to help because we're already next to you, waiting for you to put it down if it gets too heavy."

"Because you guys would stay at the table with me. You guys would stay." I say through my tears. "No more secrets. Consider you guys in the loop at all times."

"I'll tell Nico to make a group chat," Vince says, scrunching his face and turning to Tristan and holding out his hand. "That was a hell of a punch."

Seriously? "Thanks, man. Are we good?"

Tristan takes his hand and shakes it. "We're good."

Liv pulls Teags and I in for a hug, and Teags tries to wiggle her way out of it but eventually succumbs.

For the next three hours, we sit around the kitchen table, laughing as we eat, and that sliver of normal creeps back in, making me feel safer than I have in months. Around this table, there is happiness and light, and I'm not alone anymore.

Chapter Nineteen

— SOMETHING ABOUT HER BY STEPHEN SANCHEZ

"Okay, so we have all the exits covered. Let's move on to the actual event ballroom," I say as I flip the packet to the next page, Emerson, Kenner, Duncan, and Chris following suit.

Connie called me the other day to ask if I could start prepping a security plan for this big event that Bree is planning. When I asked her what event it was because I didn't see one on my calendar, she hung up on me, and thirty seconds later, I had an email in my inbox.

So, I got to work.

I still have to ask Bree about this, because if it was up to me, an event this size with the amount of publicity it will bring is way too dangerous. But I do what I'm told and try not to make much noise.

"Wait, so we'll need every single person for this? Who's going to watch the house while we're all there?" Emerson asks me, voicing the concerns I've had since I got Connie's email.

"Yeah. It's an all-hands-on-deck occasion. I'm talking to Nico about having around the clock surveillance on the house while we're at the event. He's coming over later to talk about it." Nico might push my buttons sometimes, but I love having him as a business partner. He may act like some pretty boy who wears suits and flirts with everyone, but he's damn good at his job.

"Okay. That works." Emerson nods at me.

Duncan keeps flipping pages and eyeing me, so I look at him. "Something on your mind?"

"The guest list. It has lots of recognizable names. This seems like a widely publicized event."

"And?"

"And isn't our main job to keep Bree safe? This event doesn't feel like it'll be safe. It feels like a giant arrow is pointing at Bree for Ralph to come and get her."

I sigh heavily, having the same gut feeling that this is going to be a giant mistake. Thanks to rule number eleven, my gut is usually right, but Connie isn't one to listen to gut feelings, so when I brought it up to her, she spun it around to be good publicity instead of focusing on the bad.

I'm all for spinning the narrative, but when it comes to Bree's safety, I'll always worry about that over anything the press wants to say.

"Connie has assured me it will be a controlled event. Tickets assigned to only the people on the guest list, and only certain people have plus ones." I sigh again, trying to run a hand through my curly hair, only for it to get stuck in the tangles. "Look, I voiced the same concerns to her, but I trained you guys, and I trust that all of us can make this event as safe as possible."

The four of them look between one another, and I suddenly feel like there's something they want to say, but are too afraid to. "Anything you want to add?"

They look between one another again before Emerson speaks. "Alex is still on the list."

"And? Is there a problem with that?" I ask, wondering what they're getting at.

"Haven't you seen all the news surrounding him and..." Duncan trails off, and I wish one of these guys would just say whatever they're alluding to.

"News about what? One of you just tell me what the fuck is going on."

"The media has spotted Alex cheating on Bree," Kenner spits out.

"More than once," Chris adds.

Fucking hell. "You've got to be kidding me."

"It's been all over the place, Boss. How did you not see it?" Kenner asks.

"The internet is more Nico's territory." I assumed he would tell me if anything concerning Bree came up, and now I'm pissed at him for not letting me know. "How many?"

The four of them squirm in their seats, and I already know it's not going to be a good number. Hell, anything other than zero is bad.

"Five, including the ex-girlfriend we ran into at the fashion show."

I grab the sides of my chair with my fists, my knuckles turning white from how pissed off I am. This kid can barely handle a fake relationship without cheating on someone, and that someone being Bree is making me angrier. This entire thing has only caused her more stress, and she was doing Alex a favor by helping him clean up his image. He can't clean it up if he keeps seeing other women on the side. Fuck, this is going to be a nightmare. I'm going to have to call Connie and discuss this at some point. If Alex is going to fuck around on Bree, I'm pretty sure that means he broke the contract. If I can get Bree out of this stupid fake relationship and lessen the stress she's under, I'll sleep a lot better at night. Well, I'll sleep a lot better once I can actually sleep in my own bed and not in front of her door.

"I'll talk to Connie and Bree about it, but if it was up to me, he wouldn't be on the list."

"Is that all, boss?" Kenner asks, antsy to get back to his post.

A knock on the door interrupts what I'm about to say. "Come in."

Bree's face pokes around the door as she walks halfway into my makeshift office. "Am I interrupting? I can come back later if—"

"They were just leaving, Bree. Come on in." I turn my attention back to the boys. "You're dismissed. Keep an eye on your emails for updates."

I hear a few murmurs as the four of them get up and leave, Bree smiling as she sits in front of me. I try to shift my attention to anything else—my laptop screen, the papers in front of me—but anytime Bree is near, it's hard to pull focus from her.

She's like a light in the dark, brightening every room she walks into. And even though she feels dim right now, she still shines.

I should tell her that. But I remain silent, knowing I would be crossing way too many lines.

"Vince?" I shake out of the haze I was in and look at her. "Did you hear what I said?"

"No. Sorry. What did you want to discuss?"

She smiles at me, but if she notices me staring at her, she doesn't say anything. "Connie told me she emailed you about the event I'm throwing, and I was wondering if you had any questions I could answer."

I lean forward on my desk, silently wishing it wasn't in between us but thankful that it is. I'm slowly losing control, and the last thing I want to do is make her uncomfortable, especially since my job with her is a means to an end. She knows I'm leaving after it's done, and I know I'll walk away.

Rule number fucking six. When my job is done here, I'll walk away like I always do.

But I'm personally attached to Bree. I know that already, and there's nothing I can do about it.

"Why now? Why is this event happening while he's still out there?"

"I've been wanting to throw an event for the Mental Health Foundation ever since...ever since it happened. It's an important cause to me, and I think this event could raise a lot of money and publicity for them."

God, does she even realize how great of a person she is? Despite going through this horrible time, she's still thinking about other people instead of herself. "You're a great person, Bree."

"I'm not throwing it just to get some good karma. I *actually* care about bringing more awareness to mental health."

"I know that. Anyone who knows you, understands that, Bree. I'm just worried. You were shot at a few weeks ago. Remember? Ralph is enlisting other people to do his dirty work for him, and I'm nervous with all the publicity that this won't be safe for you."

Her shoulders tense up. "But you and your team will be working the event."

"That's right."

"So, I'll be safe." She smiles at me, her eyes locking with mine.

My heart starts to beat faster, but I disregard that for now. "As safe as you can be."

"As long as you're around, I'll always feel safe."

Her voice is just above a whisper, almost as if she didn't want me to hear it, but I did. Does she really mean that? I knew she felt safe with me because it's my job to protect her, but the *way* she said it makes me think there's another meaning behind it. I want to change the subject because we're floating into dangerous territory, so I do.

"I didn't see your parents on the list of attendees. Do I need to correct that mistake?"

Bree rolls her eyes when I mention them. "It wasn't a mistake. I haven't spoken to them in almost a year."

"Oh. I'm sorry for bringing it up."

She just shakes her head. "It's okay. I cut them off around the same time Liv did."

"Neither of you talk to your parents anymore?" I stifle the urge to smile. I was never a fan of them, but I kept my opinions to myself, knowing it wasn't my business.

"Long story short, Liv cut them off because they ruined her relationship with Tristan. They meddled in her life after ignoring her for twenty years."

What the actual fuck is wrong with them? "Why did they do that?"

"Because they could. They never really gave her a real reason, which is ridiculous."

"Very ridiculous." Bree laughs when I agree with her. "And why do you not speak to them?"

Her face falls immediately. "Lots of reasons. You remember they kept the house Ralph hurt me in, but that wasn't the only reason why I decided to cut ties with them."

"We don't have to get into it if you don't want to." I reach to grab a pen on my desk, wanting to distract myself from how fast my heart is beating. When I think about what happened before I was here, before I was protecting her, I can't breathe. It physically pains me that I couldn't protect Bree, even when I didn't know she existed.

But now she exists, and she and her safety cloud my mind twenty-four hours a day, seven days a week.

I feel a hand come down onto mine, and when I look up, Bree's eyes meet mine, and she starts to move her hand back and forth. "It's okay, Vince. We can talk about this another time. I really came in here to talk about the event."

My heartbeat slows like it always does when her skin comes into contact with mine. "I have an uncomfortable question to ask you."

"Oh. Well, go ahead." She detaches her hand from mine, and I miss the contact but shove that feeling down.

"The boys brought something to my attention earlier. Did you know Alex has been spotted in public with other women?"

To that she smirks. "I'm an internet personality, Vince. Of course I know about it. Ellie sent me some articles last week. I think she was trying to be nice by showing me, but there's another part of me that thinks she wants to be one of those girls on his arm."

"Yeah, I've never really liked Ellie. She's almost too friendly with everyone, and I don't think her motives are clear."

"Wow. I never thought I'd see the day when Vince Evans talked poorly about one of my friends to my face. I should write this down on my calendar."

I stifle a laugh again because, for some reason, Bree makes me laugh more than anyone else I know. "I'm just saying. She makes it seem like she's everyone's friend, but most people like that always have ulterior motives of some sort. Just be careful, okay?"

"I'll be careful, Vince. I know if I somehow fall back into old patterns of letting people walk all over me, you'll be there to catch me."

"I'll always catch you, angel."

"I know," she whispers, tucking a loose hair behind her ear. *God, I wish I did that instead of her.*

"Special delivery!" Nico announces as he waltzes into my office, throwing a stack of something on my desk.

I look at what he's just dropped, and when I see my face on the cover of one of them, I pick it up immediately. "What the fuck is this?"

Bree snatches the magazine from my hand before I can stop her.

"Oh my God!" she squeals as she turns it around to show me. "It's your first cover feature!"

Nico laughs as Bree hands it to him. "Who is the elusive bodyguard, Vince Evans? Here's all *you* need to know about the company he founded alongside partner Nico Wilder. Aw, they gave me a shoutout on your cover story."

"If you want a shoutout, why don't you just take the cover and tell them to leave me off it?"

"Them, Vince? I can't control the paparazzi. God, Bree, I thought you were teaching him about all this shit?" Nico leans against the back of Bree's chair, and she continues giggling as she flips through another magazine.

"He's practically a lost cause, Nico." She reaches up and pats one of his hands where it rests against her chair. That small touch between them drives me crazy, but I reign that in before I do something stupid. "Five facts about Vince Evans you can't find anywhere else!"

"Wow, Vincey, did you give them the exclusive?" Nico asks.

"Are you both done now? I'd like to get back to work on these security plans."

"I think we pissed him off, princess."

Bree only continues to laugh, and I could get drunk off that sound. It's been far and few between lately, and whenever she laughs, I want to bottle it up and store it somewhere for later. I prefer hearing those than the screams and sobs.

"He knows we're kidding, Nico, but we should let him get back to work," Bree says, a hint of mischief in her tone as she scoops up the magazines. "Are you thinking what I'm thinking?"

Nico's brow raises at her, and I'm already pre-annoyed at whatever these two are planning. "I'm two steps ahead of you. Shall we?"

"We shall."

"What are you both up to?" I ask.

"We're definitely not going to flip through these and figure out a hundred new ways to push your buttons, that's for sure!" Nico salutes me.

"Don't worry. I'll make sure Nico plays nice." Bree waves as she heads out of my office and for the rest of the time I'm working, I hear her laughter float through the house a few different times, and it has me smiling at my desk the entire afternoon.

And damn, if that isn't the best sound I've ever heard.

Chapter Twenty

— NDA BY BILLIE EILISH

"OKAY, SO THIS IS what I'm wearing to Liv's event tonight! It's a simple silk slip dress. I went with the champagne one you guys voted for on my Instagram story yesterday. This one is definitely my favorite since it matches her book cover," I say to myself.

I've finally picked up my camera after a few weeks of being too afraid to film anything. I'm taking it slow and only doing a day in my life video. Most of it is probably going to get cut since most of my days consist of me not sleeping, working out, and sitting in my bed editing photos for the posts I'm allowed to make.

"I'm wearing these brand new Chanel shoes. They're sleek black heels, and they're not the comfiest, but for the outfit, I'll suffer." I laugh to myself as I feel another presence enter my room. "Okay, let's go to Liv's event!" I say before I shut the camera and turn it off.

"All set?" Vince asks me, and I nod at him, excited to go support my sister at her biggest signing to date. While I look more dressed up, Vince has opted for his usual attire—an all-black outfit, fit with an extra button undone on his shirt, and his hair looks natural, as it curls on the end, that one hair still hanging in front of his face. If I was bold enough, I'd reach over and tuck it in for him, but he doesn't seem to mind it.

"I'm ready. Liv and Tristan just got to the store and said there's already people lined up to meet her!" I say, a huge smile crossing my face. My cheeks already hurt from all the smiling I've done today because my talented sister has a huge signing tonight.

"You're proud of her," Vince states, a small smirk crossing his face.

"I am. She's been through a lot. Liv deserves all the success in the world." I stand from my vanity and grab my camera before Vince grabs the purse I was going to bring out of my closet and hands it to me. "How did you know I was bringing this one?"

"You always lay your stuff out early, and this one was on the little table in your closet."

"Always on top of things, Evans, aren't you?"

"Of course. Now, let's get going before Emerson yells at us to hurry up. He's following us to the event." He opens the door to my room for me, and as we walk down the stairs together, I feel his hand hover against the small of my back. He's not touching me, more so guiding me down the stairs and making sure I don't fall since I'm wearing tall heels.

He's barely touching me, and if I put my hand in that tiny space between us, lightning would strike. I'm sure of it.

Does he feel it, too? I hate that I'll never know the answers to these questions because once Ralph is taken care of, Vince will leave, and I'll be alone again. Connie will probably continue to ship me off on fake dates for the rest of my life, and I'll never have a choice in anything ever again.

But who am I to complain? My life has so many other beautiful things in it, but sometimes the bad outweighs the good, and it becomes all I can focus on.

Not tonight, though. Tonight is all about my sister and her amazing accomplishments.

Teags and her mom are coming to show support. Harry and his girlfriend are coming, and I think Dom might even stop by. A few other book girls I know from Instagram have told me that they're coming, and are excited to see Liv and I, and it's so adorable the way my viewers have helped champion Liv's books.

I knew I loved my audience, but they continue to shock me with the amount of love and support that they show the books that I love.

Vince opens the door for me, and the sound of something falling has the both of us pausing in my doorway. When I look around the porch, I spot a small pink envelope, and Vince leans down to pick it up.

"What is that?" I ask him, a knot forming in my gut.

Vince says nothing as he carefully flicks the envelope open and turns it upside down, a cell phone falling out of it. It's a simple gray flip phone, and Vince is pressing a ton of buttons, trying to find an answer as to why it's here.

It's obviously from Ralph. Only he would leave something like this for us to find when we're about to leave the house.

"Emerson! Did you see this get dropped off?"

"What is it?" Emerson asks, coming closer to us.

I hear Vince mutter a curse under his breath. "How the fuck does he keep getting past us?"

"I'm sure you'll figure—"

The phone starts to ring, and Vince answers immediately. "Who the fuck is this?"

I don't hear the other side of the conversation, but I notice that the vein on Vince's forehead starts to strain, whatever the other person is saying clearly stressing him out.

"Absolutely not. You can talk to me, motherfucker. Leave her out of this." *Her.* Me. It's Ralph.

Vince curses a bit more before he hands the phone to me. I take it from him, my body shaking as I pick it up, but I don't speak. I know he can hear me breathing from the other side of the line.

"Is that you, little lamb? I remember the sounds of your breathing. I don't think I'll ever forget those noises you made."

My entire body shivers at the memories he's trying to jog, but I push them down. I push them where they can't hurt me.

I silently curse him for doing this now, on a night I was supposed to be celebrating my sister. "What do you want?" I hate that my voice comes out as a whisper, but when I lock eyes with Vince and notice that he's on the phone as well, he starts to circle his hand.

"It's a burner, Nico, but try anything you can."

Translation: Keep Ralph talking so Nico can try to get a location.

"I want you, sweetheart. Haven't you known that's all I've wanted for years now? But you made me wait. You made me do this."

"Do what? Shoot at me while I have lunch? Leave me all those pathetic notes and have other people do your dirty work for you?" I somehow find a little bit of fight, but I immediately regret my outburst. I know it's only going to make him mad.

"I wouldn't have to do that if that guard dog of yours would go away. Or maybe I should take him out, too."

"Don't you dare touch a hair on his head. I'm the one you want," I remind him, ignoring the rush of panic at the thought of anything happening to Vince.

"Tell me, is he coming with you to your sister's event tonight? Or is one of his other goons tagging along?"

My stomach bottoms out, my ears start to ring, and I can't breathe. I look at Vince, and he starts to rub my shoulder, still on the phone with Nico, silently telling me he's here for me.

"I'll see you there, Bree. Unless, of course, you don't make it in time. I'd sure hate for you to miss all the fun we'll have. It's going to be *explosive*." And then he hangs up.

"No! Fuck! No, this isn't happening." I all but drag Vince to the car. "We have to go."

"Bree, angel, what's going on?"

"He threatened Liv. He's going after her. He's going after my sister."

"How can you be—"

I cut Vince off with a yell. "Because he knows about the event tonight, and he mentioned us not making it in time! Get the fucking keys and let's go! I'm not letting him take anything else away from me!" Ralph has taken my safety, my sanity, and my life from me. I'll be damned if he tries to take my family too.

"He threatened the event?"

"Yes! Now, let's go!" I drag him some more, but he stays rooted to the ground.

"No."

I release my hold on his hand and turn to face him. "What do you mean no?"

"If he's threatening that bookstore with something, then the last place I want to take you is exactly where he wants you."

"He's threatening my sister, Vince! Don't you understand? I'm not going to stand by while he hurts the only family I have left."

"Bree, it's my job to protect you, and if I drive you there, I wouldn't be doing my job."

I scoff, annoyed he can't see this from my point of view. "I understand that, Vince, but it's either you drive me with backup, or I steal the keys and sneak off on my own. So, which will it be?" I hate that I've put him in this situation. I hate the look he has on his face as I yell at him, because he's only doing his job. He's only trying to protect me, but right now, I don't care about *me*. Liv and Tristan are in danger, and if they got hurt because of me, I'd never forgive myself.

Vince shuffles through his pockets before he grabs the keys, his gaze shifting to Emerson as he rounds the car to the driver's seat. "Follow us, and call Chris and Duncan for backup. Nico's already trying to work out a trace on his end, but Ralph is too good at masking where he's calling from, so it seems like a dead end."

"Got it, Boss."

Vince slides into the car, and I'm practically sweating through my outfit as I frantically switch between calling Liv and Tristan, neither of them picking up. "Fuck! Rule number one is to always be reachable, and the fact that they aren't answering could mean a thousand different things."

"Bree, it's going to be fine. He could just be doing this to scare you."

"Ralph doesn't just say things, Vince. You and I both know he always follows through." I can barely breathe as he weaves through traffic, but the faster I can get to them and know they're okay, the better I'll feel.

"Tell me exactly what he said."

And so, I do. I reiterate every word from memory, because despite having a terrible memory and always losing things that are practically attached to me, every word of his sticks to my brain like glue on paper.

"Fucking hell. He's escalating faster than before. He really said the word explosive?"

"Yes," I say as a few tears threaten to spill over. God, I just wanted one night of normalcy. I wanted one night to pretend I could be a normal person going to support someone I love on a night that is supposed to be filled with happiness.

Leave it to Ralph to ruin every single crumb of happiness I have.

"When we get to the bookstore, you're staying in the car."

"No—"

"Bree, I'll pull this car over right now. You're staying in the car." He enunciates every word, trying to get it through my stubborn head, but he should know I'm not going to listen. Not now. Not when Ralph is threatening Liv.

"Vince, I understand you're just doing your job, but—"

"It's not just my job, Bree."

Before I have time to unpack what that means, he pulls up to the curb and races out of the car, the other Tahoe pulling up behind us. Emerson climbs out, slamming the door, and a few seconds later, I see Chris and Duncan run into the store.

I feel like a sitting duck right now. I'm all alone in the car, and if Ralph has eyes on this place, he probably knows that.

What if this was his plan all along—to get me alone without protection?

What if he comes and grabs me, and everyone is too busy inside to save me?

All my thoughts are spiraling into one big panic attack, and before I continue down that spiral, I hop out of the car and run into the store, but not before kicking my heels off. I'd rather be barefoot than have to wear those five-inch weapons. I'd probably twist my ankle trying to run in those.

I step inside, and when I'm not greeted with absolute chaos, I can breathe a bit better. My sister spots me a few seconds before I do, and I run over to her, wrapping my arms around her.

She's okay. Liv is safe.

"Bree, you're shaking. Do you want some water?"

I can only nod as she pulls back from me, her eyes consumed with worry like they always are lately. "Did Vince brief you?"

Before I can answer, Vince pops over to where we are. "Yes, I did. Why the fuck aren't you in the car?"

"I was all by myself out there. I didn't feel safe, so I came inside. You can protect me here."

His hazel eyes pierce mine, and I see him nod ever so slightly. "Okay."

"Bree!" Tristan breaks the semi-circle we have and wraps his arms around me. "Are you okay?"

"I'm okay for now, I think. What's going on?"

Vince clears his throat before he speaks. "My guys are sweeping the place, and the cops have been notified and are on the way. They should be here any second."

I turn to Tristan again. "Did you tell Teags not to come? I forgot to text her on the way because I was too busy calling you two."

"You called us?" Tristan asks, pulling his phone out and swiping a few times. "I don't have any missed calls from you."

"Me neither." Liv shows me her phone, and my gut drops again. *What the hell is going on?*

"Over here!" I hear Duncan's voice shout from the back of the store. I go to move, but Vince stops me.

"Stay here."

"I want to see—"

"Bree, *please* stay here." He grabs my shoulders, the look on his face pleading me to stay where I am. "You might not care if something happens to you, but the rest of us do. Stop throwing yourself into the first sign of danger."

"That's not what I'm doing."

"Don't lie to me, angel. I know you're tired of all this, but please hold out a little longer. Trust that Nico and I will get him. *Please.*"

"I'll make sure she stays here," Tristan says, breaking up the intense moment.

Vince walks away from the three of us, but I hear him speak as he does. "Remember what I said in the bathroom, West."

"I could never forget it, buddy."

Liv shifts closer to me and whispers in my ear. "When did they become so friendly?"

I lean over to her. "Maybe punching each other in the face helped them get closer or something."

"Chris! Get over here!" I hear Vince yell a few moments later.

I turn to my sister, her arm now wrapped around my shoulder. "I'm sorry I ruined your event, Liv."

"Don't do that, Bree. You didn't do anything—*he* did. This isn't on you." She squeezes my shoulder, and I feel some more tears fall from my eyes.

"I wish I didn't exist. You guys wouldn't be dragged into this mess if I didn't."

"I, for one, am very glad you exist, Bree. I can't imagine not having you in my life."

The kind words are helping, but I still want to disappear. I want to run as far away as I can, change my name, and stop dragging the people I love into all this. I'd leave them all if it meant they were never in danger again.

"Anyone in here right now needs to calmly make their way to the nearest exit quickly and quietly!" I hear Duncan shout, and a few seconds later, Vince rounds the corner of the bookshelves and beelines for me.

"Outside. Now," is all he says as he grabs my hand and drags me out of the store. The three of us don't argue with him as we get into the car.

"Whose chair was off to the side behind the desk you were going to be sitting at?"

"That would've been Bree's spot."

Vince only sighs heavily as he looks at me. "There was a bomb on your seat, rigged to activate when you sat down, and when you stood up, it would've gone off."

"A bomb? Like an actual explosive device?" Tristan questions, unsure if he heard Vince correctly.

"Yeah. Nico is jamming the signal for us so the cell phone detonator won't go off while the bomb squad gets here. It looked like some sort of improvised explosive device..."

Vince's voice fades as my mind takes in all of this information he just threw at us.

There was a bomb under the seat I was supposed to sit in.

I could've died tonight.

I could've killed the only family I have left and a bunch of innocent people.

My stalker almost killed me. Again.

I hear the voices of the people I love most, but none of the words will permeate my brain.

And then I start laughing. I probably look and sound like a maniac, and as I turn around to face them, they're all staring at me.

"Are you okay, sis?" Liv asks me, and I keep laughing. There's nothing funny about this situation, but I can't help it.

"No. No, I'm not okay. I'm a YouTuber with millions of followers, and I have a stalker who keeps threatening to kill me! I post about books I love, makeup tutorials, and I have a *stalker*. A whole ass stalker who can't seem to get enough of me! A stalker who threatened to kill me before while he ran his hands all over my body and thought I was enjoying myself! God, I feel like I'm going insane."

"Bree..." my sister says, her face full of concern. I don't know if it's for me or the situation at hand. "Maybe we should all head to my house."

I'm about to agree before Vince cuts me off. "No. I'm getting her out of town for a few days."

Chapter Twenty-One

— SMOKE SIGNALS BY PHOEBE BRIDGERS

If I could erase anything from my memory, it would be the past three days.

Overwhelming doesn't even begin to cut it. First, hearing Ralph on the other side of the phone pissed me off. He's taunting me, and he knows that this stupid game he's playing with Bree is getting under my skin. Then, having to deal with a whole ass bomb threat at Liv's event took about fifteen years off my life.

I couldn't get Bree out of that building fast enough. When I saw what my guys had found, it felt like the walls were closing in on me.

All I had on my mind was her. If something happened to her that I could've prevented, I wouldn't be able to live with myself. Just the thought of Bree being hurt makes my skin crawl.

I've been running on empty lately, and this threat on Bree's life has kickstarted an entire new feeling. I've been burning hot with this intense need to protect her, but my safety has never mattered, just hers.

All the thoughts that fill my mind lately are of her, and when I try to sleep, I can't. Images of her needing me and being hurt when I'm not there haunt my dreams, and when I wake up, I'm paralyzed with fear.

Even though it's never real, the dreams feel so vivid, and they've shaken me more than I care to admit.

If I lose Bree, or if that psychopath ever gets his hands on her, nothing could stop me from protecting her—not even death.

We've been here for a few days, and Bree has barely left her room. Well, my sister's room, which shares a wall with mine, even though I've barely used the bed.

I've become way too comfortable sleeping outside her room, and even being here, that fact remains the same. In my mind, I know nobody can find us out here. We're completely disconnected from everything. Both of our phones are off, and the burners I keep here for emergencies are all I've been using to communicate with Nico, Liv, and my sister. Nico has been updating me, and he hasn't gotten anywhere with finding a location on Ralph, but he's not giving up. He's even tried some dark web shit, but that kind of stuff takes a lot longer.

Liv has called a few times, and I've given Bree the phone to talk to her, but she hasn't wanted to speak to anyone. I keep telling Liv to let her be with her emotions for a few days, but she's worried about her, so she continues to call and check in.

I'm just as worried about her, but the one thing that might make her feel better is on the way here. I don't know how much of a difference it will make, but not being able to do anything to help Bree has unraveled me more than the shit we've dealt with the past week.

I've been scared to leave her alone for so long, and I even offered to have her call Dr. Anna, but she's declined every time. I'm worried she's spending too much time wrapped up in that head of hers and is going to do something stupid—like cut herself off from everyone she loves to keep them out of danger.

Or something worse, but I try not to go down that road.

The only good thing is that she hasn't had a panic attack in the past few days, so I guess that's a win, right?

A knock at the door has me pulling my gun from the strap of my waistband, and when I see my sister walk in with Nellie's leash around her hand, I drop it.

"Christ, baby brother. What the hell are you doing?"

"Sorry. You didn't tell me you were close."

"I texted you a few times that I was five minutes away." My sister rolls her eyes and releases Nellie to me, and I practically get attacked by her excitement. God, I missed her. I've been away from her for too long, and I was almost afraid she wouldn't remember who I was.

I should've known my girl could never forget me. I did raise her, after all.

I got Nellie as a baby. My sister suggested getting a dog when I was going through a rough patch a few years ago, and I brushed her off every time she mentioned it. One day, she practically kidnapped me and drove me to a shelter. As soon as I laid my eyes on Nellie, sitting all by herself in a cage, I knew she was my dog.

And now, sixty pounds later, she's been with me ever since—unless I was out of the country or on an extended assignment.

"Are you hungry?" I ask my sister, wondering if she's going to stay for a bit and catch up.

"No, but I could use some coffee and a thousand explanations as to why you're up here."

This time, I'm the one to roll my eyes, but I nod my head over to the kitchen, and Aria follows me. My sister and I look way too much alike. She's got the same brown hair as me, only hers is to her shoulders and pin straight. I was the sibling to get the curly haired gene both of our parents had. She's tall, like me, around 5' 10", so only a few inches shorter than me.

I throw a pod into the machine and place a mug underneath it, waiting for it to start working. "It's three in the afternoon. You're going to be up all night."

"That's for me to worry about, Vince. I have a long flight back to Seattle, thanks to you."

"Oh, come on, you missed me." I wrap my sister in a hug, thankful that she brought Nellie back so I can try to cheer Bree up. "Thanks for bringing her. The flight wasn't bad, was it?"

"No, it wasn't. She didn't seem scared either. I think she knew where we were headed."

"That's my girl," I say as Nellie comes over to where I'm standing in the kitchen and plops onto the floor by my feet.

After I hand my sister her coffee, I know she's about to interrogate me as to what I'm doing, so I don't let her speak before I offer her an explanation. "Bree's safety was compromised back home. I wanted to get her away for a bit until things calmed down, and this was the first place I thought of. That's all there is to it."

"I thought you sold this place a few years ago? How is it still in such good condition?"

"I was going to sell it, but I couldn't." Every time I imagined getting rid of the house that held so many memories, I got itchy. In a way, this house feels like the only string I have left of my parents. Their faces faded a bit as I continued growing up, but here, in our secluded house tucked into the mountains, I can remember everything. The shape of their faces, the hum of their laughter, and a piece of my grief heals every time I walk into this place.

Because here, they still exist. They still linger in my mind in every corner of this house, and even on the trails we all used to hike on, and I couldn't get rid of it.

"I'm glad you didn't," my sister says in a low whisper.

"Me too. I come up here more than I care to admit."

"Why?" my sister questions as she takes a sip of her coffee.

"More reasons than one." The main one being that everything seems quieter up here. This is where I come when I have to clear my head of all the shit I've seen being on the job this long.

The only place I find peace most days is when I'm hiking. I've climbed most of the mountains in this area, and getting to the top and seeing how small the world looks helps to calm the storm that floods my brain sometimes. I love to push myself to the point of exhaustion so that by the time I get to the top, I feel like I succeeded at something.

All the pain, all the sweat, all the straining of my muscles is worth it when I see the world from the top of a mountain. Everything seems to feel useless when I sit and watch the trees move in the wind, the air feeling a bit cleaner as I sit and catch my breath.

It's the type of peace you can only experience in fleeting moments because by the time you get back to the bottom of the mountain, reality seems to hit you in the face again.

"I understand that. Just promise me you're taking care of yourself. One of these days, you'll have to put yourself first, you know. Maybe you'll eventually do something just for you, and not everyone else."

I shove my sister's shoulder as she laughs at me, knowing that will probably never happen. "Keep dreaming, Aria."

Small taps coming down the stairs makes my heart beat a bit faster, and as Bree turns the corner, I practically stop breathing as I take in the state of her.

She's wearing one of my fucking shirts again. The first night we were here, she didn't want to wear any of her pajamas because they felt too much like clothes, so I offered her one of my shirts, and she took it.

But this is *not* the one I gave her, which means she went through my stuff to find another one.

That makes my pulse pound even harder.

Her eyes are still red and puffy, indicating she's still been crying, and from the look on her face, she didn't realize anyone else but me was here.

She's also wearing a pair of fluffy socks her sister gave her—pink ribbons all over with a white base—and probably a pair of shorts like normal.

That's been her usual attire, at least what I can tell from the little peeks I've seen of her in her room.

"I'm sorry, I didn't realize we had company. Let me go change. Just give me—"

"Bree, it's okay. This is my sister, Aria. Aria, meet Bree Hart."

Aria's eyes widen with excitement, and I'm suddenly worried she's either going to embarrass me or say something she shouldn't.

Fuck, I regret this.

Before Bree can turn around and retreat, my sister reaches her and pulls her in for a hug.

"Uh, I thought this was against the rules?" Bree questions, and my sister just laughs.

"Oh, Vince, you've got her to memorize those dumbass rules of yours? Oh, baby, come have some coffee while I apologize for my insane brother."

That earns a small laugh from Bree, and I could collapse just from hearing that. I didn't realize how much I had missed hearing her laugh. Even her smiles have a sound, and I've been trying to pull them out of her since we got here.

But I don't want to press too hard. It's just been far too quiet around here for my liking.

I don't know when or how it happened, but the lines are starting to blur between us, and I don't hate it. I've had way too much time to think up here, and after doing my usual rounds of check-ins every morning, all I'm left to think about is the girl I'm protecting.

But it's become so much more than that. It's not only the fact that I've broken most of my rules for her, but I've come to like spending time with her. I like when she smiles at me. I like every single thing about Bree, and even though I wish I never met her under the circumstances, I wouldn't change any of it.

It was only when I was sure I'd rather die than see a single hair on her head harmed that I knew I was fucked.

But there's nothing I can do about it now. I'm going to wait until after the assignment is over and Bree is safe to make any kind of move, especially since I don't know how she feels. The last thing I want to do is misread a situation and do something I shouldn't. For now, I'm protecting Bree because it's my job. And after, if she'll let me, I'll stay and try to make her the happiest person on the planet.

Not because it's my job but because it would be my honor to make her smile every single day until she gets sick of me.

"Nellie, come here girl!" my sister says, breaking me out of my haze, and I feel Nell get up, wagging her tail as happily as can be, and the minute Bree lays her eyes on my dog, they light up.

Thank fuck.

There's that shine I missed so much.

"Whose dog is this?" Bree asks as she sits on the floor, fully prepared to get tackled by my dog as Nell licks her entire face.

"She's mine."

Bree stops petting Nell as her dumbfounded face looks at mine. "You have a dog? Why have you never mentioned her before?"

"Vince had been on an extended assignment overseas, and then he cut that short to guard you, so I've had her for a bit. I'll admit, I'm going to miss her, but I won't miss all the shedding that comes with it. I swear this girl loses more hair than I do."

"Did you get the brush? It works like a miracle, Aria. I told you."

Another eye roll from my wonderful sister. *Why did I invite her here again?* "Yeah, yeah, whatever."

"I cannot believe you kept this a secret from me. Did you have her when you first met me, too?" I don't say a word, and my silence confirms everything Bree needs to know. "I should arrest you right here for keeping this beautiful girl from me for this long."

"I would *love* to see that. You have my permission, Bree," Aria laughs, and that even coaxes a smile out of Bree.

"I feel like I'm being teamed up on."

The two of them look between each other, and a look of understanding passes through them both. "You are."

"Got it," I say, shifting back to the coffee maker and popping Bree's favorite into the machine—vanilla. This is the first time she's been out of her room since yesterday night, so even though it's late in the day, I make her a cup.

"Are you staying for a few days? I'd love to pick your brain about what this one was like as a kid," Bree asks my sister.

"No. I've got to get back. I have an antsy husband waiting for me back in Seattle. This was just a drop in visit to bring Nellie back. I have a car on the way."

"Oh. Well, I'm sure I'll see you again at some point," Bree says before my sister looks over at me.

"Can we talk for a second?"

"Yeah. Porch?"

My sister nods at me before saying goodbye to Bree. "It was nice to meet you. If my brother ever pisses you off, give me a call. I'll straighten him out for you in no time."

"Thanks, but your brother could never piss me off. He's too busy watching everything around me to make sure I'm safe, and he takes his job *very* seriously."

Aria laughs. "Don't I know it."

"Can you guys stop talking about me like I'm not standing right here?"

The two of them shake their heads at me. "Okay, let's go, sis." I turn to face Bree, who's still on the floor, Nellie nestled in between her legs, as if she has known Bree her entire life. "I'll make us some lunch. I'll be back, okay?"

"I'll be here."

I smile softly at her before I head outside to the porch, my sister crossing her arms at me with a weird look on her face. "What?"

"You're more stupid than I thought you were."

"Care to explain, or are you just going to keep throwing sentences out and not elaborating?"

Aria punches me in the shoulder. "You're emotionally involved. You like her."

"I care about her. It's different." I'm lying through my teeth. She knows it, I know it, and she's definitely about to call me out on it.

"You look at that girl like she's the only thing that exists, Vince. I've never seen you look at anyone else like that before. She walked down the stairs, and I swear I saw your heartbeat freeze for a second."

"And what if I do, Aria? I can't break my rules for her, and she's currently my *client*! It's literally my job to protect her, and I can't let my own ridiculous feelings get in the way of that, or it could cause her to get hurt." I'd never let my feelings get in the way of doing the best job I can, and I guess there really is a first time for everything. I don't know how to navigate all the emotions Bree makes me feel, and if I can't get my head on straight, then she could get hurt.

"You've broken all of your rules for her already, Vince! You dropped another case to rush back here and protect her. In all the years you've been doing this, I've never known you to just hand off a case to someone else. You always see them through, but when it comes to that girl currently in our family's house, your rules go out the window. If you can't see all of this when it's right in front of you, then you're dumber than I thought."

"Aria—"

"I'm not done." She rubs her hands together, clearly nervous. "Don't let your fear of getting close to people because of what happened to our parents ruin something good. Because I noticed her looking at you in the exact same way when she came into the kitchen. You'll be able to protect her even if you're emotionally involved, Vince. Those two things can exist at the same time, and you deserve someone who wants to look out for you as much as you do her."

"I'm not afraid of that happening," I lie. It scares me to death, the thought of losing someone else close to me. It happened in the blink of an eye with my parents, and what's to say it'll never happen again? She can't be entirely sure. Nobody can. That's what happens when someone suddenly dies. The rug gets ripped out from under you, and it could happen again if you keep standing on the same fucking rug. "It's easier to keep people at a distance."

Aria nods her head, seemingly agreeing with me. "I know. I did it for a while before Max broke that wall down. And when I finally let him in, shit...it was the best feeling in the world. I want you to experience that because you deserve it, Vince. I'm tired of seeing you protect everyone else and go home to an empty apartment. I'm tired of seeing you jump from job to job to fill some sort of void since you felt like you couldn't protect our parents."

God, I should know that nothing gets past Aria. She hit the fucking nail on the head, and I can't even be mad at her for it.

She's right. She has always been right, and she raised me to fight for the things I want, but somewhere along the way, I fell into a hole I didn't want to get out of.

I'm a coward. I spent so long running from client to client so I didn't have time to think about where *my* life was headed.

"I'm tired of running, but how the fuck do I do this? I don't do relationships, Aria. All I've had are one-night stands where I knew I wasn't seeing them ever again."

"I do *not* want to hear about my baby brother's escapades, so I'm going to disregard that comment."

This time, I roll my eyes at her. "I'm a grown ass man, Aria."

"And I practically raised you. There is no correct way to do this, Vince. Just go with that gut of yours you love so much and do what feels right." A car pulls up, and my sister grabs the bag she brought with her. "Don't overthink it, and you'll be fine."

"Thanks, sis." *For bringing Nellie back. For the advice. For raising me even though you were just a kid yourself.*

"You're welcome," she says, bringing me in for a hug. "You better come visit Seattle soon, or Max is going to think you went and got yourself killed."

"As soon as I'm done here, I'll come visit."

"Maybe the two of you can?" she questions, and I don't say a word as she gets into the car and is out of sight. I take in the scenery around me and breathe in the cool mountain air before I head back inside.

"So, what are you feeling for lunch? There's a bunch of stuff—" I stop speaking when I notice Bree isn't sitting in the spot where she used to be. She probably retreated back to her room based on the note she left me on the counter.

Appetite diminished again. It was nice meeting Aria. You two look a lot alike.

I sigh heavily before Nellie comes over to me and licks my hand where I lean against the counter.

"Don't worry, girl. We'll help Bree. We just have to give her a little time, that's all." I begin to make lunch, and when I'm finished, I place a plate in the fridge, wrapped in plastic, just in case.

— IF I GO, I'M GOIN BY GREGORY ALAN ISAKOV

As I REREAD THE same paragraph for the fifteenth time on my Kindle, Vince knocks on my door and steps into my room. "Can I come in?"

"Aren't you already in my room? That question seems redundant."

That makes his mouth lift up, but only in one corner. "Do you want to play cards with me? Normally, I play blackjack, but it's not that fun when I play it on my own."

"Sure. Downstairs?"

He nods at me before I get out of bed, throw my blanket over my shoulder, and head to the living room. I hear the fireplace crackling before I reach the bottom, and when I get fully into the room, a blast of heat hits my face, and I instantly relax. This house can only be described as cozy. It feels like I've been transported to another world here, and part of me feels selfish for never wanting to leave it.

I don't want to go back to reality where I feel like I'm being eaten alive. I don't want to go back to where I'm scared of what's around every corner. I want to hide away somewhere, like Rapunzel in her tower, where nothing bad can ever touch me or anyone I care about again.

I've barely left my room the past few days, except earlier when I heard murmured voices, and when I got down to the kitchen, Vince's sister was *not* who I was expecting. I thought Nico had come up to give Vince an update, but apparently, Vince has a dog I didn't know about.

Nellie is asleep right in front of the fireplace, and she might be one of the cutest dogs I've ever seen. I never imagined Vince being a dog dad, and somehow, that makes him even hotter.

He's protective of me. *Because it's his job.*

He dropped everything to come back for me. *Because it's his job.*

He has a dog. *Because he probably likes animals more than people.*

"Bree? Are you in there?" he says as he looks over at me from where he sits on the couch.

"Sorry," I say as I make my way over to the couch and sit next to him, leaving enough room between us so our cards will fit. "What are we playing?"

"I figured War is a good place to start. Do you know how to play?"

I nod at him. "Liv and I used to play cards all the time as kids. She wasn't very good, though. I seemed to have all the luck."

"Well, buckle up, Hart. You might meet your match tonight," he jokes, and I can't help but let out a soft laugh.

He deals out all the cards, and the two of us play for a bit, mostly evenly matched as we run out of cards and have to create our next pile.

"I'm worried about you."

Vince's candor surprises me, but he was never one to beat around the bush. "It's your job to worry about me, Vince."

"Yeah, it is." I hear him sigh heavily. "But lately, it hasn't been *just* my job."

He can't possibly be saying what I think he is, but the rush of knots in my stomach tells me otherwise. I try to focus on anything else but how weird I'm feeling—the fireplace, the low light in the room, the breeze blowing outside—but nothing is working. Because when I look at Vince and see the soft glow of the fire illuminating his face, the gut punch is even harder than the first time. "I heard what your sister said."

I don't know why that was what just came out of my mouth, but something about the scene in here is throwing my guard off. Vince and

I have been by ourselves for a few days in this secluded house in the mountains, and for the first time since I got here, I feel like I can finally breathe again.

But this conversation could change that, and even though I'm scared to enter this new territory, it was bound to happen sooner or later.

All those stolen touches and glances have shifted something between us, and hearing what his sister said to him on the porch earlier just solidified what I already knew.

I trust Vince. I like having him around, and after he's done protecting me, I don't want to lose him. I want him by my side.

But I want him to choose that, just like I'd choose him and his presence in my life after all is said and done.

"Does what she said scare you?" he asks, his voice a low whisper.

I don't hesitate to answer. "A little bit."

"It scares me, too."

"I think you're the only person I'll ever feel safe with ever again, and when I'm with you, I feel like I can breathe properly."

His eyes soften when I say that. "It's no coincidence that you do the same for me."

"Rule number nine at its finest," I say as I yawn, a wave of tiredness hitting me like a train.

"Let's get you to bed, Bree." Vince reaches his hand out, and I take it, my blanket still wrapped around me like a cocoon.

"But we only played one round of cards," I say, another yawn forming as I sway back and forth on my feet. "I can stay awake."

"Angel, you're about to pass out. Let me get you in bed. The stress of the last few weeks is hitting you, and you need to get more rest. Do you want me to carry you?" I shake my head before he pulls my hand and practically drags me up the stairs, my blanket flowing behind me like a cape.

"Wow, I guess you really are worried about me," I say as we stop in front of my door.

When I look over at Vince, his face is a lot closer than I thought it would be. Our noses are almost touching, and I can feel his warm breath on my face.

"I'll always worry about you, Bree. I don't think I'm wired to think differently." He squeezes my hand three times before he lets go and pushes my door open, pulling his face back from mine. I hate that I miss how close he just was. It's been a long time since I was able to feel close to someone—mentally and physically. But with Vince, I always seem to want more than he gives me. "Get some sleep for once. You deserve some good rest."

"Can I talk to my sister tomorrow?" Vince has offered me his burner phone to talk to Liv a few times since we've been here, but the guilt I was feeling about putting her in danger made me not want to face her.

And that makes me feel even shittier because I shouldn't be ignoring her, but tomorrow, that changes.

I'm so tired of hiding from the world, from my emotions, from the people I care about.

"Of course. I'm sure she'll be happy to hear from you. I think she's tired of hearing me tell her I have no new information."

"You and Nico are doing the best you can. I know that, and she knows that. Don't beat yourself up about it," I say, crossing the threshold into my room and heading toward my bed. "Can we have pancakes tomorrow morning?" I ask, and I see his smile come back in full force.

"Anything you want, Bree. I even have chocolate and strawberries in case you want a late night snack."

I smile so hard that my cheeks hurt. "Thank you."

"Sleep well. I'll be next door if you need me." And then he shuts my door, and I barely touch my head to the pillow before sleep consumes me.

Chapter Twenty-Two

— EPIPHANY BY TAYLOR SWIFT

TODAY WAS THE MOST normal day of my entire life.

And it was the best day ever.

I got a full night of sleep last night, with no nightmares waking me up, no panic attacks, and no dreams. None at all.

I think this house has magical healing properties or something.

Vince and I went on a walk with Nellie after we ate breakfast, and after that, I spent the entire day reading. Some people might call that a waste of time, but spending time in my favorite fictional universes will always be one of my favorite things to do.

Vince made all of our meals today, and I even helped him make the salad we had with dinner. It was the most mundane, boring, and peaceful day I've ever had. Vince took off after dinner to run to a nearby store, and I haven't seen him since he got back, but I know he's home because Nellie ran off when I was taking a shower. She likes to come in and lick the water, and it's entirely too cute. I love having her around. There's something so soothing about Nellie, and sometimes, I think she can tell I'm feeling a bit down.

Dogs are smarter than people think. I wish my parents let Liv and I have a pet when we were younger, but they thought pets were messy and annoying.

Maybe I'll get a dog if Vince leaves…

My therapist recommended getting a therapy dog once, and I brushed it off because if I could barely take care of myself, how was I supposed to take care of another living thing? I would've felt bad subjecting any animal to my panic attacks, depressive episodes, and general lifestyle.

Now, I'm in my room, a smile on my face as I queue up my favorite classical music playlist I use while I read. I can't read or do much of anything without sound, and since I don't have my noise machine here, this works just as well.

Vince and I haven't talked about what happened last night—us basically admitting our feelings for one another—and that's fine with me. In time, maybe we'll discuss it, or maybe we'll never bring it up again. The thought of that makes my chest ache, but I don't want to make things awkward if I ask him about it.

Two knocks on my already open door pull me from scrolling on my Kindle, trying to find another book to read, and when Vince walks into my room, my heart stops beating.

Vince is wearing no shirt, his hair wet with that same one strand dangling down, his abs on full display.

My mouth is suddenly dry, and I find myself wanting to read another bodyguard romance, but I know I shouldn't. I'm practically living in one, and it would only get my hopes up, which is what I'm trying to avoid.

"Hi," is all he says, waving some sort of box in the air before he sits down on my bed and places it in front of me.

"What's this?"

"It's nothing," he says as I open the box. When I see what's inside, emotions fill my chest.

It's a night light shaped like a book. It's open, and all the pages are spread out as if someone was fanning through it. Vince bought me a night light because he knew I didn't have one here. I've been using the bathroom light, and it's worked just fine. I can't help the tightness in my voice when I speak again. "Vince, this is beautiful."

"I figured you needed one since I don't know how much longer we're going to be here. It's not a big deal."

"Yes, it is. Nobody has ever been thoughtful enough to get me something before."

"Oh, come on, you get packages every single day, Bree." He's trying not to make this seem like a big deal, but it is to me.

"Those are for me to promote. This is different." I grab his hand. "Thank you, Vince. I mean it. This is the nicest present anyone has ever gotten me."

"I saw it at the store when I went to get dog food for Nellie. It was right by the register, and I immediately thought of you when I looked at it."

God, that sentence could send me into a coma. "I didn't think anyone thought of me like that."

"Well, now you know I do. I don't only know you because I have to. I know you because it's a privilege to be around you."

I have to hold some tears back because that might be one of the nicest things anyone has ever said to me. Lately, I've been feeling a bit detached, but the fact that Vince still thinks I'm a warm human being means everything.

Nobody really notices how hard I'm trying every single day—even when nobody's looking. I'm constantly battling within myself to try and make sense of all the things I've experienced over the past few months, and it's really fucking hard. But Vince sees it. He sees me. "Thank you. Can you plug it in for me?"

He only nods as he brings it to one of the plugs in my room, and when he turns it on and shuts my light off, it illuminates the room perfectly.

"It looks good, huh?" he asks me, and I can tell he has a smile on his face just because of how he said that.

"It's perfect," I whisper, snuggling into my covers and getting more comfortable.

"I'll see you tomorrow, Bree. Sleep tight."

"You too. Give Nellie a kiss for me."

"I will, angel. Goodnight," he says as he slowly closes my door.

I answer him after it's closed. "Goodnight."

"Liv, what are you doing here?" I ask her as she opens the door to my closet, crouching in front of me.

"You called me, remember? And I got here before he did."

No, that's not right. I never saw Liv that night. "No, you didn't. I saw you outside in the ambulance when I could barely speak." What the hell is going on?

"Tristan and I are here. Let's go. Now, Bree. He's coming."

I follow my sister out of our childhood home, only to stop at the top of the stairs at a sight that breaks my heart. Ralph has Tristan and Vince on their knees, mouths taped and bodies shaking as he moves the gun between the two of them.

When he hears us, he launches into a chase, and Liv runs, but I'm frozen where I stand.

Ralph grabs me by the arm, his grip tight as he drags me down the stairs, whistling as he pulls me. I'm barely able to move, because this isn't right. Nothing about this is right.

"Little lamb, there you are. These two wouldn't tell me where you were, but I guess I found you after all, just like I always do."

I hear Tristan and Vince screaming through the tape on their mouths.

"We're going to play a game, Bree. Choose one, and the other dies. If you don't choose, they both die. Understood?" he asks me, and I shake my head.

No. No, I don't understand what's happening. This isn't how it goes. None of them are here for this; it's always just me and Ralph.

"Let them go. Please. I won't do it. I won't choose between them."

I can't choose Tristan because he'll experience a loss in a few years that will crush him and his family, and if he's not around, I don't know what will happen to the rest of them. I won't let the West family lose him too. I won't let my sister feel the ache I do every single day.

That's all it ever takes. A few seconds, and your life can change—for better or worse.

And I can't choose Vince because all he has ever done is protect me. Even though I didn't know him when Ralph first attacked me, all he has done since is make me feel safe.

Ralph is asking me to choose between the two most important men in my life. He wants me to kill one or both of them.

"Don't do this, please," I say as tears fall from my eyes.

Ralph points the gun between them and pulls the trigger twice. I hear a body fall and see Tristan on the floor, a pool of blood spreading from his chest.

No, no, no, no, no.

My sister is screaming from the top of the stairs, a guttural yell that makes my legs give out.

And then he fires two more times, and I see Vince keel over.

This time, I'm the one yelling, and Ralph fades into the background as I watch the two of them take their last breaths.

I wake with a yell. My body is drenched, and tears are streaming down my face. I can't bear to just sit in bed, and before my brain stops me, I throw my covers to the side and rush out of my room, only to trip over something and fall to the floor. Just like that night, I scramble to grab onto the carpet, but again, it doesn't work.

My scrambling comes to a halt when a pair of strong arms wraps around me, brings my back to his chest, and holds me. The familiar body registers in my head immediately.

Vince. He's alive. He's okay. He's still here. He's not dead.

A strangled sob rips from my chest as the realization hits me in the chest. "Oh, God," I chant over and over again.

"Angel, what's wrong? Am I squeezing too hard? Do you need me to get cold water? W-what do you need me to do? Tell me and I'll do it."

"Keep holding me so I know you're real," I heave, the sobs still overtaking my body. "*Please.*"

And he does. The two of us sit in the hallway for an hour, or five minutes for all I know, and he holds me until my breathing slows and my heartbeat returns to normal.

I finally was getting real sleep, and I could only get through one night before the nightmares came back. Will it ever end? Will my mind ever stop conjuring up the worst moments of my life to replay like I'm the only person at a movie? Even after he's caught, when does it end? Does it ever end for me or can I only continue to fight my way through the toughest memories of my life? My breathing starts to pick up again, and I feel like I'm an earthquake and this is the aftershock.

If this is what forever looks like for me, I'm not sure if I want it.

I just wanted one glimpse of normalcy, and I thought I had that, but the reality of my mental state slapped me back to normal.

"Come back to me, Bree. Come out of that beautiful head of yours and focus on me."

"I don't know how to anymore," I admit, feeling more defeated than I did when we first came here.

"Then I'll do it for you," he says while I feel his fingers against my skin, lightly grazing my arm. His stubble scratches against my shoulder and I can feel his breath on my neck as he slows his breathing down, silently telling me to try and match it, and I try my best.

"I thought you were dead," I whisper, more tears falling out of my eyes and onto the carpet in front of me. Vince and I haven't changed positions yet, and talking about this without facing him is somehow easier. If I can feel him, I know he's real, but if I look at him, he could disappear in an instant. "I thought Ralph killed you. H-he shot you, Vince. He shot Tristan too, and fuck, it felt so real."

I continue to cry as he speaks. "You thought I was gone, but I'm right here, angel. I'm right fucking here, and I'm not going anywhere. I'm not going anywhere," he repeats over and over again so it gets through my head. "Do you want me to call Liv and Tristan?"

I shake my head. "N-no. I don't want to bother them. It's late," I say as my breathing evens out, the words he's repeating getting through my head. "I'll never have peace again, Vince. This is what my mind does. It brings new scenarios into my head, and they haunt me for days until a new one takes over."

He lets go of me before he leans down, picks me up, and carries me in his arms back into my room. He places me on my bed gently before he crawls into my sheets and wraps his arms around me, his tattoos disappearing into the t-shirt he's wearing. "Your mind can do that, but I'll always be here to make you remember it's not real, that you're safe, Bree. So, get some rest, and if the nightmare comes back, I'll be here to wake you up from it."

"Always?" I question his use of the word.

He nods at me. "Always."

I start to drift off again, my emotions weighing me down and making my eyes heavy before they snap open again. "Vince?"

"Yeah?"

"Why were you in front of my door?" I ask, noting that I tripped over him trying to leave my room. I didn't run into him in the hallway. I tripped *over* him. The only rational explanation is that he was sitting in front of my door, but I don't know why.

I hear him sigh heavily and tense up a bit when I ask the question, and when I think he's going to pretend he didn't hear me, he answers, "I can't sleep unless I'm in front of it."

Oh. "Why?"

"One of the first nights I was back, I woke you from a nightmare. You didn't realize you were screaming for someone to stop, to get off of you, and I rushed in to find nobody there. I was relieved because I thought someone had gotten past me, and I made sure that could never happen again by sleeping in front of your door. It helped to ease my mind when all I did was toss and turn in my own bed. It was easier to wake you up from a nightmare. It wasn't every night, only a few times a week."

"You came back in March," I yawn. "It's June. There's no way you've been doing this for months, Vince."

"I have been."

"But why do you still do it here? We're all alone. It's safe."

"Force of habit, I guess." He rubs his hand against my arm like we've done this a million times before—cuddle in bed together after I have a nightmare.

"Oh," is all I can manage before my eyes get too heavy to stay open.

Fear.

That's all I felt as Bree scrambled over me, hiccupping through her words, tears streaming from her face. Pure fear like I've never felt before.

I've never been so out of control like I was tonight. And when I held her in my arms and calmed her down from a panic attack again, it felt like this was where I was always meant to be.

She was always meant to be in my arms, to be held by me.

Bree Hart is unraveling me day by day, minute by minute, second by second.

I'd give anything for her to have some relief from the confines of her own mind. But if she feels safe in my arms like I know she does, maybe one day, the panic will lessen, and the nightmares will be fewer and farther in between.

She told me before that she's broken, that she needs to be fixed.

What she doesn't know is that I'll try anything I can to show her that, even though she feels like she'll never have peace, that nobody can love her, that someone can and will.

Me. I'll be that for her. I'll be her anchor when the weight of the storms in her mind become too much for her to handle.

I look down at her sleeping in my arms, her hand fisted around my shirt as if she's afraid I'll turn to dust in the night, and press a kiss to her forehead.

Her eyes are already puffy, and I wipe some of the wet tears from her face with her blanket before I take another long look at her.

She's goddamn angelic.

My beautiful, tortured angel.

"I'll keep you safe, Bree. I promise we'll get past this, and I'll spend every single day showing you that being with you is as easy as breathing."

Chapter Twenty-Three

— SAME SEA BY LIGHTS

My eyes are barely able to peel open as a bright light hits my face. Only when I don't feel Vince next to me do I realize he's the one opening the curtains and trying to kill my eyes.

The same eyes that feel swollen, puffy, and dry from all the crying I've been doing lately. I desperately need eye drops if this is how the morning is going to go.

"Morning, Bree. You better get a move on, or we're going to be late," Vince says as he opens my *other* curtains, and I move my hand to my face, trying to shield them from the burning sensation that comes with staring into the sun.

"Are you trying to blind me?"

"No, I'm trying to get you out of bed. Come on, let's go. I've got your clothes all laid out right here." He motions to the end of my bed, where he's picked out one of my workout sets—the light pink one. My favorite one.

"Are we going for a walk like yesterday morning?"

"Something like that, but you'll love it. I promise. And you might want to get up before I let Nell in, or you'll never leave that bed ever again."

"I don't think I'd mind getting attacked with kisses to the face. I find them quite nice," I say as Vince goes to open the door. Sweet Nellie is sitting in front of it—apparently just like Vince does—guarding the path for any intruders. Her tail starts to wag as Vince asks her about breakfast, and she takes off down the stairs toward her bowl.

"I'll leave you to get dressed. Meet me downstairs?"

I nod my head and throw my covers off as he softly shuts the door.

I take a moment to steady myself. These past few days—well, months—have been emotional whiplash. Not to mention that Vince and I admitted what we did the other night, and then we slept together.

Well, we slept in the same bed together. All night. And he woke up in my room the next morning. *This* morning. And now, we're going to do something just the two of us, because we're the only two people up here in this house.

I think I just walked into some sort of forced proximity romance novel, and I find myself not wanting to get out of it.

Just be normal, Bree.

But I can't. I'm afraid Vince said all that and isn't going to act on it because he's my bodyguard. I'm literally employing him, and rule number three is no personal attachments, but he also said he had broken all his rules for me. Or did his sister say that? Either way, whatever is happening between us feels like it's up to me to figure out.

Which is easier said than done.

Wanting to banish all of those thoughts and have a calm day, I shove them to the back of my mind before I throw my outfit on, brush my hair and teeth, and shove the boots Vince set out for me on my feet.

Where did these come from? I like to think I'm an organized person, and I would remember buying these. I think I have everything I need for this surprise adventure, and when I walk down the stairs, the sight before me stops me in my tracks.

Vince is sitting at the table doing a crossword puzzle while Nellie eats breakfast like a maniac.

"Does any of the food actually make it into her mouth?"

Vince laughs, obviously very familiar with this behavior. "Sometimes. Usually in about two minutes."

I stifle a laugh of my own as Nellie vacuums up her food—partially inside the bowl, mostly outside of it.

"So, did you make me rush to get up just so I could watch you do your crossword puzzle? I thought you had something exciting planned," I tease as I swipe the pencil from him.

His gaze meets mine, a challenge in his stare before he steals the pencil back and lifts off his chair. "Ready?"

"Ready," I answer, unsure of where this day is going but excited to see where we end up together. The only thing I'm certain of is that I trust him more than anyone else.

⁂

So, IT TURNS OUT, Vince took me and Nellie on a trip to climb a mountain this morning. As we hike up the trail, Nellie leading the charge, I try to clear my head of all the things I've been thinking about, but it doesn't really work.

I hate that I feel trapped all the time, and this trip out here has helped me see that I need some new degree of separation between my personal and work life. I can't keep living like I am. I can't keep pretending like everything in my life is fine and dandy to the media when, in reality, I'm falling apart at the seams.

I've always seen myself as a genuine person, especially online, and I hate how I'm basically lying to the people who watch my videos. They've all been prerecorded since I haven't been wanting to film lately, and I hate feeling like I'm lying to the people who got me where I am.

But according to Connie, I have to do this. I have to pretend that everything is fine, that I'm in love with Alex, because it's what's best for my career.

My *career*, not me. But I get where she's coming from. Her job is to look out for me in the media and help lessen my load, but sometimes, I wish I had someone who cared about *me*, not just Bree Hart, the social media influencer.

"Care to join me, or are you going to spend all day in that pretty head of yours?" Vince asks as he jostles his shoulder into me.

"Sorry," I say as I take in the surrounding trees and rocks. "How tall is this thing again?"

"Eleven hundred meters," Vince tells me as I stare at him. "Around thirty-six hundred feet tall."

"Oh. That's tall," is all I can say.

"This? This is nothing compared to some I've climbed before."

"How did you get into all this—climbing mountains for fun?" I wonder when it happened, because I never heard him mention it all those years ago. Then again, we didn't talk that much back then—besides toward the end, when we started to become more friendly. But it was more of a professional relationship. Somewhere during these past few months, that shifted, and the two of us are in this weird limbo between something we could be and what we used to be.

He told me the other night that he would always be here for me when the nightmares came, and I don't know how he meant that. I'm too afraid to ask.

Because everyone leaves me eventually, and it wouldn't surprise me if he left at the end of all this, too. I'd never ask him to stay, because I know how difficult it is to be around me, and I figure it would be even worse if he dated me.

It's bad enough that I have to see all the social media posts about how hot he is, and most of my comments talk about him, too. It's...weird. Some people *really* don't care about their digital footprint anymore.

"I'm not really sure exactly when it started, but it's one of my favorite things to do. The house we're staying in was owned by my parents, and they used to take Aria and I up here all the time when we were kids. Anytime I'm in between cases or have some time off, I try to climb another one."

"Seems like a very active hobby. I think my legs would fall off if I tried to do this more than once," I say as I wipe my hair out of my face. I regret not throwing it up before we left, but I wasn't sure what we were doing. My long blonde locks are falling in every direction in front of my face, and I regret not throwing a scrunchie on my wrist.

Vince laughs when I say that. "Says the girl who runs on the treadmill until she can't breathe. I swear, you run more than any other person I've ever met."

I knock his arm with my hand. The two of us have slowly crept closer to one another, and I don't think either of us has noticed. "Well, I can't exactly argue with that."

"Exactly."

"Have you climbed this one before?" I ask, wondering if the reason he doesn't have a map is because he knows the way.

"This will be my fourth time, actually."

My eyes practically bulge out of my head. "You're insane, Vince, but I get why you like it so much."

"Yeah?"

"Yeah. There's something so special about being in nature and hearing all these sounds that remind you you're alive in the first place. The birds are chirping, the wind is blowing across my face, and hearing the dirt under my boots kind of puts everything into perspective."

"Wait until we get to the top."

"Is the view worth it?"

"Absolutely. That's my favorite part of all this. When you get to the top and you see the world from the peak, it all seems so...pointless. Going through all that effort to climb and then getting to the top and seeing everything from a different perspective helps me to remember what's important in my own life."

I can only nod my head in understanding. "I can't wait to see it."

"Only about two thousand more feet to go, but there's a small opening up ahead where we can rest. I have snacks and water for us and Nell."

"Sounds good to me."

We walk in silence until the opening comes into view a few minutes later, and I pause on the rock to take it all in. I see another mountain in the distance that looks a little smaller than the one we're climbing, and Vince was right—everything does look so much smaller from up here, and we aren't even at the top yet.

Vince hands me a granola bar and a water bottle, our hands brushing, and I feel goosebumps start to spread across my skin.

Did he feel it, too?

He looks down at where his hand is outstretched, then up at me, before he shakes out of the haze and grabs some water for Nellie.

God, all these minor touches between us are going to drive me insane. It's definitely not one-sided, based on the way he keeps looking at me.

About halfway through my granola bar, I see Vince's hand in front of me, and when I look up, he's holding a hair tie out.

"For your hair. I can tell it's been bothering you."

I stare in disbelief at his hand before I take it from him. "Where did you get this?"

"I keep one on my wrist, just in case."

If I was standing, I might've collapsed. This rock is barely holding up my weight after hearing him say that. I don't want to jump to the conclusion that he keeps it on his wrist for me, but it sure looks that way. *How have I not noticed that before?*

"Thank you," is all I manage to say before I stand. "Ready to keep going?"

"Let's hit it," he says as he collects Nellie's travel bowl and puts it into his bag. "Come on, Nell. Let's go, girl."

And I know for certain that I'm fucked as he continues on the path up the mountain because I can't stop staring at his ass and thinking about how nice it is to be in his company all the time. Especially like this—us together on a hike. It's something he loves doing, and the fact that he's sharing it with me makes me think he doesn't mind my company too much, either.

THREE HOURS AND SOME conversation later, we've finally reached the peak. The two of us are the only ones up here, and it feels otherworldly when we break through the trees that block the top of the path. All I can see is blue sky and white clouds as we hike. My legs feel like jelly, and I can barely feel them as I lay down on the first flat patch of rock I can find.

"Oh my God, my legs don't exist anymore. I can barely feel them."

"Come on, angel. You don't wanna miss the view. It's better from the other side." He reaches down and grabs my hand, pulling me up. The feel of his hand in mine as we walk to the other side of the peak has me thinking way too many things.

But the entire time we were climbing, I didn't try to escape my mind. Vince and I kept up a pretty good conversation, and even in the quiet moments when we weren't speaking, my head remained silent.

For the first time in months, I didn't feel like escaping the moment. I wanted to be there listening to the sound of Vince breathing as we walked, hearing my own as I trudged up the mountain, feeling more alive than I have in years.

Vince was right. Hiking really does have some sort of healing powers, because I've never been so out of my head than I was when we were climbing.

"Close your eyes," Vince says as he stops abruptly. Nellie continues in front of us and sniffs the rocks a bit before she lays down, soaking up the sun.

"Are you going to throw me off the top? Was this all a ploy to murder me? I have to admit, this is pretty smart of you. We're all alone up here and—" I stop when I see him glaring at me, his eyes narrowed on my face.

"You of all people are the lowest on my murder list, Bree. You should know that."

"Aww," I say, a smile gracing my face. "Okay, since I trust you, I'll close my eyes."

"Thank you," is all he says before he tightens his grip on my hand and starts us forward. A few seconds later, after he turns my body slightly left, I feel his hand on the small of my back. "Okay, you can open them now."

The view in front of me is the most magnificent thing I've ever seen. It feels like I can reach up and touch the clouds, and the air feels cleaner up here for some reason. The sky's the most beautiful shade of pale blue, and miles and miles of trees cover the ground below. We're practically surrounded by mountains in every direction, and as I take it all in, everything seems so small.

God, it's heavenly. I turn to Vince behind me. "Thank you for bringing me up here."

"It's nice to get a new perspective sometimes, and I think after all you've been through, you needed a moment to clear your head."

And I don't know what possesses me in this moment, but before I can stop myself, I stand on my tiptoes and press my lips to his.

It's a slow and tender kiss before Vince takes control and starts to kiss me back. God, I knew he would be good at this. He wraps his arm around my back and anchors me to this moment, and I feel heat spreading through my entire body, from my toes to my head.

He feels it, too. He wants this as much as I do, and—

And then he pulls back, the two of us panting more from the kiss than we did the entire time we were walking.

"We shouldn't be doing this, Bree."

"Why not, Vince? I can see how you look at me because it's the same way I look at you. Didn't you feel what I did during that kiss?"

"We can't, Bree. I'm your bodyguard, for fuck's sake, and whatever's been going on between us can't happen!" He runs a hand down his face, torment visible in his features. "No matter how much I want to kiss you again."

Well, at least there's that. "I'm not some sort of forbidden fruit, Vince. I'm a grown ass adult fully capable of making her own choices."

He runs a hand through his hair as his chest continues to heave. "You're my client, for starters, and you're just a—"

I cut him off. "Don't do that."

"What?"

I slowly start to move toward him as I speak again. "Don't call me too young, too naive. Don't tell me I'm just a kid latching onto you because of our proximity, because it's so much more than that, Vince. I feel like I'm myself when I'm with you, and you treat me like I'm a human, not just some sort of thing everyone else seems to know."

"Bree, I wasn't going to do that. You're just going through way too much shit lately, and I don't want to add to it. My job is to protect you, and I don't want whatever feelings I'm having to muddle that. Because if something happens to you and I could have avoided it, I wouldn't be able to live with myself."

I take a deep breath. "I understand that, but I'm strong, Vince. I've lived through more things in the past few years than most people will experience in their lifetime. I chose to kiss you, and I'm choosing to tell you that I like spending time with you because you make me feel *alive*, and I like who I am when I'm with you."

He takes a small step toward me, and my breath hitches as he reaches up to my hair and pulls my ponytail out. My hair spreads down my sweaty back as the two of us continue to stare at one another.

"You're one of the strongest people I've ever met, Bree, and throughout the past few months, you've been unraveling me," he says as he takes part of my hair in his hand and starts to wrap it around his fist. "Do you understand how difficult that is? I've trained to always be alert and focused, but when I'm around you, my control slips."

He tugs on my hair, not too hard to hurt but enough to lift my head back so I'm face to face with him again. "Oh yeah? Is that so?"

"Mhm. And you were wrong earlier. You *are* a forbidden fruit. You've been dangling in front of me this entire time, and I can't have you."

"Why can't you have me, Vince? Who says you can't?"

"My rules, baby." He lifts his other hand to graze against my lips, and my body shudders. The tension between us could snap at any moment, and it's only been a few minutes since I kissed him, but I already want more.

I try to make my voice strong, but it comes out in a whisper instead. "Fuck your rules, Vince. You've already broken most of them for me anyway, right?"

"I have, angel."

"And you named your company after me."

"It seems I did, huh?" He smirks at me, that one hair falling in front of his face as he inches toward mine.

"Why?"

"I don't have an answer for you. It seems you've been under my skin long before I came back to you." He lightly brushes my lips with his, and I need more, but he doesn't give it.

"Vince..."

He moves to my neck, and I feel him lightly bite my pulse point before he moves back to my cheeks, forehead, nose. "Fuck it," he whispers as he gives me what I want, smashing his lips to mine.

Compared to the last kiss, this one isn't gentle. It's possessing every cell in my body as he slips his tongue into my mouth, and I let him have control.

I've never felt like this before—wholly and truly possessed by another person. This kiss is better than any of the sex I've had. Part of that might be because I chose to kiss him the first time, and this time, he chose to initiate it.

We've both chosen each other, and that's all I could ever want.

His teeth nip at my bottom lip as he pulls away and rests his forehead against mine. "Fuck, Bree."

"What?"

"Now that I know what you taste like, I'm ruined."

"Oh yeah?" He nods against my head, and I can't help a laugh from slipping out. "Well, there goes rule number two."

"What do you say I throw out all the rules and keep kissing you whenever I feel like it?"

"I'd say you should've done that a while ago, but I'll take it."

"Be careful what you wish for, angel. A man obsessed may look appealing in those books you read, but it's my mission to blow those fuckers out of the water. Do you think you can handle it?" he says as he cradles the back of my neck and brings my mouth close to his again.

"I can handle anything you throw at me, Vince. Bring it on."

And then his lips lock with mine again, and we spend the rest of our time on top of the mountain losing one another in stolen kisses and touches.

Chapter Twenty-Four

— MY TEARS RICOCHET BY TAYLOR SWIFT

Forty-five minutes into our drive back, I finally get service again. Vince gave me my phone before we left, and it was fully charged and ready to go. For the first time ever, there were no notifications on it, and it made me feel like I could breathe.

Vince is convinced that after this big stunt Ralph pulled, he'll go underground for a few weeks. Nico traced a few leads but came up empty, so that's the assumption we're operating under, but Vince has still added extra security for my house and my sister.

Speaking of Liv, I should give her a call. I was able to chat with her a bit, but for the most part, I was completely disconnected. Vince might be onto something with the mountain air because up here, I feel nothing but peace. It feels like my batteries have been swapped out for fresh ones, and I finally feel like myself again—as much as I can in my current situation.

Neither of us has discussed the kiss from the other day, and neither of us has brought up the *other* kisses that have occurred since then.

Or the fact that Vince slept in the same bed as me for the past four nights.

Or that every morning, I woke up clutching his shirt, only to look up and see him smiling at me—like we did this every morning.

Or the fact that we're blurring the lines of our relationship and neither of us wants to talk about it. Truth be told, it feels liberating. I like having this one piece of my life to myself for now, and even though I don't know what we are, it's nice knowing Vince chose to steal all those kisses from me.

He *chose* me. The thought is hard to wrap my mind around, and for now, I'll take all these stolen moments with him until our relationship goes back to what it used to be.

Just a bodyguard and his client.

A bodyguard whose hand is on my thigh as we drive home...

But a bodyguard, nonetheless.

I'm about to open my mouth to say something, but my phone chiming a million different times makes me pause. I feel Vince's hand tense, and as I pick my phone up in one hand, I place the other one on top of where his rests on my thigh.

"Is everything alright?" he asks me.

"Uh, I don't know. My phone is *blowing* up, but there's a few things from Liv." I haven't talked to her since before Vince and I kissed. There's around twenty voicemails timestamped from this morning. The pit forming in my stomach has me terrified, so I pick up the phone and call her. She picks up almost immediately.

"Thank God. Are you guys headed back?"

"Yeah, we just got back. What's going on, Liv? Did something happen this morning? Did they catch him?" I'd lie if I wasn't the slightest bit excited that this could be the case, but hearing Liv sigh heavily across the phone tells me that isn't why she left me all those messages.

"It's our parents."

Fuck. "What about them?" Neither of us has had any contact with them in a year. What the hell could they be doing now? I thought they forgot Liv and I existed.

"Bree...I don't know how to tell you this." I hear her sniffle across the line, and the pit in my stomach grows heavier, my heart beats faster, and I start to get warmer.

"Tell me what, Liv? You're scaring me. Are they okay? Did something happen to them?"

"No, but something might if I ever fucking see them again," I hear Tristan say, realizing I'm on speakerphone.

I switch my phone to connect to Vince's car so he can hear, too, wanting to cue him in on this if it involves something big. "Vince is on too. Liv, what's going on?"

"They leaked your story in an exclusive interview. It aired this morning, and now the whole world knows what happened," Liv says, her voice breaking, and if I could hear through the ringing in my ears, I'd probably say she sounded angry, too.

"No..." is all I can manage.

My own parents leaked the details of what happened to me on the worst night of my life. The *one* thing I had for myself, the one thing I didn't think I would ever share with anyone online, was leaked because of my parents.

I feel the car come to a stop on the side of the road, and I exit, needing to get out of the car, my mind, and my body. I need out. Vince stays in the car; I know he hates my parents, but Liv is probably telling him the entire story of why we don't talk to them anymore. He already knows that they kept the house I was attacked in, but he doesn't know the rest.

All I can do is scream toward the sky and hope somewhere that my parents hear the echo of it and realize how much they've hurt me. Will they ever feel bad? Will they ever care about us more than themselves, money, and their jobs? Will they ever reflect on their lives years from now and regret the things they've done?

I can't see them ever doing that, because in order to feel bad about something, you have to have emotions in the first place.

They're cold, soulless versions of what I wished my parents were, and I'll forever be that little girl who chased them around the house. Only now, I'm chasing the versions of them I wish existed, and my legs will disappear before I ever reach them.

Vince doesn't know about our childhood and how they ignored Liv and smothered me. He knows about how they concocted some plan to break her and Tristan up because they hated him. Liv is probably telling him the rest of it, and I'm grateful for that because I can barely get two words out.

Liv is the only one who ever understands because she grew up in the same household. I can confidently say that they are no longer our parents anymore.

Not after this. Not after all they've done. This was the final cord for me, because this is unforgivable.

I'm done. So fucking done.

I hear the car door slam before Vince all but crushes me in a hug. His strong arms wrap around me, and I can feel my thoughts start to make sense. That's what he does for me—he calms every bone in my body. He might be engulfing me in his strong grip, but I've never felt safer. I can *breathe*.

And when he pulls back, I know I have some things to fill him in on.

"Take your time, angel. I don't need it all right now. We can do this in pieces."

"They're my parents, you know? You grow up with them, and they're your biggest role models, your biggest fans. And I thought it was good for a while, but when I was old enough to understand things, I realized they didn't give a shit about either of us. They started to work more and talk to us less. The thing I remember most growing up is Liv feeding me every single night. She was always there, and she used to help me with my homework. When I got my period for the first time, she explained it all to me."

Tears start to come, but I keep going. "Liv has always been more of a parent than they ever were. Despite her feeling so alone and alienated by our parents, she was the person I leaned on the most, and some days, I regret doing that, but I was just a kid. Hell, she was just a kid too. And as the years passed, and I started to gain a following online, they started to pay attention to me. *Only* me."

"I feel the same way about my sister. She was nineteen when our parents died, and in an instant, she turned into my legal guardian. It was...insane. One minute, we both had parents, and the next, one of us was becoming one. I think that's why she doesn't want kids as an adult. She had to deal with me growing up as an asshole teenager who just wanted his parents back."

"I'm sure you were a wonderful kid, Vince. Let her know that, despite it all, she raised a wonderful man. She should be proud. *You* should be proud of who you are, because I know your parents are proud of who you've become, despite it all."

I swear, I see tears rush to his eyes as he presses a quick kiss to my forehead. "Thank you."

"Thank *you*. You do way too much for me, and I feel like I rely too much on you sometimes."

"Christ, angel, do you realize how much you cloud my thoughts? Do you understand that I never want you out of my head? I don't mind you relying on me because it feels good. It feels good to be wanted by someone, and when that person is you, it feels even fucking better. So, lean on me, rely on me, knock me the fuck over for all I care, but don't you dare apologize because I'm welcoming it with open arms." He pulls me into his embrace again, wanting to be closer, and I bury my head in his chest as a few tears escape.

When we pull back, Vince doesn't let go of my hand as he squeezes it, a silent way of telling me to keep going with my story. "Liv chose to be my anchor. She chose to fill the role of the parents we never had.

But my parents never dismissed me. They would always harp me about something—my next video, my next brand deal, anything they could. It felt like they cared more about the money I was bringing in, rather than me or Liv. I was burned out a few times, struggling to get out of bed, to feel like a person, to brush my hair, and they never let up. I was in school, trying for college, trying to manage my overnight fame all as a teenager. It was hard, and eventually, college faded away because I was already making a decent amount of money. But I never made that decision—my parents did. They thought college was a waste, but I saw college as an opportunity to get the hell out from under their roof. So, I started to accept more brand deals that would take me away because it helped me breathe a bit easier. Liv was in college, so I never felt bad leaving."

"You just hated coming back," he says, his voice tight with an emotion I can't place.

"This place, that house, my parents—they never felt like home. It felt like prison I was sentenced to for life. And then Ralph came into the picture."

"I hated them from the start, you know. That first day I met you, I disliked them."

I smile at the thought of him already clocking that without ever meeting them. "You probably listened to that gut of yours."

He laughs under his breath. "It hasn't been wrong yet."

"I know." I squeeze his hand back, sending a thank you through my hand. "You've read the police report. You've seen the damage he left behind with what he did. There's really not much else to say about it."

"Bree, I know it's tough, but I can tell you're lying."

Of course I'm lying. "If I told you the truth, you'd look at me differently."

"No, I wouldn't."

"Yes, you would." Even I look at myself differently since that night. I thought I was strong, a fighter, but that night showed me a different Bree.

"Bree—"

I cut him off. "Vince, don't—"

He cuts me off. "Don't you get it? There's nothing you could ever say to me that would make me look at you any differently. So say it, Bree. Tell me every thought racing through that head of yours."

Tears leak out of my eyes, but my breathing steadies as I all but whisper. "I didn't fight back."

"What?"

"I didn't fight back!" I yell. "I laid there frozen while he touched me, while he whistled, while he changed my life. I. Did. Nothing. I'm a fucking coward! A coward who couldn't do anything but sit still and do what I was told!"

I'm breathing heavily again, and I've taken a few steps away from him. I never thought I'd be a pacer like Liv, but right now, I am.

I turn to look at Vince, and he has a solemn look on his face. "Angel...come here." His arms are out wide.

My feet move of my own violation, and when I feel his arms wrap around me, I force myself not to break.

"Just because you didn't fight back doesn't mean you wanted that to happen to you. As far as I'm concerned, you're a fucking fighter, Bree. You fight every single day to heal from what he did, and I'm proud of you every single day for not letting him win."

Tears flood my eyes. I'm done being broken. I'm done letting others have a say over *my* life, and I'm going to take my goddamn life back if it kills me.

Because here in his arms, where nothing can touch me, I believe I can do anything. And taking control of my life, my story, is exactly what's on my list.

"Did Liv say anything else?"

"Connie is doing her best to control the fallout, but there's something else."

I move my head on his chest to meet his gaze, and more sorrow fills his expression. "Keep it coming, Vince. I might as well know about all the bad shit I'm walking back into."

"There are some leaked messages between Ellie and Alex floating around. He's also cheating on you with her, it seems. There's a message from her telling him that you're too traumatized to be a good girlfriend, that she could show him a better time, and another one stating how you weren't actually raped and should just get over it and stop acting like a victim." His face twists in disgust as he recites the messages, and before I can stop it, I burst out laughing.

What the fuck even is my life? "Let me guess, the messages were first, and some reporter called my parents, offered a bunch of money for the full story, and they took it?"

He can only nod.

"How much?" I ask, wondering how much my parents made telling *my* story to the world.

"Two hundred and fifty thousand dollars."

I laugh again. "That sounds about right."

"Are you okay? Do you want to go back to the house? We can stay for a few extra days."

I shake my head. "No," I say as I start to walk back to the car. "I have a few conversations to have. We should get going."

I might be headed to my parents' house, but that will never be my home.

As far as I'm concerned, I haven't found my home yet, and I don't know if I ever will.

But I'll fight like hell for it, and maybe one day, *one day*, it will all work out for me.

Please let it work out for me.

— MAD WOMAN BY TAYLOR SWIFT

I STORM INTO MY parents' house, not bothering to knock because I know they're home. Vince and I passed about fifteen different news vans on the way in. I know my parents, and they must be rolling over with all this attention on them. I don't think they fully thought this through—exposing my story to the public. After all, the reason they moved to this house in the first place was because my fame became too much for them, especially after Ralph was caught. I had more attention on me than ever, and now, it's worse.

I hope they're uncomfortable. I hope they're afraid to leave their house while the story floats around. It's *everywhere,* which means that only another huge story can dethrone it. I hope they start to understand that this is what I feel like every time I leave my fucking house—mobbed, terrified, nervous, and like my privacy is always being invaded.

They deserve to feel a fraction of how I've felt because they did this to themselves when they aired *my* story to the entire world.

I stand in the foyer after slamming the door open, knowing they'll find me in a minute, and I feel Vince behind me as I hear the slow, calculated steps of my parents. When I see them both appear on the staircase in front of me, I hold their stares.

They look surprised to see me, as if they weren't expecting me to show up after they did what they did.

"Were you scared one of the reporters somehow made it in here?" I ask them, and before they can answer, I speak again. "That's how I feel every time I hear a door slam, or a loud noise, or whistling. For that fraction of a second, you felt what it was like to be me. It doesn't feel great, does it?"

"Bree, it's lovely to see you," my mom says, walking down a few more steps but not meeting me at the bottom.

"Vince," is all my dad can seem to say.

All I hear is Vince grunt a response back, not wanting to say a single word to them.

"I've barely heard from you guys since you moved, and after Liv told you guys off, I considered you to be cut off from me, too." I take a steadying breath before I continue. "So why, after all this time, are you choosing to keep using my name to get your fifteen seconds of fame? Why the fuck did you tell *my* story to the world for two hundred and fifty thousand dollars? Is that how much I'm worth to you? If it is, as far as I'm concerned, you two don't deserve to have the title of parents."

All I hear is my father sigh heavily before he rolls his eyes at me. "You seem angry, Bree." *Seriously?* That's all he has to say?

My mother's heels click against the floor. "We got laid off a week ago, and we have yet to find jobs, so money has been tight. You must understand why we did it."

"You expect me to hear you out after what you did? Not only did you tell a story that wasn't yours to tell, you got *paid* for it. And you got to sit comfortably in those fancy interview chairs while you did it. You two told my story! You didn't live through it, and you fucking told it anyway! Where do you get off doing that?"

"We got laid off because of you! We lost our jobs because of our fucking last name! Your name is everywhere and very recognizable now that you're with Alex. The partners got tired of reporters camping out in front of our offices and disrupting work hours," my dad yells at me from the top of the stairs before he comes stomping down, his finger pointed right at me. "All of this is because of you, so don't blame anyone but yourself, Bree!"

Before I can snap back at him, Vince steps in front of me and grabs my father's hand. "Lower your voice when you speak to her, and if you lay a finger on her, I'll kill you." My father only laughs as he keeps his finger pointed at me.

"Vince, it's okay," I say as I put my hand on his bicep. "Dad, I appreciate your misplaced anger, but none of this is on me. I didn't ask to get famous, I didn't ask to get assaulted, and I didn't ask to be fucking stalked."

I step around Vince but keep him close since I want to leave here as soon as possible. I only have a bit left to say, and then I'm gone.

I'm fucking done. These two people in front of me are no longer my parents. They're merely two people who conceived me, but Liv is the one who raised me. She's always been all I've ever needed.

"If you needed jobs, that might've been easier before you went on a fucking talk show for the whole world. If you're blaming me for this, then maybe you should take a long, hard look in the mirror, because I never asked to be born."

"The only reason you exist is because your sister was a failure from the moment she stepped out of the womb. You wouldn't be here if it wasn't for her low potential," my mother states, a cold bite to her words.

Tears fill my eyes as they talk about my sister like that. "Liv was only two or three when I was born! How the hell could you deem her a failure only a few years into her life?"

"She was slow to develop, but you...you were practically gifted from the time you were born. We always had high hopes for you, Bree, but you chose a different route over what we planned for you."

I scoff at them, already knowing what they wished I would've become. "Law school, right? You wish I would've followed in your footsteps and become successful that way instead of this, right?"

The two of them nod their heads. "It's too much now. We did what we had to."

"That's your excuse? You told the story of the worst night of my life to the entire world because *you had to*?"

"And the money, of course." My dad smiles as he steps back to stand by my mother.

"Holy fucking shit," I hear Vince curse behind me.

"I want you both to open your ears because this is the last thing you'll ever hear me say to you. By doing this, you've taken *everything* from me. You chose money and your fifteen seconds over protecting your own daughter. Fuck. You. Both. And Liv is not, and has never been, a fucking failure. She's a best-selling author whose words will make a lasting impact on her readers, which is more than you'll ever be remembered for. One day, none of us will exist, but her work, her stories, and my videos will live longer than you ever will."

Tears fall from my eyes as I grab Vince's hand and walk out of their house, knowing the two of them won't say anything back to me anyway. As I walk with my head down towards our car, I hear another door slam, and I jump.

A few seconds later, I feel Liv's arms wrap around me. I recognize her perfume, and when I feel her squeeze me, Vince lets go of my hand so I can wrap my arms around her.

And I break.

"I'm here, Bree. I'm here," she says as she rubs circles on my back. I hear Vince and Tristan mumbling something, but all I can focus on is my sister and how comforting her touch is.

"How did you know I was here?"

"Vince texted me. He thought you might need a shoulder to cry on."

I detach from my sister and turn to face him, a silent thank you passing between us. His eyes are full of longing, like he wants to comfort me, but there are cameras everywhere, and we can't do anything—not in public, and not until we've talked about everything in full.

"Thank you for coming over here for me."

Liv tucks a stray piece of my hair behind my ear as tears fall from her eyes. "Always, Bree. You're my family, and family is there for each other no matter what."

"I love you, sis. Thank you for everything you've done for me. I don't think I'll ever be able to—"

"Bree, stop. I'm your older sister. You should know by now that I would do anything for you. Driving over here was the easiest decision." She hugs me one more time before we pull back and take a look at the house our parents inhabit.

I think the two of us have known for a while that we would never invite them back into our lives, but today was the final nail in the coffin. Liv and I are on our own now. Our parents are mere flecks of dust that will eventually fly away as our stories continue.

But, actually, Liv and I aren't on our own—we have each other. And we have Tristan and the entire West family to surround us with love whenever we need it. The two of us have made our own little family, and that's all I'll ever need.

As long as I have Liv, everything will be okay. As long as I have Liv, my home exists.

"Ready?" Tristan asks us as he pats Vince on the shoulder. *Are they buddies now?* Liv and I nod at the two of them.

"I'll follow you back," Vince says, moving toward me as we walk back to our car. I can feel his hand behind my back—not touching me, but guiding me to the car, and that almost touch has me buzzing with energy.

Or that could be because of knowing how Vince's lips taste.

Or the adrenaline of the past few hours is running out.

Despite the craziness of the past few years, I know who my real friends are. I know who I want to go through life with. I'm certain it was meant to be me and Liv against the world. Now, thanks to Tristan, we have a few more people headed to our final destination with us.

Friends by chance, family by choice. I think home is something we can create, and I'm one thousand percent sure I have one with Liv, Tristan, Vince, Teags, and the rest of the West family.

Chapter Twenty-Five

Vince

Two Weeks Later

— I, CARRION (ICARIAN) BY HOZIER

SITTING NEXT TO BREE in this stuffy conference room is testing my patience. It has barely existed in the past two weeks, and waiting for Connie for the past hour has been even worse.

My leg bounces as I try not to get up and walk out of this room, but Bree told me this was important, and since she hasn't seen Connie in a while, we have to stay here.

It doesn't help that all of my thoughts are clouded with her—the girl who sits on my right. Ever since we spent those days together in the mountains, I've been itching to do all the things we could while up there—grab her hand, caress her face. All those small touches and stolen kisses can't happen while we're back home, and it's killing me.

Bree is off-limits when we're in public—hell, even in private. We haven't had a chance to talk about everything, but I don't think it's top of the list for either of us. We've barely had a minute to breathe since we got back.

I know that my number one to-do is to find Ralph and beat the shit out of him for all he's done to Bree. This fucker can't hide forever. He'll slip up, and Nico and I will catch his mistake.

All I want to do is be able to show Bree that I'm not just beside her because it's my job. I genuinely like being around her, and I can't imagine a life without her being in it.

I'd give her everything I was able to if she'd let me. If she asked me to stay after all this was over, I'd say yes in a heartbeat.

But for now, my main priority is to protect her with everything I can. Because Ralph is still breathing, and that means Bree is still in danger. I won't rest until she feels safe, even if it kills me.

"Do you want me to get you some water?" I ask, breaking the silence that engulfs the room.

"Yes, please," she says with a smile.

Fuck. How does one word affect me so much? *Please.* The moment she says that word, I'm gone. Six letters is all it takes for her to crumble all my walls.

Please, Vince.

Anything you want, angel.

I get out of my seat and grab a water from the table across the room, and just as I'm about to sit down, Connie walks in.

"Sorry to keep you guys waiting. It's been a hectic day," she says as she sits across from us. "How was the mountains?"

I hand Bree her water, and my fingers graze hers. Fuck, just that small touch, and I'm losing focus. *Get it together, Vince.* "It was much needed, especially after everything that has happened."

"Good. Now, down to business, if that's okay." Connie looks at me, and I nod in agreement. "Let's start with Ellie. I think you should release a statement. It's short and simple, basically stating that you did not condone any of the things she said and that you're handling it with her in private."

"Okay. That's fine with me, but I don't have to talk to her, do I? Because I don't think she'll like what I have to say."

Connie shakes her head. "No. I'll be handling all correspondence with her team."

"Good. What next?"

"Alex and the contract, I'm afraid."

"What about it?" Bree asks. She told me before this that she was going to try and see if she could get out of the contract, since he's basically been cheating on her in public for weeks, and I hope she can because that fucker never impressed me.

It's obvious he's still in love with that one girl or whatever, and I hate what he's doing to Bree, even if their relationship is fake.

"Well, I'm sorry to say you have to see it through. And before you yell at me, there's technically only one fake date left. I can schedule it for after your event since we don't want any bad publicity attracted to it, but since it's the last one, his team and I agreed you two should be seen one last time together, for good measure. We'll leak that you both have agreed to remain friends and wish each other the best after you separate due to busy schedules. He'll go back to California, and that's that."

I hear Bree sigh heavily as she plays with the end of the bow. I swear, they keep getting bigger and longer, but it matches her outfit, and she always looks amazing in whatever she wears. I don't understand fashion, but anything Bree wears, she pulls off.

"Fine, but triple-check that he's not on the guest list for my event. He's ruining everything else, and I'll be damned if he ruins this too."

Connie nods her head and jots down a few notes, and then she looks at me. "How's security coming, Vince?"

"It's all set. I sent the plans over yesterday, so they should be in your inbox."

"Wonderful, I'll look at them later, but I'm sure it's perfect." Connie rifles through her stack of papers before she looks back at Bree. "I'll have the finalized guest list sent to you within the week. I added all your last-minute invites while you were gone, and I finalized the seating chart."

"Thank you, Connie. I wish I could've done it myself, but—"

Connie cuts her off. "Sweetie, don't. I'm just glad you're okay and got some well-deserved rest. You deserved it, but now it's back to work."

Bree only nods her head, and a few seconds of silence later, she stands from her chair. "Now, if you'll excuse me, I have to go meet my sister."

Connie crosses the room and engulfs Bree in a hug.

"Angel is getting ready to go. We'll be down in five. Get the car ready."

Kenner speaks back to me. "Got it, Boss."

Bree turns around and looks at me. "Are you ready to go wedding dress shopping?"

I give her a knowing look. "Are you kidding? I was born ready. Let's go."

"I'm right behind you," she says as she throws a wink in my direction.

— NOTHING MORE BY THE ALTERNATE ROUTES FT. LILY COSTNER

"Ooh! What about this one?" Teags asks as she pulls out a fully black dress.

The rest of us—my sister, Parker, and Cassie—stare at her in disbelief.

"I think that's more your style, Teags," I tell her, and she starts laughing almost immediately.

"Yeah, right. Imagine *me* of all people getting married and shopping for frilly dresses." She puts the dress back on the rack, and the rest of us laugh to ourselves, knowing full well that one day, she's going to regret saying that. She practically just jinxed herself.

The five of us are at this small boutique in Philadelphia that Tristan rented out for a few hours. He not only wanted Liv to be able to have fun with this whole thing, but he also wanted to make me feel as safe as I could.

That's why I can't wait to have him officially be my brother-in-law. Tristan West is the perfect man for my sister, and I can't wait to see them spend their lives together.

Tristan proposed a week ago while Liv and him were book shopping. He had it all planned out; it was the most adorable thing I've ever heard. He planned a scavenger hunt that took them to places that meant a lot to them—the grocery store they worked at, the baseball fields, a classroom where they first started passing notes, and more.

"Wait! I have an idea!" Cassie says, almost spilling the champagne in her hand. "We should all pick two dresses for Liv, and she can model them for us! Rather than just perusing, we can make this more fun!"

"Cassie, maybe you've had enough champagne?" Parker reaches for it before she pulls away.

"It's a mimosa!" Cassie counters, and the rest of us laugh.

"Cass, a mimosa is supposed to have orange juice in it," Liv tells her, a huge smile gracing her face. I know she's missed Cassie a lot, and this is the first time they've seen each other since college. Cass has been super busy with her job and some family troubles, but I'm glad she's back. Her energy has been missed.

"There's orange juice in here! Just a few drops is all I need." Cassie smiles and sets her glass down as she swipes through the racks.

I let my laugh flow from my lips as I lock eyes with Vince, who's standing close to the entrance, staring back at me with a hint of something in his gaze. It looks like he's thinking or imagining something, but I can't tell what. I know Emerson and Chris are around somewhere, but my gaze always finds Vince.

The two of us are locked onto each other's eyes until Liv breaks it by tapping me on the shoulder.

"Hey, are you okay?"

"Yeah, I'm all good. Are you excited to live your Disney princess dreams?" I ask as I see Parker and Cassie carry way more than two dresses into Liv's changing area. The store associate that's in here is also carrying two drastically different options into the room, probably due to what my sister said she wanted in her dress.

"I'm actually very excited. I never imagined this would be so fun. All I imagined when I thought of planning a wedding was stress, but Tristan is making the process fun. So far, it's been okay."

"It's only been a week, Liv."

"Yeah, but it's going to be a small wedding. Thank goodness, because I want it to be about everyone celebrating life, not just about us."

I smile, loving that even on the most special day of her life, my sister is still thinking about everyone else. "It's going to be a happy day, Liv. I can't wait."

"I think we deserve a happy day, don't you? Especially after the past few years."

I reach down and grab her pinky finger with mine. "It's going to be the best day ever, I promise."

"Well, when it's your turn for all this, I promise I'll make it the best day for you as well, Bree. You of all people deserve to feel it with whoever catches that heart of yours." I swear, I see her eyes move toward the door where Vince is standing, but I could've been imagining it.

"Thanks, sis. Now excuse me while I peruse the gowns and find some I know you'll love."

"I'll leave you to it." She smiles as she walks over to her dressing room.

Around fifteen minutes later, I carry my two selections to her room. I'm the last one, of course, and I join Teags on the small couch at the end of the small runway. This boutique is *adorable*, and Tristan told me his card had already been put down if Liv finds something. He's absolutely sure she'll find *the* dress today, especially since the fashion expert of our family is here—which apparently is me.

I wouldn't call myself an expert, but I love fashion. It's one of those things that makes me happy—putting an outfit together and it coming out exactly how you pictured. It's nice to have access to some cool vintage pieces, and I've even done a few collaborations with different brands.

But I hate the word expert because there's always going to be some new trend that I don't understand, and fashion is like everything else—the trends come and go as they please.

I look around at the rest of the store while we wait for Liv to come out in her first dress.

"Vince is over there," Teags tells me as she points in his direction.

"I wasn't looking for him," I lie.

"Yes, you were. Something in the air between you two is different. Care to tell me what the hell happened in the mountains while you were away?" She smirks as she sips her drink.

Dammit. I should know nothing gets past her. "We might've kissed."

"You guys—" I clamp my hand over her mouth before she shouts that statement to everyone. I feel her trying to bite my hand, so I let go after a few seconds.

"I feel like you enjoyed that too much."

Teags just shrugs with a smirk.

"How much dark romance have you been reading while I was gone?"

"I don't know, maybe an entire fifteen-book interconnected mafia series, but stop changing the subject. You kissed your bodyguard? Once or a few times? Come on, Bree, don't skimp on the details. Your sister writes smut, and I know you have the vocabulary to describe it in detail."

"Are you guys ready?" Liv asks from behind the curtain, cutting our conversation short.

"Yes! Get your beautiful ass out here, Livs," Cassie says from the other couch.

"You're not getting out of this that easily. I'm coming over at some point, and we'll be discussing that kiss in detail."

"*Kisses*," I say, a smile gracing my lips.

Teags' eyes go wide, and I swear she's about to lightly smack my arm, but Liv comes out of the dressing room and draws all of our eyes.

My sister walks out in a skin-tight mermaid gown. There's a slit up to her knee, and the straps of the dress sit on her shoulders. It's stunning, but I can tell by Liv's face it's not the one.

"You look absolutely gorgeous, Liv," Parker says.

"Agreed," Cassie says, her voice tight with emotion.

"It's beautiful," Liv says as she smooths the dress down. "But it's not the one."

"Well, we've got three hours left, Olivia. We'll find your dress. Let's try another one," the attendant says as she picks up the train and walks back into the dressing room.

An hour and a few drinks later, the five of us have turned into a mess of tears as we keep talking about Liv getting married and reminiscing on our favorite memories. It's been a really nostalgic day, and I file these moments away for later so I can remember them when I'm feeling down.

Most of my days aren't normal, and I appreciate these little pieces of paradise where I can be myself. Today, I'm just Liv's sister, and that's the most wonderful thing I can experience. I feel my phone buzz in my purse, and when I pull it out, a smile creeps up my face.

Vince: Are you feeling okay?

Bree: Never better. And I actually mean that for once.

Vince: Do you need anything? Water? Tylenol? Different shoes? Tissues?

Bree: I'm okay, but thank you for letting me have today. I know public spaces aren't great for me right now.

Vince: I'd do anything to see that smile on your face as much as it has been today.

Vince: You deserve some good days amidst all the chaos, Bree. Don't ever forget that.

Bree: Thanks for giving me good days to remember.

Vince: I didn't plan this, Bree. It's Liv's day.

Bree: I'm not talking about just today, Vince.

Parker's voice interrupts my conversation with Vince as Cassie tells another story. "Remember when Liv tried to grab that letter he slipped under our door? I swear her eyes were about to bulge out of her head when you invited him into our place for the first time."

"I like to think of that night as a turning point for them, and I wanted to confirm my suspicions. They were, of course, correct."

"What suspicions?" Teags asks Cass.

"That they liked each other. It was glaringly obvious to everyone except for them. I look back and laugh at how in denial the two of them were."

I smile at every story the four of us tell while Liv gets changed into her seventh or eighth dress. I lost count after five, if I'm being honest.

"I remember when she first told me she had a boyfriend. I was out of town, and she called me screaming. I think it was the day after it became official, and the only thing she would tell me about Tristan was his name. I kept asking for specifics, but she was too giddy to say anything. After the call, I'd ask her one question a day, and that was all she was willing to answer." I stop to laugh, my body starting to warm at the memory of seeing my sister's face light up about something, especially back then when all the two of us did was complain about our parents to one another.

"Anyway, I finally got some real answers, and just from that first call, I knew. I knew Tristan was going to be her forever person."

"Trying to get the romance author to admit her feelings was the hardest feat I've had to endure," Cassie tells us.

"The irony of that is insane," Teags chuckles under her breath.

"I'm glad we're here, though. It may have taken a bit, but I'm glad we all finally made it," Parker says, and I feel Teags tense up beside me.

"Not all of us made it," I hear her whisper under her breath, and I grab her hand to offer some comfort. To my surprise, she doesn't pull away. She lets me rest my hand in hers, and a few seconds later, Liv walks out, her eyes wet with tears.

This is the one.

My sister is wearing one of the dresses I picked out, and the attendant gives her a few tissues to blot her eyes. The dress is white, corseted at the top, before the ball gown falls into a huge skirt. The silk of the skirt contrasts nicely with the layering on top. The sleeves are a loose silk that falls on her shoulders, and a separate part wraps around her neck.

"Guys..." Liv says as she looks at all of us. "This is the dress."

All four of us agree, and I'm pretty sure we're all crying at this point.

"The train attaches if you prefer a longer one, and the skirt is detachable, which would be great for the reception."

"It's perfect, Liv," I say as I get up and stand beside her. I grab the veil from the attendant, and I throw her hair in a quick makeshift bun before I slide the veil into her hair. I fluff it down, and when I step back and admire my breathtaking sister, tears start to flow.

She deserves the sun, moon, and stars, and Tristan is the only person on the planet who would build his own spaceship just to get each one for her.

"This is the one," she says as she blots some tears from her face. "I'll take it."

"Wonderful. I'll get an order sheet ready for you, and we'll schedule a tailor appointment for you in a few weeks."

Liv goes to take the dress off, and I'm stuck here reminiscing about when we were kids playing pretend in the basement. Now, Liv is actually getting married for real, and we're all grown up. The thought hits me in the chest, terrifying me. When did we get here? How did it show up so fast?

I used to think time dragged on, but that was when I was stuck around people who only wanted me for my follow count, or my parents who wouldn't let me breathe.

Now, I feel lighter. I have true people around me who want me because of who I am, not what I represent on the internet.

Just years ago, Liv and I were playing pretend, and now it's real. All the scenarios we enacted as kids—Liv having a book signing, getting married, and giving our dolls the life we wanted—are coming to life right in front of my eyes.

And as Liv and our friends walk out of the boutique, I can't help but send a message to the universe to slow the fuck down.

Because I don't want life to speed up so fast that I can't remember all these moments.

These are the good old days that everyone talks about, and despite having a stalker on the loose, I'm not going to let him take any more of these moments away from me. They're mine to live, and he'll have to pry my life away from my cold, dead hands.

Chapter Twenty-Six

— SEVEN BY TAYLOR SWIFT

"Okay, start talking before I explode," Teagen says as she sits down on my bed.

"Hello to you too, Teags. How was your morning?" I joke, knowing that the reason she came over was to hear about the kiss.

"It was fine. Now, get on with it. I've given you two days to figure out how to describe whatever transpired between you two, and I'm expecting juicy details, babe."

I get up from my desk chair and all but skip over to my bed. Teags is sprawled out, her long legs hanging over the side of my bed, and I sit across from her, my legs crossed underneath me. I look over to the door to make sure it's fully closed, and when I'm sure it is, I look at my best friend.

"It was the best kiss of my entire life."

Her eyes light up as if we're talking about a romance novel instead of my actual love life. "I fucking knew he was a good kisser. He's just got that energy, you know?"

"I know, Teags. I experienced it in real time."

"God, I'm so jealous. Okay, what else?"

I ignore her jealousy comment because she *has* a boyfriend. Does she keep forgetting that on purpose? There's definitely something going on with her, but since she came over to talk about my life, I won't press.

Not today, but at some point.

"He keeps a hair tie on his wrist for me, just in case. Every single time he touches me, I feel like I'm going to fall over from butterflies. I feel insane, Teags, like truly insane about all this. I kissed him the first time, but he chose to kiss me again…and a few more times while we were back at the house."

"Bree Rose Hart, are you serious!"

"Yes! Ugh, Teags, I never thought I'd feel like this. And even though nothing is official, it feels like it could be."

"You have hope again, Bree. It's nice to see that light back in your eyes, and I'm glad you have a tiny sliver of something good amidst all the shit you're going through."

Tears fill my eyes, but I will myself not to let them fall. "Thanks, T. I'm glad I have you by my side through all this. You've been a constant in my life these past few years, and I'll always be thankful to Liv and Tristan for bringing us together." I grab her hand, expecting her to pull away, but she doesn't.

"I'm thankful too, Bree."

"I don't know when we'll talk about next steps. I assume he wants to wait until Ralph is caught."

Teags nods her head. "That makes sense. Things might be a little calmer when that happens, and all his rules probably prevent him from doing anything while the media is watching you like a hawk."

"Well, when we were on top of the mountain, he said he didn't care about those anymore. He told me I was unraveling him, and that's not easy to do…" I trail off, my face getting hot.

"Oh, so he's *obsessed*." Teags face is neutral for a few seconds before she explodes in laughter.

"Get your laughter out now, Teags. I know you probably think this all sounds like a bodyguard romance. So laugh it out, and then say something when you're ready," I say as I playfully hit her arm while she continues laughing.

"It sounds exactly like something Liv would write, and I kind of love it. You deserve this, Bree," Teags says as she runs a hand through her dark brown hair.

"You deserve to feel this too, girl. I take it that things with Gregory are still the same?" Talking with her about her relationship is like pulling teeth. They could've broken up, and Teags wouldn't have told anyone.

"He asked me to move in with him. In Arizona."

"Arizona? Across the country Arizona?"

"That's where it is, yes," Teags says as she gets off my bed and leans against my bookshelves. "I haven't given him an answer yet, but Tristan thinks it's a terrible idea."

"Well, it's definitely a big decision," I tell her, not wanting to voice my true opinion until she wraps her own head around it. I don't want Teags to be that far away from me, but if she does end up moving with him, I'm not going to stop her.

It's her life, and even though I would miss having her around all the time, if it's what she wants to do, I'll support it.

"I'm not sure what I want to do yet, but I still have time before I have to make an official decision." Teags pulls a few books off my shelf then puts them back, and I can tell this situation is making her nervous. She can never sit still when something is bugging her, kind of like my sister, but instead of pacing like Liv, she has to keep her hands busy.

"Well, we could dance it out or scream it out. It's up to you."

Teags turns around to face me, and I know she's remembering when Ralph first came into the picture how we used to go to my backyard and yell into the night. Any time we wanted to, we did it. Teags used to sleep over a lot back then, and I barely slept or got out of bed, and that was one of the things that helped—screaming it out.

"I could use a good scream," she says as I throw one of my pillows to her. We can't go outside because Vince's team is out there, and I think they would look at us like we're insane.

I grab one for myself, and the two of us look at each other before we yell into them for a few seconds, and I can feel some of the stress melt off my shoulders. After we're done, we burst out laughing before my door slams open, and in runs Vince with his knife drawn.

"Are you guys okay? Is there someone here? Wh—" He's looking between the two of us, and I feel bad, but I can't stop laughing.

"We're okay. Just alleviating some stress," Teags tells him.

"By screaming?" His eyes narrow, and my laughter stops. *Shit.* I guess I didn't really think this through.

"I'm sorry. It's something we used to do outside, but..."

He sighs heavily as he catches my drift. "My men are outside."

"We didn't want them thinking we'd gone crazy from cabin fever, so we thought pillows would muffle the sound. I guess they didn't," Teags laughs.

"Not really," he says as he looks at me. "Next time you want to scream, come to me."

My face gets red, and I know he's not insinuating where my mind went, but the thought still makes my face get hot.

"Does that offer apply to me as well?" Teags chuckles.

"I didn't mean it like that. I just meant that I could tell my men to leave, and I'm going to quit while I'm behind. Have a nice day, you two. Let me know if you need anything." And with that, he shuts the door behind him, and the instant we're alone, we burst out laughing.

"Oh, he's got it bad for you, Bree. I've never seen Vince so flustered. It's kind of cute."

"That's probably the third or fourth time I've seen him flustered, and I kind of love it. He's always in hyperfocus mode, but I like making him unravel when we're alone."

"I can't wait to see him in action at your event. I bet he'll have even more of his guard up since you're the one throwing it." Teags plops onto my bed. "Are you excited about it?"

"I am. It's been a long time coming." I pause before I think about telling her who else is coming, and it slips out anyway. "Dom is coming in place of his parents."

"Oh," is all she says, but from the way her eyes got bigger, I know that's not all she's feeling. "That's nice. It'll be good for Tristan and Liv to see him again."

"Hide your excitement all you want, but I'm excited to see our friends and family all dressed up."

Translation: I'm excited to see Teags drooling over Dom in the black suit he's probably going to wear. I'd never tell her that, though, because she would deny it, citing that she's with Gregory now and her crush on Dom doesn't exist anymore.

But Gregory isn't coming to my event. He has some sort of work emergency to deal with, and Teags is going stag.

"Me too. Now, can we continue our rewatch of *Pretty Little Liars*? We stopped on one of the best parts of season five."

"Of course, Teags," I say as I pull my blanket up to cover the two of us, and we settle in as I start the episode.

These days will always be my favorite, and I know that no matter where Teags ends up, she will always and forever be my best friend.

And no distance will ever change that.

Vince

"You kissed her?" my sister all but yells through the phone.

"Technically, she kissed me first," I say as I throw my knife onto my desk before I settle into my chair. Nell nudges my legs and lays beneath my desk before I see her eyes flutter shut.

My sister called me after I burst into Bree's room, thinking there was someone inside. I heard the two of them screaming, and I sprinted up the stairs, only to find them laughing when I opened the door.

I swear, those two together could cause a heart attack, but I was glad to hear Bree's laugh back. Even if they scared the shit out of me, hearing that was like music to my ears.

And then Aria called me, and I blabbed about the kiss. I didn't mean for it to slip out, but I've been slowly freaking out the past few days.

I broke my rules. I broke the rules I put in place because without them, I wouldn't be as good at my job. Bree and I broke my rules on our trip up the mountain.

That's not even the part I'm freaking out about. It's that I don't care that I broke my rules for her.

I'd do it again, too. Except I'd kiss her first. I wouldn't pull away, and I'd prove to her that I'd choose her again and again. Bree possessed me with that kiss, and I'm terrified of how that made me feel. I've never been in a serious relationship because all I've done since I became a bodyguard was move from place to place. It was easier that way, but I'm thirty-four now, and I'm tired of all the traveling.

For the first time in my life, I want to plant roots. I want to stay, and the only reason I want to stay is so I can be by Bree's side. I want to choose her because it's what my gut is telling me to do.

And God help me, I want it. I want her. I don't want to be just her bodyguard anymore. I want to wake up next to her every morning, and

I want to show her that I don't give a fuck about anything the media has to say.

I can handle it. I know I can, and if she can't, then I'll handle it enough for the both of us.

"Okay, but you kissed her, right?" Aria questions, wanting to get the full story, so I tell her every detail. By the end of it, I'm practically out of breath. "So what's the problem, Vince?"

"The problem is that I'm terrified of fucking this up! I've never done relationships, sis. I don't know how to fucking do this."

"Vincey, you're so adorable," she says as she laughs across the line.

"I'm going to hang up on you, Aria. I swear to—"

"Chill out, baby brother. All I'm saying is that you have to talk to her about it, plain and simple. I don't know why people always think it's such a complicated thing. Have a conversation with her and go from there. Lay it all out on the table—your feelings, where you want to go from here, everything."

"But what if—"

"Stop. It's okay that you care about her, Vince. It's okay to fall for someone, even if she's technically your client. You're not breaking any rules—your own, maybe—but you yourself just told me you didn't care about that."

"I don't. I'd break every rule of mine again if it meant I could have her."

"So tell her that, you idiot."

"Okay, there's no need to name-call, Aria. We're thirty years old."

I hear her scoff. "And you're acting like some sort of lovesick teenager. It's rather cute, actually. I've never seen you like this before."

I roll my eyes at her, even though she can't see me. "Why did I tell you all this again?"

"Because I give great advice. Listen, I have to go. Max needs me for something, but let me know what happens. I'm on the edge of my damn seat over here. Love you, brother."

"I love you too, sis."

I hang up the phone and toss it onto the stack of papers on my desk.

I hate that Aria always seems to be right, but I do think a conversation with Bree would help.

Maybe after her event is done, I'll ask her to have a talk with me.

Yeah, I think to myself. I like that plan. She'll have one less thing on her plate, and I already know it's going to be a successful event, since she's the one who planned it all. Bree never does anything without her full attention, and I'm excited to see it flourish and hopefully bring her real smile back to her face.

The one thing I'm absolutely sure of is that I'm completely fucked in the head over Bree Hart.

And so help me, I never want to be cured.

Chapter Twenty-Seven

— BETTY BY TAYLOR SWIFT

As I STEP INTO my dress, I hear a knock on my door.

"Can I come in?" Vince's voice permeates the wall, and I can't help but smile.

"Yes," I say, and when the door opens, my mouth drops.

Because Vince Evans is standing in my door frame in a full navy blue suit that looks like it was made just for him. It molds to every muscle in his body, and his hair is curly and all over the place, but in a styled way.

He's fucking beautiful, and I know what his mouth feels like on mine.

I think it got about ten degrees hotter in here, and when I look down at my pale blue dress, I notice the two of us are matching.

"Did you plan on matching with me tonight?"

He smirks as he steps closer into my room. "No, but Nico insisted I wear navy blue because he's wearing maroon and didn't want to clash with me."

I giggle as I imagine that conversation. "Well, you look wonderful."

"Thank you," he says as he roams his gaze over my body. I opted for some blue chunky pumps, and my hair is curled down my back, tied with a long white bow. My makeup is simple, so I decided to go with a dark pink lip gloss. Vince must notice because his eyes linger on my lips for a few seconds before he returns to my eyes. "There are no words to describe how enchanting you look tonight, Bree."

"Thank you, but I'll look better when I lace my dress up. Can you help me?" I say as I turn around, the threads of my dress hanging to the ground.

"Of course," he says as he moves closer to me. I feel his hands grab the threads before his face moves closer to mine from behind. My heels give me a bit of height, but he still has to bend down toward my ear. "How do I do this?"

"You just take it and cross it through the holes and then tie it off at the end." My voice comes out in a whisper, and as his hands start to work across my back, my entire body gets hot.

Can he feel what he does to me? Does he know how much I want him to kiss me again? I thought all the stolen touches from before were enough to drive me crazy, but since we kissed, every touch has felt a thousand times worse.

He ties off the end of the threads in a small bow, my dress now fitting me like a glove. I turn around to thank him, but he's a lot closer than I thought.

His eyes are piercing into mine, and I notice his hands are still wrapped around my waist, as if he can't bear to let me go.

I'm staring straight into his eyes, and for this fleeting moment, I pretend he's mine, that we're going to this event together. For this moment, I can pretend we're a real couple, that he helped me get ready, and maybe I tied his tie for him because he needed my help.

Maybe one day, that will be real, but for now, the two of us are in a delicate stage of in-between. We're not anything, but we're also not nothing, because I know what he tastes like, and I've felt his mouth against mine.

"Are you ready to go?"

"Just a few more seconds, please," I tell him, still looking into his eyes.

"For what?"

"To pretend it's real. To pretend that you're mine," I whisper.

He leans down and presses a kiss to my forehead. "We're as real as the air you're breathing, Bree. You have me, angel. I promise you, I'm not leaving your side."

"You have me too, Vince." He smiles at me, and if this wasn't my event, I would stay here all night, lost in the feel of him. "We can go now. I can't be late to my own event."

"Wherever you go, I go, Bree." He grabs my hand. "Let's make this the best night ever, okay?"

I can only nod as we descend the staircase, and he whisks me off into the night with a smile on my face the entire time.

Nothing in the world can hit me when Vince is by my side. The two of us deserve some light after all the dark we've endured, and tonight feels like the beginning of something new, something good.

And I can't wait to see where it leads us.

As I WALK INTO the ballroom with Vince behind me, I'm stunned at how many bodies I see filling the space. I knew we had invited a ton of people, but actually seeing them all inside the ballroom for a good cause makes my heart soar.

"Bree!" I hear from across the room, and when I move my head to the right, I see all of my favorite people standing together, looking in my direction.

Liv and Tristan look beautiful in their matching attire, both of them in gray. Nico is wearing a maroon suit, while Teags is wearing her signature color—black—with some bright red heels and lipstick. My best friend is absolutely beautiful. Dom has just returned with a drink in his hand, and he's opted for his usual all-black suit. His jet-black hair makes him look even more dangerous than he normally is.

My heels click as I walk across the ballroom, and I wrap my sister in a hug when I reach them.

"Bree, you look absolutely beautiful," she whispers in my ear. Her eyes move behind me. "You don't look too bad yourself, Vince, but my sister has you beat."

I can hear him laugh as I turn to let him into our circle. "I'm not going to argue with that, Liv." His eyes move to everyone else. "You guys clean up well."

"Who are you again?" Dom asks, and I have to fight the urge to laugh.

"Vince Evans, Bree's bodyguard," he says as he shakes Dom's hand.

"Oh, right. It's nice to meet you."

"Yeah, you too. Your parents are jewelers, right? I recognize your last name," Vince tells him. I knew he had dossiers on my social circle, but damn.

"That they are." Dom rolls his eyes, and I wonder how close he is with his parents. That's the same way I would talk about my own parents when people found out they were both lawyers.

Tristan starts to laugh as he turns to Dom. "The fact that Vince knows more about your parents than I do is crazy. You told me they were rich, but I didn't know why. Vince, thank you for your service." He raises his drink to him, a smirk on his face.

"Before I put my foot in my mouth again, I'm gonna make my rounds and check in with my guys. Nico, care to walk with me, buddy?"

Nico only smiles at him before the two of them head to leave, but Vince catches my arm and leans down to my ear.

"Save me a dance?" he questions.

"You're the only one I want to dance with anyway," I tell him, my cheeks flushing.

"I'll be around if you need me, angel. Have fun, okay?"

I nod at him as Nico drags him away, and when I turn to face my friends again, they're all looking straight at me. "What?"

"The amount of sexual tension between you two is crazy. Is he your bodyguard or your boyfriend? Or both?" Dom asks before Tristan smacks his arm.

"Dom, shut the fuck up."

"Come on! It's a valid question."

"Is that right?" I say to them, and all of my friends nod their heads. "Damn, okay."

"We don't have to talk about this here, Bree," my sister says. "But it's nice seeing you happy again. No matter what you two are, I'm thankful your smile is back on your face."

"Me too," Teags says as she rolls her eyes. *Aw, her love language.*

"I'm so thankful my parents didn't make me bring a date to this," Dom says, looking at me. "Thanks for denying my plus one, Bree. You've saved my life."

"You're welcome?" I say, confused as to why he's so happy to be here stag.

"Your parents would force you to bring a date? What kind of parents do you have, Dom?" Liv asks him, a curious look in her eye.

"Pushy ones who won't get off my back," Dom says as he downs his drink. "Now, if you'll excuse me, I have to mingle."

"I'll join you, Dom. It is my event, after all," I say as I tell my friends goodbye and join the crowd of people.

This is my least favorite part about events—mingling. It always feels so fake. But being able to talk about why the foundation is so important to me will always mean the world.

"So," I say to Dom. "I don't know how long it took me to realize your family owns Graves Jewelry."

"I'm not exactly an open book when it comes to them, but yeah, the family business has been passed down for generations. I'm next in line to learn, but not before I clean my act up." Dom smiles as he glances at me.

"Is that so?"

"I've gotta please mommy and daddy if I want my inheritance. I have an entire trip planned next summer to prove how good of an employee—I mean, son—I am."

That was totally on purpose. "I bet you'll prove a lot of people wrong, Dom. To be fair, I'm glad you're here in place of them. It's always good to see you."

The two of us break off in separate directions. Connie pulls me to the side an hour later, her phone in one hand and her clipboard in the other. "Are you ready for your speech? You've got around three minutes."

"I'm ready."

Connie looks around at me, her eyes almost bugging out of her head. "D-did you not write anything down? Where are your note cards?"

"I don't have any. I'm speaking from the heart, Con. It'll be fine." I smile, hoping it eases her, but it doesn't seem to be working.

"I believe in you. Sort of," Connie says as she speed walks away to the stage, and everyone quiets down. "Hello, everyone, and thank you so much for coming. This event has been an absolute blast, and we've already surpassed our donation goal, so thank you so much!" A round of applause ensues before I feel a hand caressing my arm. I don't even have to guess who it is.

"Liv, I'm going to be fine. You know I don't hate public speaking as much as you do," I say as I spin to face my sister.

"I know you'll be amazing, Bree. I just wanted to stand with you before your speech. And I'm sorry that our parents did what they did."

"Don't apologize for their mistakes, Liv."

"I'm not. Well, I did, but I wasn't trying to. I'm just so proud of you, Bree. I feel like I don't say it enough, but I am so damn proud of the woman you've become. Look at all this good you're doing for others, even when you're going through something nobody else can understand. It's remarkable, Bree. You are remarkable."

I pull her in for a hug, our heels making us the same height. "I am who I am because of you, Liv."

"You are who you are because of *you*, Bree. I had nothing to do with who you've become. And no matter what you say, I'm not taking any credit. Now, get up there and show everyone why I'm the writer in the family," she jokes as she squeezes my hand before she heads back to Tristan, slipping into his side like she was always meant to be there. Tristan's eyes meet mine, and he gives me a thumbs up before I hear Connie introduce me.

That's my cue.

I walk up the short staircase before I hug Connie and stand behind the podium. I take a deep breath as I look out into the crowd, the ballroom filled with more people than I could've imagined when I first started organizing this event.

"Thank you all for coming. I'm so excited to be hosting this event in honor of the Mental Health Foundation, and the fact that we've already passed our donation goal is...insane. So, to anyone who donated, thank you so much. One hundred percent of your donations will be going directly to the foundation to bring mental health access to communities where it's not easily accessible."

I pause for the applause, and before I speak again, I lock eyes with my family in the front of the small stage. I knew this wasn't going to be easy, but seeing them here to support me makes the nerves settle in my stomach. And then I spare a glance at Vince in the back of the room, and the look of pride on his face is enough to send me straight through the floor.

He throws me a wink, and I smile to myself. "I know a lot of you have probably heard about my life through the internet. I've been putting myself out on the internet since I was a teenager, and I've had my best and worst moments broadcasted for everyone to see. A lot of people have had a lot to say, especially in the past few months."

I look to my sister for some extra strength, and I take another breath to steady myself. "But my story is my own, and nobody should be able to tell it for me. I talk to my therapist every single day. Since that night in May, I've had panic attacks, PTSD-induced nightmares, and so much more behind closed doors. It's been hard, and it's been the biggest fight of my life, but having someone to talk to about it has made it easier to carry. It was easy for me to have access to a therapist, but others don't have that luxury. This foundation is so close to my heart, so thank you all. I hope the rest of your night is magical. Thank you."

I walk off the stage, and I'm immediately met with Teags and my sister pulling me into a hug before Teags lets me go to take a sip of her champagne.

"Might want to slow down, Teags," Dom says as he tries to take her flute from her.

"I'll bite you, Graves. Don't touch my drink when I'm having a good time," she snaps back, and our eyebrows raise. I can almost guarantee we're both thinking the same thing.

Vince's hand around my center surprises me, and before I have time to say anything, he whisks me to the dance floor, just as a song comes on that I immediately recognize.

Faithfully by Journey.

"Did you pick this song just for me?" I ask him, wondering if he remembers that the first time he escorted Liv and I home after we met, this was the song playing on the radio.

"Of course I did. Now, let's get lost in the music for a bit, okay?"

I can only nod at him as my grip on his hand tightens, and I let him lead while we dance. I'm not the best dancer, but Vince seems to be amazing at it. He's got this confidence about him when he dances, and with the way he's looking at me, I could melt into a puddle on the floor.

I'm hyper-aware of all the cameras, but I'm also aware of his hand on my back, guiding my movements. The way his hand feels in mine is too good, and I hate that the song is almost over because I could dance with him all night and never get tired of it.

I like being close to him like this. It almost feels more intimate than our other interactions. Our entire relationship can be explained through how we're dancing. He's the one guiding me, holding me steady and safe, and I'm the one naturally following his lead. The two of us make so much sense, but all these other factors keep getting in the way, and I can't wait until those walls aren't blocking us anymore.

I want to be able to dance with him any time I want. I want him to kiss me like nobody's watching, even if we're surrounded by people. I want us to be real.

But I have to wait for that moment, and I'd wait forever if it meant I could have him for real in the end. I'd wait as long as it takes if Vince is by my side the entire time.

I'm about to ask if he wants to dance to another song before murmuring ensues by the door, and a few people start to cheer.

"What's going on, guys?" Nico asks me as he appears by our side.

"I'm not sure," Vince tells him. "You two stay here while I go check it out." His head flicks to where Emerson and Duncan stand, but then a familiar face pops into view, wearing a suit and that same pretty boy smile he shows everyone in Hollywood.

Alex is here, even though he was not on the guest list.

"Bree! My beautiful Bree," he says as he all but slides over to where I'm standing with Nico. He grabs both of my hands before he leans into my ear. "Play along, okay?"

"What?" I whisper at him before he pulls back from me and gets on both of his knees. "What the hell are you doing here?"

"Bree Hart, the worst things I've done in my life are the things I've done to you these past few weeks. I am so sorry for breaking your trust in me, and I'm sorry you found out from someone other than me. It was a mistake, a slip-up, a casual thing with all of them. It meant nothing to me."

"Alex," I say, nervously looking around at the scene he's now created at an event that means way too much to me. I can't believe he's done this. Now, all of the coverage tomorrow is going to be about this moment instead of the foundation. "Please get up."

"Not until you forgive me. I wanted to make a grand gesture here in front of everyone to show you how sorry I am. A big gesture like in one of those books you love so much."

"And you thought showing up and crashing my event was the best way to do that?" I question, a smile on my face but anger in my tone. I all but yank him off the floor and drag him to a small, private area outside the venue. By the time we're outside, he drops the phony boyfriend act. "What the hell are you doing here?"

"My team told me I should make a big show of faith to you, to show the media we're doing better than ever. Did it work? Do you think they believed it?"

"Oh my God, you're such an idiot," I say as I pace around on the cobblestone beneath my feet. I have no idea how I'm supposed to go back out there and continue the night after the scene he made. I'm hoping Connie is trying to end the event early or make some other gesture that could get people to forget about this, but I doubt it will help.

"Bree, I thought this would be okay. Why are you freaking out right now?"

"Because this event meant something to me, and you ruined it with your stupid declaration! Now this is all people are going to be talking about for days! And why the hell did you think apologizing for cheating on me in front of everybody was a good idea?"

"The main part was over! I thought it would be okay! The only thing I wanted to do was show the media we're still together despite me being a young idiot. I figured showing up here, at your event, was the best bet to get people to notice."

Is he blaming all this on the fact that we're young? "Well, you thought wrong, Alex! Oh my God, this is a mess," I say as I place my hand on my head and a few seconds later, the door opens, and in comes Vince and Nico. The two of them are staring at Alex, both looking rather murderous, but Vince's gaze shifts to mine.

"Did he touch you, Bree? Did he break the fucking rules again because he's an idiot who doesn't care about anyone but himself?"

Vince starts towards Alex, and I place my hand on his chest. "No, he didn't, Vince. I'm fine. I'm just pissed is all."

"If you touch her without permission again, I'm calling this deal between you two off, and then I'll kick your pretty boy face in."

"Vince..." Nico warns as he wades into dangerous territory, but Alex doesn't let up.

"It's funny, Evans. Did I see the two of you dancing before I came in, or did my eyes deceive me? I don't want to make any assumptions, but those looks you shared were very telling." Alex smiles, and Vince takes another step forward before Nico grabs his arm.

"He's not worth it, buddy. If you go back out there after kicking his teeth in, the media will go even crazier than they are now."

"Please don't make this worse, Vince. I'm fine; he didn't touch me."

"But he ruined your night." Vince clenches his jaw.

"Not all of it was ruined," I tell him as his muscles start to relax. "Alex, we have one more fake date left. After that, you're free to date and fuck whoever you want, as am I. Please leave before you make things worse. Connie will be in touch with your people."

"Okay," he says as he opens the door. "I miss you already, Bree. I'll see you soon, baby."

I know he's saying all that because people can hear him, and it pisses me off. Where the fuck does he get off doing all this at my event?

Did he really think that showing up here and making some bold statement was going to make everyone believe we were all fine and dandy? Did he think I was going to kiss him, hold him in my arms, and forgive him just so our contract would hold up? He's an even bigger idiot than I thought. What happened to that guy in the bookstore all those weeks ago? Where did the real Alex go, and why does he keep up this stupid persona when he's fine as is beneath his exterior?

I turn to face Nico and Vince, who both have the same look on their face—concern for me and anger at the situation, I assume.

"Are you okay?" they both ask me at the same time, and I can only nod.

"I'll be fine. How bad is it out there?"

"According to my guys, bad. I don't even know how Alex got in, and someone's getting fired or demoted when I find out—"

I walk up to Vince and put my hand against his chest, hoping it will be enough to calm him down. "Vince, stop. If Alex wanted to get in, he would get in. I'm sure it was nobody's fault."

"She's right, Vincey. That kid has more tenacity than we did at his age. Look, I'll try and get some of the headlines featuring Alex taken down by the morning so your event has the front page, Bree."

"Thanks, Nico. I appreciate that."

"Anything for you, princess." He smiles at me, and I only roll my eyes.

"Nico, get the fuck out and meet me by the entrance," Vince commands, and he leaves without a fight. When the door closes, Vince and I are alone again, and my body becomes all too aware of how close he is to me. "Are you okay, baby?"

Baby. I don't know why that term of endearment makes my heart beat a little faster. "I am now," I say as I wrap my arms around his middle and press my body to his. "Now I feel a lot better."

I feel his chest rise and fall, as if he's laughing, before his arms tighten around me. "I'm glad he didn't ruin your night completely." His hand grabs my chin and tilts my head up to meet his. "You even sparkle in the moonlight, Bree."

"Stop making me blush, Vince, or people are going to think we're doing something out here."

"The pink of your cheeks is my favorite color, Bree, so why would I stop? Let them think we're doing something. I can handle anything that all those nobodies say about us."

And then he presses his lips to mine, kissing me how I've wanted to be kissed since we danced in each other's arms. His lips take over, and his tongue swipes into my mouth as the two of us breathe heavily under the starry sky.

"More, Vince," I tell him, and he grips the back of my neck, kissing me deeper and rougher than the first time.

Fuck, I think to myself. This is what I needed; *he* is what I needed.

He pulls back from me, breathing heavily as he centers himself. "Bree, I'd love nothing more than to get lost in your lips all night, but we should really get you out of here before it gets too crowded outside."

I steal one more kiss from him while we're alone, before the cameras come back to us and I have to pretend like I don't know what his lips feel like on mine.

Chapter Twenty-Eight

— THE LAKES BY TAYLOR SWIFT

"ARE YOU READY TO go? Kenner and Chris are going to clear a path," I tell Bree as she smooths out her dress. I hate that Alex decided to crash her event, and just seeing his stupid face pissed me the fuck off.

How fucking stupid is he?

I hate that the first thought that ran through my mind was that Bree is mine and not his, because I hate how possessive and insane that sounds.

But she'll never be his in the way that matters. The two of them are faker than those teeth of his.

"I'm ready, I think. Does my hair look okay? I feel like it's written all over my face that we just made out. My lip gloss is all over your lips now." I smile as I bring my hand to my lips. *Yup, there it is.* "Do you want me to wipe it off?"

"No."

Her cheeks flush when I say that. "So, how do I look?"

"You still look as beautiful as ever, Bree," I tell her as I press one more kiss to her forehead, the blush creeping up her cheeks again. "There's my favorite color again."

"Vince, stop making me swoon so much."

"Never," I say as I open the door for her. "Your friends want to say goodbye, so we'll stop for them and then we'll leave, okay?"

"Okay. That sounds good."

I push the door open, feeling Bree follow behind me like always. I shift my gaze around the event and notice that a decent number of people have left, and I speak into my earpiece.

"We'll be out soon. Is the path clear?"

"It's settled as best as we can. There's a lot of fucking people out here, boss," Chris tells me, and I sigh heavily. This is going to be a shitshow, and my only hope is that I can get Bree out of here safely. Alex really fucked things up. I'm sure half the cameras out there are because of his surprise appearance.

A few minutes and lots of hugs later, I softly touch Bree's arm. "Time to go, Bree. It's getting crazy out there."

"Okay," she says as she turns to her friends. "I'll see you guys. We should have dinner at my place soon."

"That sounds good, Bree," Tristan tells her before he looks at me. "Take care of our girl, Vince."

"That's all I wanna do, Tristan."

"I know, man," he says as he throws his hand out for me to take.

"Bree," I say, reminding her that we have to go.

"Sorry. Okay, I love you all. Thank you for coming. Vince has guards for each of you when you leave. I'll text you all when I'm home!" Bree follows me to the door, and before we leave, I let her collect herself.

"It's going to be rowdier than normal. Chris tried his best, but it might be a tight squeeze."

"I'll be okay, Vince. As long as you're in front of me, I'll feel okay."

"Good. I'm going to open the door," I tell her, and when I open it, flashes of lights are all I see. It's a fucking zoo out here, and I can barely see two feet in front of me. "Everyone back the fuck up!"

I feel Bree grab onto my suit jacket as I push forward. I can't see any members of my team, and that thought makes me want to turn around and get the hell back inside, but either way, I'm fucked. As long as we can make it to the car, we should be fine, but even that is proving difficult.

"Back the fuck up! You'll get your fucking pictures, just move!" I yell, and a few photographers listen, but not enough.

I take a few more steps forward, but something hitting me in the face makes me pause, and the next thing I know, all I see is darkness.

IT'S A FUCKING MADHOUSE out here, and I'm holding onto Vince like he's my only lifeline in a storm, which he kind of is. He keeps yelling at them to back up, but nobody is listening. They never listen, and all I want is to be safe in my car.

Why do they only care about pictures? Can't they tell that this is unsafe? I can barely see ahead of me as the flashes go off. I'm so tired of feeling like some sort of zoo animal. It feels like I'm trapped in this glass box, and nothing I can do or say will help me get out of it.

The only time I feel free is with Vince, and all these stolen moments we've had together have let me breathe a bit easier in the past few weeks.

When I feel his jacket slip from under my touch, I start to panic.

What's going on? I wonder, and a few seconds later, Vince falls to the ground, his face way too pale and his skin hot to the touch.

"Vince? Vince! Vince, what—" I search his features for any sign he can hear me, but his eyes are closed, and I have no idea what all this white stuff is on his face. Where the fuck did this come from?

I grab his earpiece and start to scream into it. "Nico! Chris! Emerson! Anyone, please help. Vince is down. I repeat, Vince is down in front of the building."

I don't bother to hear any responses, and a few seconds later, Nico and Chris show up.

"What happened, princess?" Nico asks me as he finds Vince's pulse. "His heartbeat is slowing down."

"Everyone back up! Back the fuck up!" Chris shouts, and they *finally* listen.

"I-I don't know what happened. He just went down, and he has all this stuff on his face. Why does he look like that, Nico? What the fuck happened?"

"We'll find out. I'm calling 911," he tells me as he pulls his phone out.

My mind starts to panic at the millions of possible outcomes, and seconds later, Vince's body starts to shake.

"Fuck! Turn him on his side," Nico tells me as Emerson helps. I'm frozen, again. Yet another time that the panic takes over my body and I don't do anything.

I hate myself, and tears flood my eyes as the ambulance pulls up. The EMTs hop out, stick Vince with something, and a few seconds later, his body stops seizing.

They strap him onto the gurney in record time, and Emerson hops into the ambulance with him as Nico finds out where they're headed.

"Princess? Come back to me. Vince is going to be okay. He's in good hands. They're taking him to the hospital, but Vince would kill me if I didn't take you somewhere safe—"

"Nico, take me to the fucking hospital right now, or I'll get there myself!" I yell through my tears.

He takes one look at me and nods as he shoves everyone else out of the way before the two of us are finally in the car. There's no doubt that

Nico is breaking a few too many traffic laws, but I can't find it in myself to care.

Because as soon as my phone dings in my pocket, I know with complete certainty that it's my fault.

Chapter Twenty-Nine

— PEACE BY TAYLOR SWIFT

As I sit beside Vince in his room, Nico offers me some food, but I decline, just like I have the past ten times he offered.

I can't find it in myself to eat, not when Vince is in this hospital bed because of me.

The doctors told us that whatever was thrown at him was laced with fentanyl—a fuck ton of it. Enough of it must've been inhaled through his nose, and that caused the seizures.

They told us if we had gotten here minutes later, Vince might have died.

He might've died, and his death would have been on my hands.

"Princess, Vince will kill me if he finds out you haven't eaten. It's been hours. Just take something, please."

"I'm fine, Nico."

He sits down on the armrest of my chair as I continue to stare at Vince. I've never seen him so vulnerable before, and tonight will forever be ingrained in my mind.

Vince is here because of me.

He's hurt, and this is all my fault.

Ralph is trying and succeeding at taking out everyone I love.

It's all my fault.

"Bree, stop beating yourself up. We don't know what happened yet. I'm downloading the footage from the ballroom. I'll have it soon, and we'll—"

"It's my fucking fault, Nico. How am I not supposed to beat myself up?" I say as I get out of the chair, wanting to shrink into the walls of the hospital.

"For starters, Vince knows the risks. He chose to come back and do his job, which is to protect you. And we don't know for certain that Ralph had anything to do with this."

I can only manage a scoff at him as I throw my phone in his face. "Read that and then tell me it's not my fucking fault, Nico."

His face scans the text I got earlier, and I see his eyes narrow at my screen as he finishes it. "Fucking hell."

"He wasn't even aiming at me. He was going for Vince because I made him a target! I was the one who did this to him, Nico! Even if I didn't throw the fucking fentanyl at his face, I'm sure as hell at fault!"

"Bree, don't do that. Don't blame yourself for this."

"He was protecting me, Nico! He was ahead of me, and Ralph knew that, and he almost died! Vince almost died because of me," I say as I collapse, my head between my hands. "I know it's his job, and I know Vince would kill me for feeling like this, but I can't help it."

Nico comes over to where I am on the floor and grabs my face. "Listen to me, Bree. Vince came back for you because he cares about you. I've seen how he looks at you, how you look at him. I know you two mean more to each other than being a client and bodyguard. He's going to be okay, Bree, and when he wakes up, he'll tell you the same thing I am—that it's not and will never be your fault."

"The darkness always seems to follow me. If I was you, Nico, I'd leave the room. Who knows what could happen to you while I'm around."

"Bree, don't."

My chest heaves as I barely get the words out. "Nico, I can't do this anymore. I can't—"

"You're enough just as you are, Bree. It's going to work out, but you have to trust us."

I'm fucking terrified. What if Vince never wakes up? What if I leave the hospital and something happens? What if his sister never sees him again because of this?

Oh, fuck. *His sister.*

"Someone needs to call Aria and tell her what happened," I tell Nico through tears.

"I talked to her an hour ago. She's trying to get a flight, but the next one doesn't leave for a few hours."

"What about Nellie? Is someone at the house with her—"

Nico cuts me off with a hug, my tears leaking down my face as the exhaustion from the past few hours starts to hit. I don't even know what time it is, and part of me doesn't care. All I want to know is that Vince is going to be alright. I'll sleep when I know that for certain. "Nellie is fine. Aria is coming, and Vince is going to be okay, too. Now, please, eat something before you're the one who ends up in one of these hospital beds. I don't want to face Vince if he wakes up and you're down the hall in a hospital room."

I sigh as I take one of the sandwiches and sit back on the chair. It's tough to get down, but I do it, and by the end of the sandwich, I feel a bit stronger already.

"The doctor told me he probably won't wake up tonight, so if you want me to take you home, I can."

"I'm not leaving his side, Nico."

"I figured as much. I'll go get us some cots to sleep on. And here," he says as he throws a bag at me. *Where did he get this?* "I asked Emerson to run home and get Vince a change of clothes for when he wakes up. There's also pajamas in there for me and you."

"Thanks, Nico."

"Anything for you, princess. I'll knock before I come back," he tells me as I grab one of Vince's shirts and throw the pair of shorts in here on. I don't hear Nico come back, because as I sit down in the chair beside Vince's bed, exhaustion takes over, and I fall asleep.

Two Days Later

MY EYES FEEL AS heavy as rocks when I try to open them. *Where the fuck am I?*

"Jesus, it's fucking bright in here," I mumble as I bring my hand to my head. My body feels so fucking heavy, as if I'm being weighed down by a freight train.

"Vince?" I hear a familiar voice say beside me.

"He's awake. I'll go get the doctor," I hear Aria say. *Aria? What the fuck is she doing here? Am I hallucinating?*

I feel a hand slip into mine, and even though my grip is loose, I sure as hell won't be letting her go.

Bree's face comes into my line of sight, and I notice how puffy and red her eyes are. "Were you crying over me, angel? You should know I'm harder to take down than that."

She practically laughs through her fresh tears. "You scared the shit out of me, Vince Evans."

"You scared all of us, Mr. Evans. We're glad you're back," a doctor says as Aria comes back into the room and heads toward the edge of my bed. I notice Nico on the other side with Bree, and he smiles when he looks at me.

"Glad you're okay, buddy."

"You didn't give me CPR, did you?" I ask him, and he just laughs.

"No, but that can be arranged," Nico jokes back.

"Can you guys stop joking around?" my sister threatens, but I know she's just as glad to see me awake.

"No thanks," I say as I look at the doctor. "What happened?"

"You absorbed fentanyl through your nose when that pie got thrown in your face. It was laced in whipped cream. Around five milligrams, which is almost twice the lethal dose."

I hear Bree sniffle as she wipes her eyes. "Excuse me," she says as she leaves the room. My sister's eyes follow her out of the room, and when she looks back at me, her eyes sadden.

"Is she okay?" I ask Nico.

"Not really. I'll explain later," Nico says, turning his attention back to the doctor.

"We're going to keep you for a few days. We'll be giving you lots of fluids, and taking more blood soon to get an accurate reading of how much entered your body. I'll be back later on my rounds."

My sister follows the doctor out, no doubt to ask a thousand questions, and as the door clicks behind them, I turn to Nico. "What's going on?"

"Bree's blaming herself for what happened to you."

Fuck. "Why? I'm her bodyguard, for fuck's sake. It's my job to—"

"I told her all that, but Ralph sent her a text about what happened last night. He did this. It's confirmed. He's escalating, and he's not just going after her anymore. He's going after everyone she cares about because he knows it hurts her just as bad." Nico swipes through his phone for something, and then he shows me a screenshot of the message Ralph sent.

> **Unknown: I guess I've moved onto your inner circle now, Bree. It's so delightfully fun to see you all up in arms over your loved ones getting hurt. You're such a caring person, sweetheart. It's one of the things I love most about you.**

> **Unknown: But they're keeping you from me, and I cannot have that. So, I can do this one by one, or I can try to get them all at the same time before I whisk you off into the sunset, never to be heard from again. We can finally be together, Bree. Isn't that something? It's all I've wanted for years, and we're so close to having it.**

> **Unknown: Tell that bodyguard of yours to stop touching what's mine; if he survives, that is. R.**

Fucking hell, this guy is batshit crazy.

If I had the strength, I'd throw Nico's phone across the room, but I can only manage to toss it across my bed. "How did you get that?"

"I took Bree's phone while she was asleep and screenshotted it. I also emailed it to myself, just in case."

"That's an invasion of privacy, Nico."

He runs his tattooed hand through his hair, the bags under his eyes telling me he hasn't slept. "What did you want me to do, Vince? The girl was breaking down on the floor of this room, blaming herself, and I did what I do best. I tried to trace the signal from his phone, but it was another burner, another fucking dead end," he shouts, running a hand through his hair. "You're not the only one who cares about her. I was willing to do anything I could to help, so I hacked her phone. Her password was way too fucking easy to guess."

"I understand that, but—" The door opening has the two of us pausing, and Bree comes back into the room, her eyes still puffy and her face wet with tears.

She's still blaming herself, and nothing I say will help her realize I'd do it all over again the same way if it meant she wasn't the one getting hurt.

"Did you tell him?" she asks Nico, and he nods. "Good."

"I'll leave you two for a bit. I have to head to the office and see if they've made any progress. I'll be back later."

"Thanks, Nico. For everything," I tell him as he leaves, and when I turn to face Bree, I can't tell what she's thinking. Normally, I can read her like a children's book, but right now, she has closed herself off, and I have a feeling I'm not going to like what she's going to say.

"Vince, I—"

"Come here, angel. Come lay next to me," I say as I pat the side of my bed.

"No, I—"

"Please, Bree. I just want to hold you while I explain how none of this is your fault."

That causes her tears to fall harder. "How can you say that, Vince? How can you sit there after what happened and still try to make me feel better? You saw what he said. You saw what he's doing, and you still want to say none of this is my fault?" Her blonde hair is cascading down in front of her eyes, as if she's using it as a shield.

"That's exactly what I want to do, because it's not your fault. You can't blame yourself for simply existing, Bree. Ralph is the one doing this to *you*. It's not the other way around."

Her head falls to her hands, and even before the words are out of her mouth, I know what she's going to say. "If you want off my case, I understand."

"Don't pull away from me, angel. Don't do this. Not now. Not after all we've been through." I move my hand to cup her face, and she leans into my touch. All hope might not be lost because of that tiny movement. "I've had this insane urge to protect you ever since I've met you. You remember that day, don't you?"

"Yeah, I do. You let me write notes to you so I could protect my voice."

"Even through those notes, I could tell you were a spitfire."

That earns me a small laugh. "I don't recognize that version of myself anymore."

"I don't either. But do you remember the day I left?" I ask her, because every single second of that day is ingrained in my head.

"Every moment," she tells me.

"I wanted to turn back so many times. I fought with myself on the drive because I knew I couldn't go back to you. I knew there was no reason for me to go back, but I wanted to anyway. I feel pulled in your direction, even when we were apart, Bree."

"I wanted to ask you to stay, but I didn't. There were a lot of things I wanted to say to you that day, but I didn't, because I figured you wouldn't have stayed."

"Since the day I met you, I've wanted to shield you from anything bad that could hit you. It's the strangest thing. With all my other clients, it was normal. I would take a case, complete it, and that was that. But with you, my mind was constantly going. I was taking more precautions than necessary, and I couldn't tell why. When I came back, the urge was ten times stronger."

"But when you're around me, all you are is in danger, and if you didn't wake up from this, I would've blamed myself for the rest of my life." She sniffles, and I reach over to the tissue box to hand one to her. "Thanks."

"I know the risks of being around you, Bree. I don't give a fuck if I'm in danger, because as long as I'm around you, I have all I need."

"Vince, don't. I've told you before that my life isn't peaceful. It's not calm. It's...crazy and insane, and we'll always be under a lens, and—"

I cut her off, because nothing she could say could change my mind. It was always meant to be me and her, and I'll spend however long I need showing her that I'm not going anywhere. "I'm not going to regret choosing you, Bree. I don't know why you think you're not worth it, that being with you isn't worth it, because the feelings I have for you are real, and they're strong as fuck. That might scare the fucking shit out of me, but when I think about choosing you and having a life together, all those scary feelings diminish, and all that's left is peace. That's what you do for me, and all I want is for you to choose me back so I can prove to you that you're easy to love."

She just shakes her head at me. "What if it's not enough? What if choosing one another isn't enough? I can't ask you to throw yourself in the deep end because you can't predict what will happen."

"Baby, none of us can. But you deserve to be loved and chosen, not almost. Let me prove to you that I'm choosing this—us. You can't push me away before we even have a chance to try."

Her head tilts down, and her face looks puzzled as she stares back at me.

"Where have I heard that before?" She touches her bracelet, and the memory must come back, because a few seconds later, her eyes pierce mine, shock lacing her features.

"What's going on, Bree?"

Chapter Thirty

Five Years Ago

— INVISIBLE STRING BY TAYLOR SWIFT

"Can I get some water, please?" I ask the bartender as he grabs a glass for me. As soon as he puts it down, I drink it all in one go.

"Refill?"

"Yeah, thanks." I didn't realize I felt that dehydrated. That tends to happen when I'm at these events, but this one having a dance floor was something Ellie and I didn't expect. She loves to pull me out of my comfort zone, and that includes dancing.

I'm not one for it, but with the right song and energy, I can be.

Ellie is way more extroverted than I am, and I always enjoy being around her at these events. Don't get me wrong, I love being a part of this world, but it gets exhausting sometimes.

And most of the time, I can't tell if someone wants to talk to get to know me or if they know who I am and just want to use me for their own gain.

Somedays, I feel like this path wasn't meant for me, that maybe one day, my entire fanbase will fizzle out, and I'll be alone again. Social media is not a set job, especially in the future. Sure, it works now, but what happens if it all goes to shit? What am I going to do then? I have no education in anything, no college degree, nothing.

Not to mention, my love life doesn't exist, and the only other person I have in the world is Liv.

What do I do if my life falls apart? What do I do if the people around me end up leaving? What do I do when it all becomes too much to handle?

God, I can't think about this right now. I *should* be having fun with Ellie and dancing until my legs give out, but I can't. I'm too busy being worried about what could happen if I'm alone for the rest of my life, which is looking more likely every single day.

What the hell am I doing with my life?

The bartender places another water in front of me, effectively stopping my spiral, and when I go to put it down on a napkin, I notice some words scribbled onto it.

You deserve to be chosen, not almost chosen. Choose the path you want for you, not anybody else.

I feel like I've seen that quote before, and I rack my brain trying to figure out if it's from a book I've read or something I've seen scrolling on Pinterest.

"Excuse me," I say to the bartender. "I was just wondering if you know who wrote this?" I hold up the napkin.

"Some guy who was here. I think he left about an hour ago, right before the event started."

We're at a hotel, so it would be impossible for me to figure out who exactly left it. "Thanks, I guess."

I've never believed in random things being signs for something, but this definitely feels like one. Whoever that guy was, he might be onto something. Maybe I deserve to choose my own path from here on out. Maybe I deserve to feel like I have some control over my own life—rather than my parents controlling every single part of my career.

From now on, I'm making my own choices, and I know exactly where to start as I throw some cash down on the bar and walk out of the hotel.

Now

MY HEAD SHIFTS OUT of the memory, and when I turn to Vince, he's looking at me like he remembers something, too. "Were you the one who wrote that on the napkin?"

"I was…" He trails off. "Holy shit. I was at that hotel in between clients, and the last one I was protecting was always talking about choices and how they were taken from her. It stuck with me, and I was trying to remember what she said, so I wrote it on the napkin. I meant to pocket it, but I got a phone call that I had a new case starting the next day, so I had to rush to make my next flight." He turns to look at me, his eyes full of wonder, and I feel a smile break through my face.

"That napkin was the reason I got my bracelet engraved. It feels weird saying this, but I never had something speak so fully to me before. Obviously, there were books that had done that, but that napkin being on the bar felt like some sort of sign. It was the exact thing I needed to hear in that moment, especially since I was at that event because my parents told me to go."

He grabs my hands, looking at me like I hung the moon and stars. "It has always been you and me, Bree. We just didn't know it."

"I guess it has been." I smile as I squeeze his hands.

"I don't think I ever believed in anything until I met you. I always felt like I was chasing something, but I never really felt like I had caught anything. But then you came into view, and that first time I saw you, I wanted to protect you. I don't know what it was I just felt like I needed to. Even back then, I knew you were special. I think my subconscious knew you would turn into more for me."

"You were the first guy I ever felt safe with after what happened. I think I somehow knew you'd be important to me, but I only thought of you as a guard and a friend, not what you are now." I blush at the end of my sentence, and Vince notices as he reaches for my hair and tucks part of it behind my ear.

"And what am I now, angel?"

"You're mine—at least I think you are."

He reaches for my chin and pulls me closer, softly pressing his lips to mine. "I choose you, Bree. For however long you'll have me, I will always choose you." He whispers the words against my lips like a plea.

"I choose you too, Vince Evans, for however long you'll have me," I say as I get up from the chair and crawl into bed with him, resting my head against his body.

"Can you believe it, Bree? Can you believe something had tethered us together before I even knew you existed? God, that's fucking crazy."

"Are you complaining?" I ask, a laugh bubbling up my body. "It got us here, didn't it?"

"It did, and God, I'll forever be thankful for that fucking napkin." He laughs, his voice a little groggy.

"Well, now that we have that out of the way, you need to get some rest, Vincey," I say as I look up and brush his face with my hand. "You almost got yourself killed for me. When you doze off, I'll be the one protecting you, and I take my job *very* seriously."

"Is that right?" he asks, a hint of playfulness in his tone.

"That's right. Now rest so you can get better, and we can go home."

"Home? I don't think I've ever had one of those before," Vince tells me, and that makes sense, since he never bothered to settle anywhere. My heart breaks for the version of himself that never let him have a home, but that just means I'll try my hardest to make sure he has one from now on. "I'm happy I have one with you, Bree. I'm happy you're letting me choose to be by your side, even if you think I'm going to run in the future. But like I said, I'm not going anywhere, and the only peace I want in life is the peace that comes from being in your orbit."

My heart is melting out of my chest at his words, and I can't think of anyone else I'd want to embrace the chaos of my life with. "You bring me that peace, too. That will always be enough, Vince."

He presses a kiss to my forehead, and a few minutes later, I feel his chest rising and falling in a steady rhythm. The next few days are going to be rough, but this time, I'll be the one helping Vince get through it. It's my time to return the favor.

A single napkin led us both here, and now, we're tied up in one another, and neither of us wants to let go. It's crazy how some things in life work out, but I'm thankful I ended up being at that hotel the same day Vince Evans was there.

I knew that day would change my life, and looking back on all that I've endured, I'd do it all again, knowing this is where the two of us would end up—tangled up in one another and never letting go.

Chapter Thirty-One

Three Weeks Later

— SAFETY NET BY ARIANA GRANDE FT. TY DOL-LA SIGN

"My final read of this month was this new hockey romance that just came out. I'm obsessed with it, and I would recommend it to anyone who loves the sports aspect as much as the romance in sports romance books. This one had such a beautiful mixture of both," I say to my camera as I put the book down. "Thank you to the author for sending me a copy along with some goodies! I absolutely adore chatting in your messages about how unwell I was."

I pause to set the book down, and when I notice Dr. Anna calling me, I quickly say an outro before I snap my camera shut and answer my phone.

"I'm sorry for the wait. I was filming a video and thought I had a bit more time."

"That's alright, Bree. How is everything going? I have to admit, when I got your message earlier, I found myself a bit nervous. I haven't spoken to you in a few weeks, so I assume we have lots to catch up on."

That's the understatement of the century, but for once, not all of what I have to talk about is bad.

Thanks to Vince—my boyfriend—I've had more good days than bad in the past few weeks. After he was released from the hospital with a clean bill of health, we came back home and spent some time with each other. I barely left the house, and Vince and I took two weeks off.

We went on walks around my property, made a bunch of sweet treats, binged *Ted Lasso*, and he even taught me some new self-defense moves, with Nico's help.

Nico clocked us dating when he found me asleep on top of Vince. When I woke up, Nico was sitting in the chair with a huge smile on his face.

And that was that.

I haven't told anyone else that we're official; Vince and I have simply been enjoying each other's company without all the cameras and judgments that could possibly come with it.

"Yeah, I have a lot to catch you up on. I'm not really sure where to start."

"Why don't we start with how you're feeling today? You sound cheerier than usual. Is there a reason for that, or is it one of those days where the pot of water is on a low simmer?"

"There's definitely a reason. I've found myself in a new relationship, and it's going well. Really well, actually."

"Wow, Bree. That's not what I'm expecting. When and how did this happen?"

"Well, it's a long story, but you remember my bodyguard, right?" I launch into the entire story. It sounds insane when I say it out loud, but I wouldn't change anything about our relationship.

"That's wonderful, Bree. It sounds like this new relationship is good for you, and I'm happy you have someone who chose you for once, despite your interesting career."

Yeah, my career. Because of that and the media attention, Vince and I have decided to keep our relationship on the down low. In the public eye, I'm technically still dating Alex. We have one fake date left, and then our contract is over. I tried to get Connie to void it since he's been seen with a bunch of different women—even one of my so-called friends.

He hasn't been spotted since he showed up at my event, and I'm thankful for that, because I don't know how much more of this cheating scandal I can handle. My comments everywhere have been a shit show, and since I don't talk about it online, my side of the story will never be told.

If I said anything, I would breach my NDA, and that is something I do not want to do.

Vince hates that I still have to be a part of this thing with Alex, but since there's only one more date, and he'll be near me during it, he thinks it's best if I finish out the contract. That way, we'll be free of Alex, free to show off our relationship anytime we want.

And you bet your ass I want to show my handsome boyfriend off. I swear, Vince gets prettier every time I see him, and I can't help it if I want to take a thousand pictures of him working out and laying in my bed with me.

I've spent too much time hiding in the past few months, and for the first time in a while, I want to shout to the world that I'm happy.

"Thanks. It feels good to talk about something positive with you for once. It always felt like I was talking to you during a spiral."

"I'm here for you during any mood, Bree. Now, what was the reason you asked to meet today? I assume it has something to do with your new relationship?"

I twist the bracelet on my wrist, nervous to even bring this up. My mind knows the answer already, but it still lingers in my head, and it won't leave. I figured talking to Dr. Anna about it would help soothe me, and I hope I'm right.

"I've been thinking about the next steps in the relationship—physically. After everything with Ralph, I'm scared of being touched in an intimate way again. My mind knows Vince would never do anything like that, and he's never pushed me to do anything, but I'm still nervous."

I hear her scratching down some notes across the line before she speaks. "Bree, it's completely normal to feel this way. You were in a situation that took some of your power, and it's normal to feel scared about entering that space again, especially after how long it's been."

"But I know Vince is Vince, not him...so why do I still have these feelings?"

"You're considering giving up a part of yourself that's been tucked away for a long time, and after the trauma you went through, those doubts are normal. Some people take that control back immediately, and some tuck it away to save for someone safe they can trust. Some never want to feel it again. It's different for everyone, and there's no right or wrong way to go about it. All that matters is that *you* feel comfortable in your decision."

"Thank you. I thought I was crazy for wanting some of the things I did. I still feel like I'm insane for feeling like this. Other than Tristan, Vince is the only man I've felt safe with after what happened." I know he would never hurt me, and he hasn't even brought up the topic of sex or being intimate, but I've been wanting it with him. Except these feelings make me believe I don't deserve to want him that way.

"What are you afraid of, Bree? What's keeping you from taking this step?"

I take a deep breath before I answer. "I'm afraid I'll get flashbacks to what he did to me. I'm nervous I'll freeze like I did that night and completely ruin the moment, and Vince will never want to be intimate with me again."

"You're afraid he'll leave you if you're too afraid or scared to take that step," she tells me, and all the pieces fall into place.

That's what my fears always come down to. I'm afraid I'm too broken.

"Yes, I am." Even though Vince has told me, and shown me, time and time again, that he's not going anywhere. "When will I stop feeling this?"

"I'm not sure, Bree. But what I can remind you of is that Vince isn't him. He's not Ralph. All he's ever done is protect you, listen to you when you need someone to hear you besides me. Every time you talk about him, I can hear your smile from across the phone. I know you trust him, but maybe bring this up to him and see what he thinks. I'm sure if you mentioned that you wanted to take it slow, he would be on board with it. I assume he's letting you control that aspect of your relationship since he knows what it means to you."

"That makes sense," I tell her.

"Talk to Vince, and I'm sure all of your fears will lessen. Baby steps are okay, especially when it comes to being intimate. It's perfectly normal to take it slow, and there's nothing wrong with wanting to do that."

"Thank you."

"Of course, Bree. I hope to hear more good things from you soon, okay? Text or call any time," she tells me as she hangs up.

I sit with what she said for a few minutes.

I trust Vince more than anyone, and I know he'll respect any decision I make.

— AS YOU ARE BY THE WEEKND

AFTER AN HOUR OF overthinking how I'm going to talk to Vince, I decide to rip the band-aid off. I get up from my desk and head downstairs. I knock on the door of his office twice before I hear him mumble for me to come in, and as I peek my head around the door, his eyes meet mine, and a smile lifts his face.

I did that.

He sets whatever he was working on to the side as I plop myself onto his desk. "Hi."

"Hi, baby." He leans forward and presses a kiss to my forehead. "How was your call with Dr. Anna?"

I sometimes forget he knows my entire schedule like the back of his hand. "It was great. We had a lot to chat about."

"Is that so?" He tilts his head at me as he studies my face. "It seems like it was a good talk."

"Mhm. But I came down here because I wanted to talk to you about something." I reach out and grab his hand, threading my fingers with his. There's nobody in the house except for Vince's team outside, so we're all alone in here, which means that I can grab his hand when I want. Just because I can, I press my lips to the back of his hand a few times, peppering small kisses where our hands are threaded together.

"You can talk to me about anything, Bree. What's up?"

"Well, we're in a relationship now, and with that comes certain...physical elements." I pull my eyes from his, suddenly way too shy for this conversation. "Have you given any thought to that part of our relationship?"

"Not too much. I knew we had to have this conversation at some point, but I didn't want to pressure you or anything. I knew you'd come to me when you were ready."

I smile at him. Of course he's letting me make the decision. Could this man get any more thoughtful? "Well, I'm ready, so I think we should have a chat."

"Now?"

"Unless you're busy working, and I'll come back later," I say as I fake leaving, but he grabs my hand and practically drags me back to sit on his desk.

"Bree, sit your pretty ass down on my desk, and we'll talk. I always have time for you, angel. You should know that."

"I do know that," I say as I press a kiss to his lips. "So, where should we start?" I ask, unsure of how to do this. I've never laid out boundaries like this before, so I have no clue where to begin. I smooth out my dress as some nerves take over. It's a new light gray mini dress I got online the other day. Dresses have always been my favorite go-to summer attire, and before autumn hits, I want to wear as many as I can.

"Well, we should have a safe word, just in case."

"And if I say that at any time, you stop?"

"Of course. Do you have any ideas?" he asks, and I blurt out the first thing that comes to mind.

"Pineapple?"

"Is that what you want it to be?"

"Yes." It would be easy to hear, since I hope I'm not talking about fruits during sex. "Okay, what else?"

Vince leans forward in his chair and rolls up the sleeves of his button-down shirt before he speaks. "How about we start with what you don't want me to do. Are there any hard no's?"

"A few, actually." I take a deep breath before I recount the things I absolutely don't want. I was afraid this would bring me back to that night, but so far, I feel okay. His presence and proximity is helping me see only him and not think about anything else. "Don't hold or pin my hands above my head, and don't choke me so hard that I can't breathe. I'm fine with some light choking but nothing too crazy. Just don't be forceful, and we'll be fine." I stifle a laugh, because talking about this feels so strange for some reason. "How about you?"

He pinches his eyes together as he thinks. "I'm pretty okay with most things, I think. It has been a while since I've been with anyone, but I do have one rule I always follow."

I raise my eyebrow at him. "And what's that?"

His head comes forward, and just as I think he's about to kiss me, his lips hover in front of mine. "You come twice before I do, baby. How does that sound?"

My cheeks flush, and my core aches at his insinuation. Just the thought of Vince's hands and body making me come is spiraling my thoughts. I rub my thighs together as he presses a soft kiss to my lips. I'm practically breathless when I answer with a whisper, "That sounds good, Vince."

As soon as his name leaves my lips, he groans. "Bree, don't say my name like that. I'm barely hanging onto my control right now as it is."

"Then let go of it. Show me what it looks like when you lose control." I'm baiting him. He knows I'm baiting him, and I'm hoping he'll take it, because the way I feel about him right now is overwhelming. I've never needed anything as much as I've needed him, in more ways than one, and I'm *aching*. My entire body feels tight with need, and for once, I want him to lose a little bit of that control he always has around me. "Please?"

That's all it takes before he stands, swipes everything off his desk, and crashes his mouth to mine.

God, yes.

His hand comes to the back of my head as his tongue threads with mine, his other hand exploring every part of my body he can touch. It's gentle and rough, two contradicting things, but I'm glad he's not treating me like something breakable. He's taking his time, as if he's been wanting this for so long and doesn't want it to end. He brushes my breast ever so slightly, but just that small touch sends shivers down my body. "Lay down, angel."

I comply, letting my back connect with the wood of his desk.

He bunches my dress above my waist as he throws his chair behind him, letting my legs hang off the side. He kneels on the floor, his face perfectly in line with my pussy still covered by my underwear. "God, Bree, you're so fucking beautiful." His hand finds my center as he teases me before he stops.

"Vince," I moan, wanting more.

His face meets mine, his features covered in lust. "I was going to take my time," he presses a kiss to my lips, "but it seems like you need something from me."

One hand finds my pussy as the other traces my hard nipple. I'm writhing on his desk, my body begging for more. "More. Please."

"Do you want my fingers or my tongue, baby?" Vince asks me.

"Both. Anything."

"Both works for me. How about one orgasm with each? I think I'm okay with that."

Before I can say anything, I hear fabric ripping, and when I look down, Vince is tearing my underwear off my body with his teeth. I watch as he puts the torn lace in his pocket. I'm almost fully exposed to him now, sans my dress, and Vince looks at me like a man starved. "Jesus, Bree. You're soaked. Is this all for me?"

"Yes," I say, breathless with anticipation for what's to come. This isn't what I expected when I traipsed down here, but I've never felt safer. I know it's him. I know Vince only wants to take care of me, and from what I've seen, he's been wanting this just as badly. I bet if he stood up, his cock would be hard and ready.

"Can I taste you, angel? Will you let me out of this torment so I can find out if you're as sweet as I think you are?"

"Yes."

"And you remember your safe word?"

"Yes, Vince. I swear, if you—" My words are cut off by his tongue swiping through my pussy. His mouth is on me, and I suddenly can't think of anything else. He focuses his attention on my clit, licking and sucking on it until I'm squirming against the desk. I grab onto the sides of it with my hands, needing something to hold onto as he devours me.

"Jesus, angel. I knew you'd taste sweet."

"Fuck," is all I can manage as his tongue flicks against my clit before I feel him swipe through my entire pussy. My hips buck against his face, and his hand replaces his mouth against my clit as he comes up to my lips.

"Do you want to fuck my face, Bree? Do you want to take control of your pleasure and take from me what you need? I'm already on my knees, baby. All you have to do is ask, and I'll let you do whatever you want to me."

I can only moan as an answer, because my entire body is quivering at his words before he goes back to sucking on my clit.

Oh my God. I'm already close. It's been like one minute, and I can barely handle what he's making me feel. It's been so long since I've felt anything close to this, and Vince is unlocking new sensations I never thought I'd feel. His mouth is claiming me as if I'm his last meal, and I feel my orgasm building.

"Vince..." I trail off, unsure if I'm making any sense.

"Give me the first one, Bree," he says as he goes back to sucking on my clit. Stars explode behind my eyes as my legs shake, and I grip the desk tight. When I come down from that one, I feel two of his fingers enter me, but he doesn't move them. "You okay?"

"I'm fantastic," I say as I meet his eyes, his pupils enlarged as he stares back at me.

"Good. Now give me another one." He pumps his fingers in and out of me, his movements never wavering. "Do you know how beautiful you look like this, Bree? All spread out on my desk like a good girl, taking what you need from me?"

"Vince," I moan. God, his words are making me feral, something I never knew I needed.

"I've never seen a prettier sight. And don't worry about the desk, baby. Feel free to scratch it if you need to." He curls his fingers, hitting a spot I haven't hit in years, and it feels so fucking good.

"More," I plead, his eyes looking into mine as I squirm on his desk.

"Harder or faster, baby?" he asks as his thumb sneaks up to my clit and starts to circle it as his fingers continue pumping.

"Harder," I tell him, and he listens beautifully as his strokes go from fast to deeper. His lips meet mine in a rough kiss, and I feel my orgasm building again.

"Come for me, angel. Show me the best sight I've ever seen one more time." And that's all it takes for me to explode all over his fingers, and by the time I'm done, I'm exhausted.

"Fuck..." is all I can manage to say, and when I meet Vince's face, I see him licking the fingers that were just inside me.

"I thought your mouth tasted good, but it's nothing compared to your pussy, Bree. God, I could feast on you all fucking day," he says as he grabs a tissue to clean me up.

"I wouldn't be opposed to doing that all day as long as I get to have some fun in return." I smile at him before I see a familiar piece of fabric peeking out from his pocket. "Can I have my underwear back?"

"Nope. Those are mine now, but I can help you go get a new pair. I don't want you walking around with no underwear on." He looks around at the destruction of his office. All of his papers are scattered on the floor, his chair now in the corner of the room, his pens all over the place. At least his computer wasn't on his desk; I'd hate to have broken that.

"Careful, your possessiveness is showing," I joke.

Vince only laughs as he lifts me off of his desk and carries me up to my room. "You're mine now, Bree. You're going to have to deal with me not wanting to share you with anyone else. Is that okay with you?"

"That's perfectly okay with me." I smile as he nudges my door open and softly sets me on my bed.

"That wasn't too much, was it?" he asks as he heads into my closet.

When he comes back out, kneels in front of my body, and slides my underwear on me, I smile. "It was perfect, Vince, but I'm exhausted."

"Take a nap," he says as he smooths my dress down and grabs my blanket from the end of my bed.

"Will you join me?"

"I will." He presses a kiss to my lips as he goes to leave. "As soon as I clean up my office."

Chapter Thirty-Two

— CARDIGAN BY TAYLOR SWIFT

"Wait, you guys kissed weeks ago, and I'm only hearing about this now? What the fuck?" my sister snarks, throwing a middle finger to us on the other side of FaceTime.

"I'm sorry! I never knew the right time to tell you with all the wedding stuff."

Teags is still laughing as my sister's jaw drops further open than it was before.

"Liv, I'll spill all the details at some point, okay? But help me get ready. It's the last fake date in my contract, and I cannot wait for today to be over so Vince and I can be a real couple."

"Are you guys not a real couple?" Teags asks.

"Yes and no. We have to hide right now, but in a few weeks, we won't have to anymore." I smile, excited that I can finally show off my relationship to the world. My *real* relationship. I'm not jumping right into it since Vince and I decided to keep us mostly private for the time being.

I can still post pictures without his face or maybe a soft launch to the world a few times. I just have to be careful about any noticeable features. But for the next few weeks, our romance is just ours, and I'm thankful something is going according to my timeline for once.

"I'm happy for you, Bree. You've got that glow about you, and it's nice to see you happy again." My sister sniffles across the line, and Teags nods her head in agreement.

"Before Liv makes us all cry, show us the outfit, hottie," Teags says, and I laugh as I run into my closet and change.

My hair's already done. I decided to straighten it today, and I threw my favorite light pink bow to tie back my hair. My usual jewelry sits on my fingers and neck, and as I slide on one of my favorite floral print sundresses and a pair of sandals, I feel a little more like myself.

I grab my phone from my vanity before I set it up so my girls can see the full outfit.

"Damn, sis! I love that dress," my sister smiles.

"Normally, I hate the color pink, but you look beautiful in it, so I guess by proxy, I like it," Teags says, and I laugh. Her hating colors other than black will never cease to amaze me.

"Thanks, guys, but—" Two knocks on my door halt my words as Vince strides into my room, wearing his usual—an all-black ensemble.

"See, now Vince's outfit is something I could see myself in. He's got it down," Teags says as I see Vince's face twist in confusion.

"Hi, Vince!" my sister practically shouts.

"Liv. Teags. Nice to kind of see you guys," Vince says, waving toward my phone before he locks eyes with me. "We have to get going, angel."

"Oh my God, is that his nickname for you?" my sister says as my cheeks heat up.

"I've got to go, guys. I'll text you later," I say as I hurry to end the call. "I just have to get my purse..."

My words trail off as Vince lifts the purse I was going to bring and throws it around his shoulder. "Already grabbed it. Is everything you need in it? Sunglasses? Lip gloss? Tylenol for when Alex eventually annoys you?"

I smack his arm lightly. "You look absolutely adorable with my purse around your arm."

"It's part of my boyfriend duties. You're never allowed to carry anything again as long as I'm around," he says as he wraps an arm around my waist and presses a kiss to my temple. "Let's go, baby. I don't want us to be late."

I cock my head at him. "You mean you want this to be over as soon as possible so we can finally be together without Alex hanging over our heads?"

Vince surprises me with a kiss, and I melt into him before we walk down the stairs to the car.

THE CAR SLOWS TO a stop in front of a small coffee shop, and before I get out, cameras are flashing. Deja vu hits me square in the chest as I think back to the first fake date we had. It's crazy to think about all that's happened since April. Now it's August, and so much has changed.

Connie promised that only the photographers we wanted here would be here, but the sidewalk is lined with what looks like at least twenty-five photographers, even more spectators across the street.

I sigh heavily before I put my sunglasses on, Vince's eyes meeting mine in the rearview mirror. I see Emerson and Chris get out from the car behind us, trying their best to clear a path.

Vince moves to get out of the car, but I practically jump through the middle console to grab his arm. "Wait."

"Are you okay?"

His eyes dart all over my features as I answer. "You'll be okay in front of me, right?" I ask, and his eyes soften immediately.

"Bree, I'm fine. I recovered, and this isn't as crazy as last time. I'll be in front of you the entire time, and I'm not going anywhere." His hand reaches for my face, and I lean into his soft touch, the world around me ceasing to exist when we're together. Thank God for tinted windows.

"I don't want you getting hurt because of me again."

"I'd put myself in the line of fire a million times over if it meant you were safe," he whispers, his lips dangerously close to mine.

"Don't say that, Vince."

"I meant every word, angel. Every day, I wake up in your arms thankful that it was me he hit, not you. Now, let's end this fake dating contract so we can go back home and I can soothe all your worries." Vince taps my nose and exits the car.

I lean back in my seat, take a deep breath, and when my door opens seconds later, I grab Vince's hand. The two of us rush inside the small shop, effectively avoiding all the cameras.

"Good?" he asks me when we get inside.

I do a quick sweep of the place and spot Alex in the back, not looking in our direction. "I'm good."

My sandals glide against the floor, and when I sit down across from Alex, his mask slips back up, and his fake smile takes a seat at the table. "How lovely it is to see you again, Bree. You're looking like an angel today."

"You can't call me that," I tell him, his face twisted in confusion. "That nickname belongs to someone else."

"My apologies."

The two of us sit in silence for a few minutes as we drink our coffees. Alex bought me one before I got here, and he got my order right, which surprised me when I took my first sip.

"Can I ask you something?" I say, slicing through the silence that engulfs us.

"Go for it," he agrees, taking a sip of his coffee.

"Why do you hide who you are from the world? Why do you act like an asshole in public when I saw a glimpse of the real you in that bookstore months ago? That version of you was much more...real, and I liked your company that day. It was different."

"How do you know that was the real me? Maybe that was another persona I put on that the media seems to love."

I sigh heavily before I answer. "Because I've done the same thing. I've worn the same mask, faked the same smiles when cameras were around, and I eventually got sick of it. It's hard adjusting yourself to different situations, so why do you do it?"

He takes a moment to think about his answer, and before I think he's going to give me some fake answer, the mask drops. "It's easier. Hollywood assumed I was this young asshole, so instead of fighting it, I embraced it. You have to be tough, and a bit of an asshole, to show people you have what it takes." He runs a hand through his hair. "If people assume I'm some playboy, when I actually do it, nobody's surprised. It's a good way to keep my name in the headlines, but I guess too much of it won't help me get cast in things if all directors see when they look at me as a womanizer. That's where you came in."

"And Lily? Where does she fit into all this?" I ask, wanting to know the truth I've suspected the entire time.

"We're...complicated. The two of us never seem to fit. Every time it was going well, one of us would mess it up. I'd compare us to two perpendicular lines. We've crossed paths, but then we keep going without one another since it never seems to work out how we want it to."

Wow, that was incredibly poetic and not at all what I was expecting. "Do you want to know what I think?"

"It can't hurt, right? Hit me with your best shot, Bree." He smiles sadly.

"I think you're so afraid of messing up the long-term you both seem to want that you run away before anything bad can happen. You keep yourself at an arm's length to protect your heart, but one of these times, you'll realize that the possibility of getting your heart broken is worth it in the end."

"And why will it be worth it?" he asks, his eyes lifting to meet mine.

I turn my head to where Vince stands against the wall, locking eyes with him as I speak. "Because feeling true love is the best feeling in the world." I turn my head to Alex again. "And I'm a person who would rather experience it all with the possibility it ends poorly rather than lock myself away and never feel it at all."

I used to be a girl who thought she was never destined for love. It felt easier to lock myself away and fall into romance novels where the couples live happily ever after.

But Vince was the person who changed that for me. He sees me for who I am, and despite my insane life, he chooses to stick by me, day after day.

I never thought I'd have someone in my life like Vince Evans, and I'll fight like hell to keep him safe from the claws of my lifestyle.

"That's a beautiful statement." He sits back in his chair. "You've changed a lot since that first meeting. You look nothing like that girl from the boardroom."

I smile to myself. "It's been a hectic year, Alex, but I'm hoping after all is said and done, we can still be friends."

"I'd like that, Bree. I'm sorry for being an asshole and for disrupting your event. I'm an idiot, and if I could go back in time, I'd do it all differently."

"Well, you can't go back," I say as I stand up from the booth. "What's done is done, but what you *can* do is focus on the future and who you want by your side when things get tough. I see how you look at her, Alex. Maybe Lily is a grand gesture kind of girl."

He stands up from his chair and looks at me. "Hug it out?"

I nod and his arms wrap around me, camera flashes peeping through the window as we pull apart. "Thank you for asking this time. We'll chat soon."

"I wanted to make sure that bodyguard of yours didn't chop my arms off for not asking. I'll probably need a bunch of advice at some point, so don't block my number after you leave."

A laugh escapes me as I grab my purse. "I won't. Take care of yourself, Alex."

"You too, Bree. Let me know if you ever need anything."

My sandals tap across the floor as Alex leads me over to where Vince is, his hand against the small of my back. "Ready to go?"

He only nods, a weird look on his face aimed at Alex, before a cold blast of air conditioning causes my body to shiver. Without thinking, Vince shrugs off his jacket and puts it around my shoulders, as if it's the most natural thing he's ever done.

"Ready to run?" he asks me, and I smile before I grab his hand.

"Let's go."

He opens the door, a path already cleared by Emerson and Chris for us, and we're able to run straight into the car, so much so that I can't even hear any of the questions the paparazzi asks.

Vince shuts the passenger door and glides around the car, sliding into the driver's seat a few seconds later. "So, what now?"

"Well, Connie and Alex's team will leak that we've parted amicably, and it'll probably float around on the internet for a few days until something else diverts attention from it."

"Ah. Got it," Vince says before he puts the car in drive. "You two go ahead. We'll follow you home," he says through his ear piece.

I grab my phone and text the girls.

Bree: I'm free of Alex! Though our last conversation was pretty deep. I think I gave him relationship advice?

Teags: You gave your fake boyfriend who's now your fake ex-boyfriend relationship advice for him and his famous ex-girlfriend when you never believed you were meant for love?

Liv: My head hurts.

Bree: Yes, I did.

Teags: Just making sure I had all the facts straight.

Bree: Liv, Vince is coming to your wedding as my date, not just my bodyguard.

Liv: I kind of figured.

Bree: Just making sure. I'm so excited.

Teags: Yay, love!

I laugh to myself, Vince's jacket falling slightly off my shoulders as I do. When I pull it back up to normal, I feel like a creep when I lower my nose to smell it.

Citrus and sage notes enter my nose, and I breathe it in, memorizing it for later.

"Are you smelling my jacket?"

My eyes bulge from being caught in the act. "I have no idea what you're talking about."

He only grunts in response, and when I look over at him, his features are tight with an emotion I can't place. Anger? Annoyance?

"Is everything okay, Vince? You look...tense."

"I'm fine."

"Based on that response, you're most certainly not fine. What's going on?"

His knuckles tighten around the steering wheel. "He touched you."

I tilt my head at him. "Is this about the hug? He asked before he did that, Vince. I swear—"

"Good, but even so, I can't help it."

"You can't help what?" I ask as I adjust my legs in my seat. His voice is deeper than usual, more lethal, and I'm getting turned on just listening to him speak.

"The urge to kick his teeth in for touching what's mine, Bree. You turn me into a goddamn maniac. I'm not worried about him, but I still hate that his hands have touched your skin. Just saying that makes me sound crazy." His eyes turn to mine, fire burning inside them. "The things I think about doing to anyone who touches you... God, it makes me feel insane, and I don't give a flying fuck."

I clench my thighs together before I grab his hand from where it rests on the gearshift, placing it on my leg as he continues to drive.

Eventually, I untangle my hand from his. The coffee shop is about an hour away, and we're about fifteen minutes from home when my leg falls asleep and I have to adjust how I'm sitting, which causes Vince's hand to slip higher where it sits on my thigh.

He looks over at me, an unspoken question in his gaze. "Is this okay?"

I don't answer. Instead, I move his hand slightly higher so it's tucked under my dress. His fingers are mere inches from me. If he was to touch me right now, he'd feel how wet I am. He'd know I've been turned on since he admitted to being jealous of how Alex touched me.

He knows we were fake, but he still got all riled up anyway.

And fuck, if his possessiveness didn't turn me on almost instantly.

His eyes keep hovering between my eyes and where his hand sits, and I know he's too much of a gentleman to go any further, so I bait him a little bit.

"Vince..." I whisper, trailing his hand towards my pussy. "Touch me. Please."

"We're almost home," he whispers, his control dangling by a thread.

"I'm aching, baby. Please," I say as I set his thumb over my clit and start to move it. "I can't wait until we're home."

"Fuck, Bree," he says as he takes over the motion, his finger dipping underneath my underwear as he continues to drive. "You're fucking soaked. Did you like hearing how insane I felt? Did you like when I claimed you as mine?"

Fuck, this feels good. Before I can answer, Vince thrusts a finger inside me, and I moan in the passenger seat.

I'm about to open my mouth to say something when his phone rings, and Nico's name flashes on the screen.

"He always has the worst fucking timing," Vince grumbles as he removes his hand, licking the finger that was just inside me before he answers the call. "What the fuck do you want?"

For the rest of the ride home, Vince's hand rests on my thigh as they talk business. When Vince parks in my garage, I lean and whisper in his ear.

"We'll continue this later. I'll meet you in your room." I don't bother to see the look on his face because I can feel the heat of his stare as he watches me walk inside.

Vince

— SO IT GOES... BY TAYLOR SWIFT

"We'll continue this later."

Those four words haven't left my mind, and all throughout the meetings Nico made me sit through, it's all I've been able to think about.

Bree Hart is my fucking undoing, and I never want to be put back together.

She makes me fucking feral. Never in my life did I think I would be the type of guy to finger someone in my car as I drove home, but that's exactly what I did. Since we talked about the intimacy in our relationship, I've been wanting her to make the first move.

And fuck, has she surprised me. My girl is catching me off guard more than I care to admit, but God, if I didn't love the way she grabbed my hand and took what she wanted, what she *needed*.

It was almost the hottest thing I've ever seen.

The thing that tops that list is remembering what she looked like writhing on top of my desk last week, her dress all bunched up as I finally tasted her. Every time I step foot into my office, I hear the echo of her moaning my fucking name as she came all over my face and my fingers.

Making Bree Hart moan is like hearing angels sing.

I've been sitting in my room catching up on some pictures that the guys sent me of Nellie while I've been gone. Since I was recovering, Nico and the rest of our team helped to take care of Nell.

It was weird, but it feels nice to have a solid team I can trust to take care of things. I don't say it often, but I love the guys I work with. They feel more like family lately, and I couldn't be more thankful for that.

For the first time in my life, I feel like I belong—not only beside Bree, but with the people Nico and I hired. They've all been with us since the beginning, and it feels good to have such a trusted environment around me when I'm not used to having anyone.

I have roots now, I think. I've officially settled into who I want to be, instead of chasing after something I'd probably never find. I'm done running, and it's finally time to build a life of my own—here, with Bree and her family.

No more jumping from case to case, trying to protect as many people as I could because I couldn't protect my parents.

I have Bree now, and she's all I need.

As if I summoned her, two soft knocks tap against my door, and when I open it, my jaw drops.

Because Bree is standing at my door in nothing but a black lace bra, matching panties, and black heels, red lipstick painted on her lips.

Holy fucking shit.

"Can I come in?" she asks, a sly smile gracing her beautiful features.

I can barely speak, so I nod my head. I close the door and turn around to see her sitting on the edge of my bed.

I feel like I'm on autopilot as I grab her chin. "Look at you, dressed in black, making me all flustered, Bree."

"I promised that we would finish what I started. I don't break my promises, Vince."

She's doing a number on me right now, and I can barely think, barely breathe, without wanting to rip her clothes off and touch every single part of her body. I want to feel her long nails drag down my back, leaving marks I'll see the next day.

But not yet. Not tonight. Tonight, I have other plans for her.

I get down on both of my knees in front of her and place my hands on her thighs. Thighs that I want my head buried between. Thighs that I dream about suffocating me for just another taste of her.

I take one of my hands and drag it down her face, her jawline, until I cup the back of her neck and force her to look at me. "You're in control tonight, angel. Where do you want me?"

Her cheeks flush instantly, and I bet if I dipped my fingers into her pussy, she'd be wet.

All mine.

"Take your clothes off and lay down."

"Yes, ma'am," I say, immediately following orders. I never thought Bree bossing me around would get my dick this hard, but holy fucking shit, I don't think I've ever been this needy.

I lay down on my bed, fully naked, and I reach for my cock, but I see Bree shake her head.

"Don't touch. Not yet, Vince," she says as she pulls her bra strap down over her shoulder. "Eyes on me, okay?"

I nod, no longer able to speak, because this feels like some sort of fantasy come to life. I see Bree focus on my dick, her eyes widening, no doubt at my size, and it takes all my control to stay where I am.

But I'm following orders.

Her eyes lock with mine as she slowly strips her bra off, her perky tits bouncing. God, what I would give to have those rosy nipples in my mouth.

I've never been so feral over anyone before, and Bree has no idea what kind of man she has turned me into.

Bree slides her panties slowly down her body and steps out of each leg before she throws them to the side. She's now standing fully naked in front of me, looking like sin in human form.

She's fucking ethereal, the low light in my room making her look sexier than ever.

My cock jerks, and I'm practically squirming, needing her touch, needing *her*.

"Angel, you better get over here soon, or I'm gonna come just looking at you."

"Patience, Vince," she says as she crawls toward me. Bree Hart is crawling toward me, looking at my dick like she can't wait to have it in that pretty mouth of hers.

My cock flexes again, the idea of that happening making it too much for me to handle.

She ends up sitting on my stomach, and I'm about to beg her to touch me, to do anything, when I see her lick her hand. She reaches around and grabs my cock as she starts to pump, and any and all rational thoughts in my head are gone.

Her hands are soft, warm as she takes me in one hand and runs the other down my chest.

"Fuck, baby. Please don't stop."

"Is this what you need, Vince? Is this what you want from me?"

I'm about to say yes when another idea comes to my mind. "I want that sweet pussy of yours on my mouth. Can you flip over for me and sit on my face?"

"W-What? You want me to..." She trails off, a little shy as her hand moves off my dick.

"I know you're in control tonight, baby, but I need another taste of you or I might die." Dramatic, but Bree is like a drug I crave all day, every day. The first time I tasted her, I knew I had found my new favorite meal, and I'm fucking starved. "Do you trust me?"

"More than anything."

"Then get up here and sit, angel. And while I taste your sweet cunt, you can put that pretty mouth of yours around my dick and smear that lipstick."

"Okay," she says, smiling with excitement. She turns around, about to take her shoes off, when I stop her.

"Keep the heels on, baby."

She nods her head as she positions herself above my face, her mouth perfectly in line with my dick, and she surprises me by licking the head, just that little contact driving me absolutely fucking crazy.

"Bree, I said sit on my fucking face, not hover."

"I—"

"Suffocate me for all I care. I'll gladly enjoy my last seconds on Earth with my tongue buried in your pussy."

That's all it takes for her to lower herself further onto my face, one whiff of her sweet pussy enough to make my dick even harder, and just like that day on my desk, I devour her. She's already fucking soaked, and the minute she takes me to the back of her throat, I practically black out.

Her mouth feels so fucking good—warm, wet, and fucking tight as she sucks my cock, one of her hands braced out to steady her and the other wrapped around the base.

I'm not going to last long, and I don't even fucking care.

I take a long lick up her entire pussy, causing her to squirm and moan, the vibration creating an entire new sensation.

"That's it, Bree. Do you feel what you do to me? Do you like knowing that you unravel me? How does it feel knowing you brought me to my knees earlier?"

My dick pops out of her mouth, her hand still working up and down my cock as she answers. "It feels good, Vince. So fucking good."

My hands tighten around her thighs, forcing her to stay where she is so I can access her clit with my tongue. I nip at her pussy, her legs squirming before she takes me back in her mouth.

Her moans around my dick are getting me close, but what sends me over the edge is Bree cupping my balls, massaging them in her hands, and before I can stop it, I'm coming down her throat.

Stars are exploding behind my eyes as I come harder than I have in my fucking life.

"Fuck, Bree." I moan, barely decipherable to my ears as all the sounds mix together. The feel of her mouth still sucking me dry makes my dick hard again as soon as I'm done.

That's what she fucking does to me. It's the first time she's touched me, and I can't get enough. I'm ready to go again, but my girl hasn't even come yet.

That changes now.

"Flip around and grab the headboard, angel. I wanna see that gorgeous face of yours when you come all over my mouth."

She complies, her legs shaking already.

"Don't be afraid to grind your pussy on my face. Take whatever it is that you need from me."

"Vince, fuck," is all she can say when I nip her clit. I grab her ass and steady her body on my face. It fits perfectly in my hands, and I squeeze it a few times, memorizing every fucking inch of her beautiful body.

"This pussy was made for me, baby," I say as I lick, suck, and devour her. I feel her body start to shake, and I know she's about to come. "Come for me, Bree. Let everyone know who's doing this to you."

Her legs tighten around my head, and a few seconds later, I feel her coat my tongue and face as she comes. Her screams are like music to my fucking ears as I hear her nails grip the headboard, scratching hard as I silently wish she would do that to my back.

Maybe in the future...

I lick up every drop of her release, and as she slumps against the mattress, I grab her and pull her towards me. "Come here, beautiful."

She can barely speak as I grab a blanket, throw it over us, and wrap my arms around her.

"Tired?"

"Exhausted, but I feel so fucking good, Vince. So good." She slaps my chest with her palm as she kicks her heels off her feet.

I grab her face, kissing her until she's breathless, her lipstick smeared. Her face is shocked, as if I did something she wasn't expecting.

"What? You don't think we taste good together?" I smirk, winking at her through my own Bree-induced haze.

"I guess I wasn't expecting you to kiss me after I—"

"Get that thought out of your head right now, Bree." I never understood why some guys are fucking weird about that. I don't mind tasting myself on Bree's lips. I like knowing that her lips were just wrapped around my dick. "Do you want to stay here tonight or go back to your room?"

"I think I need a shower before bed, but I don't want to walk around naked with all the cameras."

The cameras. "If anyone saw you in that set you walked over here in, I'm going to have to kill them."

"Oh, shit," is all Bree says through a giggle. "I was too nervous to think about that when I walked down the hall."

"Fuck. Let me—"

"Don't bother Nico. You know if he watches it back, we'll never live it down. Plus, you shouldn't kill your best friend over something like this."

"He's not my best friend. You're my best friend," I say to her.

"I'm your girlfriend, Vince. Nico's your best friend."

"You're both to me, angel. Nico is my business partner turned acquaintance turned annoying guy who pushes all my fucking buttons."

"Exactly, and you wouldn't kill your best friend."

I grab Bree's chin and kiss her deeply before I pull back, my forehead against hers. "I'd make it look like an accident, baby."

Her legs twitch. "Does that turn you on? Knowing I'd kill someone for looking at you the wrong way?"

"No," she lies, her pink cheeks and shortness of breath giving her away.

I kiss her again, this time pushing my tongue into her mouth, and she opens for me. *Good fucking girl.* "Take one of my shirts and head to your room. Turn your shower on, touch yourself, and wait for me."

"I thought I was in control tonight."

"Don't worry, you are. I'll let you grab my hair and drag my face wherever you want it, angel. I have to solidify something with Tristan about the wedding first."

She throws her legs over my bed. "Please don't mention my brother-in-law before you bury your face in my pussy."

"Sorry. I'll make you scream my name a few more times if you do as I ask. How does that sound?"

She only kisses me, one of my shirts falling to her knees like a dress, before she saunters out of my room. When I hear her shower turn on a few seconds later, I smile to myself, knowing that tonight is just getting started.

Chapter Thirty-Three

— SHAKE IT OUT BY FLORENCE AND THE MA-CHINE

"God, I'm so nervous, I might throw up," my sister says as she paces back and forth in the West's kitchen.

"Livvy, there's nothing to be nervous about. All you have to do is go get married. It's one step! It's simple!" I say, trying to calm her nerves but knowing that nothing except seeing Tristan will probably help. I'm trying to make sure her dress doesn't get wrinkled or torn, but all her moving around is making my job impossible.

My sister looks absolutely beautiful in the dress. Her dark brown hair is curled down her back, her veil keeping her short framed locks out from her face. Her veil is almost as long as the dress, and the flower clips that trail all throughout her hair peek out just enough to where you can notice them. "Tristan is going to love the clips."

"You think so? God, I'm definitely going to throw up. Tell Teags to grab a bucket along with that water bottle." My sister continues to pace, her heels clicking across the floor.

"I have the water but no bucket," Teags says as she comes back into the room, her pale orange dress fitting snugly against every curve of her body. I don't know if I've ever seen her in so much color, and she looks absolutely stunning.

"You need to wear more color, Teags. You look fucking amazing," I tell her, and she cocks her head at me.

"Take a long and good look, because I have to wear black for the next year to combat this color. No offense, Liv."

My sister is too busy panicking to pay attention to us, and when I look down at my pale pink dress—satin, with a bowknot at the neckline—I smile to myself. I love that Liv let us pick our own dresses. There was only one rule: pale colors only.

Teags adhering to that rule goes to show how much she cares about today being perfect.

Cassie and Parker slip inside through the doors to the backyard, and when they notice my sister pacing, they shoot me a look, and I tilt my head, signaling for them.

"Liv? Everything is almost ready; are you okay?" Parker asks, and my sister doesn't stop pacing. I have no doubt that Liv would never run out on Tristan, but something has her really up in arms, and I have no idea what it could be.

"Tristan looks absolutely stunning up there, Liv. Everyone does," Cassie says, a slight shake to her voice. As Maid of Honor, I decide to step in and figure out what's going on.

"Cassie, tell them to ready the music and grab the groomsmen. Pair up and get ready to walk down the aisle. Liv and I will be right back," I say as I grab my sister's hand and drag her to the nearest bathroom so she can't escape. We get inside, and I lock the door and turn to her. "Okay, today is supposed to be only happy emotions, so why are you freaking out? I know it's not Tristan, so out with it."

Liv takes a few deep breaths as she pulls at her dress, another nervous habit. As she opens her mouth, I find myself afraid of what she could say. "What if I end up like Mom and Dad in a loveless marriage with kids who hate me and no real love in my heart? What if this ends exactly like them, Bree? What if Tristan and I turn into them years and years down the line? God, I'd rather die than have that happen."

I sigh deeply as I let my sister's fears sit in the air for a few seconds before I can get them to dissipate. "You and Tristan aren't our parents. You're afraid of nothing, Liv. That could never happen. Do you want to know how I know that's not going to happen?"

"Yes, please."

I feel tears creep into my eyes before I answer. "Because that man out there looks at you like you're the only person on the planet. You and Tristan have fought so hard to get here, Liv. You guys have been through hell and back, through some of the worst things two people can go through, and yet you made it." I grab Liv's hands in mine, staring directly into her eyes so my words sink in. "This is your finish line, Liv. This is your sunrise. One chapter of your life is ending, and with it, all the bad shit you two endured. This is the beginning of your new day, your next chapter, and I don't know two people more deserving of this than you and Tristan."

"But we could turn into them in twenty years, Bree. They were happy at one point, and then they had us and—"

I squeeze my sister's hands as I cut her off. "You're not them, Liv. You never will be." I feel a few tears fall as I start to sniffle. "Because you were the sister who made me waffles in the morning when our parents forgot to make us breakfast. You were the sister who helped me with my math homework when I didn't understand why there were letters instead of numbers."

Liv starts to laugh through her tears as I continue.

"And you were the sister who has been there for me in every way that matters. *You*, Liv. Not them. You. I know it's scary embarking on this new chapter, but with Tristan by your side, anything is possible. You two have the love you write romance novels about. I'm sure of it."

She wipes her eyes, careful not to smudge her makeup, as she nods. "You're right, Bree."

I pop my shoulder at her. "Of course I'm right," I say as I fluff her hair and check to make sure her makeup is okay. "Now, are you ready to get married to the love of your life?"

She lifts her chin high. "Hell yes, I am."

The two of us exit the bathroom, and when we see all our friends standing in the kitchen, I feel Liv's tension start to loosen beside me.

Parker, Cassie, and Teags stand by the table, all holding glasses of champagne and staring at my sister as if they know she was just crying. Theo—Teags' brother—Dom, Harry, and Ethan all stand by the snack table in their suits, looking fashionable as ever.

"Liv, I'm free tonight if you decide to run out on that idiot, just so you know." Dom smiles at her before Teags smacks him on the arm.

"She's marrying my brother, you incessant idiot."

"Livvy knows I was only joking," Dom says as he heads toward Liv. He wraps her in a hug before I hear him whisper something in her ear that I can't quite make out. I break off from Liv as all the boys head over.

"Cassie, is everything all set?"

"We're all good. Just waiting on Liv and we can start. Tristan is worried we're going to miss the sunset, but I think we timed it out perfectly," Cassie peeks out the window, and sure enough, the sun is just starting to descend. By the time their first kiss happens, the sun will be setting at the perfect time.

Liv and Tristan wanted a small wedding, so only his family, their friends and significant others, plus Vince and Nico, are here. You can't really get any smaller than this.

The one thing they requested was that they get married as the sun sets, and all of us cleared our schedules immediately to make August 29th the perfect night for a wedding.

"Alright, boys, she's going to be a married woman in an hour, so hands off," Theo jokes. "Bree, what are the pairings for the walk down the aisle?"

"Well, Harry is officiating, so he can walk down alone first. Ethan, you're with Parker. Cassie, you're with Theo. Dom, you're with Teags." I smile at the end of my sentence, and I turn to see her eyes turn murderous.

She'll thank me later. I feign innocence as I peek my head out the door and give a thumbs-up to Tabitha—Tristan's mom. Liv doesn't know this, but fairy lights decorate the entire yard, illuminating the space and creating the most beautiful environment for their small nuptials.

"Okay, one by one, you guys. When the people in front of you reach the three-quarter mark, that's your cue," I tell them as I join Liv in the back of our small line. "Can I say one more thing before this gets going?"

"Of course, Bree."

I say nothing as I lift my pinky to her and smile. "I promise you're going to live a long and beautiful life with Tristan, and this is going to be one of a thousand amazing days you'll experience the rest of your life."

She lifts her hand and locks in the promise with me. "And I promise that when you get married, I'll say the same thing to you." She pauses, willing her tears not to fall as she speaks again. "We really made it, didn't we? From our fake basement weddings to the real thing."

"We made it, Liv, and I could not be happier to walk you down the aisle toward the love of your life. So, let's go," I say as I grab her arm. Liv grabs her bouquet off of the table—a sunset mix of lilies, roses, and baby's breath—and I grab my small one before we step into the backyard.

The music changes to an instrumental version of one of Tristan and Liv's favorite songs, and all the guests rise as Liv and I make our way down the aisle. The bridesmaids and groomsmen are now in the front row, only Theo and Harry beside Tristan as he finally turns around and sees Liv for the first time.

Tears immediately fall from his eyes, and his hand goes straight to his heart, as if he felt it skip a beat. Theo pats him on the back as he offers his brother a small tissue from his pocket.

My eyes wander to Vince, and even he has a smile on his face. He throws a wink in my direction, and I throw a smile back, letting him know I'm okay.

As Liv and I reach the end of the small aisle, I give Liv's hand one last squeeze as I let her go. Tristan grabs me before I step to the side and engulfs me in a hug, wrapping both his arms around my body.

"Thank you, Bree," he whispers into my ear.

"Anything for you, bro," I say with a smile as we pull back. A smile crosses his face before he focuses back on my sister, and I swear, I see his eyes sparkle when he looks at her.

Harry says all the usual things during the ceremony, even a few jokes here and there, and after all of that, my eyes wander to Vince as we get to their vows.

"Okay, I have to go first because I know I'd never be able to follow whatever you're going to say, but I'm gonna try my best," Tristan says as he grabs some paper from Theo and unfolds it.

He clears his throat before he starts. "I've never been more thankful for a single cup of coffee in my entire life, Liv." Everyone laughs as they remember how they met. "If I knew that day that my life would change this much, I would have slowed down to really take it all in. If I had known that day that I would meet the girl who would change my life, I would've at least stopped to buy you flowers first. Liv, my entire life, all I've wanted to do is run. Run from things I was afraid of, run from this town, run from my feelings about anything and everything. But you...you were the first thing I ever wanted to run toward. You were like a magnet drawing me in that I didn't want to let go of, that I couldn't let go of, no matter how hard I tried to convince myself I should."

Liv sniffles, and I hand her a tissue from the pocket of my dress.

Tristan continues. "Olivia Hart, I know I've made some mistakes, and I'll probably make a thousand more, but I know you'll be by my side regardless. Through thick and thin, you've been there for me. You've held me through storms and some of the worst feelings I've ever had. You are the love of my life. You're my sunset, pretty girl, and there are not enough words to describe the feeling of waking up every single day to your beautiful face. I might not have words, but I'll spend every day proving to you that I love you a little more than the day before. My girl. My sunset. My Livvy. I love you so fucking much."

My tears are falling, and I notice everyone else's are, too. I think every single person here can agree that these two deserve lifetimes of happiness, and seeing them get their happy ending is way too emotional for me.

"Oh, God, I don't know how I'm going to be able to speak after that, but I'm going to try my best," Liv says with a slight laugh.

"For my entire life, I never thought anybody noticed me. But one day, this guy ran into me, spilled coffee all over me, and decided to help by giving up his hoodie. I thought growing up that I was meant to be a girl who ghosted through life with nothing to tie her down, and one day, I'd just float off into space, never to be heard from again." Liv looks up from her cards and stares at her future husband. "Until you, Tristan West."

I smile again, my cheeks already hurting, and I lock eyes with Vince in his seat again. He's smiling with his whole face, and I even see some tears on Nico's.

Vince can tell my eyes are on him, and he shifts his gaze to me, my body heating at his stare.

Maybe one day, I'll be standing across from him like that. Maybe one day, we'll get the happy ending my sister sees for me.

Maybe it has always been him and I.

Maybe.

I'm tired of that word. I want this with Vince. I want to be happy forever, and I want to go to sleep every night with him by my side, and

I'll do whatever it takes to get there with him. Nothing can stand in my way—not the media, my stalker, nothing.

"Tristan West, you are better than any fictional man I could create. I recently realized that every single male love interest I create has a piece of you in it because you make me want to live in real time, not hide away in the worlds I create. You make me feel like my voice matters, that I matter as a person and a writer. Even if I go broke, even if the world falls apart tomorrow, I'll be thankful I got to experience a fraction of the love you've given me. Never again will I feel like that lost girl begging for someone to hear her, to see her, because you fill my days with love, light, and laughter." Liv pauses to cry a bit, and Tristan reaches over to wipe tears from her face. "For however long we live, I'll always feel like I belong somewhere as long as I'm with you. I love you so much more than any love story I could create. Forever, Tristan West."

"Forever, Olivia Hart."

⚘

"Come on, angel. You owe me a dance," Vince says as he pulls me onto the makeshift dance floor. Tristan curated a playlist for tonight, and one of my favorite songs is playing as Vince and I sway to the slow beat.

Liv has barely left the dance floor, along with all of her friends, they've been dancing all night long. Nico and Teags are sitting at a table together, talking about who knows what, and I notice Tristan and Dom watching them.

Teags is still with Gregory, but she hasn't mentioned moving to Arizona since she brought it up the first time, and I have no idea what's happening with that. Is Teags leaving? Is she staying?

"Come back to me, Bree. I know you're worried about Teags, but stay in this moment with me," Vince says as his hand brushes up and down my back. He looks absolutely stunning in a light gray suit—the one Nico bought for him—with a matching tie to my pale pink dress.

"I'm sorry. I'm here, I promise." I smile at him, and his mouth lifts up at the corners. Vince presses a kiss to my temple as we continue dancing, the song almost over at this point.

When it ends, Theo steps up to the microphone. "All right, everyone gather around. I've got a few things to say."

Theo taps the microphone a few times before beginning. "Since the moment I saw Tristan and Liv, I knew my brother was going to make this girl his forever. For one, it was the first time he had brought a girl home to meet the chaos that was our family, but it was also the first time someone fully embraced the chaos that comes with being a member of the West family. We're loud, rambunctious, and not easy to deal with, but Olivia here matched our energy, even though she looked terrified the moment she walked in the door."

Theo stops on account of all of us laughing, and I smile, remembering how Liv said the same thing about their family.

Our house was always quiet, since our parents often worked rather than being with us, and when Liv was describing what it was like that Thanksgiving, I'll admit, I was a little jealous.

Now, we're here celebrating their love loudly and openly, and I understand how Liv felt that night. The West family is magic, and I'm so glad our two families have merged to create one loud, crazy family.

Theo turns to where Tristan and Liv stand. "It's been an insane year for all of us, and I'm glad you two have found your way back to one another amidst the craziness." He takes a deep breath before his eyes shift to the dark sky. "And I know we're missing a few people today, but I know Dad and Tobias are up there somewhere, smiling down on you guys and wishing you all the happiness in the world. I know they would be so proud of who you've become, Tristan." Theo's eyes shift to my sister. "And I know that Tobias loved you like a sister, Liv. My dad would be proud that Tristan managed to love someone like you. To Tristan and Liv. May your days be filled with love, light, and sunsets for the rest of time."

Cheers cry out around the party, and Tristan barrels his brother in a hug, holding him tight. Liv wipes a few tears from her eyes as she looks over at me, her eyebrow raised as I detach from Vince's hold and head to the microphone.

"I don't know how I'm supposed to follow that, but I'll make this short and sweet so we can all stop crying. I love you guys, but holy shit, it's been a long time since I've cried this much over something so joyous."

A few laughs echo around the party, and I focus my attention on my sister and her *husband*. God, that feels insane to say, but I couldn't be happier for them.

"Liv, I am so proud of the woman you've become, and I'm so thankful the two of us are here, surrounded by people who love us, celebrating this special occasion. We aren't used to this—the laughter, the love—and I'm grateful we can experience that now. You two are the definition of love, and Liv, I know you're the author here, but I don't think even *you* could write a book that captures the love you two share. We all love you so much, and I am so proud of who you've become. And Tristan, you're now officially my favorite brother."

Everyone laughs as Tristan cocks his head at me. "I'm your only brother!"

"Exactly!" I say as he wraps me in a hug, my sister following shortly after. "I love you guys."

"We love you too, Bree." My sister whispers at me before she pulls back. "Now, let's get back to the party!"

Everyone cheers, and I see Vince chatting with Harry about something as I feel another presence by my side.

"That was a wonderful speech, princess."

I look over at Nico, looking dangerous in his all-black suit, as he looks down at me. "Thanks, Nico. What were you talking to Teags about earlier?"

"Nothing I care to share. Your friend has some rather...interesting tastes in things. Her brain kind of scares me, but I wouldn't say that's a bad thing."

I turn my gaze to find Teags sipping another drink, looking tipsy as Tristan goes over to her. Their conversation looks a bit heated before Teags stomps away into the house. Tristan follows her, and so do I.

Heading through the door, I stop when I see Teags headed to get another drink.

"What's going on?" I ask, hoping one of them can answer my question.

"My sister is being an idiot," Tristan sighs. "Teags, listen to me, please—"

"No, Tristan. My decision has been made, and nothing you do or say will make me reconsider. So let it go, and we can talk about it another time. Or not, because it's my life, not yours," Teags says as she stuffs a cracker into her mouth, swaying on her feet.

"There's no way you're driving home tonight. You can either stay here with Mom or go home to that boyfriend of yours. What's it going to be, sis?"

"Tristan, I can take her home—"

"Bree, it's fine, babe. You and Vince need time together. You two just became a thing, and I don't wanna fuck that up for you." Teags moves her eyes to her brother. "I'll get home, don't worry about me. Stop trying to dictate my life, Tris. It's your goddamn wedding day; you should be with your wife, not worried about me."

"Teags, you're my sister. I'll always worry about—"

"Uhh, is everything okay out here?" Dom asks as he steps out of the bathroom, his suit jacket abandoned somewhere and his white sleeves rolled up, showcasing his arms full of tattoos. *Has he always had those?*

"Everything's fine. As a matter of fact, since you're not drinking, can you take my sister home? I know you have to leave soon anyway," Tristan asks him as Teags looks like she's about to hurl.

"Tristan, I don't need a babysitter, so stop—"

"Not another word, Teags. Just accept my help and get your ass home so I can enjoy my honeymoon and maybe, when I get back, the two of us can talk without you yelling at me." Tristan throws car keys toward Dom.

"I can always ask Nico to take her if—"

Dom cuts me off. "It's fine. I'm sober and a fantastic driver." Dom turns his head towards Teags. "Do you need me to carry you, or can you walk?"

Teags just scoffs at them before she sets her drink down and walks out the front door. "Does she have her shoes? Or her purse?" I ask, knowing the answer is probably no.

"I'll fucking find them," Dom says as he grabs his jacket and follows Teags outside. He points at Tristan before he leaves. "You owe me."

"Just make sure my sister gets home, please. And don't fucking touch her!" Tristan's plea is cut off by Dom slamming the front door, and I hear him sigh as he turns to me. "What the hell am I going to do with her?"

"She'll cool off and you guys can talk. What the hell made you so pissed in the first place?" I ask, hoping he'll tell me.

"Her choices. She's been making some impulsive ones lately, and I wanted her to actually think them through."

"That's extremely vague and not at all annoying."

"It's her life, Bree, but moving to Arizona with someone she's only known for a few months is fucking crazy." Tristan leans against one of the chairs, his head between his arms.

"So it's official?"

"Yeah."

"She told me about it like a month ago before everything got crazy, but her decision wasn't finalized. Even though I'm going to miss her like crazy, I'm trusting she knows what's best for her. And if she says Gregory makes her happy, then I believe her."

"But I don't think he does, Bree. Not only does she barely talk about the guy, but the look in her eye when she does... It doesn't feel like he's the one for her."

I put my hand on Tristan's back. He's reminding me so much of Liv right now. The two of them sometimes can't turn the parenting part of themselves off, but I know he just wants what's best for Teags. "Sometimes, you have to let someone make a decision that you know will turn out horribly before they're able to see it. Teags will learn from her own mistakes—if this one turns out to be one. Neither of us knows how this will end."

He sighs heavily before standing. "I'm just worried she's running because of Tobias. I'm worried she's going to make the exact same mistakes I did and regret it for the rest of her life."

"It's her life, Tristan. I know you'll always worry, but is Teags turning out like you really the worst thing in the world?" I chuckle.

"Yes and no, I guess," Tristan says as Vince steps into the room, my purse dangling off his shoulder.

"I've been looking for you. Are you almost ready to go? You have that brand meeting tomorrow, and I want to make sure you get some rest."

Tristan laughs when he says that, and I turn to him. "Is something funny?"

"You guys are adorable together."

"It was a nice wedding, man. I'm happy for you," Vince says as he puts his hand out to Tristan. They shake, and Tristan pulls me into a hug before he goes back outside.

Before I have a chance to say anything, Vince leans down, kneels in front of me, and takes my heels off. When he stands, he scoops me into his arms and carries me out to the car.

"Careful, Vince. A girl could get used to this," I tell him.

"You should get used to this, Bree. You deserve all of it and more." And then he opens my door for me, places me into the car, and the two of us drive home, his hand interlocked with mine the entire time.

Chapter Thirty-Four

— SOMETIMES BY ARIANA GRANDE

It's been way too quiet the past few weeks, and I've barely slept soundly knowing that any day, the other shoe could drop when we're not ready.

Bree and I have been enjoying each other's company lately, but the two of us have this nagging feeling that something is hanging over our heads. She still has nightmares, and even though they've diminished in frequency, they seem worse every time.

The other night, she shot up screaming so badly that I thought she was physically hurt. It turned out she thought Ralph killed all of us and left her to deal with the fallout.

It fucking guts me that I can't take her pain away. The one thing I know for sure is that if I see Ralph, only one of us is leaving alive, and it'll be me.

That fucker won't be breathing by the time I'm done with him.

But that's exactly why I'm currently doing what I'm doing. I wanted to show Bree that just because times are tense doesn't mean we can't have moments to ourselves.

I'm only making her dinner, but I wanted tonight to be special, so I'm also attempting to make chocolate-covered strawberries. She must have some sort of magical touch when it comes to these things because I cannot get the damn strawberries to stay on the skewers.

"Shit!" I say as another one falls into the pot of chocolate.

"Boss? Is everything okay?" Emerson asks me as he floats into the room.

"How the fuck does she make this look so easy?"

He only furrows his brows at me. "Uhh..."

"I'm trying to make Bree's favorite dessert, but I can't fucking figure it out."

Emerson walks over to the kitchen island and leans against it. "Do you need some help?"

"Yes, but wash your hands first." I point at the sink with a skewer, and he heads over.

A few seconds later, the two of us are at work, Emerson is dipping strawberries, and I'm stirring pasta. It pisses me off that *he* is able to get them to stay on and not me. Is it because of how big my hands are? All I wanted to do was make something for Bree to cheer her up, and I couldn't even do that without needing help.

Emerson and I work in silence for a few minutes until I hear Bree descend the stairs, and everything isn't set up yet. *Shit.*

Her blonde hair is the first thing I see. When I notice what she's wearing—a black minidress, matching heels, and a big ass bow in her hair—my heart stops beating. "Hey guys! Something smelled good, so I hung up with Liv early. Can I help?"

Without taking my eyes off the girl who is somehow mine, I speak. "Emerson, get out."

The second I hear the door shut, I rush her.

"You look absolutely beautiful, but I told you we were just doing a night in."

"Liv told me to wear something cute, so I threw an outfit together. It only took like fifteen minutes, and I'm wearing your favorite color…" She trails off, her face turning pink.

I press a kiss to her lips. "I've already told you that my favorite color is the pink of your cheeks when I make you blush. And you wear that rather beautifully, too." I pull one of the kitchen chairs out for her and motion for her to sit down. "I'm almost done. Just sit and relax while I plate this stuff."

"Are you sure you don't need—" Bree tries to get up, but I stop her.

"Angel, I've got it. Just relax, okay?" She nods, and I can't help what slips out. "Good girl."

I can almost hear her cheeks flush as I turn to stir the pasta. A few minutes later, Bree turns on some music, and it plays softly in the background as I strain the food. I plate it, not beautifully, but when I sit down next to Bree, her smile lights up the entire room.

Making Bree Hart smile is one of my favorite things to do. Since I've known her, all she's done is retreat inside her head. Being able to see that fucking smile means she's out of her head and living in the moment.

"Thank you," she says as I pour her some water. "This looks great."

"It's one of the only things I know how to make. Aria used to make it all the time." I smile at the memories of Aria trying to help me study while she almost burned the house down.

"You don't have to answer if you don't want to, but what was it like when you were younger? I feel like you never really talk about your childhood."

"Well, it was a long time ago. I am thirty-four years old, so I guess it feels like forever ago at this point."

Bree tucks a loose strand of hair behind her ear. "It's okay, Vince, I—"

"No, baby, it's fine. I don't mind," I tell her as I grab her hand resting on the table. "I had a good childhood. My family was like any other normal family, I guess. My parents worked for a non-profit together, and they loved making a difference in our community."

"That's nice." Bree smiles at me. "Where did you grow up?"

"Seattle. Really rainy place, and I don't regret leaving, because I'm not the biggest fan of the rain. Aria still lives there, so I go visit her every so often."

"I love the rain. It's perfect reading weather." Bree smiles at me as I take a bite of the pasta. It tastes just how I remember it, and I love the way that so many different things can hold memories for a person.

"You know, you've never actually told me what your favorite book is. I've seen you reading a million things over the years, but I never knew which was your favorite."

"It's a hard question, Vince." She pauses to take a bite and practically moans into her fork. I have to bite my lip, because I didn't do this just to have us end up in bed together.

When it comes to anything physical, Bree has all the power, and even that makes my dick hard. I like watching her take control and beg me for what she wants—what she needs.

"This is so good. It's been a long time since someone other than Liv and Tristan have cooked for me."

"Don't expect it too often. I'm not the best chef, but I can follow a recipe. Though Emerson did have to help me with the strawberries and chocolate."

"So that's why he was here earlier. You couldn't figure out the skewers, could you?" Bree smirks, noting my struggles before I even voiced them.

"No, and I think you have magical powers because you make it look easy."

"You can't stab a simple strawberry, Vince? My big, strong boyfriend can't stab a fruit with a skewer?" Bree is full on laughing in her chair, and I'm almost afraid she's going to fall out of it.

"Yeah, yeah, laugh it out. You've officially found something I can't do."

"I'm totally going to call TMZ or something. This will be on the front page by tomorrow."

I roll my eyes at her, and for the rest of the dinner, the two of us trade stories back and forth. It's nice—being able to let go and just be myself. I don't have to always be on around Bree, and I can turn the bodyguard part of myself off when it's just us.

I'm still a protective son of a bitch, but the only thing I care about is making her happy. I want all her smiles, all her laughs, and every shy smile when she thinks I don't notice she's turned on.

She was practically moaning around her fork all through dinner. Every time she'd do it, she would look for my reaction, which is how I knew she was turned on.

"You know, you still haven't told me your favorite book," I say as I take our plates to the sink, and Bree trails behind me. I start washing, and Bree has a towel, so when I hand her the plate, she dries.

It's so normal, and I know she's appreciating every second of tonight because she doesn't get a lot of these moments in her life. And it's my job to make sure that, despite everything going on, she's still able to remember she can be a normal girl sometimes, not just a social media personality.

"If I had to pick, it would be an entire series. It's got one of the best fictional families ever, and I could reread the second book for the rest of my life and never get tired of it."

"So, found family is your favorite trope?"

Her eyebrows shoot to her hairline. "Yes, but how did you know that?"

"You and Teags get forty octaves higher when you talk about the books you've read. I heard you guys one day when I was in my office."

Bree only giggles. "Ah, that makes sense."

We spend a few more minutes cleaning up, and when we're done, I pull the strawberries and chocolate out for her. "I have a surprise for you."

"Vince, I hate surprises, and the dinner was enough of a treat." Bree plays with part of the bow that hangs from her hair before I set a small black box in front of her.

"Open it, angel."

"Vince—"

"Bree," I say as I open it for her. I don't know why this girl is so weird about accepting gifts, but once she sees what it is, her mouth drops open.

"Touch bracelets?"

"You've seen them before?"

"Yeah, just online, but why did you get me these?"

"It's technically for both of us. Now we have matching bracelets," I tell her as I slip it onto her wrist. "I figured we could use them in public. It kills me sometimes that I can't grab you and kiss you, but I can send you a message through this so you know I'm thinking about you."

Her eyes get a bit misty. "This is perfect, Vince. I'm sorry I can't parade you around in public, but as—"

I stop her unnecessary apology with a kiss. "Angel, I don't need the entire world to know about us. The only thing that matters is that we know it and the people who love us know it, okay? We could be a secret forever, and I'd still be the luckiest man on the entire fucking planet."

"I'd never keep you a secret for that long. Once this is all over, you'll be annoyed with how many pictures I take of us." She grabs my face and kisses me again, only this time, she slips her tongue into my mouth, and I wrap my arms around her so I can pull her closer.

"Bree, we still have dessert," I tell her as I pull away.

"I want a different dessert right now," she tells me as she hops onto the counter, pushing the bowl of strawberries and chocolate away. "I want you, Vince. *All* of you."

Is she saying what I think she is? "You do?"

"Yes," she says as she lifts her dress up. "I thought it was obvious when I came down here with no underwear on."

Jesus fucking Christ. I have to stop my mouth from watering as I look at her bare pussy underneath her dress. "Well, I need my dessert first, don't I?"

"Wh—" is all she can say before I hike her dress up and lick her entire pussy in one swipe. God, I could do this all fucking day. The sweet taste of her makes my dick twitch against my jeans, and as she lays against the counter, I grab her thighs and move her towards my face.

"You walked down here like this? You're a bad fucking girl, Bree," I say as I snake two of my fingers up to her mouth. "Suck. Get them nice and wet for me, baby."

I only hear a strangled moan, but she does what I ask like the good girl she is. My fingers are slick when I take them back, and then I push both of them into her pussy while my mouth works her clit.

"Fuck! Vince," is all she can say before her moans and pants take over.

My tongue is lapping at her clit, my fingers thrusting in and out of her, and I don't let up until she comes all over my hand. I lick my fingers clean, still craving the taste of her even though my face was just buried in her sweet cunt.

Bree's orgasm haze diminishes after a few seconds, and even on her shaky legs, she hops off the counter and gets on her knees.

Oh, fuck. "My turn," she says as she reaches for the buttons of my jeans. Before she does it right here, I pick her up off the floor and throw her over my shoulder. I don't bother to pull her dress down, but when she starts to complain, I smack her ass.

Hard.

Her squirming on my shoulder and pressing her legs together lets me know she liked it, so I do it again.

"If you're going to get on your knees for me, I want you on your knees in my bed, where nobody can walk in on us."

"But—" I shut her up with a hard smack to her ass.

"And if I'm fucking you for the first time, I want it to be in a soft bed so you're comfortable."

"Aww, that's nice," is all she says behind my back.

"Trust me, angel, there's nothing nice about what we're about to do."

Chapter Thirty-Five

— SLOW DOWN BY CHASE ATLANTIC

I CARRY BREE INTO my room before I throw her on my bed, her dress still hiked up above her hips. I drink her in as she sits on her elbows, cheeks flushed, thighs glistening with arousal, her eyes hooded as she looks up at me.

My beautiful fucking angel. My beautiful Bree.

Ever since I tasted her, I've been craving the feeling of her unraveling around my dick. I know that once I feel her tight pussy wrapped around me, I'll be ruined.

And I'm perfectly okay with that.

"Vince, take your pants off," she orders as she crawls over to where I stand at the edge of my bed. "I want to feel you, baby."

I grab her chin in my hand. She's in control, but that's not going to stop me from bossing her around. "Unbutton my jeans and take my dick out."

Her cheeks flush harder as she does what I tell her. Her hands take their sweet time pushing my jeans and boxers down, and as I step out of them, I'm caught off guard by her mouth wrapping around the head of my dick.

"Fuck, baby."

Her mouth takes me deeper, and the only sounds I hear are the ones she's making as she groans around my dick. *Fuck,* I have to stop myself from coming down her throat.

"That's it," I coax her as she takes me entirely—all nine inches. "You look so beautiful with my dick down your throat, angel."

Her eyes all but roll to the back of her head, and when she cups my balls, I have to pull out.

This girl fucking unravels me, and before we take the last step, I want to double-check. "Are you sure about this?"

"Yes," she breathes. "I'm not going to break, Vince. I don't want you holding back. I'll be fine. I'm aching for you, so hurry the fuck up."

"Whatever you need, baby," I say, kissing her fiercely until she moans in my mouth. "How do you want to take it?"

She only groans in response. "I don't fucking care, Vince. Fuck me like I'm famous."

I stifle a twin groan. "Get on those pretty knees of yours and face the mirror."

She complies immediately, ass in the air as she looks at me through the mirror. I'm glad I didn't move it, because this view is one of the hottest things I've ever seen.

I stroke myself a few times before I lean down to her ear. "Do you remember your safe word?"

She nods into my bed.

"Good. Use it any time and I'll stop immediately, okay?" I say in a soft tone, and she nods again. I grab a condom from my side table and roll it on before I lock eyes with her in the mirror and thrust into her tight pussy in one, punishing stroke. It doesn't take much; her pretty pussy has been dripping for me.

"Oh fuck," I hear her moan into my sheets.

"Christ, angel, you're so fucking tight."

"I feel so full, Vince. God, you feel so good. I need you to move."

"You haven't taken all of me yet. Just relax and let me make you feel good, baby." I slowly thrust in and out of her, letting her adjust to my size before I lose my control. It's so fucking hard to think of anything but the girl in front of me, and I'm slowly losing every single shred of my sanity.

I'm fucking ruined. Bree's never taking another dick again. Her pussy was made for me, and so was she.

"Faster, Vince, please. I'm not going to break, I promise," she moans as I continue my same pace.

"I'm not doing this for you, baby. If I go faster, I'm going to lose control."

"Lost control then. Please, I *need* you to go faster, harder, anything," she begs, and that one word unravels me before she says it again. "Please?"

My control snaps, and then I'm ramming in and out of her pussy, her moans and pants buried in my sheets. I'm worried I'm going to split her in half, but her legs wrap around me as she pulls me even deeper than before.

All I see is red as I feel her pussy tighten around me. She's strangling my dick; I should've known that sweet Bree likes to be fucked like I hate her. Her pussy clenches when I praise her and when I degrade her, which makes no goddamn sense.

But I don't really care, right now.

I grip her hip as I slam into her, her face still buried in my sheets. I can't have her missing the beautiful picture in front of me, so I grab her lightly by the back of the neck and lift her head.

"Do you see us, angel? Do you see how good we look like this?"

I feel her nod as I continue thrusting into her. "Vince..."

"What would the world say if they saw sweet, innocent Bree watching herself get fucked in front of the mirror?" I ask, my hand moving toward her clit.

"Don't stop, Vince."

"I won't, baby. I'll give you what you need, don't worry," I say as my finger circles her clit. Her legs are starting to shake, but I want this to last a little longer, so I slow down. "But you need to be punished for walking around without underwear."

"What? Vi—" I slap her ass before I lean down to her ear.

"Has anyone ever touched you here?" I ask as my finger circles her ass.

"N-No. Nobody," Bree pants as I slowly fuck her, the pace torturous.

"Do you want me to play with your ass, Bree?"

"One finger," she states. "I'll try anything once."

"Good fucking girl," I say as her pussy tightens around me. I take my dick out, wet my finger with her arousal, and thrust back inside of her. Her knees give out a bit, so I use my left arm to steady her. "Let me play with your ass while I fuck you, okay?"

She nods, and I pick up my pace before I slowly circle her ass with my finger. I press in only a little at first, and I hear her moan as I get knuckle-deep. I thrust in and out of her pussy while I continue to fuck her ass with my finger.

"Oh God, Vince," she all but screams as her legs start to shake and her orgasm takes over. I feel her pussy clenching around my cock, and my own follows, still feeling her spasming around my cock.

"Fuck, Bree, you feel so fucking good," I say as I thrust through my release, her moans still indecipherable as her body goes limp under mine.

After I regain my composure, I dispose of the condom and return with a warm towel so I can clean Bree up. She came all over my sheets, but I can't find it in me to care.

That was the best sex of my life—not just because it was good sex, but because it was with Bree. Sex with her feels so much different than all the meaningless flings I had while on the road for my job, and I know it's because I was meant to be here with her all along.

I clean Bree up, and she's fast asleep as I carry her to the shower. We smell like sex, and I know Bree would hate to wake up tomorrow naked and unclean. The girl hates going to sleep without showering, and she might hate me when I wake her up, but she'll thank me tomorrow.

"Baby? Wake up. We're gonna shower, okay?"

She only grumbles in response. "I can't feel my fucking legs."

"Then I did my job. How are you feeling?" I ask her as I place her on my counter.

"I feel fantastic. How do you feel?"

"The same. I hope you know that your pussy is mine now." I lean into her, pressing a kiss beneath her ear. "And your ass too. That's fucking mine."

She shivers where she sits on the counter, and her eyes lock with mine, heat still blaring in her gaze. *Is she still turned on?* "I'm yours, Vince. I told you that from the start."

"Good, baby. Now, let me fuck you in the shower."

"It's like you read my mind." She smiles before I carry her into the shower. The two of us spend all night getting lost in one another's bodies before we eventually fall asleep, tangled up in one another like we were always meant to.

Chapter Thirty-Six

**— WOULD'VE, COULD'VE, SHOULD'VE BY TAY-
LOR SWIFT**

I'M COUNTING DOWN THE minutes until I can leave this show.

Don't get me wrong, I adore fashion, but all I can think about is going home with Vince, watching a movie, and cuddling on the couch.

I've officially become someone who would rather stay in with my boyfriend than be working on a Saturday night. Plus, it's September; Tristan's birthday is coming up, and I don't have a clue what to get him.

What do you get a guy who has everything he already wants?

The designer comes out, signaling the end of the show, and everyone stands, applauding her work. I did see a couple pieces I have my eye on, and this show felt more like art than it did clothes.

I lock eyes with Vince, his gaze already on me as I tilt my head toward the exit. His hand goes to his ear, probably letting Emerson, Chris, and Duncan know we're leaving as soon as this is over. There's some sort of exhibition dinner after the runway, but Connie told me all I had to do was make an appearance tonight. I haven't been going to many events, and since this was one close to home—about an hour away—Connie said a small appearance would work.

Since the break-up hit the internet, people haven't seen me, so the speculations were crazy. Some people thought I cut my hair and changed my whole look, some said I was heartbroken, some thought I had moved on a few times since.

And those people weren't wrong. Vince and I have moved on quite a few times since Alex has been out of the picture, and all of it has been on my terms.

I stand up from my front-row seat and saunter over to him.

"Ready?" he asks as his hand slides to my back.

I smile at him. "Yeah, let's go."

Vince steps in front of me, and I feel Emerson and Chris flank me from behind. Duncan is most likely outside with the cars, and I'm counting down the steps until I'm safely inside.

Ralph hasn't said a single word lately. No notes, no texts, nothing. And although Vince has been trying to distract me for weeks, my mind still races every time I leave the house.

As we leave, a few people try to stop us for interviews, and I can hear people whispering about me and Alex, even though they think they're being quiet. I sigh heavily before Vince stops and throws his arm out behind me.

"Is something wrong?" I ask, but before he can answer, I spot a familiar face up ahead, her gaze locked on me.

Ellie.

Her heels click over to where I stand, Vince's body still covering mine, but I tap his arm, signaling for him to move out of the way.

"Are you sure?" he asks me.

"It's fine. It was bound to happen sooner or later," I say as she comes into my personal space. I'm unsure if she's going to hug me, slap me, or something else. I have no idea what she's thinking, and if she came over here to apologize, I won't be accepting it. What she did was inexcusable, and for what? A few clicks on a post? A few stories about her online? A chance to steal my fake boyfriend from me when he wasn't mine in the first place?

She, like my parents, had no right to do what she did. I don't even know how she found out about it, but I couldn't care less.

She flips her hair behind her shoulder as she looks me up and down. "It's nice to see you out of the house, Bree. You look good tonight."

I glance down at my outfit—an oversized suit jacket belted at the waist, thigh-high black boots, and a tan bow that drapes down my back. I dressed myself tonight, and I look good, but her tone says otherwise. God, I hate all this petty shit.

"Can you just say what you came over here for and let me get on with my night, please?"

She smirks and rolls her eyes at me. "It's nice to see all this hasn't dampened that tongue of yours, Hart. I thought playing the victim for so long would make you forget who you used to be."

Playing the victim. "I feel bad for you, Ellie. Having to tear others down to get anyone to pay attention to you; it's sad, really. Tell me, did you really like Alex, or did you just like what he did for you in the media?"

She only scoffs for an answer, and I notice some cameras have made their way to watch our interaction, but I'm not giving them more fuel.

"I bet you were asking for it, Bree. I bet you secretly liked it. What were you wearing to entice that guy so much?"

"Pajamas. In my own fucking house." It's always so interesting how everyone—including the media—seems to blame the victims. In no world is anyone ever asking to be assaulted. It makes no goddamn sense. Can't we start blaming the people who touch others without their consent? Why does nobody ever ask what they were wearing? Why does nobody ever ask why they didn't stop when the other person said no?

I step closer to her so only she can hear me. "I'm not playing anything. I didn't entice him, and I sure as hell don't need to explain the worst night of my life to someone who decided to blame me and not the person who attacked me in my own home. I'm a goddamn survivor, and I spend every day trying to heal myself. The last thing I'm worried about is you. Now, if you'll excuse me, I'm heading home."

I step around her, cameras flashing as they watch me walk away, but I can't find Vince. I look around as Emerson steps in front of me, Chris behind me. "Guys, where's Vince?"

"The boss had to take a phone call from Nico. He said it was important, but we'll get you to the car. Vince is meeting us there."

I nod at Emerson, but Vince not being around has me more on edge than I'd care to admit. What is Nico telling him? Did they catch Ralph? Is my sister okay?

Way too many scenarios play in my mind, and as I slide into the car, my emotions overwhelm me. I don't know if it's the cameras, the flashing lights, the conversation with Ellie, or Vince being gone, but this car suddenly has no air.

> **Bree: Liv, please answer. Is everything okay?**

> **Liv: I'm here, Bree. Do you want me to call you?**

> **Bree: No. Has anything hit the news tonight? About me?**

> **Liv: One second.**

It feels like an hour before she answers.

Liv: I don't see anything new. What's going on?

Bree: Vince is on the phone with Nico, but I don't know what's going on.

Liv: Where are you?

Bree: A show. About an hour from home.

Liv: Do you want me to bring over some dessert? I can have it ready in no time.

I smile at my phone; Liv's answer for everything is always dessert.

Bree: Sure, Liv. I'll let Vince know when he gets back.

Liv: See you soon.

My nerves have dissipated slightly, and when Vince finally gets into the car, a scowl on his face, my stomach drops. It's not good news. It wasn't a social call from Nico.

He meets my eyes in the rearview, and his entire face changes. His eyes soften, but I can still see underneath the mask.

"What happened?"

He looks down before he answers. "Nico called. Someone gassed all my guys outside your house and broke in."

Someone. No, not just someone. "You mean Ralph?"

"Yeah, angel, I do." His voice deepens, and I can feel the anger rolling off him in waves.

"How are your guys?"

He runs a hand down his face, clearly stressed, and I'd give anything to be able to take a fraction of that away. The guys who work for him are like family, and I know he feels responsible for them. "They're all awake, just disoriented."

"Are they okay? I'll pay for anything they need, medical care, anything."

"Bree, you don't have to."

"Vince, I will," I say as I grab his bicep. "It's not your fault. They knew what they signed up for, right?"

The tension in his shoulders lessens, but I know the weight is still there. "I know, but—"

"No buts, Vince. They're fine. They're alive. Ralph could've killed them, but he didn't. Is Nico meeting us at home?"

"Yes. He's pissed that he didn't catch someone being in the house until after my guys were hurt. He thinks Ralph looped the security footage to make it seem normal, and he's angry he didn't catch it in time."

"Then what are we waiting for? Let's get the hell home," I tell him, and he starts the car, Emerson barely in the passenger seat before Vince speeds off toward my house.

⚘

VINCE SPEEDS INTO MY driveway, parking the car in an instant alongside a few others.

"Nico's here already," Vince tells me as he opens my door, Emerson joining him.

I'm already on edge, but seeing Vince's men being treated outside my house is unsettling me even more.

"Thanks," I say as I get out. Before I can say anything more, Liv and Tristan rush towards me.

"Vince, Nico wants to talk to you," Liv tells him before she turns to me. "You're staying out here."

"Why?" I ask, noting my sister's face full of concern. "Livvy, what's going on? What did you see?"

"Nothing that you should see, Bree." Tristan tells me as he and Vince trade a look.

Vince tilts his head at Tristan, and the two of them head inside, Tristan's hand on Vince's bicep as he whispers something to him. I can't see his face, but the way his back just tensed up means that whatever Tristan told him wasn't good.

"Please tell me what's going on, Liv. I need to speak to Vince's men and see how they are. I really don't have time—" A loud noise from inside my house causes me to jump, and before Liv can stop me, I rush inside.

What I see when I enter stops me in my tracks.

My house is covered with pictures.

Pictures of me.

Grocery shopping, getting into my car, at different events over the past few months, at my own event. The most frightening one of all is the one of me crying over Vince passed out on the concrete.

Oh my God. They're *everywhere*. Literally. Pictures are taped up and down the walls all around me—the kitchen, the staircase, Vince's office, and I bet there are even some in my room.

"Bree..." I hear Liv's comforting tone behind me, but all I can focus on is the state of my house.

"Where's Vince?"

"Up here!" Tristan yells from upstairs.

"Bree, don't come up here!" Vince yells back.

I rush up, trying not to look at any of the pictures surrounding me, but when I get into my room, my once safe space, my sanctuary, I freeze.

Because all I can see taped up around my room are pictures of me from the worst night of my life. The night Ralph took everything from me. The night that haunts me every moment of every day.

He took pictures? I don't remember a camera, but maybe it's something I blocked out. In some, tears are streaming down my face. In others I'm simply laying against my bed with a fearful look in my eyes.

I can't breathe. Images of that night are rushing back into my head, flooding my memories with things I've tried to heal from. Ralph has set me back months in recovery because of these reminders, and my legs turn to jelly before I sink to the floor.

But Vince, Liv, and Tristan catch me before I drown.

"I-I can't do this anymore."

There will never be a time I'll be able to forget that night, and thanks to Ralph—who took pictures of me crying, of me begging him to leave me alone, of me frozen on the ground—these pictures will always be somewhere. They could eventually get onto the internet, and people will not only know what happened to me, but they'll be able to see the evidence of it.

I was only twenty years old in these pictures. Twenty. I was practically a kid when my safety was taken away from me, when my sanity was ripped out from underneath me.

I was only twenty when my life was taken out of my own hands.

Even though I'm a few years older, the pain still hurts. The memories cut into my head like knives, and I miss who I used to be before. I was so naive to think I had any control over my own life back then, and I was an idiot to think that just because Ralph was in prison, he could never hurt me again.

Every memory haunts me while I sleep, and even though the pain might get better over time, it will never leave me. How could it? How could I simply forget about the worst night of my life?

That's the one thing I hate about my mind: I can't remember the good days I had as a kid, and pieces of my life are so blurry that I don't know if they're real or if I made them up.

But the worst night of my life will stay with me forever. I can remember the temperature outside that day, everything leading up to that night burned into my memory. I remember exactly what pajamas I was wearing, exactly what book I was reading that I can no longer look at on my shelf. It was merely sitting on my bed as I doodled on my iPad, but I still can't look at it.

I'm falling. I'm falling so hard into my mind that I might not come out after this.

I feel safe here in my head. Please don't make me come back out. I'll get hurt. Or worse, I'll get killed by my stalker, and he'll win. He'll win this sick game he's playing with me. Please don't let him win. Please don't have my sister watch as I get lowered into the ground if he succeeds.

I can't do that to her because then she'll be alone. She'll be the only Hart sister to exist if that happened, and I don't know if Tristan could save her.

"Angel, look at me," Vince says, his hands around my face as tears fall. I move my blurry gaze to his, and his thumbs caress my cheeks. "Focus on me, okay? You're strong. I'm going to find him, and I'm going to fucking kill him for what he's doing to you."

"Vince, I-I can't do this anymore. Please just let me drown."

"Not a chance, baby. You've got all of us around you, and none of us are letting you sink. Let us carry you, Bree. Let us help." Vince is begging me, his voice strained as he tries to help.

"You'll get hurt. Everybody around me always gets hurt," I say through my sobs.

"We're all willing to take that chance, Bree. You're not doing any of this alone anymore," Vince tells me, and I hear Tristan and Liv agree behind me.

"We'll take care of each other, Bree, just like we always have," my sister says as she kneels next to me on the floor. "You just have to let us."

They're sitting at the table with me. "Okay," I whisper.

"Ralph might've taken a lot from you, but he'll never take us away, Bree. We're fucking here for you, no matter what," Tristan says.

You can't promise that, I think to myself. Ralph has escalated, and I'm scared to think about what else he's capable of. He has people helping him, which makes him even more dangerous.

"Let's go downstairs. Nico's taking pictures of everything, and he got this room already," Tristan says, motioning us out of my room.

"One second," I say. Before I leave my room, I stand in front of my bookshelves lined with pictures from the worst night of my life, and I rip every single one to the ground. "Okay, I'm ready."

Chapter Thirty-Seven

— ICE CREAM MAN BY RAYE

It has officially become a party in my house as we all congregate in my living room.

All the pictures have been taken down and stored where I can't see them, thanks to Nico and the work of his people.

Liv hasn't left my side as we sit on the couch, her rubbing circles on my back to comfort me. Tristan is standing with Nico and Vince, no doubt trying to pretend he has any sway in the decisions to be made about my security. He'll try his best, though, citing that as my only brother, he knows what's best for me.

He's too sweet.

Teags has been silently brewing across from Liv and I on the floor. She has barely said a word, and I can practically feel the anger rolling off her. I'm not sure what she's angry at—Ralph, the situation, Tristan, or all of it.

Until Ralph is arrested again, I'll never be safe. The people around me will never be safe.

This is all my fault. I know that, earlier, I told Vince it wasn't his fault, and I stand by that. It's *my* fault. The reason they're all here is because of me.

"How the fuck didn't you catch that? Your entire job is security, Nico!"

"I caught it, just not immediately. It was sophisticated, Vince. I'd try to explain it to you, but you're too irrational right now," Nico argues back with him. I hate seeing us like this. It's way too tense in here, and everyone is going to start blowing up at one another soon if we don't think of a plan.

"I'm not fucking irrational. I'm pissed! My guys are all being treated because they were *gassed* by this fucker, and you're telling me you have no idea how he was able to hack your system and loop the feed?"

Nico runs a hand through his hair before he fixes his suit. "I'm *working* on it. It's going to take a bit because we're also reinforcing our fucking firewalls. You have every right to be pissed at me, but take a fucking breath."

"Don't fucking say that to me. What the hell are you going to do about Bree's security? I'm down half my men."

"I'm fixing it, Vince. More than one person will watch the cameras for anything suspicious, and I've called in more men for you while the others rest and heal."

"That's not fucking good enough!" Vince yells, and the entire room goes quiet. "Bree doesn't feel safe, and my job is to make sure she is, so we need to figure out a fucking plan!"

"You're not the only one who cares about her, Vince. This entire room is full of people dedicated to keeping her safe!" Nico shouts back at him. "We can do that if you stop fucking yelling!"

"I say let him yell. Vince has spent too long being broody and uptight. This is probably helping," Teags says, her gaze moving to Tristan. "Sometimes, you just need to yell out your feelings."

"Teags, don't. We're focused on Bree right now, not the fact that you're throwing your life away for some boy you barely fucking know."

"Did you hear that?" Teags says as she gets in her brother's face. "You said *my* life, so *you* should stop fucking worrying about it so much."

"Teags—" Liv says, only to be cut off by Vince.

"Can you guys chill out with the family squabble, right now? We have bigger things to worry about."

"Guys—" I say, and the four of them—Nico, Vince, Teags, and Tristan—start arguing in circles with one another. God, this is a mess. Nothing is going to get solved if we don't stop yelling at one another.

This is exactly what he wants. He wants everyone I love to turn on one another so when he comes for me, we'll be disorganized.

"Enough!" I yell as I stand up, and the four of them quiet down as my anger comes back in full force. "All of you need to sit down and listen to me, because I'm done being a bystander in my own life while you make choices for me." I wait for them to sit before starting again. "I'm not going to a hotel, and I'm not leaving my house."

The five of them raise their arms to interrupt me, but I shoot them all a look.

"This is my fucking life. I feel safest in my own home, the one I bought with my own fucking money and that you two," I look to Vince and Nico, "know how to guard best."

"But—"

I cut Vince off. "No. There are cameras here, a state-of-the-art security system, and men all over the place. Plus, you practically live in my bedroom, so if anyone was to get past *all* of that, they wouldn't get past you. Isn't that what you said to me the first night you came back, Vince?"

He nods at me, a glint in his eyes. I can't tell if it's pride or something different. "I did say that."

"Exactly. It's my fucking decision, and I'm staying here." I look over at Nico. "It's not your fault. Ralph's gotten smarter since he got out. None of us could have seen this coming, and the only person to blame is the person who has been fucking up my life for five years."

"Exactly," Liv agrees, her face shining with delight that I'm finally speaking up for myself and my safety.

"I won't leave my goddamn house for months if that's what it takes for Ralph to finally come out of hiding. I trust you guys to keep me safe, and you have, but I feel safest in this house. If he wants to come for me, he'll come to our fucking turf."

"You're saying you'll have the advantage if he comes back?" Nico questions, and I nod.

"It's my house. He might've cased the last one, but he doesn't know about all the panic buttons or all the other security measures you two psychos installed."

"She's right, Vincey." Nico jabs him in the arm, only for Vince to glare back at him.

"And Bree," Teags says as she gets off of the floor. "Rule number fucking eight."

I cock my head at her, confused as to why she's bringing this up now. "What about it?"

"If you need help from any of us, ask. Stop running when all we want to do is help you."

I grab my best friend's hand and squeeze it. "I will. I promise."

"Wait a second, that's it." Vince turns to Nico. "He had pictures from when I was hurt of you and Bree around my body."

"And?" Nico asks.

"Rule number ten," Vince states, a glimmer in his eyes.

"Always watch the watchers," Nico and I say at the same time.

"You think he's been watching you guys this entire time? The whole world knows what he looks like; that wouldn't make sense," Tristan says.

"He could have some sort of disguise, or maybe he dyed his hair. Regardless, there's enough pictures that we might be able to find him," Nico says as he pushes off the wall. "I can try to find similar faces in the crowds. I can work with that," he says as he dials someone on his phone as he leaves the room.

Vince heads towards me. "I'm sorry for all the yelling."

"It's okay. It's been a long and overwhelming day," I tell him as I press a kiss to his lips. "I'm okay, Vince. I bounce back quicker these days."

"You're so fucking strong, Bree. I'm so proud of you."

"So are we. You'll be sleeping alone tonight, Vince, because Liv and I are staying the night. Tristan too, but the girls will be in Bree's room. You two can cuddle in bed or on the couch in your room if you want." Teags smiles at Vince as she pulls me away, and the three of us head up to my room to prepare for an impromptu girls night.

"You can take one of the other guest rooms," I hear Vince say to Tristan.

"I won't steal your couch, dude, I promise," Tristan laughs back, and if I didn't already suspect it, I think they might be becoming friends.

Chapter Thirty-Eight

— FROM EDEN BY HOZIER

WAKING UP ON MY desk for the third night in a row is starting to give me a headache.

I don't mean to keep dozing off down here, but I can't—no, won't—stop until I can find Ralph and end this fucking cat-and-mouse game once and for all.

I need to find him before he hurts the one person in the world I don't want to live without. I thought eventually, as we dated, the feeling would fade, but somehow, I wake up every day wanting her more than the last.

Not just physically, but emotionally. Bree Hart has cemented herself on my soul. She's part of me now, and there's nothing that would make me stop wanting her—stop needing her.

For the past few days, while Bree is stuck inside her house, I've been working myself to death to try and figure out where this fucker is. Nico and I have found some similar faces in photos, but none have been Ralph.

I check my clock and see that it's now two in the morning.

Fuck. I was supposed to head back up to Bree at midnight. Liv and Teags are sleeping in the guest rooms, and Tristan has taken over my old room since I've moved into Bree's.

The three of them have been staying over more and more lately. I don't mind their presence, but I know Bree is nervous. I know she loves having them all around, but I can see the fear on her face when they offer to stay another night.

She's the one in danger, yet she's still worried about everyone else but herself.

I run my hand down my face, exhausted, as I stand from my desk and drag my feet to Bree's room. I can't wait to pull her body to mine and hold her until the morning comes. Falling asleep next to her never gets old, and waking up to her beautiful, shining face every morning has filled whatever weird hole I had in my body from all the years I spent alone.

Now, this house is filled with more people than just us.

And I don't hate it. It's nice having some extra noise around. It reminds me of when I was growing up. My parents and sister always had music on, always chatting about something, and my house was filled with noise.

Then, my parents passed, and everything was quiet. The absence of noise created an even bigger absence without my parents. It's like their bodies were the soul of our house, their love so loud that it filled the room. Aria and I used to creep down the stairs after they put us to bed to watch them dancing in the kitchen.

There was no doubt in my mind that they loved one another, and instead of chasing the kind of love they had, I ran away from it.

I seeped further and further into the quiet because after their deaths, it was all I knew. It became my new normal.

But Bree has brought that noise back, and someday, I'll tell her how thankful I am to be in a house full of music, laughter, and chatter.

I softly open the door to our room, and as I take my shirt off and crawl into bed, I don't feel Bree's warm body. Instead, the bed feels cold, as if she hasn't been here for a while.

Where could she have gone? I assumed if she was roaming around that house, she would stop in my office and force me back upstairs, but that didn't happen.

My mind races as thoughts of the worst scenario fill my head. Nico would've texted me if one of the panic buttons was pressed, and the alarms would have gone off, so I try to calm my mind, but it doesn't work.

Where the fuck is my beautiful girlfriend?

I check the bathroom and her closet, and she's not in either having a panic attack, so that I count as a win.

I knock on the room next door, and when I get no answer, I open the door to yet another empty room. Liv and Teags are nowhere to be found, either.

Fucking hell.

I head to my last resort, and after a few knocks on my old door, Tristan opens it. He rubs his eyes, his hair looking like a mess since I just woke him up. "Dude, it's so fucking early. What the hell is going on?"

"I can't find the girls."

That causes him to perk up immediately. "What do you mean?"

"They aren't in their rooms, and I can't find them."

He runs a hand through his hair before he turns around, throws a shirt over his head, and walks by me. "I'll check up here, and you check downstairs?"

"Sounds good to me," I say as I book it down the stairs, my feet moving of their own volition. I keep the lights off, because if something did happen to them and they're stuck somewhere, I have the advantage. My eyes are already adjusted to the darkness. I take my phone out, texting Nico to double-check on the alarms.

Vince: No buttons were pushed? No silent alarms going off?

> **Nico: All good. Wanna tell me why you and Tristan are going crazy or not?**

> **Vince: We can't find the girls. Can you get a visual?**

> **Nico: On it.**

I pocket my phone as I search the first floor of Bree's house, and minutes later, Tristan meets me downstairs.

"Anything?" I ask.

"Does it look like I found them?" He motions to the empty space around him, panic in his tone.

"Fucking hell," is all I say. "Where the hell are they?"

"Do you think…" Tristan trails off, not wanting to finish his sentence. "Fuck!"

I can't fucking do this right now.

I storm outside to the front of the house where my guys are at. They all turn their heads to look at me, surprise on their faces when they see me in my fucking pajamas. Not the best impression to make this early in the morning, but I couldn't give a fuck.

"Do you guys know where the girls are? They aren't in their rooms."

"Well, sir—" Wilson says, but Tristan cuts him off.

"Where the fuck is my wife?" Tristan yells, and before he starts swinging, Wilson points to the left. Deep in Bree's yard, I can see three silhouettes doing…something. I'm not quite sure what.

I see one of them turn around and start to run in our direction, and the two others follow suit a few seconds later.

As soon as I see Liv's face, Tristan and I breathe a few sighs of relief.

"Pretty girl, what the fuck were you guys doing? We thought—" Tristan stops himself as he looks over to where they came from and the egg carton in Liv's hand. "Seriously?"

"Sorry. We left you guys a note on the counter. Did you not see it?" Bree says as she smiles at me.

Tristan and I exchange looks with one another before he bursts out laughing.

"Just get it over with," I tell him, knowing what's about to happen.

Tristan just keeps on fucking laughing.

"What the fuck is happening?" Teags questions, an annoyed look on her face.

"This dude," he says as he grabs my shoulders, still laughing, "is a trained bodyguard!"

"We're all aware of that, Tris," Liv says, a confused look on her face.

I'm rolling my eyes as Tristan speaks. "He's the one who swept the first floor looking for you guys, and he didn't catch the goddamn note on the counter!"

"Fucking hell, before you die from a laugh attack, can you maybe think about how stressed I was thinking that all three of them were tied up in the back of a van somewhere?"

"You thought we were what?" Teags scoffs, as if we were the ones being ridiculous.

"We thought you guys were hurt, but it turns out, you were throwing eggs at Bree's goddamn tree. Typical fucking Hart sisters. God, I love you guys." Tristan presses a kiss to his wife's forehead before he grabs her hand. "Don't fucking scare us like that again, though. Especially not now."

"Baby, Teags and I were just trying to make Bree feel better," Liv says, melting into her husband's frame.

"It worked, if that helps." Bree smiles at me, hoping to ease some of my frustration.

"Plus, your men could see us the whole time, but you two went straight to freak out," Teags quips, sounding bored.

"Can you fucking blame us?" I say as Bree slips her hands around my waist, her simple touch lessening the tension in my body. "Is this like a thing you guys do? Why the fuck are you so calm about this?"

"Trust me, dude. Throwing eggs at a tree is a rite of passage in this family. You, Nico, and I can try it sometime. It's fucking awesome," Tristan says as he smacks my shoulder. "Can we please go to bed, pretty girl? I'm officially stealing you away. You guys spent all night reading before you came out here."

"Let's go," Liv says as Tristan picks her up and carries her inside. "Sorry to scare you two! Maybe next time, keep an eye out for a giant piece of paper explaining everything, or talk to your guys before you go crazy! Just a thought!" Liv all but yells before Tristan pushes the door open.

"You would think a professional bodyguard would be able to see a simple note, but maybe you're getting old, Vincey." Teags jokes before she too heads inside, leaving Bree and I standing on the small path in front of her house.

"I'm sorry, Vince. Teags and Liv heard me having a nightmare, and they all but dragged me out here to relieve some stress."

Fuck, that kills me. My girl was having a nightmare, and I wasn't there to calm her down. But since I wasn't, I'm glad her sister and Teags were there. If it wasn't gonna be me, I'd rather have it be them. "Why didn't you come get me, angel?"

"Teags said you were asleep, and I didn't want to wake you because I know you've been burning the candle at both ends because of me, and—"

"Baby, I'd never sleep again if it meant you were safe. Don't worry about me. I'll be okay."

Her happy gaze wavers for just a moment, but it's quick enough for me to catch before she masks it again. *She doesn't believe me.* "I know, Vince, but I'll always worry about you."

"I'm not going anywhere, Bree. I'll be here for you until someone drags my dead body away, and even that might not be enough to stop me from protecting you."

"Don't say that." Bree smacks my chest.

"Sorry," I say as I press a kiss to her forehead. "Can we go inside? I'm fucking freezing, and I don't want you getting sick from being out here all night."

I can feel her roll her eyes at me from here. "It wasn't *all* night. It was an hour, max."

"Autumn is on the way, which means it's fucking cold at night, so I don't care how long it was. Let's go get you warmed up," I say, and before Bree has the chance to quip back at me, I throw her over my shoulder and head inside.

Fifteen minutes later, my girl is fast asleep in my arms, and I follow her to sleep a few minutes after.

And all night, I dream of the beautiful girl next to me, but just before I wake up, she floats away.

Chapter Thirty-Nine

— GILDED LILY BY CULTS

A LOUD THUMP STARTLES me awake.

As I shift my arms beside me, I feel nothing but empty space. Vince must've fallen asleep at his desk again. It's been a week since this became our new night routine, and I hate that he's overworking himself like this.

He's overdoing it because he's trying to protect me, and since they have no new leads on Ralph, Vince has been searching for a crumb of anything to point to his hiding place.

Something about this entire situation feels off in my gut. Why would Ralph attack Vince's men? Why would he leave them alive? Why go through all this trouble just for me?

I suppose it never made sense in my head, and I don't know why I thought it would make any sense now.

I grab my phone to check my messages, and sure enough, there's one from Vince.

> **Vince: I'll be up soon. Don't stay awake for me; it's going to be another long night.**

That was about two hours ago, and I try to send a message back, curious if he's still awake or asleep at his desk, but it won't send. I try to reset my phone and see if that does anything, but it still doesn't work. I even try to send one to Liv at home, but that damn red error keeps popping up.

Maybe it's the rain and wind blocking the signal?

"Ugh!" I say as I throw my phone down my bed. I rip my blankets off, and I'm about to throw my slippers on when I hear something ringing.

But it's not my phone.

I'd know that ringtone anywhere.

Whistling. It's the same exact cadence and tune.

My gut drops, and I search around my room to find it and destroy whatever is making the noise. My eye catches on a ripped-up corner of my carpet and something flashing on my wall.

Thank God my night light is still on. It's just bright enough that another light blinking could catch my eye, but I still feel okay enough to get out of bed and rip my carpet up.

A small flip phone lies underneath, and someone is calling it.

Breathe, Bree, I tell myself before I grab it and answer the call, already knowing who's on the other side of the line.

"I think you've got the wrong number."

"Oh, little lamb, how I've missed your voice."

A shiver shoots down my body when I hear him speak. I'm not cold, especially in my new satin pajama set, just disgusted with this person and everything he's done to me.

He's not making me a victim. Not again. Even if I have to fake it until I make it, I'm going to fight back.

"I haven't missed yours. Soon, I won't have to hear it anymore since you'll be behind bars again. I hope they saved your cell because once we find you, it's over."

"We, huh?"

I have to get Vince. He's right downstairs, and I bet I can keep Ralph talking long enough for Nico to trace the call. I go to get up off my carpet, but Ralph's voice makes me pause.

"If you go near that bodyguard of yours, I'll blow his brains out right in front of you. Stay where you are, Bree."

The low, malicious threat makes my heart race. *He can see me. He's watching me.* "You're bluffing."

"I shot at you once, Bree. Do you think I won't do it again? How about we test that theory, and I'll paint the walls of his office with his brains? He looks like he's asleep, so maybe I'll fire a warning shot to wake him up."

Fuck. Fuck. Fuck!

"Don't you dare touch him," I say as my head spins. "What the fuck do you want?"

He only chuckles over the line as if amused by the question. "Get in the closet, Bree. I'll be up soon, and nobody is going to ruin it this time."

"Good luck getting in here," I say, trying to steady my shaky voice. "My place is surrounded. You'll be dead the minute you step on my property."

"If you don't do what I say, I'll kill every last person you care about, Bree. And then when I take you, you'll have to live with the knowledge that you could've stopped it. You're making me threaten all this, Bree. Don't you get that? Just do what I tell you like the sweet, innocent girl you are, so I can have my way with you how I know you want it!" His voice is low, almost like he himself is hiding, but I don't know where. If he's in my house, the alarm would've gone off, but it hasn't. Maybe he's outside?

Fuck, I'm scared. Terrified. All the feelings from last time are coming back in full force, and I can't do anything to stop them. "No." My voice is barely a whisper, but I manage to get the word out.

"You can't say no to me, sweetheart," he says, and the phone pings a few seconds later.

Pictures come through—ones of Liv and Tristan at home, Teags outside on the tire swing at her mom's house, another of Vince at his desk.

"One message to my guys, and all of them are gone, Bree. So get in the fucking closet, and wait," he bites, and my head empties of anything else I have up my sleeve.

I could go get Vince. But what if he shoots him?

I could message them all a warning. But my phone isn't working.

Could I use the burner to message them? I doubt it, since Ralph bought it. He probably has some sort of bug in here that can view the messages I send.

I'm officially out of options. I can't scream since Ralph will probably hear me. I can't hang up because that will make it all worse, especially if he's watching me.

Fuck!

"Don't you dare fucking hurt them."

"As long as you do what I want, they'll be fine."

I don't believe you.

I lower the phone from my ear as I head to my closet and shut the door behind me. I try to look for any sort of shoe I can use as a weapon, but he's much bigger than me. There's no doubt in my mind that he'd get angrier and take it out on me if I didn't succeed in taking him down.

Fuck. My panic button is underneath my side table, and I didn't fucking press it.

Maybe a hanger? No, that won't work. They're all soft and velvety.

Fucking hell, why didn't I follow rule number five? If I had a knife, I could hurt him before I could make it downstairs. I'm sure a stab to the stomach would make him falter.

"I'm in the closet."

"Good," is all I hear, but it's not through the phone. Before I can turn around and see where he is, his hand comes over my mouth, and he has me in a headlock. "Don't make a sound, little lamb."

I feel something prick my neck, and the entire world goes dark.

I FEEL LIKE I got hit by a bus.

My eyes flutter open, adjusting to the darkness as memories of what happened rush back.

Vince is in danger. My family is in danger. Ralph was hiding in my closet waiting for me. I got lured into one of his games yet again.

God, I hope this is the end. I hope that whatever he has planned is over tonight, and I hope it ends with him behind bars or dead, and not the other option.

He might kill me this time.

No, he's not going to win. He doesn't get to win anymore. Not after all he's put me through. Not after all I have to lose.

I sit up, and what I see makes my body go cold.

I'm in my old house, the one where all of this started. The house my parents kept after Ralph assaulted me inside it.

It's not just the house I recognize—it's the room. My old room surrounds where I sit on my bed, and when I realize what he's doing, I panic.

He's recreating that night. He's giving himself a redo. He's keeping his promise.

"This isn't over, Bree. No matter where you end up, I'll find you. If you can't count on anything else, count on that. You're mine."

I shiver where I sit. When I look down, I notice he dressed me in the same pajamas I was wearing that night. The same book sits on my bed, next to my iPad. It's all the same. Every detail cemented in my head sits in front of me.

For him, this night is the memory of when he finally got his hands on me.

For me, it was the worst moment of my life.

And both of us remember every detail.

I'm gonna be sick.

How long did it take him to do this? Did he recreate my old house just for this? I thought a family was living here after my parents sold this place, but I wouldn't know if it went back on the market. I've tried to erase this house from my memories. I don't come back to visit, don't even drive near this street.

Is that why he spent most of this year taunting me instead of actually doing anything? He was waiting until the house was perfectly set up so he could make me relive it all. This is his final move. This is his endgame.

This is the grand finale.

I practically force myself to calm down. I don't feel his presence in the room yet or in the house, as a matter of fact. There's a stillness to the air that's putting me more on edge, which was exactly his plan.

Ralph is taking my safety nets away. He's not going to let anything interrupt us this time.

I try to move from my bed, but as I pull my arms from my sides, a rattling sound breaks the silence.

He handcuffed me to the bed. I try to move my feet, and the same sound comes.

I'm trapped. I can't escape even if I wanted to.

I'm a sitting duck, and Ralph is coming for me.

Even if I try to scream, I doubt anybody will hear me.

A crash downstairs startles me, and memories of that night rush back into my mind.

At least this time, I know it's him. He lost the surprise factor. I'm still afraid, but I know what's coming.

But this is probably going to end differently, and that's terrifying. I don't know his plan. Is he going to kill me quickly? Is he going to finish what he couldn't the first time? Is my family alright? He had pictures of them all, and there's no doubt in my mind that he would follow through on the threat if I didn't cooperate.

"Bree," I hear a voice say. "I'm coming for you, little lamb."

I all but gag at the way his voice sounds, and then the whistling starts.

I can hear it more clearly since I'm not hiding in my closet, and as he ascends the stairs, the same step creaking under his weight, I look around for something I could use as a weapon. I find nothing as I hear his footsteps echo through the hallway, getting closer and closer as my breathing picks up.

I'm panicking. I'm falling apart. I'm going to die.

But this time, I'm not going down without a fight. Even with my legs and arms secured to my bed frame, I'm going to do anything I can to hurt him.

"I'm almost there, Bree. Are you ready for me? Are you shaking with excitement over being back here? I know I am."

Don't throw up. Do not throw up, Bree.

He knocks on the door, no doubt another taunt because he knows I'm strapped down, before it creaks open, and he stands in my doorway.

He's wearing the same outfit from that night, same boots, the same ski mask so most of his face is covered.

My pulse is thrashing underneath my skin, and I try to pull my legs to my body, but the restraints don't allow me to move much. I want to hide, but I can't. I try to shake my wrists out, but that doesn't work either.

I'm panicking. I can barely breathe, and he's watching me struggle because he knows I can't leave. I feel his gaze on me, and a few drops of cold sweat run down my face.

"God, Bree, do you know how long I've been dreaming of this? Of your fight? God, it turns me on just thinking about it." He comes over to the bed and stands at the foot of it.

"The only thing I've dreamt about is you being dead," I bite back, not wanting to play into this stupid game. I'm not his victim. I'm not the mouse he's trapped and can do with as he pleases.

If he wants me to succumb to him, he'll have to kill me.

He scoffs a bit, as if I said something crazy, and I lower my gaze from his, not wanting to look this sick fucking freak in his eyes.

"Sweetheart, I know that's not true." He comes closer to me, his hand grazing my face before he forces my gaze into his. His eyes are dark—almost black—as he looks at me. "God, you're so beautiful, and it's all *mine*. I'm the only one who will see you for the rest of time."

That's not true. No. Vince and Nico have to know I'm missing by now. It has probably been hours since Ralph took me, and they should've got an alert that someone was on the property, right?

Please be looking for me.

I should try to get some information from Ralph, but playing into this game of his is something I'd rather not do.

He lowers his head, and I flinch as he nips at my ear, my body shivering with nausea. "See? Even your body reacts how I knew it would."

"How long was I out?"

"I only gave you a mild sedative so I could transport you here. It took me two hours to set everything up for your arrival. Isn't it perfect, Bree? Isn't it just how you remember it?" His eyes sparkle at his masterpiece, and I have to hold down my nausea as he looks around the room. "Everything is the same. We needed a redo, Bree, and this is it."

I'm torn. Do I play into his games, or do I try to overpower him? Maybe if I'm good, he'll uncuff me. Fuck it, I have to try, right?

"I-It looks wonderful," I choke out, my throat feeling like I swallowed cotton balls. "Exactly like I remembered it." It's not a compliment, but to Ralph's ego, it is.

"God, I knew you would love it. I know you so well, little lamb." His hand comes back to caress my face as he sits next to me. "We're meant for one another, Bree. I know you know that now. I knew this would convince you."

He kisses my neck, and my body starts to shake with fear. I don't want this. I don't want him touching me. "Get off," I whisper.

"Bree, if you ruin this, I'll fucking kill them. I'll kill them all. So sit still and let me touch you."

He'll kill them.

"No," I whisper. "You won't kill them because then you'll lose me."

"I'll do whatever I have to do to keep you here forever, Bree. Don't fucking test me."

I'm done listening to his rules. I'm going to fight, and I might die trying, but I'm not letting him do this to me again. I'm not letting him keep taking things from me. "Get the fuck off me!" I scream.

"Bree, don't you fucking ruin this again!" he roars as he slaps me across the face.

Fuck, that burns, but I keep fighting. I try to squirm from underneath him, but he's too strong, and when I hear something rip, I think it's my pajamas.

But then my mouth is covered, duct tape pressed against my mouth, and I can barely breathe as the panic sets in.

"You're going to shut the fuck up, and you're going to sit still so I can have my way with you!"

The last thing I hear before I pass out is Ralph mumbling something I can't understand.

Chapter Forty

— DAYLIGHT BY DAVID KUSHNER

A NOISE HAS MY head jerking up from where it lays against my desk.

"What was that?" I say over comms, and when nobody responds, I head for my front door. As I swing it open, my guys guarding the house meet my gaze. "Anything to report?"

"No, sir," Chris tells me, and I take a breath.

"I'll be upstairs with Bree. We'll talk in the morning," I say as I look at my watch. "Well, when the sun's up and the shift changes."

"Got it. Have a good night, boss."

"You too. Call me if anything changes," I say as I close the door, and I all but drag myself up to Bree's room. I've got to stop falling asleep at my desk. I'm working myself dry, but we still have nothing on Ralph. We've been checking paparazzi photos for similar faces and Nico's running facial recognition on the crowds, but all we have is a load of nothing so far. Some crowd members have DUIs, but Ralph hasn't been spotted in any photos.

Yet again, we've reached a dead end, and I have no idea how the motherfucker keeps hiding from us. It's pissing me off.

I open the door to Bree's room, the glow of her night light making it easy for me to get to her closet so I can change into comfier clothes.

But when I get in and see its contents all over the floor, my guard flies up. Bree is organized as fuck. She never would've gone to sleep with this mess.

My pulse picks up, and when I rush to her bed, she's not there.

A note sits on her pillow, along with a picture of her sleeping—or passed out, I'm not sure which.

Fuck! He fucking has her. He was under this roof, and since I wasn't up sleeping with her, he grabbed her.

I grab the note, and the urge to kill him gets stronger.

Checkmate.

– R.

My heart is beating out of my chest as I pull my phone out, dialing the first person on my speed dial.

"It's too fucking early—"

I cut him off. "Bree's gone."

"I'll be over in ten," Nico says as he curses and hangs up the phone.

I race down the stairs and throw open the door. "Get the day shift up, now! Bree's missing and Ralph has her. Search the entire fucking property. Nico's on his way."

"On it, boss," Chris says.

"Get Emerson and a few others to search the back. Chris, you take the front." I take a deep breath and wish for my sanity to return, but it doesn't. "Find her!" I scream before I head back inside to my office to check the security cameras.

I should've been notified if something happened. I should've been up with her. God, this is all my fucking fault. Bree is somewhere with that sick fuck, and I could've stopped it, but I wasn't there.

I wasn't there. It was the only promise I made her, that I would always be by her side, and I fucking broke it. I failed.

"What the fuck happened?" Nico shouts as he storms into my office.

Ten minutes, my ass. But I don't care how many laws he broke to get over here. I'm just glad he's here. "I have no idea. I'm pulling up the cameras now."

"Why didn't any of us get an alert that the property was breached?" Nico asks, and before I tell him I don't fucking know, Emerson calls me.

"Did you find her?"

"No, but we did find an abandoned plate in the bushes behind her house." He rattles off the letters and numbers, and Nico plugs it into the system as I pull up the cameras from her backyard.

"Thanks, Emerson."

"We'll keep looking," is all he says before I drop the call.

"The plate belongs to a stolen car. It was reported missing a few days ago from a house across town. A white Ford Fusion."

I search the cameras for any sign of it. It takes a few minutes, but then I spot it doing laps around Bree's gated neighborhood a few days ago. I zoom in on the plate, and it matches the one we found, but there's no way to tell what Ralph could have switched it to.

Nico paces around my room. "How the fuck did he manage to kill our system again? It's pissing me off. I reinforced our fucking firewalls and made sure they were stable!"

"That's not what I'm worried about right now," I bite out, my jaw tense as I think about what he could be doing to Bree. "I don't think he would leave the state. Ralph is a psychological motherfucker. He likes to play with Bree's mind, and crossing state lines with her would mean too many eyes on him."

"So where would he take her then?"

"I don't fucking know!" I say as I swipe everything off my desk. That felt good, but my pulse is still thrashing, and I can't fucking breathe.

He got to her. He took her. He might fucking kill her.

Bree is the love of my life, and if I lose her, I'm losing a piece of my soul. There would be no coming back from that. I'd rather die a thousand times over than let something happen to her, something that I could've saved her from—that I could've stopped.

I need to fucking focus, but my mind can't stop thinking that Bree could be hurt. He could be touching her again.

Again. There's that fucking word I hate.

"Nico, I don't know what to do," I say, fear overtaking my mind. For the first time in my life, I don't have a plan. I don't have next steps. All I can think about is what he's probably doing to her, images flooding my mind.

"We need to think. Where would he take her where nobody else would interrupt? That's what he wants, right?"

"Wait, the bracelet I got her should have tracking," I say as I tap my bracelet a few times. I hope that wherever Bree is, she can tap back or at least know I'm coming. "Can you track it using mine?"

"Yeah, I can. As long as she isn't very far, I should be able to."

I yank it off of my wrist and throw it at Nico. He tinkers with it for a few seconds, plugging a bunch of shit into his phone as I lean against my desk, needing support to keep standing.

"I can't get an exact location, but she's still around here. Vince, she's not far. Think—where would this sick fucker take her?"

"Knowing Ralph, he's been planning this for a while. He's been taunting her for months. He had a few opportunities to grab her, but he didn't."

Nico runs a hand through his hair. "With his last girlfriend, the last place she was seen was the spot where they had their first date."

My mind flashes through tons of different places before it lands on where this all started: her old house. The first time he got his disgusting hands on her was in her old room, and he left me that note on her pillow, knowing that I would be there to see it.

"I know where they are."

Chapter Forty-One

— PTOLEMAEA BY ETHEL CAIN

I DON'T WANT TO be here.

I'm not safe.

He's hurting me.

He's going to kill me.

Please, make it stop. Make it fucking stop.

I chant it over and over again in my head. Screaming is no use to me. Now, I'm praying to anyone who can hear me—if anyone or anything is even out there.

Ralph is on top of me, stroking himself as he watches me struggle against the handcuffs he has me in. He runs his free hand over my body, and even though my pajamas are still on, I can feel every hard ridge of his hands, just like last time.

Tears are streaming down my face, and they haven't stopped. My head hurts from where he knocked me out, my limbs feel weak from whatever sedative he gave me, and my face hurts from where he slapped me.

My wrists and ankles are burning, screaming at me to stop fighting, stop trying, because it's no use. The metal is cold against the scrapes on my hands and feet, but I'm not stopping.

Ralph likes my fight, so he's getting off to this. He's *enjoying* this. He loves watching the tears stream down my face as I fight for my freedom. He tells me it's because he loves me.

Obviously, he doesn't. He's just fascinated by me. I'm the next in line of his obsessions, and he's going to kill me just like he killed his girlfriend.

I'm trying not to throw up as I watch the door behind him for any sign of help, but it never moves.

I'm all alone.

I'm fighting, but it's no use.

I do it anyway. I'll fight against him until I'm sick of it.

"My perfect little fuck puppet. Now I can do this properly."

My lungs start to seize under the duct tape, and I feel like I'm gonna pass out. Maybe I should, just so I can't feel whatever he's about to do to me.

Ralph's warm, clammy touch makes me squirm, and I wish I had access to my legs so I could try and knee him—he's barely paying attention as he strokes himself.

Ew. Ew. Ew.

I keep squirming, hoping he'll at least get off of me, before he chastises me.

"That's it. Fight me, Bree. I know this is what you want. And you'll take it. God, you look so fuckable bound underneath me." He's drowning in his own lust while I'm fighting the nausea crawling up my throat. "Fuck, if it feels this good, it can't be bad, can it, little lamb?"

I scream through the tape over my mouth, hoping he'll take it off, but he doesn't, and I keep thrashing, so much so that he loses his balance.

"I won't let you ruin this again, Bree!" he screams as his hands wrap around my throat, and all my air is cut off. I'm frozen as his hands squeeze so hard that it feels like my eyes are about to pop out of my head.

Stop! Please, stop.

"You need to be punished. And if I kill you, then at least I can have my way with you!" His hands are still cutting off my airway, and my lungs are seizing underneath the duct tape, my hands and feet thrashing as I try to loosen his hold, but he's too strong for me.

This is it, I think to myself. At least I fought this time. At least I tried, right? That's all I'm able to do, especially when someone else is making all the decisions.

Tears leak out of my eyes, burning as they slide down my face.

I love you, Liv. You're the best big sister I could've had.

I love you, Teags. You're the only person I can call a true friend.

I love you, Tristan. Take care of my sister for me.

I love you, Vince. And I'm sorry I never said it when I had the chance.

I speak all these things in my mind, hoping that after I'm gone, they'll all know that, in my last moments of being Bree Hart, I loved them.

In my last moments, I choose to think about them and not what's happening because if I'm leaving this world, I'm leaving it with good memories.

As my breathing starts to slow, the tears continue to fall, and I swear I hear something crack before I pass out.

"HALF OF YOU ARE with Nico. Go around the back of the property and enter through that door. The rest of you are with me. We're going in the front," I say to my men as I adjust my bulletproof vest before we pull up to Bree's old house.

It looks just like I remember it. I haven't been back here since I left the first time, and I never thought I would be.

Leave it to Ralph to bring her back to the one place she's been trying to forget.

I know he's here. The white Ford Fusion is parked in the driveway, and all the lights inside are off. He's taunting Bree, playing the cat-and-mouse game he loves so fucking much.

Good thing he won't be breathing properly in a few minutes. Once I find this fucker, I'm going to fucking kill him.

"Everyone ready?" I ask as I take the safety off my gun.

I hear a string of agreements across our comms, and the police we called lead the charge.

"Pennsylvania State Police!" they shout as they breach the door with a battering ram, the rest of us rushing inside. While Nico's team clears the back of the house and the guys I'm with clear the first floor, I head straight upstairs to Bree's old room.

She has to be in there, and I bet Ralph is with her.

I stride up the stairs two at a time, feeling Emerson behind me. I run over to her door and kick it open, and what I see makes my body go cold.

Ralph's standing over Bree, who appears to be passed out, bound to the bed with duct tape over her mouth. She's not moving, and I can't see if her chest is rising and falling.

All I see is red before I tackle him off the bed, my gun getting lost in the struggle, and all I see is the smirk on the fucker's face as he looks up at me from the floor.

"Did you enjoy my note? I definitely enjoyed finally getting a piece of Bree's sweet—"

Instead of letting him finish, I punch his fucking teeth in. I grab his shirt with one fist and punch him with the other, wanting the blows to hurt. He fucking touched her again, *hurt* her again. He doesn't get any of my fucking mercy. My knuckles are killing me as I pound his face in, blood splattering on the carpet, but my pain doesn't matter.

Just his. And he needs to feel all of it.

"You're a fucking coward!" *Punch.* "It doesn't feel as good being on the receiving end, does it?" *Punch.* "You touched her, and I should fucking kill you!"

It could be five or ten minutes later, and his face is a mess, the black mask wet with blood.

Good, I think. I should kill him right now for all he's done. I should let him fucking die.

"Boss...I think he's down," a voice says to me, but I keep hitting. Somehow, it's not enough. None of this will ever be enough for the rage I feel.

"Vince! Stop it!" Nico says as he pulls me off Ralph. "He's down."

"He deserves worse," I bite, but Nico slapping me in the face somehow brings me back to reality.

"Go help Bree while I sort all this shit out."

I turn my head to where Bree lies on the bed, her chest finally moving as I rush over to her. Tears are spilling down her face, and her eyes are red as fuck, practically bulging out of her head.

She's alive, I remind myself a thousand times as I look at her.
I didn't lose her.

I rip the duct tape off slowly, and she starts coughing immediately. She has marks on her neck like the ones Ralph gave her before, and just seeing that is making me want to finish what I started with the fucker.

"G-get...me...out," she coughs through her words, her voice barely audible.

"Holy shit," I hear Nico mumble from behind me, the scene in front of him settling into his mind. We've protected some high-level people, but neither of us has seen anything like this before.

It's going to haunt us forever, and we didn't even experience it. Bree did.

God, it hurts. It really fucking hurts that I can't take any of her pain away right now.

"Fuck, angel, one second," I say as I scramble for the handcuff keys. "W-where are the k-keys? Someone find the fucking keys!" I scream.

"Here, boss," Emerson says as he hands me them. "They were on the table."

Yeah, that makes sense. Yet another taunt. The keys to her freedom were sitting two feet away from her, and she could never reach them.

I undo all the cuffs as fast as I can, but not before seeing the red marks on her ankles and wrists. My heart lurches; she fucking fought him. She fought against him hard, so hard that she's bleeding from where he bound her. *God, what the fuck.*

Her body is shaking as I hold her in my arms, her head tucked into my shoulder, as if she can't bear to see anything else in this room. *I've got to get her out of here.*

"I've got you, Bree. You're safe," I say as I pick her up and take her outside, the area surrounded by ambulances and some news vans pulling up. *Fucking hell.* This is going to be all over the fucking internet by tonight.

Can't they give her some time to recuperate before they start blasting her trauma everywhere? Do these people have any fucking courtesy?

Bree shakes in my arms as I set her down in one of the ambulances, a female EMT immediately coming over to check her out. I don't leave her side for a second. I can't, because I'm afraid she'll slip through my fingers if I let her out of my sight. I know Ralph is done. I know he's out of the picture now, but the fear is still there.

Bree could vanish at any moment, and I'll lose her again.

I could've lost her tonight, and I fucking failed at protecting her. Ralph somehow managed to get through our fucking defenses. Just as

I mention the fucker in my head, his body—still alive—gets dragged out of the house. I notice his hands are cuffed in front of him, and Nico comes over to me.

"He'll live, but he won't see anything but concrete for the rest of his life."

"Good," is all I manage to get out.

"Can you tell us what happened, ma'am?" an officer asks Bree.

"W-well, I was…" Bree trails off, still coughing, and before she tries to speak again, I answer for her.

"Can't you do this another time? She can barely fucking talk."

The officer nods at me before leaving. Nico pats my back as my guys filter in and out of the house. Bree starts to talk, but I can't understand what she's trying to say.

"Liv," is all she can say. "A-and T-Teags."

"What about them, princess?" Nico says in a soft tone.

"Shooters," she scratches out before coughing a few more times. "Watching th-them and y-you."

"I found the phone, princess. Don't worry. Those were from a few days ago when Ralph was casing your house. I found the same stolen car outside Liv's place and the West house on the same day. They're okay."

She nods at me before someone calls out her name.

"Bree! Where the hell are you?" I recognize Liv's voice just as she locks eyes with me, her gaze shifting to her sister, who sits on my right. "Oh, fuck."

Liv and Tristan rush over to us, and Liv hugs her sister, Bree's arms shaking as they slowly go around her body. Bree's wrists and ankles now have gauze wrapped around them, the bleeding and scrapes covered in ointment so they can heal.

But there's no gauze for her mind. There's nothing anyone can do—besides Dr. Anna, maybe. Ralph terrorized her again tonight. Just like before, he's left invisible marks in her mind and memory that she'll never forget.

I think that hurts Bree more than the restraints. She has to heal from tonight, from what he did the first time, from everything in between.

She's strong. She'll heal, and I'll be with her every step of the fucking way.

I love her, and I'm going to do everything in my power to show her that after all this, I can still love her as much as I did before. I'll love her through every panic attack, through every bad dream, through every good memory we create together. Maybe those will override the bad ones in the future.

I can only hope.

"Are you okay?" Liv asks but then stammers a second later. "Actually, don't answer that."

Liv knows the answer already, and she can see the bruises on her neck. She probably has déjà vu, and I can see the fresh tears on her face, Tristan's too. He looks at my hands, then back up at my eyes, a question in his eyes that he doesn't dare speak.

Is that from Ralph's face?

I only nod back at him, and he does the same to me before the EMT returns.

"Your vitals look okay. Besides the elevated heart rate and scrapes on your wrists and ankles, you'll be fine," the EMT says before she packs some things away. "I'm recommending you go to the hospital to get your throat checked out and—"

Bree's head shakes in my arms.

"No need for a hospital," Nico says. "I have a specialist coming who can check Bree out at home."

"In a different room?" I ask Nico, wanting to make sure Bree doesn't get panicked walking back into the room where Ralph took her.

"Of course. She'll meet us at the house."

"T-Thanks, Nico," Bree whispers.

"Anything for you, Bree. You should know that by now." Nico motions for us to leave, and we follow him to the car, Bree still in my arms because I can't bear to put her down.

I almost lost her. I almost lost the most important person in my life tonight.

And if I had walked into that house a few minutes later, a few seconds later, she might not be here. Her heart might not be beating in her chest, and everything that made my world bright, colorful, and beautiful would've been gone.

My beautiful fucking angel. My beautiful Bree. The only girl I'll ever love.

A fighter.

A *survivor*.

Chapter Forty-Two

— FAITHFULLY BY JOURNEY

"This might sting a little," the doctor says as she massages my throat. It feels like I have sandpaper in my airway, and suddenly, I'm catapulted back to the last time I felt like this.

It's over, I remind myself. Ralph can't hurt me anymore. Vince made sure of that when he punched his face in.

For me. He did that for *me,* and I don't know how I'll thank him for saving my life.

But I feel just as broken as before, like I'm watching all this happen from outside my body. I don't know how to get back. I don't know how to go back to normal after this. What is normal? What does it mean to be normal? I've got no fucking clue, but with Vince and my family by my side, I'll get through it. I know I can. I just have to trust they're at the table with me. They'll carry some of the weight because they love me.

They stayed with me through all this. They love me, and when they need me to sit at the table with them in the future, I'll be the first one in my chair. After all they've done for me, it's the least I can do.

Ralph is gone. Now, maybe I can move in the right direction without worrying about the other shoe dropping.

The doctor finishes her assessment and scribbles a few things down on a piece of paper before she hands it to Vince.

"I'm prescribing some medicine to help with the pain. Keep her hydrated, maybe tea with lots of honey, and try some lozenges to help with coughing and her voice. It should heal over the next few weeks." She looks at me. "Try not to overuse your voice, and you'll be fine. The bruises should heal and put some ointment on your wrists and ankles to help those."

"Thank you, Doctor," Vince says as he leads her out of the room. I hear him and Nico saying something before Vince returns, picks me up off the bed, and walks over to the shower before turning it on.

He strips off all my clothes for me, and I let him because it feels nice to be taken care of, especially by him. He's gentle as he places me in the shower, joining me a few seconds later.

"Careful of your bandages, angel," Vince says, his voice rough with emotion. It sounded like that sentence was hard to get out, and all I want is to make him feel better.

He hasn't taken his eyes off me since we left the ambulance, and I know he's blaming himself for what happened. It's what I've been doing the entire time too, but if Dr. Anna has taught me anything, it's that none of this was my fault. It wasn't Vince's either. It was Ralph's. He's the one who shoulders the blame for all of this.

The hot water hurts as it beats down on my bruises and scrapes. It has to be almost morning, and I can't wait to sleep for two days straight. My body is tired. My mind is equally drained, and it might take me a few days to adjust to feeling like I'm not being hunted all the time.

But my life is mine again, and I can finally breathe a little better knowing I have some of the control back. It's taken months for me to feel okay again, and even though Dr. Anna and I are going to be having lots of conversations about tonight, they don't scare me. It might take a few sessions to come to terms with what happened, but I'm stronger now.

In fact, I'm looking forward to talking about tonight, healing from it, and leaving it where it should be left—in the past, out of my head.

For the first time in my life, I don't want to spend all my time safely in my head. I want to *live*. I want to experience all the things I can with Vince, my sister, and my best friend. Tonight has only cemented that for me. Time is so fucking precious, and nobody knows how long we have on this floating rock in space.

I don't want to waste any of that time in my head and ignore the people around me who I love more than anything. As much as I love books, reality is where I want to be more than ever.

Vince pours some shampoo into his hand to wash my hair for me, his hands massaging my scalp as he does. *God, this feels good.*

I lean back into his embrace, the water beneath us running slightly pink, his hands all red, scraped, and bloody.

"I-I'm bandaging your hands after this, Vince," I whisper before I cough a few more times.

"Angel, don't strain your voice. You can take care of me after I take care of you." He rinses out my shampoo before he grabs the conditioner and massages it into the ends of my hair.

I notice his hands are shaking, and I don't know if it's because of how much they hurt or if it's something else. He lets the conditioner sit as he grabs a loofa and squeezes some of his body wash onto it. Vince washes every inch of my body—twice, as if I'll disappear underneath his touch if he doesn't.

"V-Vince," I say as I turn to face him and notice tears falling from his eyes. I almost thought it was from the shower, but he's not the one underneath the spray. "Baby?" I reach up to his face.

"I almost lost you tonight, Bree. Y-You almost..." He trails off, not wanting to say the rest of his sentence.

"I'm right here," I whisper as I take his hand and place it over the pulse in my hand.

His head dips to my forehead as he takes a deep breath, trying to regain his emotions. His arms wrap around my body, and I let him hold me as I feel his chest heave. He needs this as much as I do because while I feel safe wrapped in his embrace, he needs to know that I'm still here. He needs to feel my heart beating in my chest.

We need this. We need each other.

We chose this. We're choosing each other, just like we did all those weeks ago when he was in the hospital.

"I love you," I whisper into his ear. "I'm in love with you, Vince."

His breath hitches, and he pulls back to face me, his eyes wet with tears. "What did you say?"

"That I love you. I choose you. I *love* you," I say in my clearest voice possible.

"God, angel, I love you too," Vince says before pressing a soft kiss to my lips. "I'll choose you for the rest of my fucking life," he says with another kiss against my lips. "Do you remember that conversation we had in the car? About finding peace in someone you love?"

I nod my head, kind of knowing where he's going with this.

"That's what you do for me, Bree. I used to feel so restless whenever I took a case, but with you, fuck." He runs a hand through his hair. "Everything's quiet. You bring me that soft, tranquil peace that I've always needed but was always too afraid I would never find."

I open my mouth to speak, but Vince shakes his head. "Don't hurt your voice, Bree. Just let our love hang in the air, okay?"

I nod before he pulls me back into his embrace, the soap washing off my body as I trace a heart across his back with my finger.

He rinses the conditioner out and turns the shower off before he dries me with a towel. I try to silently tell him he needs to sit down so I can wrap his hands and knuckles, but he refuses until I'm dressed.

He throws one of his t-shirts on my body and gives me a pair of his boxers. I have to roll them at the waist a few times to fit comfortably.

After he throws some clothes on, he grabs my hand, leads me back into the bathroom, and does my entire skincare routine for me. After he washes his hands, he grabs my lotion and carefully lathers my legs. He avoids my ankles and the gauze around them, not wanting to hurt the raw skin underneath.

Is he doing my entire night routine? I'd be surprised, but of course, Vince knows every step. He's that attentive, and I just fell a little bit more in love with him.

When we walk back out to his old room, Nico is standing there with a few bags packed, his face lifting as soon as we come out.

"Are you guys ready?"

I look between the two of them, confused.

"We're heading to Liv and Tristan's house. Teags is meeting us there. Connie too," Vince tells me. "Just to get ahead of things, and I don't want you going back in that room if you don't have to."

I smile softly at him before I mouth a 'thank you' to him, and he kisses my forehead.

Nico leaves the room, and as I go to follow suit, Vince stops me. "No matter what's thrown our way by the media, the internet, and the chaos of our lives, I'll love you through it all, Bree. We'll do this together going forward, and I can't wait to love you for the rest of our lives."

"I love you, Vince. And I'm glad I'm still here to be able to tell you that. Thank you."

A single tear falls from his eye before I wipe it away. We head to the car where Nico is packing our bags into the back, and as I take in the state of the house that protected me for four years, the house that saw me at my best and worst, I wave goodbye.

It was good to me, but it's time to leave the past where it should remain.

And the future has never looked brighter for me, especially when Vince slides into the back seat and threads his fingers through mine. He's my future now, and together, we'll build a home full of light, laughter, and love.

"Are you two lovebirds ready?" Nico asks us from the front seat.

"We're ready," I whisper, and Vince squeezes my hand three times as we drive away.

Chapter Forty-Three

One Month Later

— GET WELL SOON BY ARIANA GRANDE

"Uhh, this one?" I say as I hand Bree a book.

"Oh, everyone has been telling me I need to read this one. Great choice, babe!" she says as she adds to it the pile. "November is going to be a month of variety, thanks to Vince."

I'm not used to being in front of the camera, but I'd do anything to see her beautiful smile. She asked if I wanted to film a video for her channel, so that's exactly what we're doing. Apparently, she's hard launching our relationship to the world.

I had to ask her what that meant, and she explained it to me without making too many jokes. Now, though, Nico keeps making fun of how old I am. He's only three years younger than me, so if I'm old, then what is he? That fucker still pushes my buttons, but he is my best friend, so I guess that's what he's supposed to do.

"Okay, how about you pick three more? I usually read ten to twenty books a month, and we're only at ten. I think I can handle a few more."

I'm standing in front of her specialized shelf in Liv's guest room. We've been living here for a month as we search for a home of our own. As soon as we hear from our realtor, we'll be out of their hair and finally starting a life together. I cannot fucking wait. I've grown way closer to her sister and Tristan, but I know we're all itching to get our privacy back. I know Bree and I miss Nellie, too. She's staying with my sister until we get back on our feet.

I hate moving around with Nell this much. I know dogs need a stable place, and my entire life has been unstable. Now, Bree and I are building a home together, and Nell will finally have a permanent place to call home, with a yard big enough for her to play and roll around.

As for Ralph, he's officially back in a supermax prison. That motherfucker will never see freedom again, and I couldn't be happier. It's the *least* he deserves for what he put Bree through.

All the hired help he had is also in prison. The four fuckers got sentenced to life with the possibility of parole for being accomplices.

This is the first regular video Bree is uploading after everything happened. Two weeks ago, she uploaded an unedited, hour-long video telling her entire story. She didn't leave a single thing out, and I couldn't be prouder of how she handled it.

She didn't let her parents tell her story for her, and now, her version—the correct one—is out in the world. News outlets called her brave for the video, and her followers have been nothing but kind to her.

Bree is also starting a foundation for survivors. She brought the idea to Connie last week, and she loved it. It's the perfect way to shift the narrative off Ralph, and onto all the good Bree can do helping other survivors.

I'm so fucking proud of my girl.

There's been a few tough moments, of course. Bree still has nightmares, and she wakes up the whole house when she screams, but instead of just me being there to calm her down, Liv and Tristan are there to help.

Gone are the days of Bree running on the treadmill until she passes out. Now, she's got a family to help her down from the memories haunting her.

"Vince, come back, baby," Bree says as she grabs my chin in her hand and turns me to face her. "Are you okay?"

"I'm perfect," I say as I kiss her before I pull back and peruse her shelf. I reach for three books—one with a pink cover, one simplistic one, and the last one blue with some flowers on it. "These."

"Are these your final choices?" she asks me, a gleam in her eyes.

"Yes," I tell her. "All of these better be five stars, or I'll make it my mission to outdo myself next month."

"Is that so?"

"Yes, angel, it is," I say as I kiss her again.

"Okay, great," she says as she films her outro. When she's done, she closes her camera and all but tackles me in a hug. "That was so much fun. Thanks for doing this with me."

"Bree, I'd do anything for you. And I enjoyed myself. I like seeing your eyes light up at all these books. It's adorable."

Bree's lips meet mine, and I kiss her with all the passion that she makes me feel before a few knocks and the door opening interrupt us. *I can't wait until we have a house.*

"Oh, shit, sorry," Liv says as she tries to leave.

"It's okay, sis. What's up?" Bree says as she moves her hair out of her face. She's still on top of me, and she might not feel that awkward, but I do.

"Tristan wants you guys to help hand out candy."

"We'll be right out!" Bree says as she gets up and heads for the closet. She grabs our costumes, and I chuckle when I see what she chose for us. "What?"

"Nothing. It's perfect."

I put on my costume—Mario—while Bree puts on hers—Princess Peach—and the two of us walk out to the living room to meet Tristan and Liv.

Tristan starts laughing immediately when he sees us. "Oh, Bree, you've outdone yourself."

"You guys look adorable," Liv says as she grabs her camera and snaps a few pictures of us.

"I've never seen Mario so stone-faced." Tristan laughs.

"You're one to talk. Your costumes don't even match. I thought we were all doing couples costumes. How is a cowboy and some lady from ye old times matching?"

The two of them just look at each other, their eyes sparkling as Tristan pulls Liv onto his lap. "You just don't get it, Vince."

"Fucking explain it to me then."

"One day when you're older," Tristan says as the doorbell rings. "That's our cue."

The four of us traipse over to the door, and as we swing it open, four kids dressed as ninja turtles greet us. We give them their candy and shut the door. Bree and I head to the couch where some scary movie is playing, and I hear Tristan talking quietly to Liv behind us.

"What are you saying, pretty girl?"

"I'm saying that we should try. I want one."

I smile to myself at the thought of the little family we all have getting bigger. Liv and Tristan would be wonderful parents, and Bree would make the best aunt.

I never had a huge family, and Bree gave me that back. She's never had one either, but together, we've created our own.

It took us a while to get here, and maybe some other people would've taken a different route, but we decided to take the road less traveled by. Even though it was full of bumps and bruises—literally—I couldn't be happier knowing we made it.

Bree chose me, and I chose her right fucking back.

"Are you okay?" Bree asks me, her head on my shoulder as we watch the movie.

"I'm better than okay, angel. I've got all I need right here," I say as I press a kiss to her forehead. "I love you."

"I love you too."

<h1 style="text-align:center">Chapter Forty-Four</h1>

<h1 style="text-align:center">Thanksgiving</h1>

— BACK HOME BY ANDY GRAMMER

"Fuck, I'm so nervous," I say as I adjust the rings on my fingers.

"Why? It's just Thanksgiving with the West family."

"I know, but this time feels different," I tell him as we get out of the car. The West house looks like it always does around this time of year—decorated as fuck. Tristan always helps his mom put decorations up, and he did the same with our new house this year, no matter how much I protested. He insisted, so I bought a bunch of decorations, and he and Vince spent all day decorating our house.

We moved in the second week of November, and unpacking has been insane—especially with how many books I have. Still, it's been fun decorating our house together. Vince doesn't have the best eye for decor, but he tries his best. We've chosen every piece together, and it's been the best time, creating our own little corner of the world for just us.

I'm excited to celebrate Thanksgiving at the West house. We put all holidays on hold because of Ralph and everything going on. We celebrated my birthday in February before all this happened, but we missed Liv, Tristan, Vince, and Teags' birthdays. And basically every other major holiday besides Halloween.

Vince knocks on the door while I hold the chocolate-covered straw-berries we brought—

the only thing I know how to make.

Liv and Tristan are already here, but I'm not sure if Teags is, though. Her flight was supposed to get in around now, and she told us she was taking an Uber—even though I told her Vince and I could pick her up. Gregory isn't coming with her, so it should be a fairly nice night.

Teags moved to Arizona with her boyfriend a week after everything. It was sudden, and Tristan is still pissed at her, but Liv has declared tonight argument free, so they better behave.

Tabitha—Tristan's mom—opens the door and immediately pulls me in for a hug.

"Bree! You beautiful girl. I'm so glad you're here," she says in my ear, and I have to stop the rush of emotions creeping into my body.

"Me too," I say as I pull back. "This is Vince, my boyfriend."

Vince holds out his hand to her, but she pulls him in for a hug too. "I know who he is. I watched your videos, Bree. You got yourself a handsome one."

Vince blushes, and I stifle a laugh. "Nice to meet you, ma'am."

"Oh please, none of that," she laughs. "Call me Tabitha. We're prac-tically family."

"Sounds good, Tabitha," Vince says as he grabs my jacket from my shoulders and places it on a hanger.

She walks back into the kitchen, the house smelling like cranberries as Vince and I walk through it. Theo and Tristan are trying to get a fire going, and when Tristan spots Vince, he pulls him in for a hug.

It still weirds me out to see them interact, but over the past few months, they've gotten close. It probably has something to do with Liv and me. We practically forced them to be friends since they're dating two sisters who are all but attached at the hip.

Regardless of how it happened, I'm glad the two most important men in my life like each other. While they're talking, I head to where Liv is working in the kitchen.

She wraps me in a hug, the brown bow in my hair snagging on her wedding ring. "Shit, sorry!"

"It's okay, sis. How are you? How's the next book coming?"

She sighs as she turns around to mix the mac and cheese. "It's okay. My next release is with my editor."

"I'd believe you if your tone wasn't so strained. What's going on?"

"It's nothing. Starting is always the worst part. Sometimes it's hard, and I can't get the characters in my head to translate to the page. I feel like I know them really well, but when I type the words out onto the page, they become real people. It's hard to explain, but I'll get through it. The first thirty percent is always difficult."

"I'm sure whoever they are, everyone will love them. You have a gift of writing characters who feel like real people. People will love them, and if you need anyone to read your manuscript, I'm always available."

"Thanks, Bree. I might take you up on that."

"Fucking finally, Liv! God, it's only taken four books for you to let me read them early."

She elbows my side as she continues to melt the cheese in the pot. "Isn't this amazing?" she asks me as she looks around.

"Yeah, it is," I agree. We never had holidays like this when we were younger. Now, thanks to the West family, we'll never know what it's like to be alone every holiday. It feels good having people to celebrate the little things with.

Liv and I spent our entire lives alone, only spending moments with one another since our parents didn't care for us. Now, that's changed. Who knows, if Liv and Tristan never met, what would've happened, but there's not a doubt in my mind that we still would've ended up here. Life is funny in that way, and I smile as I take in another holiday surrounded by love and laughter.

"I never thought holidays could be like this," I say as tears fill my eyes.

"You know, I always thought we missed out on a big part of our childhood by not having these moments with our own family." Liv pauses to wipe a tear from her own eye. "But today just goes to show that you can still find that family when you're older. Life doesn't end when you grow up, even though we always think it does."

"You're right, Liv," I say as I lean my head on her shoulder. "I love you."

"I love you too. Now, Tristan was supposed to set the table, but he looks busy talking, so do you mind doing it? The plates and everything are sitting on the table. You just have to put them out."

"Yeah, I can do it."

"And make sure to set a place for Tobias too. It's tradition."

I smile sadly to myself. "Of course."

I'm halfway done setting the table when I feel a presence behind me. "Boo!"

I turn around, and my best friend's face meets mine. I grab her, squeezing her until she pushes me off. "I'm so glad you're back. Face-Time doesn't cut it."

"I know, I know. I'll be here for a few days, but do you mind if I stay with you and Vince? I don't know if I can handle being here for an entire week."

"That sounds perfect," I say, noticing her red-rimmed eyes but opting not to ask her about it. She probably wouldn't tell me anyway or would make up an excuse as to why her eyes are puffy. Teags will tell me on her own time, just like she always does.

"Where's mom?"

"Last I saw, she was trying to find the parade on the TV."

"Thanks," she says as she leaves the dining room.

"Now, you all know the drill," Tabitha says as we all sit down for dinner. "One thing you're thankful for."

"Ugh, do I have to go first?" Teags complains.

"You're still the youngest, so yes," Theo tells her, and she flips him off.

"Teagen!" her mom chastises as we all laugh.

"Sorry, Mom." She runs a hand through her hair. "I'm thankful for being here today."

"Great. Now Theo."

He sighs heavily before answering. "I'm thankful I only have a few more stops on Tobias' old bucket list. I love traveling, but I'm getting tired."

I forgot he was doing that. Tobias left them all letters after he passed, and Theo's had Tobias' bucket list that he never got to complete. Theo has been trying to do it for him, and he's been all over the US. According to Tristan, he only has two or three stops left, and I think the last one is Vermont. The West family used to vacation in a small town up there, and since their dad died, they haven't been back.

It's interesting how that's the last stop on Tobias' bucket list.

"That's nice, darling." Tabitha turns to me. "You're up, Bree."

"I'm thankful for the family surrounding this table. It's been a hell of a year, and I'm glad I'm here to celebrate with you all. And sorry for swearing, Tabitha."

She reaches her hand out, and I put mine in hers. "It's okay, honey. I'm so glad you're here too."

A smile and a few tears fall from my face, but I rein my emotions in so Liv can talk.

"Livvy, girl, you're up."

"I'm thankful I got to marry my best friend this year." Liv turns to Tristan and leans into his body.

"I love you too, pretty girl. And we had the same answer, so Vince, it's your turn," Tristan tells him, and I see Vince run his hands over his pants. They're probably clammy, and I think it's funny how nervous he is.

He clears his throat before speaking. "I'm thankful I kept my promise to come back. After all, it led me here, and I can't think of anywhere else I'd want to be."

His eyes meet mine, and my cheeks flush. I love this man more and more every single day, and I'm so fucking glad we found one another. He's been the best part of my life for so long, and in a weird, fucked up way, I'm thankful I met him all those years ago.

"Mom, what about you?" Theo asks.

"I'm thankful that all of us are here, and I hope that, wherever your father and Tobias are, they can see us. Actually, scratch that. I *know* they see us." Emotions start to cloud her features. "Someday, we'll all be together again, but until then, each sunset will remind us of them. Right, Liv?"

"Right," Liv says, a few tears pouring from her eyes.

"Now, let's eat before it gets cold," Tabitha says, and for the rest of the night, we trade stories about our lives as we sit across the table from one another.

For so long, I thought I'd be alone. I thought I wasn't worthy of having people around me, but the people around this table changed that for me. I thought I was destined for meaningless relationships and never having control over my life.

But that's not the case.

I have a family now, one that's loud, rambunctious, a little broken, but at the end of the day, we'll always be there, and that is all I could ever need.

Not a biological family, but a chosen one. Somewhere along the way, Liv and I found our family, and I'd take the same road again knowing it would lead us here—to the ones who chose us for who we are.

This is where we were meant to be. Every laugh, every smile, heals a tiny part of me, and soon, the cracks in my heart and mind will cease to exist.

It won't be today, and it won't be tomorrow, but sometime in the future, I'll look back on this time and wish I could go back.

But I only look forward these days. And tomorrow, I'll wake up next to Vince, and he'll kiss me on the forehead and heal all the parts of me he didn't break in the first place.

I still get to read Liv's books.

I still get to have lunch with Tristan, who's officially my brother, and I call him that anytime I can because I've never had a brother before.

I still get to talk about books with Teags and have reading dates, even if over the phone.

I still get to love Vince how he deserves to be loved.

And I still get to love myself.

Because I survived. I'm alive. I've created the life I've always wanted, and nothing can take that away from me.

Epilogue

Three Years Later

— FOREVER BY NOAH KAHAN

I FEEL SOMEONE JOLT me awake, and before I think it's my own body waking up from a nightmare, I realize it's Vince.

"Angel, wake up."

"What time is it?" I ask as I rub my eyes. The sun isn't even shining yet, so it must be early in the morning.

"Like three a.m., but get up. Liv has gone into labor, and Tristan just called me."

That gets me right up.

"She's early! She's not supposed to be this early!" I shout as I clamor out of bed.

"I know, but she and the baby will be fine," Vince says as he passes by Nellie and Poppy in their beds, still sleeping soundly. Vince and I got another dog—a boxer named Poppy—about two years ago. She and Nellie are the best of friends, and it's been nice having two sets of pawprints in the house.

They're the best dogs ever and have their own corner in our room. It's all decked out with dog beds, toys, and anything else they could need.

There's even a small water bowl in case they don't want to get up and go downstairs at night.

I burst out of bed, throw on some sweats, a bra, and a hoodie before Vince grabs the car keys from where they sit in our room, and we head out the door.

"Are you driving, or do you want me to call Emerson?" I ask.

"Don't wake him up. We'll be fine," Vince says as he opens the car door for me.

Emerson, Chris, and Duncan have stayed on as part of our security team. There's obviously no need for my entire house to be guarded all the time, since Ralph is still in prison. I haven't had any other situations like that one, so Vince handed the reins over to Emerson.

Vince no longer makes the final decisions regarding my safety. Technically, I do. Emerson is my head guard, and Vince is *just* my boyfriend.

But he still likes to butt in during conversations about my safety, which I don't mind, because he still does this shit for a living. He and Nico still run their company together, but Vince is more hands-off than he used to be. He doesn't take cases anymore. He has finally put down roots, and the two of us have been enjoying our lives together.

He still works, helping Nico train the new men, but when it comes to me, Emerson has taken over. I couldn't be happier. I've trusted Emerson since I met him that first day outside my house, and I know Vince is super close to him, too.

It all works perfectly, our little unit.

"Are you ready to become an aunt?" Vince asks as he drives the car out of the gate and onto the road.

"I am, I think!" I say nervously, because what if I immediately hold the kid and it starts crying? What if it can tell that I'm kind of afraid of it?

Well, I probably shouldn't call it an 'it'.

"Are they at the hospital already, or did Tristan waste time texting us while Liv was having contractions?"

Vince only chuckles, knowing that's something Tristan would do. "I think they're at the hospital already. His first text came in around one, but I didn't hear it. He left me like a hundred voicemails talking about how if I'm not there to protect their kid, and if you missed your sister's birth, he would kill me."

"That sounds about right."

Tristan never lets anyone forget that Vince is a bodyguard. Well, he *was* a bodyguard. Anytime we go out in public, he always asks Vince to sweep the area. It has become a running bit.

My brother is the goofiest motherfucker on the planet, and he's going to make a wonderful father.

Twenty minutes later, we're rushing into the delivery unit to find Teags sitting in the waiting room by herself.

"Teags? Where is everyone?"

My best friend lifts her head from her phone. "It's just me. My mom is in the room with them. No baby yet."

Vince presses a kiss to my head. "Go, Bree. I know you'll want to see Liv. I'll keep Teags company."

"Yay me," my best friend says. "Is Nico with you guys, at least? I really wanted to ask him a few things."

I raise my eyebrow at Vince, and he only shrugs. Those two are weirdly friendly with one another, and I don't think I'd want to be a fly on the wall for any of their conversations. They seem...peculiar, to say the least.

I push through the doors and head into Liv's room, only to hear her breathing heavily.

"Livvy?"

All their heads perk up and swing to mine as I enter the room.

"Bree! Thank goodness you're here. I didn't know if you guys were going to make it," Tristan says as he pulls me in for a hug.

"How are you both feeling?"

"Wonderful!" Tristan cheers.

"Terrible," Liv says at the same time. "You better worship the ground I walk on after this, West."

"Don't worry, Liv. You'll probably get sick of me telling you that you're the most amazing, beautiful, and magnificent mother of our children. I'm in awe of you, pretty girl." Tristan leans down and presses a kiss to Liv's head.

"I know Tabitha will be with you guys the whole time, but I'll be in the waiting room with Teags and Vince. Can you two give us a second?" I ask as I walk over to the side of my sister's bed.

"We'll be in the hall. Come on, Mom," Tristan says as he shuts the door softly behind him.

"Bree, make this quick because I'm going to have another contraction soon," Liv says as she huffs.

"I wanted one last moment with just us. Just the two Hart sisters, like we've always been."

"I hate to break it to you, but it hasn't been just us for a while now, sis."

I stifle the emotions about to pour out of me. "I know, but this is different. We always thought we were alone our whole lives, and now, we're not. Now, there's going to be a small piece of you out in the world. I just want one last moment with you before you become a mom. I want to say thank you."

"For what?"

"For always taking care of me. For raising me to be the woman I am today. Thank you for everything, Liv. And if you ever doubt your ability to be a parent, just look at me and how I turned out. I'd say you did pretty damn good."

"Bree..." she trails off, emotions overcoming her. "You're who you are because of so many things, not just me."

"Yeah, but you made sure I was never alone. You were like my very own built-in best friend, and I'm so fucking grateful I get to call you my sister. I'm so thankful that, despite everything, we still had one another. You may be so many things to so many people, but you'll forever be my sister." I grab her hand, her grip loose but firm in mine. "I love you so fucking much."

"I love you too, Bree. So damn much."

"Okay, now, bring me a niece or nephew, okay?" I say as I kiss her forehead.

She nods at me, and as I leave the room, I have to wipe a few tears away. Tabitha spots the tears, resting a calming hand on my arm before she heads back in, but Tristan doesn't. He just stands there and looks at me.

"God, how did we get here?" he asks as he runs a hand through his hair.

"Your guess is as good as mine."

He smiles at me. "It feels like only yesterday I ran into her with that coffee."

"Are you nervous?"

"A little. I wish my own dad was here to give me some fucking pointers on how to do this whole thing, and Tobias, too. If he was here, he would've read all the fucking books about what to do so he would have all the answers for me."

"I bet they're really fucking proud of you, Tristan. For everything, not just today," I say as I pull him in for a hug. "You'll be a wonderful father. You have a good team, you and Liv."

"Yeah, we do," Tristan smiles before we hear Liv scream in pain. "Shit, I have to go!"

He races back into the room, and I know we're in for a long night as I head back to the waiting room with Vince and Teags.

Eight Hours Later

VINCE FELL ASLEEP ON my shoulder two hours ago, but as Tristan bursts through the doors, the biggest smile on his face, we jump up to meet his excitement.

"So?" Teags asks, nervously tugging at the ends of her hair.

"Yeah, dude, say something!" Harry says. The three of them—Dom, Ethan, and Harry—joined us around breakfast time. It's been a lot of nonstop glory days stories, alongside lots of nervous pacing and leg shaking.

Tristan stands in the middle of the waiting room, looking like he just saw sunlight for the first time. "It's a boy!"
All of us cheer, and hugs are given all around.

"And a girl!"

What did he just say?

"What the fuck?" Dom says. "Two?"

"Surprise!" Tristan says with a huge smirk on his face. "God, that was so hard to keep a secret. I almost blurted it out a million times."

"Are you kidding me?" I attack Tristan in a hug.

"Leave it to you guys to only have to do this once," Teags says, smiling at her brother like I've never seen her. "Congrats, Tris. I'm going to go call Theo!"

Tristan takes turns hugging his friends, Vince giving him a pat on the back while Tristan whispers something into his ear. God, I love how close they are. It makes Liv and I ridiculously happy that they're such good friends.

We've truly created the life we both wanted, our own little family that loves us as much as we do them.

"Do you guys want to see them?"

I hang back with Vince while Tristan's friends head in first, no doubt getting the lecture from Tristan about washing their hands. Those guys have been friends since college, and this isn't the last time they'll all be in a waiting room. Harry's wife is pregnant—around six months—so they'll be back soon.

From the good days in college to the good days as an adult.

How beautiful a sentiment like that is. I never went to college to be able to have people around me like that, but Tristan's friends always make me feel welcome no matter what. And sometimes, they too feel like older brothers to me, and it makes me laugh anytime the three of them are protective of me.

Vince steps up behind me, his hand rubbing up and down my back as I look up at him.

"Hi, baby."

"Hi, angel," he says as he kisses me. "How are you feeling?"

"Elated. Scared. Excited. Proud. Yeah, that about sums it up."

"You'll be fine holding the baby, Bree. You're not going to drop it," he says as he escorts me to the room.

"Well, now that's all I'm going to think about!"

He only laughs as we head into the room, the joy and company spreading around the room, filling it with light.

"Can you guys give us a second?" Tristan says to his friends, and they all disperse into the hallway.

"Was it something I said?" I joke, my emotions getting the better of me as I see my sister holding one of her babies. "Oh my goodness, Liv."

I notice the other baby in the bassinet the hospital provided, and Vince goes over to him and Tristan, the two of them hugging again.

"Come here, sis. I want you to meet someone." Liv says, her smile bursting from her face. She holds her daughter in her arms, and tears fall from my eyes even before I've properly met the new addition to our family. "This is Tahlia Bree West."

Sobs burst from my chest. "Bree?" I ask, making sure I heard her correctly.

"Well, we wanted to continue with the T tradition for Tabitha and his dad," Liv says as she hands me her daughter. "But I wanted her namesake to be someone strong, fierce, resilient, and beautiful, like you."

"Hi, Tahlia," I say as I look at Tristan and Vince, my eyes so blurry that I can barely see them. God, she's so fucking tiny. I've never seen a more beautiful baby. "What's the boy's name?"

Tristan takes a deep breath before he speaks. "Tobias Daniel West. The second, technically, but that just sounds like a mouthful." He takes another shaky breath. "After my brother."

"Two beautiful names for two beautiful babies," I say as I hand the baby back to my sister. "Thank you for the greatest gift anyone has ever given me."

"I couldn't think of a better middle name to give my daughter, Bree. I mean that."

And for the rest of the day, people filter in and out of the room as the new parents adjust. Lucky for them, they have a village of people ready and waiting to help.

I used to think that life was a series of choices.

But now, I think life is a series of moments we're lucky enough to have. All our life leads to these big moments, and no matter what, humans will always find their way to where they're supposed to be in the end.

I used to think that my story was going to end, that I'd be alone forever.

But now, I have a whole family surrounding me, and our story is far from over. Actually, I think it's only the beginning.

We'll be by each other forever, through thick and thin, through the good days and bad. Because, despite not being related by blood, we will always choose one another.

Of that, I'm sure.

Authors Note

This duology may be over, but there are people like the Hart sisters all over the world. I relate so much to these two in so many different ways, and being able to share them with you all has been an honor. I not only wanted to highlight romance and sisterhood in these books, but I also wanted to highlight how terrifying, confusing, scary, exciting, and magical life can be.

I didn't type The End on either of these books because they feel like such huge parts of who I am. When I came up with these sisters, I was struggling to find a purpose just before graduating from college. I was terrified, and I put all of my weird emotions into Liv and Bree. In my mind, these characters are so reflective of people everywhere, and I couldn't bring myself to say goodbye. These books will always have a piece of me, and to all of you telling me you feel a kinship with them, thank you.

It's an honor to have my characters take up space in your mind. And no matter what stage of life you're in, I promise that it will all work out. It may not be today, tomorrow, next week, or next year, but eventually, the pieces will fall into place. Eventually, you'll look back and be grateful for the road that lead you to where you are.

Maybe take the road nobody else has. Maybe try the one that only a few have gone on. Because you never know what awaits you, and though it might be terrifying throwing yourself into the unknown, do it anyway.

You'll make it through. Even if just one step at a time.

Acknowledgements

This duology would not have been possible without the wonderful people that support me throughout this process.

Lexi—Writing Bree and Liv was easy for me because of all the love you show me every single day. I can't imagine a life where I don't wake up and text you every single morning. I am eternally grateful that I get to exist at the same time as you. I love you to the moon and Saturn. Thank you for being my biggest hype woman, my number one fan, and the best sister I could ask for. None of the books I write would exist without you. So, thank you for everything that you do for me.

Hannah—Your cover designs are always so magical and I adore you so much. I've never considered myself a big sister before, but having you as an honorary little sister is an honor. You create such beautiful covers that have sat on my shelves, yours, a Barnes and Noble shelf, and hundreds of people's home libraries. I'm forever in awe of you. Thank you for everything.

Lexi & Hannah—Thank you for staying by my side through it all. I'll never have enough words to describe how grateful I am for you both. Sisters forever and ever.

Jan Boswell—Having a friend like you is such a gift. From our eight minute voice notes freaking out about our manuscripts, to chatting about our days like old women getting tea together, I'll forever cherish every conversation with you. You truly keep my delusions alive and I'm so thankful for that. I feed off of your feral energy, and for something that can be so isolating and lonely, you have been such a bright light for me. Thank you for reminding me my words matter on the days I don't think they do. I love you!

Sarah A. Bailey—I firmly believe the universe somehow knew that I needed you when we crossed paths on Threads. I truly believe that this duology would not be what it is without you. The Hart sisters will always make me think of meeting you and trading manuscripts, me eventually threatening you in your messages. Liv, Bree, and Teags are you, me, and Lexi in another life, I'm sure of it. Because no matter what path I take in any life, the three of us will always run into one another. I love you so much.

Josh—You know how much I love you. Thank you for being my biggest fan—even though you're terrified of my brain sometimes. I get it, I'm scared, too. Thank you for feeding me after I spent all night writing and would forget.

Mom—I know we don't do emotions well, but thank you for embracing my books as much as you have. Every wonderful parent I write in these stories is always an extension of you. I hope you and Theodora enjoy the parts with Vince's dog when you cuddle up and read this book at night.

My beta readers—Joana, Soph, Maine, and Holly. Thank you all for giving the best feedback and for making my story that much better. I adored seeing all your reactions to this book, and I am extremely thankful for you all. I love you guys so much!

Taylor Swift—You'll never see this, but folklore as an album has cemented itself into my bones. It's brought me comfort, delusions, and lyrics that have spoken to me unlike any album I had heard. It was truly an album that came to me at the right time. Thank you for inspiring me and millions of others across the world with your lyrics.

Ellie at LoveNotes PR—Thank you for making ARCs so much easier for me with this duology! I truly adore working with you.

Alexa—Thank you for making my story shine! I can't wait to work with you again in the future on some of the things you begged me for in the Google Doc comments!

Cassidy Hudspeth—I always adore working with you! You truly polish my stories so beautifully and I'm so thankful for you.

To the readers—You have all changed my life. Thank you for making my words matter when I never thought they did. There are not enough words to explain how much you have done for me over these years. Thank you for taking a chance on me.

To me in my last semester of college—I promise you, it got better. Now, our stories reach people from all over the world. I'm so very proud of you.

Also by Emily Tudor

<u>The Grand Mountain Series:</u>

Replaying the Game

Redefining the Rules

Reconsidering the Facts

<u>The Hart Sisters:</u>

The Road Not Taken

The Road Less Traveled By

About the author

Emily Tudor creates characters and stories about platonic and romantic love for anyone and everyone. She lives in the state of New York and loves listening to music and creating stories. She loves Marvel movies, the song *mirrorball* by Taylor Swift and buying too many books when she already has many to be read at home.

You can find her on Instagram at: @authoremilytudor
www.authoremilytudor.com